Praise for
CROSSROADS OF EMPIRE

". . . a captivating historical chronicle fused with a personal drama—Evan's quest to rediscover himself is the emotional core of the novel . . . a supernaturally charged adventure story." —*Kirkus Reviews*

"Cooper follows up *Wages of Empire* with this deep dive into the personal and political consequences of the First World War. The novel's strength lies in its intricate, real-life characters and their interwoven stories, offering a fresh perspective on World War I . . . This interplay of grand events and intimate character arcs makes *Crossroads of Empire* compelling . . . A richly layered narrative that sheds light on the human toll of conflict and celebrates an indomitable spirit of resilience amid overwhelming adversity." —***BookLife** Review*

"*Crossroads of Empire* brings to life a journey of self-discovery set against a backdrop of the war in motion. Cooper's skillful storytelling sets an unrelenting pace with the international events of the early twentieth century coupled with Evan's search for answers—about himself and his family's history. Beautifully written in a voice and in details that capture the era, *Crossroads of Empire* is a must-read for readers of all ages with high hopes for more of Evan's adventures yet to come. Five Stars—Highly Recommended." —***Chanticleer Book Reviews***

"*Crossroads of Empire* dives into the tumultuous waters of World War I, presenting a thrilling narrative enriched by a blend of historical and fictional characters. Cooper's writing is compelling and richly detailed, offering a tapestry of scenes that bring early 20th-century conflicts vividly to life." —**Literary Titan Review**

"In page after page of *Crossroads of Empire*, I was thrilled with how the plot widened with various actors added as history unfolded one step at a time. The book picked up speed as it moved along with rising tension as disparate subplots charged forward to the conclusion. I loved it! Bravo!"

—**Sylvia Boorstein,** PhD, bestselling author, teacher of Buddhist Insight Meditation, and cofounder of Spirit Rock Meditation Center.

"A novel full of gripping intrigue, tension, and lively, witty characters, including T. E. Lawrence. At the heart of the book is a father-son story like no other. Crossroads of Empire both instructs and entertains . . . great storytelling that brings history to life. Highly recommend!"

—**Alfredo Botello,** award-winning author of *180 Days*

"In *Crossroads of Empire*, Michael Cooper has again taken a historic footnote and has, with great story telling and amazing character development, animated WWI. As an example of subtle insights contained in this novel, Cooper mentions in passing a comment by Gertrude Bell disparaging Mark Sykes, whose postwar actions with his French counterpart in drawing the borders of a ruined Ottoman Empire are the basis of tragedy today."

—**Gordon Freeman,** PhD, Rabbi Emeritus, Congregation B'nai Shalom, Walnut Creek, California

AWARDS

CIBA 2023: First Place for Hemingway Prize—Wartime Fiction
2024 SF Writers Conference Writing Contest Finalist—Adult Fiction

Praise for
WAGES OF EMPIRE

"Masterful storytelling will keep you furiously turning the pages of this compelling WWI novel. A winner!"

—**Andrew Kaplan,** *New York Times* bestselling author of *Blue Madagascar* and the *Homeland* novels

"A beautifully written tale...exhibits seamless research in illuminating unforgettable historical and fictional characters...a tour de force!"

—**Professor Ronit Meroz,** Dept of Jewish Philosophy and Talmud, Tel Aviv University, Israel

"This superb historical novel is a must read . . . directly relates to issues we face today."

—**Rizek Abusharr,** Emeritus Director of Jerusalem International YMCA

"An engaging history lesson as contemporaneous as the morning newspaper, but far more enlivening."

—**John Bennison,** Rel.D–Lead Teacher: Pathways Faith Community

"The characters, historical and fictional, come to life on the page as the storyline drives relentlessly forward. Bravo!"

—**Matt Coyle,** bestselling author of the Rick Cahill novels

"Compelling novel with global insights...offers history buffs a thrilling ride."

—**Sujata Massey,** internationally bestselling author of *The Widows of Malabar Hill*

"Another finely wrought, deeply and lovingly researched novel from Michael J. Cooper that brings history and historical figures to life. The next best thing to a time machine."

—**Kenneth Wishnia**, award-winning author of *The Fifth Servant* and *From Sun to Sun*

"In this absorbing offering, Cooper explores plot strands that hold historical significance, including the Arab desire for independence, the Zionist movement, and Western interest in Middle Eastern oil and control of Jerusalem. The pace is steady, allowing Cooper to plumb various facets of the war as it unfolds, with special emphasis on its Middle Eastern front as he skillfully braids the disparate plot strands together into a cohesive narrative with suspense and tension." —***Publishers Weekly***

"With gripping tension, Cooper keeps readers on the edge of their seats as the stakes are raised with each turn of events. *Wages of Empire* is a must-read blockbuster for history buffs of all ages. The novel's masterful storytelling will leave readers wanting more. Five Stars—Best Book" —***Chanticleer Book Reviews***

CROSSROADS OF EMPIRE

MICHAEL J. COOPER

VIRGINIA BEACH
CAPE CHARLES

Crossroads of Empire
by Michael J. Cooper

© Michael J. Cooper

ISBN 979-8-88824-512-5

All rights reserved. No part of this publication may be reproduced, stored in a retrieval system, or transmitted in any form or by any means—electronic, mechanical, photocopy, recording, or any other—except for brief quotations in printed reviews, without the prior written permission of the author.

Cover photographs derived from:
Old City Jerusalem, Temple Mount (undated, post 1910); Photo credit: (c) DEIAHL, Jerusalem—Used by permission from the Protestant Institute of Archaeology.
H.I.M. William II, German Emperor—Painting by Max Koner, presented to the kaiser on July 11,1891.

Published by

3705 Shore Drive
Virginia Beach, VA 23455
800-435-4811

Also by Michael J Cooper

Foxes in the Vineyard

The Rabbi's Knight

Wages of Empire

In loving memory of my parents

Emanuel and Buni Cooper

Who showed me "the way wherein I must walk, and the work that I must do."

> *And all this hurries toward the end, so fast,*
> *Whirling futilely, evermore the same.*

—Rainer Maria Rilke, *The Merry-Go-Round—Jardin du Luxembourg*

AUTHOR'S NOTE

Crossroads of Empire follows the first book of the series, *Wages of Empire*, as a novel of historical fiction set during World War I. Both are inspired by historical events and peopled with historical and fictional characters. Likewise, both books generally adhere to the historical timeline with a few departures for purposes of craft and continuity. Such departures are noted in the Cast of Characters, and I beg the reader's indulgence for these digressions.

Crossroads of Empire traces the journey of sixteen-year-old Evan Sinclair after his baptism of fire in the first book. At the outset, Evan leaves France on a hospital ship bound for England as multiple storylines are interwoven to create a tapestry of the "Great War for Civilization." Though fought mainly in Europe, *Crossroads of Empire* highlights the combatants' growing interest in the land bridge at the crossroads of Europe, Africa, and Asia— the Middle East. There the war will determine control of the Suez Canal and the rich oil reserves of Arabia, with the diadem of Jerusalem as the ultimate prize.

While some observers at the time referred to the Middle East Front as a "sideshow," there is ample historical evidence to suggest that this piece of real estate was a central aspiration of Kaiser Wilhelm II. Indeed, one of the novel's central themes is the kaiser's obsession with Jerusalem, first demonstrated during his visit there in 1898 when he initiated major building projects, had himself crowned "king of Jerusalem," and fancied himself, Holy Roman emperor in the mold of Charlemagne and Frederick the Great. At its core, *Crossroads of Empire* holds up a mirror to current conflicts in the Middle East that are the direct descendants of promises made and promises broken during and after the Great War for Civilization.

PROLOGUE

October 21, 1912
Cedar City, Utah

AT FIRST, Janet Sinclair wasn't certain if the ache she felt in the pit of her stomach was indigestion, false labor, or a visceral reaction to the *Titanic* disaster. She was reading about the tragedy in the *North American Review* while sitting on the divan with her feet up after dinner.

From where she sat in the living room, she could hear her husband, Clive, and fourteen-year-old son, Evan, talking in the kitchen—something about an error committed by someone named Snodgrass that allowed the Boston Red Sox to best the New York Giants in the recent World Series. Instructed by her obstetrician to keep off her feet, the men in her life were taking care of the dishes. Putting the magazine aside, Janet closed her eyes and rested a hand on her belly as her attention drifted away from the talk of baseball and returned to the article about the *Titanic*.

Six months had passed since the sinking, and as she listened to the sound of water being pumped into the kitchen sink, she imagined the pumps of the great ship, laboring to keep *Titanic* afloat for a few more minutes, perhaps an hour—just long enough for the *Carpathia* to reach her. Almost asleep, she felt herself drifting, compassed round by dark frigid water, the heaving ocean beneath an indifferent black sky crowded with stars.

Beneath her hand, she felt a gentle quickening in her belly, and her thoughts turned to the water warm within, the small sea surrounding and protecting her baby. She imagined the twisting blue vessels of the cord, connecting and sustaining—

She winced as the pain came again. Stronger.

Her eyes fluttered open, her heart pounding as the tightening pain rippled through her abdomen and fear gripped her heart. *Please God, not again.* She bit her lower lip and tried to reason—*most women have false labor.*

But most women hadn't recently miscarried.

Then the pain passed, and she drew a grateful breath.

The conversation in the kitchen about baseball had ended. In its place she heard Clive whistling his favorite tune, "Brian Boru's March," sweetly and slowly. She smiled, remembering how he used to sing Evan to sleep with the tune as a baby in his rich tenor voice—the words in Gaelic, which neither of them understood, weaving a tapestry of such mystery and beauty. As she listened, her thoughts drifted back to the baby they had lost.

She hadn't even known that she was pregnant when they left their home in Oxford late in the summer of 1911 bound for an archaeological dig in Northern Syria. Clive had been awarded a four-year traveling scholarship from Magdalen College, and the whole family had been excited to embark on an adventure to Arabia. Just before docking at the Port of Beirut, Janet had experienced the first quickening of that pregnancy. Immediately sharing the glad news with Clive and Evan, they had all been happy and excited to know that there would be a new baby in their new home.

Once reaching Carchemish, they moved into a comfortable bungalow next to one occupied by two young Oxford scholars, Ned Lawrence and Leonard Woolley. Their new neighbors were welcoming and endlessly entertaining, and for the first few weeks, all was well.

Until Janet had early labor and lost the baby.

She blamed the malodorous headwaters of the Euphrates where she was forced to bathe. She blamed the lack of a properly trained obstetrician at the local field hospital. She blamed Clive. But most of all, she blamed herself.

But heartsick turned to hopeful when she conceived again, two months later—in January of 1912. Determined that this pregnancy would be different, she insisted that Clive curtail his four-year scholarship, and that they leave the excavation camp—that they leave Syria. She refused to sacrifice another baby to the substantial remains of the Assyrian and Neo-Hittite periods. She refused to bury another baby next to the tombs of Carchemish.

She had wanted to move back to Oxford, but there was no opening for Clive at Magdalen College, and there wouldn't be one for the remainder of his demyship—almost another three years. Additionally, they had promised to let their friend, Mervin Smythe, stay at the Oxford flat for the full four years.

Before leaving Syria, the university had provided a list of other possible positions, including one in southern Utah in the United States—a position that included free housing and the use of an automobile. Both Janet and Clive seized on that option, having fallen in love with images of the American southwest at a photographic exhibition in London a few years before. Clive would be allowed to shift his grant from studying ancient Assyrians in Carchemish to studying the cliff drawings of the indigenous Ute Indians.

The opportunity was well-timed; Evan would arrive in time to enter the tenth grade of high school, making a smooth transition from having completed the upper fourth form curriculum in Carchemish as provided by the Oxford High School for Boys, and Clive would be able to maintain his grant without interruption. What's more, the entire journey by rail and ship would be fully funded by the American college, the Branch Normal School in Cedar City, Utah.

They crossed the Mediterranean in a Greek Line ship, arriving in Southampton in late June, and after a few days took ship for New York aboard the RMS *Olympic* of the White Star Line. Morning sickness and rough seas had made the crossing unpleasant in the extreme for Janet despite luxurious first-class accommodations. And the recent *Titanic* tragedy had cast a heavy pall over the ship. But on balance, it had been an uneventful and pleasant voyage, and they had arrived in the sweltering heat of New York City after a week. From there, they traveled by train for another week along the transcontinental railroad to the Salt Lake Basin, and from there, a day-long trip by motorcar had brought them to Cedar City.

In the months since their arrival, Janet was pleased that the Branch Normal School had fulfilled all its promises, from Clive's work with the Ute Indians to the free use of a new 1914 Buick touring automobile to a fully furnished cottage, as well as expert obstetric consultation services provided by an outstanding local physician, Dr. Maurice Arons.

And just as she thought about Dr. Arons, there it was again—the pain, now sustained, and stronger.

Trying to steady her voice, she called for Clive. "Darling, could you come here for a moment?"

"Would you like y'r tea now, love?" Clive asked in his soothing Scottish burr.

"No, I'd very much like a word with you."

Clive was quickly out of the kitchen, drying his hands with the dishcloth, kneeling at her side. "What is it?"

She touched his face, his dark beard, salted with gray and trimmed short. She saw the fear rising in his clear gray eyes behind wire-rim spectacles. They'd been through this before.

"Any possibility it's just false labor?" he asked quietly, his hand on hers.

"I don't think so." She shook her head. "Too strong."

"How far along are you . . . thirty-two weeks?"

"Almost thirty-three—the furthest yet."

"It might be far enough—"

"I hope so."

"Let's go for a ride then, shall we?" He bent and kissed her hand, then turned his head and called, "Evan! Get the Buick running."

Evan, tall for his fourteen years, with sun-streaked fair hair and a deep tan on his face and forearms, stepped from the kitchen, his hands dripping water on the floor. "It's happening again?"

Clive nodded. "Light the headlamps and bring the car up to the porch."

Evan was out the front door in a shot, the screen door snapping closed behind him.

"What would you have me pack for you, darling?" Clive asked as he brought her hand to his lips.

"The bag's already packed—in the closet, my side."

As Clive went for the bag, Janet could hear the Buick sputter to life. Clive was back. "Any pain now?" he asked.

"No. Let's go. Now."

Haunted by the too familiar actions and feelings of despair, Janet stepped carefully from the porch. Moonlight glowed through high clouds and the steady song of crickets filled the cool air. Clive helped her into the passenger seat of the touring car, Evan already seated in the back.

Clive raised the cushion on the driver's seat and used a ruler to measure the remaining gas in the tank "A bit low, I'm afraid," he said with a frown and slipped behind the wheel. "We'll stop at Pitney's filling station before we leave town."

"But don't you have the spare gas can?" asked Janet.

"I have two of them, darling, five gallons each, but it's fifty miles to St. George, and I don't want to run out of our main gas tank in the middle of nowhere. Besides, I'll use the telephone at the filling station to call Dr. Arons."

"But won't the station be closed? It's probably about nine o'clock."

"Yes, but Bob and his wife live in the little bungalow behind the station, and he's always happy to help with emergencies." He eased the auto down the rutted driveway illuminated by the headlamps and onto the asphalt road that would lead to St. George by way of the filling station.

As the automobile accelerated forward, Janet closed her eyes. *Please, God, let it stop. Please let me keep my baby.*

After a few minutes, they pulled into the darkened filling station. Clive cut the motor and squeezed the rubber bulb to the left of the steering wheel, sounding the Klaxon horn until the house lights came on. After a minute, Janet saw the sleepy proprietor, Bob Pitney, pulling on his suspenders. "Thank God," she said with a sigh as she watched Clive follow Pitney into the office.

"Are you okay, Mom?" Evan asked from the backseat of the Buick.

Janet felt his hand on her shoulder and covered it with her own. "So far, darling. I haven't had any pains since we left the house."

"That's good," said Evan as he climbed out on the driver's side. Janet watched as he lifted the front seat cushion and helped Pitney fill the ten-gallon tank.

"We'll have you on your way in no time, Mrs. Sinclair," said Pitney.

"Thanks, Bob," she said and managed a smile. "Sorry to wake you."

"Oh, no trouble, no trouble at all. You all have yourselves a safe trip. Me and the missus will be praying for you."

"Thank you," she whispered. Looking up, she saw the electric lights of the filling station, alive with clouds of flying insects. Then the pain came again.

"Dr. Arons was on a house call," Clive said when he returned to the automobile. "I left a message with his wife for him to meet us at the hospital."

Janet heard the desperation in his voice, matching her own. She bit her lip. "Good. Let's go, please."

Clive got back into the car. Bob Pitney turned the crank, and the motor coughed and roared to life.

They were soon on the road to St. George, the headlamps carving a tunnel of light through the empty desert as Janet prayed for the pain to stop.

* * *

Clive pushed down on the gas pedal, hoping they'd make it to the hospital in time. With the Buick not having a speedometer, he wasn't sure how fast they were going, but he reasoned, *if it's fifty miles to St. George, and the Buick's top speed is about fifty miles-an-hour, we should make it to St. George in about an hour.* He pushed down harder and felt the Buick accelerate.

"How are you doing, my love?' he shouted over the noisy clatter of the motor car.

"Better now. It passed," she called back and smiled.

"Good! We'll be there in an hour, maybe a few minutes less . . ."

But as he drove, the idea of minutes and hours seemed, at once, all-important and completely irrelevant. In the crowding darkness of the desert and the empty road, time was no longer something determined by a clock, but rather a primal force, keeping its measure in the sound of Janet's rapid breathing and in the unbidden ebb and flow of her contractions.

They finally reached St. George, and everything seemed to happen in a singular but drawn-out and terrible moment: Clive, shouting and honking the Klaxon horn as he guided the automobile toward the weakly lit hospital glowing at the end of a dark street, the gurney passing beneath the stark glare of electric lights; Janet's blond hair radiating out on the hospital pillow, bright tears shining on her face; Clive sitting by her bed bounded by white partitions, a brave smile and her hand in his, the last kiss.

Then, the waiting—pacing by the swinging brown-painted doors; the single cry followed by silence; the doctor, shaken and frowning, "It was a girl, barely two pounds, too small . . ."

And Janet?

"We're trying to stop the bleeding."

CHAPTER 1

November 18, 1914
Calais, France

It was late morning by the time the convoy finally left the hospital in Boulogne, the departure delayed by the time it had taken to fill each lorry with the wounded judged sufficiently stable for transfer to England. Those left behind would remain in hospital until fit to travel.

Also left behind were scores of English dead who lay buried in the soil of Flanders and France. At the beginning of the war bodies were identified and interred in marked graves, but as the slaughter mounted into the tens of thousands, any careful accounting was overwhelmed. These unknown young men, either blown to bits or entangled in no-man's lands of mud and barbed wire, or haphazardly buried in single or mass graves, were officially "known unto God."

The convoy reached Calais as a smudge of lighter gray marked the cloud-hidden noonday sun, and the boarding of His Majesty's Hospital Ship, *Austrium*, began. A converted mail ship, the *Austrium* was unarmed and conformed to Hague Convention criteria for hospital ships with a fresh coat of white paint emblazoned with large red crosses. Nurses, doctors, and able-bodied soldiers joined the ship's crew on the quay, moving gurneys and stretchers from the canvas-covered trucks onto the ship. One of the able-bodied wounded was a tall sixteen-year-old young man with light brown hair wearing tan trousers and a brown leather jacket over a white linen shirt—a young man who answered to the name Evan Sinclair.

Once all were aboard, mooring lines were freed from the cleats, and with the fenders made fast, the *Austrium* churned through the dark blue waters of the Channel toward Dover.

Assigned an upper berth in a cramped cabin, Evan stowed his suitcase and headed back up the narrow steel stairwell to the ship's deck with his haversack strapped to his back. *I'll hardly need a bed with a crossing of only a few hours,* he thought as he headed toward the forecastle.

He felt a twinge of nostalgia being back on a steamer—less than three months after crossing the Atlantic on the *Sant Anna* out of New York to join the Great War for Civilization. He looked up at the heavy clouds darkening the sky and thrilled at the cool wind on his face. *And now, back to England!*

Standing at the forward railing, he shrugged off his haversack and, placing it at his feet, regarded the practically new boots he'd been given along with all his clothing upon discharge from the field hospital in Boulogne. He wondered about the boots' previous owner, about the roads he'd taken, about his last road. As he thought about the field hospital, he sighed and touched his lips, remembering the beautiful young VAD nurse, Sharon Meehan—her easy grace as she moved through the tent ward, her striking figure, her calm blue eyes, and her hair, the color of burnished gold, escaping from beneath her white head cloth.

Shaking the thoughts away, he leaned on the railing to look down at the water foaming along the bow. It was then that he noticed the ship turning sharply starboard, then to port, and after less than a minute to starboard. He was wondering about the erratic course when he was joined at the railing by a middle-aged man, bareheaded and wearing a green raincoat over civilian clothing.

"Good morning!" the man said.

"Good morning to you!" Evan replied and glanced up. The man had a pleasant face—a cleft in his strong chin and a part in the middle of his wind-blown hair. "What's going on with the sharp turns? Has the captain already started drinking?"

"Only tea!" The man smiled. "It's called zigzagging—standard evasive maneuvers since U-boats were sighted in these waters yesterday."

"U-boats? But isn't it clear that we're a *hospital* ship?" Evan nodded up at the Red Cross flag snapping in the wind.

"Captain doesn't want to take any chances."

With mounting dread, Evan looked over the water. The wind had risen and the Channel roiled with whitecaps. "How long before we reach Dover?"

"About two hours, perhaps longer with this rough sea and the zigzagging." After a brief pause, the man asked, "Are you worried about U-boats?"

"Aren't *you*?"

"Not really. Torpedo attacks are difficult in these conditions—even without zigzagging. And as you said, we *are* a hospital ship."

Evan stuck out his hand. "I'm Evan Sinclair," he said, then added an apology upon seeing that the man's right arm was in a plaster cast.

"No worries. I'm John McCrae. Pleased to meet you!" The man shook Evan's right hand with his left. "What landed you on a hospital ship?"

"I was wounded in Belgium."

"What were you doing *there*?"

"I was with the Flemish resistance."

"But you're an *American*!"

"British, actually. I lost my accent while living in the US."

"Alright, but what's a Brit who sounds like an American doing with the Flemish resistance in Belgium?"

"I kind of volunteered." Evan buttoned his leather jacket as drops of rain began to fall. "What about *you*? I can't place your accent."

"Canadian Expeditionary Force."

Evan studied McCrae's face. "Don't take this the wrong way, John, but most of the guys I've seen are about my age. You look like you're thirty-something." With the rising wind, he had to shout to be heard.

"Forty-one, actually. I'm a medical officer with the Canadian Field Artillery."

"Where were you wounded?"

"About three kilometers north of Ypres. Hit by shrapnel while treating wounded from the shelling we were taking from Kaiser Bill's Fourth Army. What about you?"

"Friendly fire on the outskirts of Ypres—British soldiers mistook us for Germans."

"I thought the Flemish partisans operate *behind* enemy lines."

"We'd come from occupied Belgium after opening the sluice gates at Noordvardt to flood the polders."

McCrae's jaw dropped. "*You* were with the partisans who flooded the polders?"

Evan nodded.

"Good show! That changed *everything*," McCrae shouted against the wind.

"That's what we were hoping for!" Evan sighed and added, "The two partisans who opened the sluice gates didn't make it."

"What were their names?"

"I only know their first names—Emile and Hendrik—they mustn't be forgotten."

"Emile and Hendrik," McCrae repeated. "I'll remember them. I may write a poem about them."

"But I thought you were a doctor."

"That doesn't stop me from writing poems when I'm not doctoring." McCrae pulled a folded paper from his shirt pocket. "I wrote this for a friend of mine killed at the Yser Canal—Alexis Helmer. It could have easily been written for Emile and Hendrik." He handed it to Evan.

Despite the wind, Evan managed to unfold the paper. Holding it with both hands, he silently read while leaning against the railing as the ship pitched in the rough sea.

In Flanders fields the poppies blow
Between the crosses, row on row
That mark our place; and in the sky

The larks still bravely singing fly
Scarce heard amid the guns below.
We are the dead. Short days ago,
We lived, felt dawn, saw sunset glow,
Loved and were loved, and now we lie
In Flanders fields!
Take up our quarrel with the foe
To you, from failing hands, we throw
The torch; be yours to hold it high
If ye break faith with us who die,
We shall not sleep, though poppies grow
In Flanders fields.

Evan's throat tightened and his vision blurred toward the end, but he managed to finish as raindrops fell like tears on the paper. He refolded it and held it out to McCrae. "You should publish this!"

"No. It's just for Alexis and me, and now for you. I have another copy—you keep that one."

"Thanks, but I mean it. You *must* publish this!" Evan opened his knapsack and placed the poem in an oilskin pouch as he continued speaking—nearly shouting so McCrae could hear him over the pounding water and the keening wind through the aerials. "People of Great Britain need this to give them hope and encouragement." He shouldered his knapsack. "Promise me you'll publish it."

"I promise I'll think about it—hey!" McCrae shouted and pointed. "Torpedo!"

Evan saw a bright streak beneath the roiling Chanel water, growing longer, heading directly toward them, not fifty yards away and closing. He gripped the railing and held his breath. The boat lurched to port. Heart pounding, he saw the torpedo slide by, missing the boat by about twenty feet. As McCrae bolted away, Evan shouted, "Where are you going?"

"To the bridge!"

Evan sprinted after him, mounting the slippery wooden steps as fast as he could. On the bridge he found McCrae in animated conversation with the captain. "Yes, yes, Major," the white-bearded captain was saying, "our watch saw it as well—two points abaft the beam, starboard side. We've increased our steam and turned to port. We're turning on our navigating lights so that our red crosses will be well seen—"

"Another torpedo closing fast!" shouted the watch.

"Hard to starboard, Mr. Smith," said the captain, and turning to Evan and McCrae, added, "Hold onto something sturdy."

Evan gripped an iron banister with both hands. He was scarcely able to breathe. When the torpedo hit, the concussion almost knocked him off his feet as the *Austrium* lurched and rocked in the water. Black smoke and an acrid smell filled the cabin as a grinding noise rose from the bowels of the ship.

"All stop," called the captain. "Damage, Mr. Smith!"

After a long minute came the ensign's reply, "We're listing to port, one of our propellers is gone, we've lost two boilers, and there's flooding in the engine room."

"U-boat surfacing—five hundred feet to starboard!" called the watch.

A submarine bobbed on the waves; the number nine clearly visible on the hull. "U-9," muttered the captain. "The one that sank the *Cressy* . . ."

"Why did she surface, Captain?" asked McCrae.

"The sudden weight loss of two torpedoes. I expect she'll dive again soon."

"Shall we resume evasive maneuvers?" asked the ensign.

"No point, Mr. Smith. In thirty minutes the *Austrium* will be on the bottom of the Channel. Time to abandon ship, gentlemen. Have all available nurses, medical staff, and crew move the wounded into lifeboats. Start with portside."

Evan bounded after McCrae.

Together, they helped the crew, nurses, and doctors evacuate the wounded on stretchers, lowering them into lifeboats. Evan saw that

McCrae's casted right arm was out of the sling, and he was using it as best he could. Within ten minutes all portside lifeboats were launched with at least one nurse, doctor, crewmember, or able-bodied soldier. Then they ran to fill the starboard-side boats as the sea raged beneath the rising storm.

As Evan helped to lower a wounded soldier into a lifeboat, his throat suddenly clenched, and his eyes burned. "What's that *smell*?" he shouted.

"Disinfectants!" McCrae shouted back. "The tanks must be leaking, and the stuff is toxic. We must get the lifeboats away!"

Frantically, they lowered the last wounded soldiers into a lifeboat.

"Get in!" McCrae shouted as he pushed Evan into the boat. "This is the last of the wounded, and they need a rower!"

"What about *you*?" Evan asked, coughing as he struggled for breath amid the acrid fumes and the rising storm.

"I'll take one of the remaining lifeboats." McCrae shouted back, grabbed a long pole, and pushed Evan's boat away. "Pull!" he shouted. "Pull for your life!"

Evan rowed, struggling to breathe and nearly blinded by the tears bathing his eyes. The rain came down in sheets. As the sea churned, tossing the lifeboat, Evan heard another sound—the staccato of machine-gun fire and the sound of bullets pinging off the reinforced steel hull of the ship.

Struggling to see, Evan let go of an oar and rubbed his eyes. He saw the U-boat silhouetted against the leaden sky, the mounted deck gun firing steadily, bright tracers whizzing over his head.

Ducking down, he saw a capsized lifeboat, not twenty feet away, surrounded by flailing soldiers, struggling to keep their heads above the raging water.

He worked the oars to get over to them, but a heaving wave threw him sharply to the side. As his head stuck the gunwale, the last thing he saw were the bright tracer bullets across the dark sky, like shooting stars.

CHAPTER 2

November 21, 1914
War Office at Whitehall, London

WHERE THE hell could he be? Captain Clive Sinclair wondered as he worked alone in the mapping room.

Almost four months had passed since Evan had left home in Utah after high school graduation, full of youthful idealism about joining the "Great War." He had concealed his intention with a deception of leaving with friends on a two-week camping trip to Moab and the Arches. But when his friends returned home without him, Clive suspected the truth—a truth confirmed when he found Evan's parting note at the house where it had fallen beneath the divan.

Clive had immediately decided to return to England and search for him, curtailing his fairly pointless sabbatical project of cataloging undecipherable petroglyphs of the Ute Indians of the American Southwest. After traveling by rail from Salt Lake City to Manhattan, he reached Southampton by steamer.

Hoping to perhaps find Evan at the family home in Oxford, Clive was disappointed to hear that Evan had never come by—this from his friend and colleague, Mervyn Smythe, who was house-sitting there. However, Mervyn did have some news: while traveling through Paris two months before, he had glimpsed a broadsheet, indicating that Evan, with no identification papers, had been suspected of being a German agent and arrested. But after being interrogated, he had somehow managed to escape and was now at large and being sought by Parisian gendarmes.

All the more determined to find him, Clive knew that the best place to look for Evan would also be the best place for him to contribute to the war effort—at the War Office at Whitehall. Reactivating his commission, he joined MO-4, the geographic division of British Intelligence where he was reunited with his young colleague and friend, T. E. Lawrence. Clive had last worked with Lawrence a few years earlier at the dig at Carchemish.

I wish Lawrence was here now instead of visiting with his parents in Oxford, but he had to go, Clive thought as he breathed out a sigh. *With two of his brothers serving on the Western Front, Ned had to give them some comfort.* He looked over the table and shook his head. *But grappling alone with this dreary mapping work is bloody tedious!*

Clive loosened his tie and opened the top button of his officer's tunic as his thoughts turned back to Evan. He leaned over the table, wondering for the thousandth time, *Where the hell could he be?*

A knock on the door was a welcome interruption. "Come in!" he shouted.

The door opened and a scout announced, "Colonel Hedley wants to see you, sir."

"Thank you." Clive grabbed his cap, praying that he might have some news. Reaching Hedley's office door, he announced himself, "Captain Sinclair, sir."

"Come in, Clive," Hedley sounded from within his office.

Not Captain Sinclair? Clive thought, alarmed by Hedley's uncharacteristic abandonment of protocol. Clive opened the door and saw Hedley at his desk.

"Have a seat."

Fearing the worst, Clive sat on an upholstered chair, his heart pounding in his ears.

"I have news, Clive—some good, some bad."

"Yes, sir?" he felt his heart beating faster.

"First, the good news." Hedley handed Clive a sheet of paper. "This arrived yesterday. As you can see, it's from a surgeon at a field hospital in France and addressed to Major-General Charles Callwell. here at Whitehall."

Clive's hands shook as he struggled to read through the tears filling his eyes.

. . . young Sinclair, wounded while helping the Flemish resistance flood the Polders. . . integrity, his intelligence and his bravery. . . his wounds have healed. . . should be awarded the Victoria Cross for gallantry in the face of the enemy.

"As you can see, Clive, your boy is a hero!"

"And the bad news, sir?" he asked, scarcely able to catch his breath.

Hedley stepped around the desk and placed his hand on Clive's shoulder. "After I received that letter late yesterday evening, I immediately cabled the BEF hospital for further details about Evan. I just received their reply. It appears that he was on a hospital ship for Dover which was attacked and sunk by a German U-boat in the Channel a few days ago. According to initial reports, Evan was among those who helped get others to the lifeboats, and among the last to leave the ship before it sank."

Clive felt Hedley grip his shoulder tighter as he continued speaking.

"A storm hit the Channel at time of the sinking, Clive. Again, that was three days ago. Evan is now listed as missing and presumed lost at sea."

Clive nodded slightly as he stared across Hedley's desk. Foremost among the images that rose in his mind was an evening under lamplight, sitting next to Janet's bed after Evan was born. He remembered the first time he had held him—the inexplicable heaviness of the warm bundle—his body so small, yet so substantial.

Clive buried his face in his hands, and he wept.

CHAPTER 3

November 21, 1914
Augusta Victoria Hospice, Jerusalem

NEARLY THREE months had passed since Montagu Walker and Guido von List had been dispatched to Palestine by Kaiser Wilhelm—Walker chosen because of his brazen audacity in successfully bribing Ottoman officials several years before to allow him to search for treasure on Jerusalem's Temple Mount, List because of his fervent preaching of Nordic-German racial superiority. Interactions between List and Walker had never been good, and during their time together in Jerusalem, they had only grown worse.

Especially since Walker had failed to make progress in the acquisition of certain adepts—Gunter von Wertheimer and Rahman B'shara. The two were archaeologists at the École Biblique in Jerusalem, and thought to possess secret knowledge of hidden passages into the Temple Mount.

For two weeks, Walker had been expecting a summons from List, living in anxious fear of the old man's displeasure. And when two quick knocks sounded at Walker's door late in the evening, he was not surprised, only more frightened. Fearing the worst, he drew a shaky breath, lifted the latch, and pulled the door open.

The Turkish sentry made a little bow, "Mr. Walker, Herr List would speak with you in the library."

"I'll be there forthwith." He closed the door and exhaled. *The sentry isn't escorting me—at least that's a good sign.*

Walker knew that this particular conversation would be about his failure to acquire a colleague of Wertheimer and B'shara—David Nathanson, a Jewish archaeologist who had been kidnapped soon after Walker and List had arrived in Jerusalem and set up residence at the Augusta Victoria Hospice. At List's direction, Nathanson had been held and tortured at the hospice. But after a month, near death, and apparently knowing nothing of the whereabouts of Wertheimer and B'shara, Walker had arranged for Nathanson's transfer to a hospital in West Jerusalem. There, Nathanson was treated and after two weeks was discharged to his home.

Once List heard of Nathanson's discharge, he directed Walker to bring Nathanson back to the hospice, but this time with his wife and infant son—to torture them all in order to bring the adepts out of hiding.

But Walker had failed to acquire the family. As he dressed, he thought back to the night he had arrived at the Nathanson's flat in a lorry with a squad of soldiers, only to find it empty—the family had somehow managed to slip away. When Walker had told List what had happened, he had expected a severe and immediate reprimand. But to his surprise, List's response had only been an ominous silence.

But Walker knew the response would come.

And now it has. Walker's hands shook as he put on his suit jacket, wondering why the summons had taken so long—a full two weeks. But the delay had given him time to compile an array of strategies to capture the Nathansons, which he hoped List would appreciate. He placed these papers in a leather case and headed for the hospice library that List had made his personal residence.

Reaching the library door, he knocked, and in a heartbeat, the door swung open.

"How very good to see you, Montagu. Please, come in!" List's face creased into an unfamiliar smile. "How about a beer?"

Never having seen the old man in such good spirits, he wasn't sure how to react. He also wondered at the choice of beverage. *A beer? Not brandy?* Nonetheless, he smiled. "Thanks. That would be lovely."

"Have a seat by the fire." List stepped to a wood-paneled liquor cabinet and held up a bottle. "*Der Löwenbräu?*"

"A perfect nightcap!" Walker said with feigned enthusiasm and thought, *God—a dreary, warm German beer.*

List beamed as he busied himself at the bar. "This Munich pilsner is the kaiser's favorite!"

Which explains the ghastly selection, Walker thought and said, "Given the kaiser's refined tastes, I'm certain the pilsner will be delightful!"

"And speaking of His Excellency, Montagu, you will be glad to hear that I have received glad tidings from the kaiser—good news from the Eastern Front!"

"Wonderful!" Walker sat in one of two upholstered chairs separated by a small table. "And I believe we'll soon have good news of our own for His Excellency, Herr List—I've come up with some sure-fire ideas."

"And I look forward to hearing them!" List handed him a stein and motioned him to stand. "But first, a toast!" Once Walker was on his feet, List raised his stein. "As the kaiser has famously said, 'Give me a woman who loves beer, and I will conquer the world!'" He slapped Walker on the back and raised his stein higher. "To the kaiser!"

"And to women who love beer!" Walker exclaimed. Together they drank.

"One more, my good man!" List raised his stein. "To the success of our mission!"

"To our success," Walker said and drank again.

He felt slightly nauseous as the mediocre beer filled his throat, but he pretended to admire it. "Great stuff, sir!"

"Indeed, it is," List said as he sat. "So, Montagu, let me see what you have."

"I've compiled a list of strategies that I'm sure will uncover the whereabouts of Wertheimer and B'shara," Walker said as he took out his notes. "First, we pressure the foreign diplomatic missions here in Jerusalem—in particular, a young Spaniard who recently took charge of the Spanish consulate—Conde de . . . Conde de Ballo . . . de Ballo . . ." he stammered, suddenly unable to read his own writing. He felt dizzy and his throat hurt. Rubbing his neck, he turned to List.

The old man smiled. "Please, do go on!"

He tried to focus on his notes, but there was an unpleasant and bitter metallic taste in his mouth, and he felt nauseated. He closed his eyes. Drawing a deep breath, he opened his eyes and tried again. "Conde de Ballobar," he said with great effort, his speech slurred.

"Are you feeling alright, Walker?"

"I'm . . . I'm sorry," he mumbled.

"No need to apologize!" List leaned forward and patted him on the knee. "It's called prussic acid, and given the amount you ingested, what you are feeling is *completely* appropriate."

Sitting back, List continued in a tone of amicable conversation. "Prussic acid has a rather fascinating history—first derived in the eighteenth century by the great German chemist, Carl Wilhelm Scheele—the same chemist who discovered oxygen, which makes one wonder how people were able to breathe before that! In any case, you English call it hydrogen cyanide. You have heard of it?"

Walker couldn't reply. His mouth was full of saliva he couldn't swallow. He closed his eyes and heard List's voice speaking.

"Though it's colorless, cyanide does taste of almonds, but with all the hops in the pilsner, you probably did not even notice!"

Seized by panic, the papers Walker was clutching fell to the floor as he tried to get up, but his body was too heavy. His heart pounded. He couldn't breathe.

"What is truly ironic is that hydrogen cyanide is an important precursor of amino acids—the molecular progenitors of life on earth—and this precursor of *life* is your agent of *death!* Isn't that just too ironic?"

But Walker couldn't speak, nor could he move or breathe. Confusion and darkness closed over him.

A final image rose in his mind—the face of his friend, Clarence Watson on the island of Corfu. Walker had just returned to the quay after an hour in conversation with Kaiser Wilhelm at Achilleion Palace. Leaving the palace, Walker had descended by carriage to the dock where Watson waited.

In the darkening library, Walker again saw the expression on Watson's face—when he pointed the pistol at him, and pulled the trigger, and the pistol discharged.

Watson's face was now his own.

CHAPTER 4

November 21, 1914
East End of London

SOON AFTER dawn, Chaim Weizmann left his flat on Orwell Road in London's East End and made his way to the pilot-plant distillery, buttoning up his greatcoat against the chilly air as he walked along the cobblestone lane by the Thames.

At forty, Weizmann was of medium height with fine features, a neat Van Dyke beard and dark hair receding from a high forehead. Reaching the distillery, he unlocked the door and let himself in. Pausing for a moment in the darkened silence, he lifted his eyes to admire the way the first rays of the rising sun shone through the plant's high windows, illuminating the giant steel vats and copper coils. *Time to get to work.* He hung up his greatcoat, pulled on the flywheel of the electric generator, and the lights came on.

Though this was a distillery, Weizmann wasn't about the work of distilling alcohol for spirits. Having come a long way from his native village of Motal in the western Russian Empire, he was a now professor of biochemistry at the University of Manchester and employed by the British War Office because of his discovery of a method to distill polysaccharides into the large amounts of acetone required for the production of cordite. And this was key, because cordite was the smokeless propellant used by the British for their heavy artillery and large naval guns. And without acetone, there would be no cordite.

Weizmann approached a long table that stood among the metal vats, and bending down, he removed a tray of agar plates from an incubator.

He had prepared the plates a few days before with different nutrient broths containing graded concentrations of different polysaccharides—from wheat, horse chestnuts, rice, corn, and potato. His goal—to evaluate which carbohydrate source would be best for the growth of Clostridium bacteria, central to his fermentation process that produced acetone.

Starting with the plates containing the nutrient broth of diced potatoes, he placed the first agar plate beneath a low-power microscope, infused a few drops of blue dye, angled the light obliquely, and began to examine the appearance of the Clostridium colonies. He knew that after several days of incubation, the most efficient acetone-producing polysaccharide would give rise to colonies with dense centers containing large numbers of spores. On the other hand, poorer polysaccharides would give rise to diffuse colonies with few spores, and these would yield little acetone. The central goal was acetone production, because without it, there would be no munitions for the artillery, and the British would lose the war.

This fact gave Weizmann leverage in another realm of his life because, in addition to biochemistry, his energies were directed to Zionism—the idea of a homeland for Jews in Palestine. And to realize that goal, the support of a great colonial power was vital. And for Weizmann, that power could only be Great Britain.

As he examined the cultures with each of the five different sources of starch, he noted the appearance of the Clostridium colonies and penciled the information onto a chart. As he worked, his thoughts turned to the day a few weeks before, when he had learned that his fermentation method had been selected for industrial development. This was also the day he had met the first lord of the admiralty, Winston Churchill.

He blew out a deep breath as he recalled Churchill's first words to him that day: "Well, Dr. Weizmann, we need thirty thousand tons of acetone. Can you make it?"

Recalling how quickly he had replied in the affirmative, he had to smile. "What remarkable chutzpah!" he said aloud in the empty distillery. "It's unheard of to have such a quick transition of a microbiological process from laboratory to an industrial scale! How did I have the nerve to say that?"

But he knew why. It was because he had already discovered the solution in response to a very different problem several years before. Weizmann had been appalled by newspaper reports of Belgian colonizers in the Congo forcing the native population to harvest natural rubber by threatening to cut off the hand of anyone who didn't fulfill a certain quota. As he methodically continued reviewing his slides, he heaved a sigh as he remembered the photographs of piles of hands and the photographs of natives with stumps where hands had been.

In the hope of stopping that savagery, he had sought to create an alternative to natural rubber—with isoprene from isoamyl alcohol that could be polymerized into synthetic rubber. But he needed the right bacterium, one that would produce isoamyl alcohol by sugar fermentation. He thought he had found it with Clostridium. But, to his great disappointment, he found that it produced only acetone.

Alone in the distillery, Weizmann sat back and laughed. *I felt like such a failure—instead of producing isoamyl alcohol to create synthetic rubber, I only produced acetone! But by then, thankfully, international outrage had caused the Belgium government to stop the abuse in the Congo and I no longer felt the need to prioritize that project. But I kept my notes, and three years later I had the key to the production of acetone—vital for Great Britain's munitions production!*

With a smile still on his lips, Weizmann returned his attention to the petri dishes.

The initial appeal from the British War Office had come in early August at the very beginning of the war in the form of a letter to British scientists—an invitation to provide any useful idea or invention that might aid Great Britain in the war. Weizmann recalled his excitement since he knew from a recent newspaper article that Great Britain had an acute shortage of acetone for production of the cordite needed for making munitions. The article had also stated that, before the war, England had imported acetone from Germany, a source clearly no longer available.

Weizmann couldn't wait to respond—to offer a solution to the problem facing his adoptive country in her hour of greatest need and to help win the war.

He had quickly responded to the War Office circular with his proposal for acetone production, and after a few months of review, interviews, and testing, it was accepted. Now, he was overjoyed to be actively working to solve England's acetone problem, and in the bargain, also working to leverage British support for the establishment of a Jewish homeland in Palestine. And the need for such a homeland at the present hour seemed more important than ever.

As he continued working, he considered that, with the war going poorly for Russia on the Eastern Front, it was only a matter of time before the five million Jews living in the Russian Empire would be blamed for the debacle and pogroms against them would begin. To avoid this looming catastrophe, it was imperative that a solution be found, and Weizmann was certain that Zionism was that solution.

Sitting in the quiet distillery, he continued to record the Clostridium colony data, relieved that after work, he would be taking the evening train home to Manchester. With that, his thoughts turned to his wife, Vera, and his seven-year-old son, Benji who were expecting to see him later that night.

Since starting work at the pilot plant, Weizmann had been splitting his week between London and Manchester, with four days living at home and lecturing at the university, and three days living in a rented flat in East London and working at the pilot plant. He traveled back and forth between London and Manchester at night to save time. And since Churchill had arranged with the university in Manchester to relieve him of most of his teaching duties, he was now able to spend more of his Manchester time at home with his wife and son.

Finished reviewing the Clostridium patterns, Weizmann sat back and studied the chart he had made reflecting the various sources of starch. It clearly showed that the best option was British wheat followed by American maize, with chestnuts a distant third.

He glanced at his timepiece and saw that it was midafternoon. *Excellent! I'll have ample time to reach the train station, and then, home to Vera and Benji.*

As he began closing up the lab, his thoughts strayed back to the first time he had seen Vera. It had been at a meeting of the Geneva University Zionist Club. He was a newly minted lecturer in organic chemistry, and she was a beautiful young medical student. While courting her for the next two years, he was also actively looking for a position that would give him the opportunity to do bench research in organic chemistry in addition to the requisite lecturing to students. But, when he found that job in Manchester, England, it created an immediate problem since it was so very far from Geneva. Actually, it created two problems.

The first was that, though Weizmann spoke six languages, English wasn't one of them. But, he reasoned, since he had several months before he was to arrive in England, he would immediately hire a tutor and learn English in his spare time.

The second problem was more formidable. He had fallen in love with Vera, and he didn't want to lose her. Hoping to solve that problem, he proposed to her, and she accepted. However, committed as Vera was to finishing medical school in Geneva, they agreed to maintain a long-distance engagement, remaining in contact with frequent letters and occasional phone calls. The plan was that, once she finished her studies, she would join him in Manchester. And, indeed, after four years, she did. In 1906 they married, and life was good—Vera gave birth to their first child, Benji, and after six months, she began working as director of a maternal-infant clinic in Manchester. For his part, Chaim became chair of the University of Manchester biochemistry department while maintaining an active involvement in the World Zionist Organization.

But, enough of these idle thoughts! Before I leave for Manchester, I must report my findings to Churchill.

And, as light began to fade toward evening, Weizmann took pen and paper and sat to write.

Pilot Plant, East London

November 21, 1914

First Lord of the Admiralty Mr. Winston Churchill

My dear Winston,

In anticipation of beginning to produce acetone as early as next week, I'm writing to let you know that I've conducted extensive comparisons of various concentrations of the following sources of starch for fermentation: British wheat, American maize, horse chestnuts, Indian rice and potatoes.

As I had expected, wheat appears to be the best source of starch for the purpose of fermentation. However, I recognize the current grain shortage and the fact that the food controller will not likely give us the volume necessary because of the war and its impact on the British public, not to mention the need to provide bread to soldiers in the field. I nonetheless hope that some portion of our needs might be met with wheat.

Regarding American maize, this appears to be a good alternative as a source of starch, but I share your concern about supply. The current German campaign of unrestricted U-boat warfare will likely put this source at risk. Nonetheless, I'm hoping that you might contact your American counterparts and arrange for immediate shipments of maize.

As to the other inferior sources, we will try to make-do with these if and when the first two options fail us.

I will be visiting my family in Manchester for a few days and will call upon you when I return to London.

Hoping for the best, and with
warmest regards to your family,
Chaim

Weizmann locked the pilot-plant door as evening fell over London, the ruddy sunlight reflecting off the smooth surface of the Thames. He headed for his flat by way of a small sorting station where he posted his letter to Churchill.

And now to Manchester! To hold Vera in my arms and kiss my sleeping son goodnight.

CHAPTER 5

November 22, 1914
East of Jeddah, Arabian Desert

FAISAL IBN Al-Hussein awoke to the sound of rats scampering across the floor of his bedchamber. He opened his eyes but didn't move. The room was dark but for the dull red glow that seeped from an iron stove in the corner. Through a half-open window casement, the bright winter stars against a black sky told him that dawn was hours away.

As he listened to the rats, his thoughts returned again and again to the coming revolt against the Turks. His heart began to pound—not with fear, but with pride. *After five centuries under their yoke, we are finally poised to thrust them from our homeland. But while we wait to begin the rebellion, I lie in bed listening to rats!*

Throwing off the bedclothes, he snatched up his robe. In the darkness, he could hear them—gibbering and squeaking as they scurried for cover.

He took a flint and lit the lamps along the wall facing the bed. Taking his crossbow, he grabbed a handful of bolts, returned to bed and propped himself up with a pillow against the wall. He set a bolt and waited.

But not for long.

With an eruption of squeaking from behind the glowing stove, two large rats broke into the open. As they scurried along the floor, Faisal took aim and squeezed the trigger. The crossbow fired with a flat snap and the bolt caught one of the rats in its hindquarters, smacking it against the white bricks of the facing wall. Shrieking, it twisted its body, gnawing at the bolt. Faisal sent a second bolt through the rat's head, and it lay still, apart from an unhurried trickle of blood dripping down the wall and over a section of dressed stone to the floor.

He set another bolt and waited. After a long minute a second rat emerged from behind a wardrobe and edged forward, sniffing at the blood.

Faisal fired again, and now two rats were impaled on the wall.

Outside the window casements, he could hear the wind keening through the acacia tree, its branches brushing against the veranda wall. Within the bedchamber the only sound was the sibilant hissing of embers in the iron stove.

The room felt suddenly airless and too warm. Faisal lay aside the crossbow and got up. Throwing open the window casements, he leaned out, feeling the cool air on his face. By the light of the guttering candles, he could see the winter bloom of the acacia's fragrant yellow flowers nodding in the wind. He inhaled deeply, tasting their aroma like warm honey. Looking up at the dark canopy of night, he took another deep breath, then went back to bed, leaving the window open.

Soothed by the sweet breath of the acacia and the windsong in its branches, he closed his eyes, but found himself thinking of his wife, Abdiya. *How I wish she was here with me and not hundreds of miles away!*

But he knew of the necessity and security of her sheltering with their four children in Nuweiba in the Eastern Sinai far up the Red Sea coast and across the Gulf of Aqaba. *Praise be to Allah!* he thought. *Abdiya and the children are beyond the reach of the Turks and well-protected by my faithful Tarabin brothers.*

But the yearning he felt for her made sleep impossible. Sitting up, he took his crossbow and set another bolt, deciding to watch for morning or more rats.

A week had passed since Faisal had departed from Mecca according to his father's wish that he return to Jeddah and prepare the Bedouin troops of the Hejaz for battle. His father, Hussein ibn Ali, *grand sharif of the Hejaz*, and keeper of the Holy Places of Mecca and Medina was no friend of the Ottoman Empire. Hussein had been in correspondence for months with the British government through their envoy in Cairo, Field Marshal Horatio Kitchener. This contact had been promising, though far from conclusive, with only vague assurance that if the Bedouin rose against the Turks, the British would provide gold and guns for the rebellion. It was in this regard that Hussein had directed Faisal to bring the news to the Bedouin at the oasis outside Jeddah and to gather more mounted troops from other tribes.

The Bedouin of Jeddah were of the Harb tribe, just as Faisal was, though of a different clan. He was of the Bani Salem, and they were of the Masruh. Nonetheless, they shared an unbreakable bond of loyalty and Faisal knew that he could trust them completely, because among the Bedouin, bonds of family and honor were sacrosanct.

When Faisal had informed the chief of the Masruh of the British assurances he saw that the sheikh was well pleased. The sheikh was also pleased to hear that Faisal had obtained promises of mounted warriors from trusted tribes of the Sinai—the Tarabin and the Muzeina—both fiercely loyal to Hussein.

Altogether, the Bedouin force totaled thirty thousand mounted warriors. However, to ensure victory, far more would be required, and these could only be recruited from among the Bedouin of the Arabian desert. This troubled Faisal because, while he could be certain of the loyalty of the Bedouin troops he'd already mustered, he could not be certain of the loyalty of the Arabian desert Bedouin. He did not know which of those tribes could be trusted, and it was imperative that the revolt be organized in absolute secrecy. If the Turks were to learn of the revolt, the consequences would be catastrophic. Anyone judged disloyal to the Ottoman Empire could expect to suffer a slow and painful death.

"This is not a problem, my prince," the sheikh had reassured Faisal. "I will assign Talib, one of my sons, to assist you. He is well-acquainted with all tribes in those regions."

These words had been music to Faisal's ears, and as the stars began to fade in the eastern sky, he knew that Talib would come in the morning to begin planning their journey into Arabia.

With Talib's help and with the British assurances, we will draw great numbers to the mounted Bedouin army. And with a vast multitude we may enjoy initial success in the rebellion, because winning battles at the beginning of the rebellion is key—to energize the fighters we have, and to draw others to our cause. Indeed, initial success is key to victory—initial failure is not an option.

Faisal was pleased with the assistance Talib had already provided in helping him navigate the day-to-day challenges of living in an unfamiliar environment, especially in securing Faisal's lodging from a Greek merchant in Jeddah.

With a shrug he thought, *Though I am a Bedouin by blood and the thirty-eighth generation directly descended from the Prophet, I have never really lived as a Bedouin, and I don't wish to start now. I know that once we trek through the desert, I will gladly live in the manner of the Bedouin, but now, thanks be to Talib, I don't have to. Prior to leaving for our journey, I am pleased that he has arranged for me to live in this lovely villa instead of a malodorous goat-hair tent pitched in the oasis. And the location couldn't be better—midway between the oasis and the city—with only a ten-minute walk in either direction. And the rent is a pittance! Especially since it includes the services of the old Greek caretaker, Khawaja Yanni, a most helpful and entertaining gentleman—*

Faisal's thoughts were interrupted by the song of the muezzin wafting on the cool desert air from a minaret in Jeddah through the open window, calling the faithful to prayer; "Allahu Akbar! Allahu Akbar! Allahu Akbar! Allahu Akbar!"

Out of bed without any further coaxing, Faisal took a pitcher of water set by the bed and whispered, *Bismillah-ir-Rahman-ir-Rahim*—in the name of God, the merciful and compassionate," as he washed the right hand, then the left. Then he proceeded to wash his mouth, nose, face, his head, his right arm then the left, and his feet to the ankle. After spreading his *sajjada* on the floor, and as far away as possible from the bodies of the rats, he stood, facing Mecca with arms crossed. He had to smile as he heard the words of the muezzin nearing the end of his call with, "Prayer is better than sleep."

With eyes closed and his hands raised to his ears, he began the dawn devotions with the same words the muezzin used to announce the call to prayer; "Allahu Akbar!"

CHAPTER 6

November 22, 1914
Lyme Regis
West Dorset Coast

TWO FISHERMEN trudged along the gray sand looking over the dark blue water laced by white caps. The storm that had hammered the English Channel had passed, but clouds still covered the sky, and a light rain was falling. With winds gusting up to forty knots, the half dozen fishing boats at anchor near the pier would not be going out.

"What's *that*, then?" one of the fishermen asked, peering out from beneath the dripping hood of his rain jacket.

"Where?" asked the other.

"A hundred yards hence near shore."

"My God! It's a boat!"

The two men began to run, lumbering forward in their thigh-high rubber waders.

Drawing nearer, one of them shouted, "Dear Christ! It's a lifeboat!"

Splashing into the cold Channel water, they struggled to grasp the gunwale as the lifeboat pitched in the surf. One of them fell but scrambled back to his feet.

"Oh, my God!" the other shouted as he saw a half dozen men lying in the boat.

They frantically dragged it to shore, where it tipped on its spine, and six flaccid bodies rolled onto the sand.

"I'll see if any are alive! You go for help!" shouted one of the fishermen as he fell to his knees and bent over one of the bodies, searching for a pulse.

The other pelted away toward the pier, his boots churning in the sand, his green raincoat like a fluttering cape. As he neared the pier, he shouted for help. After a few seconds, several fishermen came out of the warming shack, looking in his direction.

"Come quickly!" he waved his arms and shouted, pointing down the shore, his chest heaving. "Come quickly! Bring the cart!"

He saw them scramble down to get the long wooden fish cart kept beneath the pier for large catches—or drownings. Turning, he ran back to the lifeboat, the hood of his rain jacket blown back, his face streaked with rain.

"Are there . . . are there any alive?" he gasped out, struggling to catch his breath.

"No. They're finished."

"Look!" he shouted. "They were . . . from that hospital ship . . . the *Austrium!*"

"Impossible!" said the other as he folded the hands of one of the dead men over his chest. "The *Austrium* went down three days ago and two hundred miles from here."

"There's the name on the hull . . . as plain as day . . . *Austrium*. It must have drifted on the storm—"

"Bless me, but you're right! And such a storm."

"To think of these poor Tommies adrift . . . for three days with no food nor water."

"At least they found land—"

"What good came from that?"

"They'll have a proper burial."

The cart arrived and someone shouted, "Oh, God! Are they all dead?"

"I'm afraid so. From the *Austrium* they were, that hospital ship sunk by a Kraut U-boat. Let's bring them to Ian's pub. God knows we've used his place as a mortuary more than once!"

The fishermen left off speaking as they silently loaded the bodies onto the cart.

"Alright lads—we're the sad pallbearers, and these our own sons come back home. Let's give them their final honor."

❀ ❀ ❀

The owner of the Pilot Boat Inn, Ian Cowan, was a large man. His frame filled the doorway of the pub, and by his side was his rough-haired half collie named Lassie.

Seeing the fishermen approaching with the cart, he knew what they were bringing.

Running toward them with Lassie by his side, he shouted, "Any survivors?"

"None, Ian. These six lads were from the *Austrium*, sunk by a U-boat off Dover three days past."

"Holy Mother of God." Ian's heart sank. "What a sad catch." As he walked next to the cart, he placed his hand on the upturned head of one of the dead. "Dear boy, may all the saints guide you out of the dark and into the light."

Stopping at the tavern door, he turned and said, "We'll bring them down to the cellar, and there's a pint for each man who's done these lads kind service." He took hold of the legs of the first man, carefully moving backward with one of the fishermen taking the shoulders. "Watch your step here," Cowan called out as he stepped backward in the half-light.

As Ian carefully descended the wooden stairs, he remarked, "This young man certainly had a fine pair of boots. Lowering the body onto the cellar's stone floor, he directed the fisherman, "Go help with another. I'll bring blankets to cover up these lads until we can get them to the mortuary."

When Cowan returned with blankets, he saw all six bodies laid out in the cellar with Lassie sitting off to the side, as if guarding them. "Take a blanket, lads, but before you cover them, make sure to find their identification disk—they'll be on a lanyard about the neck." As he began to hand out blankets, he saw Lassie step gently among the bodies, sniffing at each, and his breath caught as he saw her settle down close to the young man with the fine boots and lick his face.

"Sweet Jesus, will you look at that! She's sending him off with a kiss to meet the dark boatman." Cowan shook his head and whispered, "That's a good lass."

In the silence he heard Lassie whimper as she nuzzled close to the body. Then he heard the young man moan.

"He's alive!" Cowan shouted. "The lad's alive! Bert!" he bellowed to the upstairs help. "Ring up Cottage Hospital and have them send an ambulance. We have a survivor!"

CHAPTER 7

November 22, 1914

Jeddah

FAISAL KNELT on his rug as he finished morning prayer, hands on his knees and facing east toward Mecca. He turned his head slowly to the right and then to the left, each time reciting the *Fajr's* final words; *Assalamu alaikum wa rahmatullah*—May the peace and mercy of Allah be upon you.

As he rose to his feet, he thought it likely that Talib would soon make his way to meet with him at the villa. *I'll make coffee for him as well as for the guards outside.*

Stepping toward the hearth, Faisal winced on seeing the impaled rats. *I'll have Khawaja Yanni clean that up when he arrives later this morning.* He stirred the glowing coals, and after adding kindling, he soon had a good fire. Taking a wide-bottomed copper *ibrik*, he poured in water, added ground coffee and sugar, and placed it on the fire.

I am most looking forward to speaking with Talib regarding our final preparations before we set out for the southern reaches of Arabia, he thought as he placed porcelain cups on the table, then settled on a stool to wait for the first boil. *The closer we come to Aden, the more likely we will encounter tribes loyal to my father and hateful of the Turks—*

His thoughts were interrupted by a knock at the door. "May I enter, o Emir Faisal?"

Immediately recognizing the voice of Talib, he turned from the fire and opened the door. "Good morning, Talib," he greeted the powerfully built young man, who was impeccably gowned in a long white abaya tied at the waist, his handsome face framed by a white head cloth. Stepping back to the hearth, Faisal asked, "Why do you insist on calling me emir?"

"Because, sire, your blessed father is sharif of Mecca and therefore king of the Arabs. And if he is king, you are emir."

Faisal shrugged as he stirred the coffee. "My good Talib, a king requires a kingdom, and at present the Arabs have no kingdom and therefore no king." He turned to Talib and raised his eyebrows, "However, if the coming rebellion leads to a kingdom, we may speak of such titles again." Leaning forward, he saw the foam rising in the ibrik. Taking it off the fire, he spooned some foam into each of the cups on the table.

"You've made a goodly amount of coffee, sire. Are we expecting company?"

"I made extra for the guards," Faisal replied as he put the ibrik back on the fire. When it boiled again, he filled two of the cups that were on the table, then motioned with his head toward the other cups. "Please bring cups for them, Talib." Once outside, Faisal poured coffee for each guard, and they murmured their thanks.

"*Mashkoor k'theer, ya emir!*"

"*Ahlan wa'sahlan,*" he replied and smiled inwardly at the thought of someday truly having the title of emir, with his father reigning as king of the Hejaz, or perhaps of all Arabia.

Returning to the villa, Faisal and Talib sat on the carpet and for a long minute, sipping their coffee without speaking. Finally, Talib broke the silence.

"Sire, many are wondering when the rebellion will begin."

"That depends on when we have sufficient numbers of mounted warriors, and ultimately, upon the considerations of my venerable father as to the quality of British assurances of support."

Talib appeared to fidget uneasily. "Many of the Masruh are tired of waiting."

"I understand this sentiment, Talib. I am also of two minds on this subject. On one hand, I feel within me the desire to strike as soon as we have the necessary number of fighters, but I also know that ultimate victory will require more than this. Success against the combined might of the Ottoman Empire and their German allies can only come with generous British support."

"But, sire, you have told us that we already have British assurances—"

"Yes, but not in writing," Faisal cut in. "And these assurances are only for British guns and gold. That is not enough. Beyond clearly written assurances of practical support for our revolt against the Ottomans, we also require assurances that our Ottoman masters will not simply be replaced by British masters."

Talib frowned. "Do you believe the British have such designs?"

"You have only to look at how they rule India. While they would likely be more benevolent masters than the Ottomans, my father insists that we should be the masters of our own fate. Toward this he is insisting that, in exchange for our revolt against the Ottoman Empire, and with its demise, we shall have the guarantee of Arab independence in our own lands."

"Independence in our own lands?" Talib's eyes opened wide. "Is this even possible?"

"So my father believes—from his communications with the British in Cairo."

"Has he any assurances of this?"

"Not yet, but with the war going poorly for the British on the Western Front, he believes that they grow more desperate, and that such assurances will come soon."

"But, sire, with the war going so poorly for the British, who can say if they will even prevail in this war?"

"That is a wise and sapient consideration, Talib. When I asked my father this very question, he replied that the only chance for the British to win this war is *with* our assistance, and this is the key to our leverage for demanding independence. For if they do not give us clear written assurances, we will side with the Ottomans, and under that condition the British will not only lose the war, they will lose their empire."

Talib nodded. "O prince, I am beginning to comprehend now. Indeed, if the British prevail with our help, they and their allies will divide up the carcass of the Ottoman Empire, and we will be positioned to receive a portion for a homeland of our own." He shrugged and added, "And in the bargain, the British will likely remain in India and Egypt with control of the canal at Suez."

"This is succinct and correct," Faisal replied but left off speaking as he saw a shadow of doubt cross Talib's face. "But I see that something troubles you, Talib. Speak your thoughts."

"It occurs to me, sire, that we might similarly strike a bargain with the Ottomans. After all, they are the devil we know. Would it not be possible to simply obtain from them the selfsame covenant? If we fight for the Ottomans in the war and they prevail, perhaps they will agree to grant us our independence—"

"No." Faisal shook his head. "There are three reasons I believe that this path will not lead to our independence. The first reason is that the Turks see how the Germans are winning the war and will not feel compelled to make a pact to give us independence. The second reason is that, even if the Turks were so inclined to grant us independence after victory in the war in exchange for our support, we know them all too well, and it is a certainty that they would never honor any such agreement. We would simply return to the Ottoman yoke for another five hundred years . . ."

Pausing, Faisal wondered, *Should I impart to Talib the third and most compelling reason for us to seek our independence with the British and not the Turks?*

Talib solved Faisal's dilemma when he asked, "What is the third reason, sire?"

"The third and main reason to cast our lot with the British is this, Talib: the Turks are in alliance with Germany, and the Germans are led by a madman whose true aim in this war is utterly contrary to our own."

"Are you speaking of Kaiser Wilhelm?"

"I am—the second of that name."

"But how can this be, sire? I have heard that the kaiser is a *friend* of all Muslims, that he converted to Islam and made pilgrimage to Mecca and is known as Hajji Wilhelm—"

"My dear Talib," Faisal said with a little laugh. "You repeat the lies that are being spread throughout the Levant by the kaiser's agents. My revered father, as grand sharif of Mecca and keeper of the holy places knows of a surety that the kaiser is in no way a Muslim. Indeed, it is widely known that he isn't even a true Christian!"

With eyes wide in stunned disbelief, Talib asked. "I understand that the kaiser may not be a Muslim, sire, but not even a *Christian*? How can this be? He made a Christian pilgrimage to the Holy Land and was crowned king of Jerusalem!"

"That is only because the kaiser seeks the power and the name of Jerusalem. In his arrogant conceit, he has made no secret in claiming his place in history with the ancient German King Frederick who joined the Crusades and crowned himself Holy Roman emperor and king of Jerusalem. This is the very reason Wilhelm made pilgrimage to Jerusalem before the turn of the century, and this is the reason he compelled the Turks to tear down a formidable section of the ancient stones of Jaffa Gate so that he could ride through dressed in white robes on a white horse fancying himself as king of Jerusalem! Imagine the humiliation he visited upon all Muslims, including his Turkish allies, with this act of vainglory—destroying a large part of Jerusalem's ancient wall built by an early Ottoman ruler—Suleiman the Magnificent! And riding into Jerusalem like a conquering Crusader king? I also know for a fact that the kaiser has changed the very face of Jerusalem with his lavish building over the past twenty years—a large hospice towering over Jerusalem on the Mount of Olives, the tallest church in the walled city for the German Lutherans, and a huge Christian abbey upon Mount Zion!"

"Why would he do all this?" Talib asked in amazement.

"Because his true motivation in this war is to seize Jerusalem for himself and to reign from a pagan palace he will build within the sacred precincts upon the Holy Mountain itself! A palace that will stand in place of the Mosque of Omar!"

"Nonsense!" Talib replied sharply. But after this outburst and a frown from Faisal, his face reddened with shame and his tone softened. "Sire, it is manifestly clear to me that the Turks will never allow this."

"The Turks?" Faisal exhaled a quick sardonic laugh. "If the Turks assist the kaiser to win this war, he will brush them aside like gnats and establish himself in Jerusalem on the Temple Mount as Holy Roman emperor, ruling a new German Empire that will stretch from the Rhine to the Euphrates, possessing the wheatfields of the Fertile Crescent to feed an army, and the oil of Basra to fuel a navy. He will make the Turks his vassals and we will be his slaves!"

Faisal saw how deeply his words had struck Talib—how his hand shook as he finished his coffee, how his visage had paled. Faisal rested his hand on Talib's shoulder and said, "But be of good cheer, Talib! For we are about the business of making sure this will never come to pass. Tomorrow we will set out toward Aden and in the days that follow, we will gather the faithful tribes to our cause beneath the banner of the sharif of Mecca!"

"But if the situation is so dire, should the revolt not begin sooner?"

"No, dear Talib.' He gave him a final pat on the shoulder. "As I have told you—only when we are at the peak of our strength in numbers and with clearly written British assurances will the revolt have a chance of initial success and ultimate victory."

"But, sire, you have said that the situation of the British and her allies is already dire."

"So, it is, and this works in our favor. Because when we join the fight, our contribution will be all the more appreciated by the British since it will likely turn the tide of the war, and they will be compelled to be more generous in honoring our wish for an independent homeland."

Talib seemed poised to respond when a knock came at the door. He climbed to his feet and opened the door. Faisal saw that it was the old Greek caretaker, a slight old man with a tousled fringe of white hair and skin deeply lined like a map of well-traveled trade routes in a brown desert.

Faisal raised his arm in greeting. "Welcome ya-khawajah Yanni! I am pleased that you have come early this morning."

"Bah!" the old man responded. "I come early *every* morning. A habit from the long years when I owned a grocery shop in Jeddah. And I'll have you know I didn't sell alcohol and always closed for prayers long before there were even any laws requiring me to do so!" As he stepped forward, his dirty, threadbare robe swept along the floor. Craning his skinny neck forward, he asked, "Is that coffee?"

"It is, ya-khawajah Yanni. Would you like a cup?"

"I most assuredly would, young man!"

"Young man?" Talib sputtered. "Do you not realize, old one, that you are speaking with an exalted personage?"

Amused by Talib's concern, Faisal poured a cup for the old man and handed it to him. "Here you are, sir."

"Thank you, young man," he said and finished the coffee in one gulp. Handing the cup back to Faisal, he asked, "Are you truly an exalted personage?"

Faisal smiled in response. "Come, my good man, because in addition to your usual chores, I have another for you." He took a water jug, length of cloth, and sack from the floor next to the hearth. "Take these, ya-khawajah Yanni." Stepping across the room to the far side of the bed, Faisal gestured toward the carnage of the rats impaled on the wall.

The old man shuffled forward with a wide, toothless grin. Apparently seeing Faisal's crossbow on the bed, he nodded approvingly at the rats on the blood-splattered wall. "Nice shooting, sire."

"Watch your tongue, ancient one," snapped Talib.

"Watch your tongue, ancient one," mimicked the old Greek in a high reedy voice.

Talib turned sharply. "I'm warning you—"

"You don't frighten me, boy," the old Greek snapped back as he jerked the bolts out of the wall, letting the limp rats fall to the floor. "I'm a good

Christian and under the protection of the Holy Mother."

"And will be with her soon, should you fail to curb your tongue, old one."

"I will be with her soon whether I curb my tongue or no." Khawaja Yanni sneered as he used the sharp end of a bolt to stab the rats off the floor and put them in the sack.

Faisal handed the water jug and cloth to the old man. "Here you are, sir."

"Thank you, young man. You're the kindest exalted personage I have ever met." Wetting the cloth, he wiped the stone clean and stood up. "There you are—good as new." He tossed the bloody rag into the bag with the rats. Then, looking at Talib, he held the bag open. "Plenty of room in here for you, boy."

"Why, you insolent cur . . ." Talib took a step toward the old man, his hand on the ornamented handle of the curved dagger at his girdle.

"Do not trouble yourself with this venerable gentleman, Talib," Faisal said and laughed. "He only seeks to provoke in jest, and yet serves our person well enough. Leave him the prerogative of speech."

"Thank you, sire." The old man bowed low with a smug sneer at Talib. "The fact is, sire, that though I never *sold* alcohol, I do drink—but I assure you, strictly for medicinal purposes."

"For what ailment, venerable father?" Faisal asked with bemused disinterest.

"Why, for three afflictions, sire: to give me sleep, to help me make water, but mostly to curb my lechery."

"Good sir, I charge you to continue this medicine, lest you spend the treasure of your time in lechery and not in our service."

The old man bowed low. "I will happily remain in your service, sire, and willingly will I bear the burden of my chastity." Chuckling to himself, he weaved out of the villa, dragging the sack behind him along the floor.

"Now, good Talib. Sit with me that we may plan our journey." Faisal drew a quill, scroll and a small bottle of ink from his pack and placed them on the table. "Please compose a map with your recollections of the various tribes we will encounter as we move toward the British Protectorate of Aden."

Talib adjusted his white head cloth and drew a deep breath. "Certainly, sire." He made a little bow and settled on a chair opposite Faisal by the table. Readying the quill, he spread open the parchment, dipped the quill in the ink and began drawing a map. "I will do my best to represent the relative distances, sire, though I'm not sure the proportions will be precise."

Faisal watched the feathered quill dance as Talib composed the map listing the oases, towns, villages, and the names of different tribes, speaking as he inscribed the details.

As they sat together in the quiet morning, Faisal felt both invigorated and at peace as an unhindered wind whispered through the opened window, carrying the fragrances of the desert and the acacia's sweet yellow flowers.

CHAPTER 8

November 22, 1914
Lyme Regis
West Dorset Coast

I'M LYING in darkness. On something that feels like smooth stone. I know that. I know that I'm cold. But I know nothing else. I remember nothing else.

I'm shaking. But not only from the cold. There's something important I should know. But I can't remember what it is. And I can't stop shaking.

It must be that I have no idea where I am. That must be it. No. There's something else. Something more important.

I don't know who I am. That's it.

I hear voices—many voices speaking, but they don't form words. Now the voices are close, but I can't understand what they're saying. And in the darkness, I can't see anyone. I can't see anything.

I'm not sure if my eyes are open or closed. I try to touch my face—to see if my eyes are open, but I can't move my arms. I feel my clothing heavy, cold, and wet.

Now I feel another wetness—but warm, not cold, and only on my cheek. And a warm breath. The warmth comforts me in the cold darkness.

It's a dog. I'm not sure how I know this—the word forms in my head. The dog is close to me, licking my cheek.

A voice speaks out of the darkness.

"That's a good lass . . ."

I try to get up, to call out. Now hands are lifting me up.

I see the flame of a single candle and a man's face close to me. I don't know him. But I know that I can see. I feel better and wonder where the dog is. I'm carried by strong hands. I hear footfalls on wooden steps, and the sound of many voices.

I'm in a place filled with gray light and many voices speaking at once. Faces turn to me and light glints on raised glasses. The glasses clink together. I don't recognize the faces. I can't make out what they're saying.

I see a fire burning in a hearth. I see firelight shining on a table. They lay me on the table and wrap me in a blanket. I feel the dog's warm fur against my cheek.

A man stands above me. He reaches out and pats the dog's head. "That's a good girl, Lassie." The same voice as before. He called the dog Lassie.

"If it wasn't for you, this boy would still be lying with his mates on the cellar floor. Thank God for you, girl."

He is looking down at me and touching the side of my head. "You took a nasty blow didn't you son?"

I try to say something, but no voice comes.

He calls out, "Dammit! When will the ambulance be here?"

"The roads are muddy, Ian," a voice shouts in reply.

Now the man speaks close to me. "What's your name, lad?"

I try to tell him that I don't know, but no words come.

"Not to worry, my boy. Not to worry. You'll find your voice soon enough. In the meantime, I'll check your identification disk." The man touches my neck. "It should be right here." He pulls at my shirt. "Never mind that for now." He bends low. "I'm Ian Cowan, and this is my tavern—the Pilot Boat Inn."

I try to speak again. A sound comes, but no words.

"We're in Lyme Regis," he says, "on England's southern coast." Then the man calls in a loud voice, "Margaret! Come here, please."

A woman's voice replies, but I can't make out what she's saying. "Margaret," he says again. "Have a look at our boy here."

"I'm a midwife, Ian." I hear her voice clearly now. "What do I know of grown men? If he's not with child, I'm not sure what I can do for him." I hear laughter.

"Don't be modest. I've seen you in action—with my wife and our five little ones—as good as any doctor in Lyme Regis. Give the boy a listen—just as you would a newborn babe. Make sure his heart is sound, and his lungs are good."

"Alright. Make room, then." The woman shouts.

I see the woman—Margaret, he called her. She looks down and smiles. "I'm to listen to your chest with this, son." She holds up a short wooden tube. She opens my shirt and leans down. I hear the dog growl.

"Easy, Lassie!" The man calls out, "Quiet now!" But the noise doesn't stop. "Quiet!" he shouts again. "Margaret is examining our young soldier."

The noise stops.

The woman bends at the waist. She places the wooden tube on my chest—first the left, then the right. After a moment she shouts, "As fine a heartbeat as ever I've heard, and lungs as clear as day!"

The noise returns. Someone calls for another round, and someone else asks, "But aren't we breaking Sunday Laws?"

"That's only for selling or buying the stuff!" Ian says. "And for this special occasion, I'm giving it away!"

Margaret isn't finished. She touches my chest. "There's a healed wound here—looks like he took a bullet." She touches my head. "The head wound isn't bad, but it may need a few stitches." She raises each of my eyelids, passing her hand over each eye. "Good response of the pupils. Now, give me a hand, Ian. I need to check his back."

I feel the man's arms beneath my shoulders, pulling me up. "Gently, Ian," she says. "What's this then—a haversack?"

"Indeed!" says Ian. "Perhaps his identification disk is tangled up with it." I feel Ian pulling on my clothing. A sharp pain cuts through my chest. "Ow!" I blurt out.

"I'm glad you've found your voice, son," Margaret says. "That's a good sign."

"It's tangled up with his clothing. Best I cut the strap," says Ian.

I see a knife blade glinting in the firelight. "There we are." He places the haversack next to me on the table. "But I still can't find his identification disk."

"Where am I?" I manage to ask, my voice hoarse, strange in my ears.

"Lyme Regis, my boy. You were on a hospital ship that went down—"

"Ship?" I have no idea what he's talking about.

"The *Austrium*—a hospital ship."

"Don't you remember?" the woman asks.

"No." A fear rises in my chest. "I don't remember anything."

"Not to worry, my boy. You'll remember soon enough." Her hand strokes my forehead.

"Let's start with your name," the man says. "What are you called?" When I don't respond, he asks again, "What's your name?"

But I can't remember and say nothing.

"Are you able to remember your first name?" The woman asks.

I try to remember, but I can't. I close my eyes and reach into my mind for a memory, but there's only darkness. My heart pounds with fear. I don't know my own name.

The man raises the haversack in his hand. "Perhaps we'll find some answers here."

I don't recognize the bag they call a haversack. The woman reaches in. I see something in her hand.

"What's *this*?" She asks, surprise in her voice. She holds it up for me to see. "Do you know what this is?"

I shake my head.

"It's a leather whip of some sort," Ian says and asks, "Do you recognize this?"

"No."

"Here's something," says Ian. "An oilcloth bag." He unfolds the edges and reaches in. "Now we're getting somewhere. There are papers in here, and they stayed dry." He bends at the waist, looks at the papers and shouts,

"We need more light!"

Someone hands the woman a lantern. She bends low. "This looks like a poem—*In Flanders Fields*. Does that sound familiar?"

"No."

"Look here, Ian. There's a name inscribed at the bottom; John McCrae." She fixes me with her eyes. "Is that you? Are you John McCrae?"

I've never heard the name before, but before I reply, Ian says, "This might be something—a letter addressed to the War Office at Whitehall." He opens it and reads silently. The room is quiet. I hear nothing but the dog's breathing beside me, her fur warm on my cheek.

"No less than a letter of commendation for the Victoria Cross!" Ian shouts and holds up the paper. "The Victoria Cross for one Evan Sinclair. Did you hear that? It appears our boy here is Evan Sinclair, and he's a hero—helped stop the Krauts by flooding the polders." He waves the letter above his head. "Another round on the house. Let's hear it for Evan! Hip, hip . . ."

Hurrah," shouts the crowd.

The noise startles me—coming from all around me. "Hip, hip . . ." He continues, leading the crowd.

I don't understand the noise. Ian leans close and speaks.

"Not to worry, the ambulance will be here in short order, and you'll soon be right as rain. Don't worry, Evan. That's your name isn't it—Evan Sinclair?"

I can barely hear him. The noise of the crowd is so loud. I don't understand what is happening, and the shouting fills me with terror. I turn to the hearth. A warm fire burns there. I close my eyes and the image of the fire lingers. I feel the dog's fur warm on my cheek.

With eyes still closed, I struggle to remember something, anything. But there's only empty darkness. My heart is beating fast.

I need to be quiet and think. I need silence, and the warmth of the hearth and Lassie's fur.

Nothing else.

CHAPTER 9

November 28, 1914
American Colony, Jerusalem

FIFTEEN-YEAR-OLD TIRZAH Wertheimer opened her eyes in the dark bedroom she shared with Fatima B'shara and Fatima's thirteen-month-old son, Mahmoud. Tirzah could hear the baby fussing, and she knew it was time for her to get up. She also knew that Fatima had come to bed late, having worked extra hours in the American Colony's soup kitchen in preparation for another day of feeding the growing numbers of Jerusalem's poor.

Lifting her head from beneath the warm comforter, Tirzah took a breath of the room's cold air. Blindly, she reached out and groped for the box of matches on the side table, determined to light the kerosene stove before tending to Mahmoud. Slipping out from beneath the comforter, she struck a match, lifted out the stove's circular heating unit, opened the kerosene spigot and lit the stove. After a few minutes, the grill glowed orange, filling the room with ruddy light and warmth.

Striking another match, she lit the wick of a small sesame oil lamp and went to Mahmoud. After changing his wet diaper, she took him in her arms and groped under the comforter to find the bottle of fresh goat's milk she knew Fatima would have placed there after feeding him a midnight snack. She unwrapped the bottle and was pleased to see that it was more than half full. Sitting in a rocking chair, she held Mahmoud in her arms and saw him smile as he put his hands on the bottle, touching her hand. He gulped down the milk, watching her with bright astonished eyes that gently closed before he finished the bottle.

Tirzah put him over her shoulder, patted his back, and smiled when he burped. As she continued holding and rocking him in the chair, she could almost remember her own mother, Rachel, holding and rocking her.

With a wistful sadness, Tirzah's thoughts turned to her mother—taken from her by smallpox six months before. She drew a deep breath and sighed out her thoughts in a whisper, "How I miss you, Ima. How I miss my own room in our own house. How I miss my life, my friends, being outdoors. How I miss the flowers, the trees, the open sky, the sun on my face. But more than anything, Ima, I miss you."

Certain that Mahmoud was asleep, she carefully laid him back in his crib and turned to look at Fatima. She was still asleep, her breathing even and unhurried.

Remembering how Fatima had tended to her mother during her illness, Tirzah's heart swelled with gratitude.

Feeling fully awake, Tirzah decided not to go back to bed. She sat in the rocking chair and considered what her life had become since first being separated by quarantine for her mother's smallpox— separated from her when she needed most to be with her—separated also from her father, and after Rachel's death, not even able to mourn. And after quarantine ended, they had immediately gone into hiding within the warren of rough-hewn limestone chambers beneath the American Colony.

She heaved a sigh and thought, *I'm not allowed to venture outside the compound or even go upstairs into the main Colony. I haven't seen the sky in four months. I don't mind helping in the kitchen, and I certainly don't mind helping care for Mahmoud—I love him as I would a baby brother, and I love Fatima as I would an older sister, but how much longer will this isolation go on?*

She also wondered about not having been able to attend school for over six months.

Though she spent about two hours each day tutored in English, French, German, and history by her father, and tutored in Arabic by

Fatima, it was a far cry from the classes she had so enjoyed at the Evelina de Rothschild School for Girls.

With a despairing sigh she remembered her school friends and wondered how they were . . . where they were. "I truly feel that I've been buried alive!" she whispered aloud. "And no one will tell me how much longer this will last!"

When she asked her father, he would only vaguely say, "Not much longer." And when she asked him who they were hiding from, he always told her that he was avoiding the German councilor authorities who sought to return him to Germany for service in the kaiser's army, and Rahman was hiding to avoid the Turkish authorities who would impress him into either active military service or a forced-labor brigade.

But Tirzah harbored other suspicions.

From bits of conversation she had heard from her father and from Fatima and her husband, Rahman, she had come to understand that the three of them were members of a secret fraternity that had something to do with the Temple Mount.

She had also come to understand that the German Kaiser had aspirations to build a palace on the Temple Mount, and to do that, he required information about certain hidden chambers beneath the Foundation Stone. It appeared to Tirzah that the kaiser was certain that her father and Rahman possessed that information, and he was resolved to find them. Which is why he had sent his agents to Jerusalem—and why they were in hiding.

But if that's the reason, what's all the fuss about? she thought with a shrug as she continued to rock in the chair. *Why don't they just tell the kaiser's agents what they want to know?*

But in her heart, she knew why. There was something else—something she had sensed about the young couple who had joined them in hiding a few months before. Sarah and David Nathanson had lived in one of the new Jewish neighborhoods in West Jerusalem, and David was an archaeologist who had worked for years with her father and Rahman. He and Sarah had always seemed pleasant enough; indeed, Tirzah enjoyed helping with their baby, Isser.

But, since the Nathansons had joined them in hiding, Tirzah had noticed things about David that didn't seem right; he often seemed melancholy, and his appearance had changed significantly over the past year—a few of his teeth were missing and there were scars on his face, hands, and arms—as if he had been injured in a bad accident. Tirzah's father dismissed the injuries as related to their work as archaeologists. But Tirzah didn't believe him, especially since he and Rahman had both had their share of accidents, but neither of them had any such signs of injury.

What happened to him? she wondered. *What happened to David Nathanson?*

Shaking the thoughts away, Tirzah rocked harder in the chair and considered that she had much to be grateful for. She truly appreciated the generosity of Anna Spafford, the director of the Colony, for the sanctuary she provided for them. Indeed, Tirzah never missed an opportunity to spend time with Anna, who played piano and encouraged her to sing. The music and voice lessons were bright spots in the otherwise monotonous and dreary life spent in the underground chambers of the Colony complex.

As her thoughts turned to Anna Spafford, Tirzah leaned forward, took a folded piece of paper from the table by her side of the bed, and spread it open. In the weak light of the sesame oil lamp, she scanned the sheet music of the song Anna had taught her, "It Is Well with My Soul."

Anna's late husband, Horatio, had composed the words of the song as a poem he had written years before, following a series of tragedies that he and Anna had sustained over the years: the loss of their home in the Great Chicago Fire, the death of a four-year-old son from scarlet fever, and death by drowning of four daughters when the steamer carrying Anna and the girls collided with a clipper out of Glasgow on a transatlantic crossing. Horatio had been due to follow and join them for a family holiday in England.

Tirzah closed her eyes against the tears as she recalled what Anna had told her of conveying the sad news to Horatio with a telegram of only two words; "Saved alone." Shortly afterward, as Horatio traveled by ship to meet his grieving wife in England, he wrote the poem, "It Is Well with My Soul," as the steamer passed the place where his daughters had drowned.

Set to music by the composer Philip Paul Bliss, the poem had since become a hymn sung in many Christian communities. Indeed, it was sung every Sunday at the American Colony church service. Anna had taught Tirzah the melody just last week. As they had sung the hymn together, Anna had complimented Tirzah on her beautiful soprano voice, and promised her that, once they were no longer in hiding, she would arrange for Tirzah to lead the congregation in singing the hymn at Sunday service.

Well . . . today is Sunday! Tirzah thought as she wiped the tears from her eyes.

She began to sing, though very quietly, so as not to disturb Fatima or wake Mahmoud. As she sang, she thought of Anna and Horatio and all the sadness they had sustained . . .

"When peace like a river, attendeth my way,
When sorrows like sea billows roll;
Whatever my lot, Thou hast taught me to know
It is well, it is well, with my soul."

She crushed her eyes shut, unable to continue.

After a long minute, she decided to get dressed. She slipped out of her flannel nightgown, and she put on her nicest dress.

I'm tired of being buried alive, and I'm certain that no Turkish or German conscription agents will be at Sunday service!

❋ ❋ ❋

With Mahmoud in her arms, Fatima rushed to the room her husband shared with Gunter.

Pounding on the door, she shouted, "Rahman! Rahman!"

The door quickly opened. "What's wrong?" he asked, reaching out to touch Mahmoud. "Is he okay?"

"Mahmoud is fine. It's Tirzah!"

"Oh, my God—is it smallpox?"

"No, no, no—nothing like that, but I can't find her anywhere! She's gone—"

"What do you mean, gone?"

She's nowhere to be found, and from the way she's been talking, I'm afraid she may have gone to visit the main Colony!" She looked past Rahman and asked, "Where's Gunter?"

"Taking a bath. I'll get him—"

"No. There's no time." Fatima patted Mahmoud on the back as he began to cry. "Shh, *hamudi*—here, you take him. I'll look for Tirzah."

She rushed back to her room, put on an embroidered dress, covered her head with a scarf and bolted out into the mazelike passageways. Running up a long stone staircase, she took the steps two at a time. To keep their presence in the Colony a secret, Fatima and the others had only interacted with Anna and her immediate family, and never with any other member of the Colony. But she wasn't worried about meeting any of them today. She knew that they would all be at Sunday service.

And at that moment, she knew where Tirzah had gone.

She stopped running and listened. After a few seconds, she heard it—the faint sound of singing.

She followed the sound.

The Colony congregation was singing a hymn that Fatima knew well—she had sung it herself with Tirzah and Anna, who had given them a copy of the words and told them of the hymn's special significance.

"And Lord, haste the day
When my faith shall be sight,
The clouds be rolled back as a scroll;
The trumpet shall sound,

And the Lord shall descend,
Even so, it is well with my soul."

As the hymn continued, Fatima slowly mounted the limestone steps. Turning on the landing, she moved toward a closed door at the end of the hall, knowing Tirzah was on the other side of the door. She could hear her beautiful soprano voice rising above the others.

"*It is well with my soul,*
It is well, it is well with my soul."

Fatima sat on the smooth stone steps, her head bowed, tears on her cheeks. She felt overwhelmed—with relief at finding Tirzah, with the poignant sadness of the hymn, and with the anxious realization that they might now be discovered.

CHAPTER 10

November 28, 1914
War Office at Whitehall, London

CLIVE WAS increasingly frustrated with trying to map Mesopotamia without the help of Lawrence, who had been gone for a week, spending time with his family in Oxford. But beyond that frustration, Clive was frantic that Evan was missing at sea, agonizing over the uncertainty of where he might be, praying that he was still alive.

"To hell with Mesopotamia!" he shouted and covered that map with one of the English Channel, which he had been studying as information about the *Austrium* had trickled in over the past five days. Leaning over the table, he reached out, touched the Channel's blue water in the narrows between Calais and Dover, and said aloud, "This is where she went down on the night of November 19."

He pulled a notepad from his pants pocket, flipped it open and glanced at the list of facts he had learned from Hedley and from the Red Cross. *I should organize this on the map,* he thought and wrote on a small square of paper; 19 November—*Austrium* sinks with 440 wounded on manifest; 377 survivors, 43 dead, and 20 missing.

He pinned the note to the map on the blue water of the Strait of Dover and wrote another note; 21 November—2 lifeboats ashore at Bournemouth—150 miles from Dover with 12 survivors, 8 still missing.

He pinned that note on the southwest Channel coast, then wrote another; 22 November—a single lifeboat comes ashore at Lyme Regis—200 miles from Dover with 6 dead, 2 still missing.

After pinning that note to the southern English coast, he drew a deep breath and stared at the map. "I feel that you're alive, Evan, but where?" he said, then shouted, "Where are you!?"

The map room door opened, and Lawrence said, "Sorry to interrupt." He glanced around the room. "With whom were you speaking?"

"With Evan." Clive shrugged as he walked quickly around the map table to Lawrence and placed a hand on his shoulder. "I'm *so* glad you're finally back! I really need to speak with you."

"About mapping Mesopotamia?"

"No—about mapping Evan."

"Any news since he dodged the Paris police?"

"Since you've been gone, a great deal of news."

"What's happened?"

"Briefly, this is what we know; after escaping the Paris police, he joined up with the Flemish resistance—don't ask me how. But we do know that he was wounded while helping to flood the polders, and that he recovered at a BEF hospital in Boulogne for almost three weeks." Clive shook his head. "I have no idea why he wasn't identified by the Red Cross or the BEF during that time, but look at this." Clive handed the surgeon's letter to Lawrence, and watched as he read, his blue-gray eyes wide, his jaw slack.

"My word. Nothing less than a recommendation for the Victoria Cross. Then what?"

"He was discharged from hospital, taken by lorry with other wounded soldiers to Calais, where he boarded the *Austrium,* a hospital ship—"

"Oh, my God," Lawrence cut in. "I read about that beastly attack . . . and Evan?"

"That's the question, Ned! He was listed as *missing* by the Red Cross, and now, eight days later, he's considered *lost at sea!*" Clive waved his hand over the map of the English Channel and watched as Lawrence read his notes and studied the map.

After a minute Lawrence broke the silence. "So, instead of twenty missing, there are now two, and one of them is Evan."

Clive breathed out his despair in a sigh as he leaned against the map table. "I'd like to think that he's in the warming hut of a kindly old fisherman somewhere between Dover and the Celtic Sea . . . but where, Ned? Where could he be?"

CHAPTER 11

November 28, 1914
Cottage Hospital, Lyme Regis

THE PHYSICIANS had finished morning rounds with the last patient, a young man with amnesia. They had taken to calling him "Joe Bloggs"—a place-keeper name that would stay in place until his true identity could be established.

As the white-coated house officers sauntered down the hall toward the doctor's dining room for breakfast, the consultant, Dr. Barlow, sporting a gray Harris Tweed jacket with white shirt and bowtie, remained behind, standing in the hall with the Ward Sister as the door settled closed.

Barlow turned to peer over his pince-nez spectacles through a window in the upper half of the door. "Joe's back to writing in his journal."

"It's certainly not for lack of trying he hasn't regained his memory," said the nurse. "Do you believe he will?"

"Too early to tell, but his journaling is encouraging, actually therapeutic."

"It certainly keeps him busy, Doctor, but how is it therapeutic?"

"It helps him retain his *recent* memories, that is, everything *after* the event. It also gives him hope he'll recover memories from *before* the event. And that's the key—that hope—it gives him a chance to avoid the melancholy we often see in these cases."

"What do you believe caused his amnesia, Doctor?"

"A number of things—the near drowning, prolonged exposure, malnutrition, the concussion from that blow to the head . . ." He fell silent and turned to look out a window at the bare branches of a spreading horse-chestnut tree. When he spoke, his voice was a whisper. "There's another possibility."

"What might that be?"

"Joe was in that lifeboat for three days and nights—in that storm with no food, no drinkable water, constantly bailing to stay afloat. He watched each of his mates die, and he could do nothing to save them. Nothing. Three days watching them die." He turned and fixed the nurse with his eyes. "Consider the *desperation*—the *horror*. Perhaps he simply *needs* to forget—to wipe it all away."

"Are you referring to shellshock?"

"Yes. An emotional rather than a physical injury. We're seeing more and more of that sort of thing—whether it's called shellshock, bullet wind, soldier's heart, or battle fatigue—whether it's expressed as amnesia or some other physical or emotional manifestation. In forward units it's affecting over ten percent of our troops."

"If he were to regain his memory, do you believe it might be a mixed blessing?"

"A mixed blessing at *best*, Ward Sister. At worst? Suicide. For the present he's often angry about his amnesia, but it may be the only thing standing between him and the full horror of terrible memories." He turned back and looked at Joe Bloggs. "That's what I fear most—that he may not survive remembering."

❋ ❋ ❋

Diary Entry November 28, 1914
Cottage Hospital, Lyme Regis

THEY TELL me it was a U-boat that sank the hospital ship I was on. But I don't remember—not the hospital ship, not the U-boat—nothing. Nothing from before I woke up in the tavern. Not even who I am.

But I'm trying—every morning and evening—keeping this journal, trying to remember everything I can.

I remember arriving here, at this hospital in Lyme Regis, though I haven't really needed any medical attention. The gash on the side of my head is pretty much healed.

When I ask when I can go home, I never get a straight answer.

But I know why. How can they send me home when no one knows who I am and where my home is?

The doctors and nurses speak with me every day—trying to help me regain my memory, encouraging me to write in this journal. They tell me I had a brain injury since I almost drowned and had a blow to the head. They tell me I was in bad shape when the lifeboat washed ashore. But at least I was alive. The five other guys in the boat weren't so lucky. But I don't remember them at all. Nothing.

But I'm trying to hold onto the memories I've made since I woke up, especially since I don't have any old ones. Problem is, I'm even finding that difficult, which is why I'm writing everything down.

So, what do I know? I know that I like bangers and mash, and I don't like haggis. I know I like fish and chips, but I don't like the little fish looking at me from a stargazy pie. I know the day-shift nurse is nice and the night nurse is mean. I know that when the doctors ask me about my father, I feel anxious, and when they ask me about my mother, I feel sad. But I have no memory of either of them. Nothing.

Ian Cowan, the owner of the tavern where I woke up, comes to visit every day, and always brings his dog, Lassie. He tells me that if it weren't for her, no one would have known I was alive. I like to pet Lassie—the warmth of her fur was the first thing I remember when I woke up.

Ian says he wants me to live with him and his family when I get out of here—until we find "my people"—whoever they are.

There's a leather jacket hanging on a hook next to my bed along with a haversack. Ian says I was wearing both when they found me—the straps of the knapsack so tight he had to cut them away. In the haversack there was a long leather strap he says is some kind of a whip. There was also a waterproof oilskin bag with five pieces of paper. The most promising one is a letter of commendation to Whitehall written by a doctor at a hospital in France about Evan Sinclair—the person they think I might be. There's also a handwritten poem, "In Flanders Field," signed by John McCrae who turns out to have been a Canadian surgeon. There are words to a song, "Brian Boru's March," in Gaelic and English. Last, there's the name and address of a woman in Bath—Sharon Meehan, and in the same handwriting, a few lines from a Persian poem. I keep those papers by my bed and study them a few times a day—the only connection to what might be my past. But, so far, I recognize none of it.

Fact is, those papers may not even belong to me. Ian thinks they do, since they were in the haversack I was wearing when they found me. But what if I was carrying the haversack for one of the guys in the lifeboat who died? Ian doesn't have an answer for that, but he came up with a way we can find out.

A few days ago, he had my photograph taken, along with one of the letter to Whitehall. They developed both and made copies. These were sent by courier with a cover letter to the doctor at the hospital in France, to Whitehall, and to the woman in Bath, asking if the person in the photograph is Evan Sinclair. There's been no response so far, but it's only been a few days.

I'm trying to feel hopeful that I'll find out who I am.

They gave me a copy of my photograph, which I'm looking at right now. I use it as a bookmark in my journal—to find my place, and to remember what I look like without having to look in a mirror.

In the meantime, Ian insists on calling me Evan. And I tell him that might not even be my name. I practice writing it over and over—Evan Sinclair—but it doesn't stir any memories. If it was really my name it should be familiar to me, but it isn't. Not at all.

During Ian's visits, he shows me newspaper reports, which along with the surgeon's letter shows my history or, as Ian says, "reconstructs my past." According to this, I was with the Flemish resistance behind enemy lines in Belgium, which can only mean that I'm from Belgium. But that doesn't make any sense, since I'm told there are two types of people in Belgium—Flemish Dutch and French-speaking Walloons—and the name Evan Sinclair is neither. The other thing is that I speak English, and a little French, but I don't know any Dutch. And Ian tells me that my English isn't really English at all, but American or possibly Canadian. He's got his money on Canadian, because John McCrae, who wrote the poem I have a copy of, was Canadian.

Ian found out about McCrae from a newspaper report about the sinking of the *Austrium*. The first mate, who survived, said that McCrae was a Canadian doctor who was on the bridge with the ship's captain after almost everyone else had abandoned ship. The German U-boat had surfaced and was firing on the *Austrium* and the lifeboats. The captain ordered the first mate and McCrae to fire up the ship's remaining boiler and then leave on the last lifeboat. But after they lit the boiler, they couldn't reach the lifeboat because of the machine-gun fire from the U-boat. The first mate said that he and McCrae sheltered behind the gunwale as the *Austrium* rammed the U-boat. The last thing he remembered was the explosion when they collided. By the time he was rescued, the *Austrium* and the U- boat were on the bottom of the English Channel, and there was no trace of the ship's captain, and no trace of John McCrae.

I think I'll go to breakfast now. Then I'll go for a walk. I've been walking a lot—around the hospital on rainy days, and outside when the weather's fair. When I go outside, I wear the fancy boots I had on when I washed ashore. The orderly who helped me dry the boots, tells me they're Italian and very expensive. He offered to buy them from me.

I repaired the straps of my haversack with a needle and thread I borrowed from the nurses' station. I wear the haversack on my walks to keep my journal and papers with me. I also keep the long leather whip coiled in the haversack. I'm not sure why. Sometimes I take it out and hold it in my hand. It has a comfortable feel to it, like it might really be mine.

Outside my window this morning, I see an unusual sight—blue sky! So I'm looking forward to a long walk after breakfast. I find I'm able to walk farther and faster every day, and I'm starting to feel fully recovered. Except of course, for my brain—empty of all memories from the time before.

And that empty darkness scares me more with each passing day.

CHAPTER 12

November 28, 1914
American Colony, Jerusalem

TIRZAH RAISED her voice with the congregation in the closing hymn of the worship service, the Doxology.

Praise God, from Whom all blessings flow; Praise Him, all creatures here below; Praise Him above, ye heavenly host...

As a child of a Jewish mother and a Lutheran father, she recognized the hymn for what it was—a hymn of praise to the triune God. And she knew that as such, it was equivalent to the *Kaddish*—the Aramaic expression of praise at the closing of the Jewish prayer service, though this prayer also served as an expression of mourning—*Kaddish Yatom*—the orphan's *Kaddish*, to be recited throughout the year following a parent's death.

As Tirzah sang the Christian words of praise in English, the Aramaic Doxology echoed in her heart as she embraced her mother's memory:

Yit'gaddal ve'yitqaddash shmeh rabba, Exalted and sanctified is His great name, Blessed and praised, glorified, and exalted...

With the service over, Tirzah made her way through the crowd toward the door in the rear of the large upper room that served as the Colony's chapel. Wiping tears from her eyes, she realized that her sudden presence among the Colony worshipers had created quite a stir. She walked faster, nodding and smiling in response to greetings, pretending not to hear the pointed questions as to her name. Managing to reach the door, she opened it and was relieved to see Fatima in the hall, dressed in a traditional embroidered Arab dress.

"Come, my dear. Make haste!" Fatima said in a tense whisper. "I'll help you leave here quickly."

Tirzah felt a wave of gratitude as Fatima guided her away from the chapel, across the landing, down a narrow staircase of smooth limestone, and through a door leading into a central garden. Crossing quickly through the garden, they entered another section of the compound, descended long flights of steps, and finally passed through a small doorway into an arched rough-hewn passageway lit by torches set along the walls. Here, Fatima slackened the pace and Tirzah, feeling that she owed Fatima an apology and explanation, spoke up.

"Thank you for rescuing me, and before you scold me, I apologize. I know it was wrong to join the service. but I felt so horrible being cooped up, and I was certain that no one would know who I am."

Fatima turned to Tirzah, placed her hands on her shoulders and said, "What's done is done, Tirzah. We can only hope that no ill will come of it."

"But, how could anyone at church know who I am, and besides, why would it even matter? I know that my dad and Rahman are in hiding from the German and Turkish authorities because of the war, but I don't understand why I must hide."

"There's far more at stake, my dear, far more—"

"What's at stake?" she asked. "For years, I've overheard whispered conversations between you, Rahman, and my parents—about the Temple Mount and the kaiser, but I've never understood what you've been talking about. Is that the real reason we're in hiding?"

"Your father had intended to tell you, but between Rachel's illness and her death, between the quarantine and the war, he didn't want to further burden you. He was waiting for the right time." Fatima paused, then added, "I believe that time is now." Fatima turned and led the way through the subterranean passageway. "Come, my dear. Let's find him."

Tirzah felt relieved that the veil of ambiguity might finally be lifted. She followed Fatima, looking forward to speaking with her father, wondering what he might tell her. When Fatima came to a sudden stop,

Tirzah nearly collided with her. "Sorry," she said as Fatima opened a barely noticeable door and slipped through.

Once through the doorway, Tirzah found herself in a corridor she recognized as one that led to the kitchen. And once she entered the kitchen, she heard her father's voice.

"Thank God Fatima found you!" Gunter ran to her and caught her up in his arms in a firm hug. "Where—"

"You should know that I found Tirzah in the main Colony at Sunday service," said Fatima."

Tirzah's heart pounded as she saw a look of horror and disbelief cross her father's face.

"Oh, my God, Tirzah! What were you—"

"Gunter," Fatima cut in, "before you speak with Tirzah, I need to talk to you!"

"Tirzah, weren't you listening to me when I told you that you must never—"

"Gunter!" Fatima cut in and put her hand on Gunter's arm. "Let me speak with you now, please." She gestured with her hand for him to follow her.

Staring at Tirzah, he nodded, "I'm happy you're back, darling, but we most definitely need to talk," Gunter said and turned to follow Fatima.

She watched him leave the kitchen, mortified by what she had done, but excited in the expectation of what he might have to tell her. She was also relieved to be back in the comfortable familiarity and warmth of the kitchen.

"We were worried about you," said Rahman as he poured water over the lentils. "We're happy you're back and look forward to hearing about your adventure this morning in the Colony. But that will wait till after you speak with your dad."

Tirzah nodded. "Where's Sarah? I thought she'd be helping here this morning."

"She's with David—looking after Mahmoud and Isser," Rahman replied.

"I very much look forward to returning to the boys once I've spoken with my dad . . ." Tirzah left off speaking when she saw Gunter return to the kitchen followed by Fatima, who began putting on her apron as she spoke.

"Rahman and I will get things ready for the soup kitchen while you have a chat."

Tirzah saw her father nod toward the doorway. Together they left the kitchen.

❈ ❈ ❈

Gunter drew a deep breath and stared at his hands, gathering his thoughts as he sat with Tirzah on a divan in the subterranean commons of the Colony compound. All the anger he had felt earlier was gone, replaced by a self-reproach at not having explained everything to Tirzah earlier.

After a few moments of silence, he began to speak, though in a low voice. "This is a conversation I have waited long to have with you, my darling girl—"

"Why are you whispering, *Aba*?" she asked.

In response, he nodded in the direction of the Nathanson's nearby room. "Though David and Sarah are dear friends, the secrets I have to convey are for your ears only."

Seeing Tirzah nod her understanding, Gunter continued. "I had hoped that your mother and I would have this moment with you together . . . and in a very real sense she's here with us now." Gunter turned to look at Tirzah and saw tears on her cheeks. Taking her in his arms, he whispered, "I want you to know that all I'll tell you flows from both of us."

He took a handkerchief from his pocket and handed it to Tirzah, drying his own eyes with his shirt sleeve. "So," he said and breathed out a sigh, "let's have this long-awaited talk. Your mother and I were bound together by the love we had for each other, and this bond of love included you as our child."

"Yes, Aba," Tirzah said as she dried her eyes. "I always felt that connection with you and Ima."

Gunter fixed Tirzah with his eyes and continued in a low voice. "And you should know that, years before those bonds of love were forged, Rachel and I were connected with each other by the bonds of a hidden fellowship, and in this fellowship, we were connected to Rahman and Fatima, along with others—adepts and comrades living in this world . . . and the next. While we were careful not to speak of this in your presence, we knew that, over the years, you overheard us speaking, and that you may have had some inkling of this secret fellowship . . ."

As Gunter paused to consider how to proceed, Tirzah spoke up. "Indeed, I did, Aba, and I'm now ready to hear the truth of it."

"And the truth of it is more wonderful and complicated than you might ever imagine." Bending toward her, he continued in a whisper. "My darling girl, ours is an ancient fellowship with origins that span the arc of history and beyond. In fact, our story begins in the darkness before history—before this city was called Jerusalem or *Al-Quds* or Aelia Capitolina or Ursalimmu. As you know from your studies of scripture, Abraham traveled here from his home in Ur of the Chaldeans—to the Holy Mountain where he was blessed by Melchizedek, the priest of the most high God—El Elyon. Indeed, our original name—the Children of Melchizedek—harkens back to the ambiguity of this personage and the mystery of our origins."

"If Children of Melchizedek was the original name of your fellowship, what is it now?"

"For the last few centuries, we've been known as Guardians of the Temple Mount."

Tirzah frowned. "That sounds like a military order."

"In a way it is, but we don't guard the physical Temple Mount as much as we keep the secrets of a spiritual city within it—"

"A *spiritual city within it*? What are you talking about?"

"The Upper Jerusalem, my child. Not this place of stone and dirt and bad smells." Gunter waved his hand toward the walled city just a quarter mile south of the compound, "But rather a place not made by the hand of man—a Jerusalem that fulfills its name—a city of wholeness, a city of peace. A place between the worlds where we meet our best selves and our better angels." Seeing the confused look on Tirzah's face, Gunter sighed. "I know this is challenging to grasp. It's like Hamlet says, '*There are more things in heaven and earth, than are dreamt of in your philosophy.*'"

"I love that quotation, Aba, but it doesn't explain anything." Tirzah raised her shoulders. "Is this Upper Jerusalem even real?"

"An excellent question, which I'll answer with a question of my own: is a rainbow real?"

When Tirzah frowned in response, Gunter decided to rephrase the question. "Is a rainbow something that can be seen by any number of people under certain circumstances?"

Tirzah nodded. "Yes—under certain circumstances . . ."

"Yes. And I would submit that the reality of a rainbow requires the following circumstances: Number one—that the sun is low in the sky in the evening or morning. Number two—that there is moisture in the air, such as during or after rain. And three—that there is an observer." Gunter paused and looked at Tirzah. "Would you agree?"

"Yes."

"But what if the observer is blind? Would the rainbow be visible?"

"Not for that observer."

"So, it is with this."

Tirzah sat back and crossed her arms. "So, you're saying that, when it comes to seeing this spiritual city, most people are blind?"

"Yes."

"And so, most people will never be able to see it?"

"Regarding that ability, another quotation from Shakespeare comes to mind; *Some are born great, some achieve greatness, and some have greatness thrust upon them.*"

"Are you saying that I might someday have the ability to see the Upper Jerusalem?"

"You already *have* this ability, Tirzah. You were born great! Your mother and I knew that from the start. We were just waiting for the right time to tell you."

"And why is that time now?"

"Because now you must be aware of the special danger we face. Now you must understand the real reason we are in hiding."

Tirzah raised her shoulders. "Do you mean it's not just you avoiding service in the kaiser's army and Rahman avoiding the Turkish labor brigades?"

"Those considerations are real, but there is a far more profound reason." Gunter sat forward. "The Guardians of the Temple Mount have lately attracted unwanted attention—"

"From the kaiser?"

"Yes. He's desperate to access the secrets of the Temple Mount and has dispatched his agents to Jerusalem—an Austrian occultist, Guido von List, and an English treasure hunter, Montagu Walker. They seek us relentlessly and will stop at nothing to find us."

"Is that what happened to David?"

"Yes. They believed that he was also privy to the secrets of the Temple Mount, which is why List and Walker captured and tortured him at the Augusta Victoria Hospice. However, since he is, in truth, not one of the fellowship, he could tell them nothing beyond our home addresses, and this he gave them only after long days of torture. But by then, we were already in hiding here." Gunter drew a deep breath and exhaled in a deep sigh. "When David couldn't provide any information after weeks of torture, Walker was satisfied that he knew nothing and released him to a hospital in West Jerusalem where he recovered and returned home after two weeks. But List was increasingly angered by their inability to locate us and settled on another plan—to bring David back for further and more extreme torture along with Sarah and Isser. List believed that, if we were to hear that the whole family was being tortured, we would give ourselves up to save them."

"Would you have done that?"

"Yes, but we learned of List's plan just in time to get David and his family out of their home in West Jerusalem, and to bring them here, into hiding with us. Anna Spafford graciously agreed, and here they are."

Tirzah appeared puzzled. "But, how did you know of List's plan?"

"From a couple of righteous Turkish soldiers who befriended and protected David when he was held at Augusta Victoria. They got word to us about the danger to the whole family. Though I've never actually met them, knowing they're on our side is reassuring since the threat from List and Walker continues. Thankfully, they don't know we're in hiding here since only Anna and her immediate family know of our presence here—none of the other hundreds of American and Swiss members of the Colony know anything about us."

"Until today," Tirzah whispered and shook her head.

"Don't be too hard on yourself, my girl. No one among the congregation would have any idea who you are. And, even if a suspicion was raised, there is another powerful factor protecting us here."

"What would that be? The righteous Turkish soldiers?"

"Yes, but more importantly, the neutrality of the United States in the war. Neither the kaiser nor his Turkish allies want to give the Americans an excuse to enter the war on the side of England. Toward this they have forbidden any aggressive action against the American Colony."

"So, we're still safe here?" asked Tirzah.

"For now."

CHAPTER 13

November 29, 1914
Cottage Hospital, Lyme Regis

"GODDAMN IT!" Joe Bloggs shouted at the blank page of his journal.

He had intended to make an entry after morning rounds, but his mood was as dark as the heavy clouds covering the sky. He couldn't write a single word.

He studied the photograph of himself, hoping to jog his memory. But the image did nothing to stir the dust that seemed to obscure any remembrance. All memories remained cloud-hidden, like the morning sun.

A thunderstorm had blown in from the Channel during the night, and he had slept fitfully. Morning found him exhausted and angry since the heavy rains made for muddy roads, ruining any chance of going outdoors.

As a peal of thunder rolled over the West Dorset Coast, he gripped his pencil and stared at the blank page. His brain felt encased in an impenetrable black husk.

"Goddamn it!" he shouted again, and grabbing the journal, he charged out of the ward in his hospital gown. Seeing Dr. Barlow further down the hall, he ran toward him, brandishing the journal over his head.

"What's the problem, Joe?" asked the doctor, taking a step backward.

"You know what the problem is—nothing's coming back!"

"It's going to take time," Barlow said and placed a hand on his shoulder. "You just need more time."

Leaning into the solid comfort of the doctor's hand, Joe's anger gave way to the despair he was trying to push away. "I feel like I'm drowning in darkness."

"You must be patient—"

"I have no patience to be patient!" he snapped, then asked, "That's a joke, isn't it?"

"A weak joke, but yes."

"I'm sorry, Doctor," he said and tried to smile. "But I just can't bear this. Has there been any response to the letters you sent?"

"It's been less than a week, Joe. I'm certain we'll hear from them, but there's no telling when. It may be some weeks—"

Joe drew a deep breath as he silently considered why he couldn't go to these places himself. *Perhaps I'll do just that!* he thought and asked, "Where is that BEF hospital in France?"

"Boulogne-Sur-Mer on the northern French coast."

"And the War Office?"

"At Whitehall in London," Barlow gave him a final pat on the shoulder. "Who knows? We *might* hear from them sooner, but in wartime, communication is difficult. It might take a long while—"

"I understand," he said and lurched away. He had decided to take the initiative.

"Where are you going?" Barlow shouted after him.

"To the library. I'll try to write in my journal there."

"But it's nearly half ten. Doesn't Ian visit with Lassie about now?"

"I'll let the nurses know where I'll be."

At the nurses' station, he leaned over the counter. He was about to speak when he noticed a strand of the nurse's blond hair escaping from beneath her white cap.

A vague memory formed and hovered at the edge of his mind. Staring at her cap, he tried to will the memory forward, to remember.

"Is there something wrong with my cap, Joe?" she asked, raising a hand to it.

"No," he said quietly. "Your cap is fine. I just wanted to tell you that if anyone calls for me, I'll be in the library."

As he headed down the hall, he wondered about the nurse's blond hair and her cap—a recognition that seemed just out of reach. *Was that a memory? I should keep track of those . . . ?*

He found the library deserted—the half dozen worn oak tables surrounded by sentinels of high-backed wooden chairs and ceiling-high bookshelves. In the silence, the pneumatic door-closer wheezed on its metal arm, and the heavy door settled closed with a muted click. He closed his eyes and leaned back against the door, enjoying the stillness.

With a slow release of breath, he let go of all thoughts about the nurse's cap, deciding that he would begin a list. Sitting at one of the tables, he opened his notebook to a clean page and wrote *Possible Memories* at the top. Below that he made his first entry: *Nov 29, 1914—Nurse's cap and blond hair at nursing station.*

Standing up, he scanned the empty library and saw a collection of reference books next to the librarian's desk. He pulled out a heavy atlas, sat back at the table, and began leafing through the pages. He came to a map of England, which included the Channel and the French coast. Tracing the southern English coastline, his left index finger came to Lyme Regis.

Okay, I'm here. Now, where's that BEF Hospital?

He scanned the French Atlantic coast northward till he came to *Boulogne-Sur-Mer.* For a moment he looked at the two map points—the hundreds of miles and the blue water of the Channel between them. He let out a low whistle and shook his head. *That's quite a distance, and I'd also need a way to cross the Channel . . .*

Shifting his gaze to London, he measured its distance from Lyme Regis. *Only a hundred and fifty miles. I could walk, hitch rides, and be at the War Office in a few days.*

Turning pages, he came to a detailed map of the roads of southern England. On a clean page of his journal, he wrote down the main roads between Lyme Regis and London. As he wrote, unbidden words rose in his mind. He turned back to his page of possible memories, entered the date, and wrote: *Quis hic locus, quae regio, quae mundi plaga?*

He stared at what he had written with a sudden sense of excitement. "That's *Latin*!" He said aloud, breaking the silence of the empty library. "How do I know Latin?"

With a racing heart, he wrote what he somehow knew to be the English translation:

What place is this, what region, what quarter of the world?

He was closing the notebook when the library door opened.

"Top of the morning to you, Evan!" Ian Cowan said as he entered the library with Lassie close behind. "How are you feeling?" Ian coughed into his fist, then cleared his throat. He took off his gray raincoat and hung it, dripping, over an empty chair.

Lassie bounded forward and placed her head on Evan's lap. He patted her head, not caring that it was damp.

"I'm fine, but how are *you* feeling, Ian? That sounds like a nasty cough."

"Got caught in the downpour last evening while loading kegs into the tavern. It's just a sniffle, Evan—nothing to concern yourself about."

"Why do you insist on calling me *Evan*? That may not even be my name."

"Oh, you're Evan Sinclair alright. I know it, and soon, so will *you*!"

"What are you talking about?"

Ian stifled another cough, leaned close, and said, "It's like this. I've spent a fair amount of time in Scotland, especially around Edinburgh. Your last name, Sinclair, is well-known in those parts. So, last week, I sent a cable to a prominent member of the Sinclair family near Edinburgh on the chance he might know something of you or your family. He cabled me back immediately, very keen about the prospect that you may be a relation. He suggested I send a photograph of you by special expedited postal delivery. Which I did, and he replied in a similar fashion." Ian drew an envelope from his jacket pocket. "This is his reply. It arrived this morning by postal courier." He put the envelope on the table.

Evan leaned forward, surprised to see a regal crest in the upper left-hand corner of the envelope above elegantly embossed script, which he read aloud, "James Francis Harry St. Clair-Erskine, fifth earl of Rosslyn." He looked at Ian. "Who, the hell, is *that*?"

"A Scottish earl who's certain that—" A paroxysm of coughing cut him off. When it was over, Ian drew a deep breath. "Read the letter. It's from the earl's personal secretary."

Evan drew a folded sheet of smooth, buff-colored paper from the envelope and read:

27 November 1914 Rosslyn Castle Midlothian, Scotland

My Dear Mr. Cowan,

Following the rapid exchange of cables between you and the earl, it was with great interest that he studied the photograph of the young gentleman in question. Given the importance of clarifying his identity, His Lordship requested that I send this missive to you in like fashion—by expedited postal delivery.

I am pleased to inform you that the earl indeed recognized the young gentleman. He's quite certain he met him with his parents when they visited Rosslyn Castle several years ago. To refresh his memory, the earl consulted the St. Clair/Sinclair genealogical chart and found that Evan's father, Clive Robert Sinclair, is fourth cousin to His Lordship, and Evan, his fourth cousin once removed.

The earl is anxious to assist the young master in any way he can. In that spirit he would be pleased to host him at Rosslyn Castle once he is able to travel.

With gratitude and warm regards from the Earl,
Your Humble Servant,
Mr. Roger Fraser, Secretary to His Lordship,
James Francis Harry St. Clair-Erskine, Fifth Earl of Rosslyn

Evan placed the letter on the table, shaking his head, his heart pounding. "Thank you, Ian! I can't begin to tell you how much this means to me."

"It's high time you had some good news, Evan." Ian paused and smiled. "May I call you Evan now?"

"Please do, since that would appear to be my name." Evan laughed. "This is *very* good news. I'm going to see this cousin as soon as I can."

"Absolutely. Just as soon as you're released from hospital—"

"No, Ian. That could take *months*. The consultant told me as much today." He tapped the paper with his index finger. "This guy recognized me in that photograph. He knows who I am! He met me along with my mother and father. He's *family*!" Evan exhaled a sigh and asked, "Do you think they'll let me go if they see this letter?"

"It's possible, I suppose." Ian coughed and cleared his throat. "But what about your medical treatment?"

"*What* medical treatment? My head wound is healed. All I do here is scribble in a journal during the day and try to get some sleep on a noisy ward at night. It's driving me crazy." He placed his hand on Ian's arm. "And speaking of medical treatment, *you* should see one of the doctors here about that cough."

"It's naught but a chest cold. I'll be fine soon. It's *you* I'm concerned about."

"Listen, Ian, you went out of your way to create this connection for me, and I'm so very grateful for that—for *everything*! Now I want to follow through. I *must* do that—to reconnect with my life, to remember my life. Will you help me?"

"Certainly, I will, but you really must speak to the physicians before you leave." Another salvo of coughing followed.

When it was over, Evan said, "But they might not agree—" He left off speaking as he noticed Ian sweating, his shirt collar wet. "You really need to see a doctor, Ian."

"Stop trying to change the subject, Evan. Promise me you'll let the medical staff know your intentions. Show them the letter. They'll no doubt write the earl and make arrangements to transfer your care to a hospital near Rosslyn."

He decided not to argue. "Alright. I'll discuss everything with Dr. Barlow first thing on rounds tomorrow morning." He placed his hand on Ian's arm. "But I need you to promise me two things . . ."

Ian stifled a cough and asked, "And what would those two things be?"

"The first thing is that you allow me to speak to the staff about this business with my cousin Harry and Rosslyn Castle. Please promise that you won't say a word to them about it?"

"Fair enough. I promise to leave that to you. What's the second thing?"

"Promise me that you'll see one of the doctors about that cough."

"Very well. If it continues tomorrow, I promise to consult with one of the doctors," Ian said and unleashed another barrage of coughing. When it was over, he wearily pushed back the chair and stood up. "Sorry for the quick visit, but I really must be going—expecting a delivery of ale."

"But you need to *rest*, Ian. You mustn't tax yourself so!"

"Alright, I'll let the lads do the heavy lifting."

"Good." Evan said and put his hand on Ian's shoulder. "You must take care of yourself, Ian. You're the only friend I have."

Ian smiled at Evan and, looking down at Lassie, tapped the side of his leg. "Come on, girl. Say goodbye."

Evan bent low, gave Lassie a good scratch and a kiss on the head. "Goodbye, Lassie," he whispered, "and thank you." He shook Ian's hand and noticed it felt cold. "Thanks for all you've done, Ian, and promise me again that you'll tell no one about my cousin Harry, and that you'll see a doctor."

"I promise on both counts." Ian put on his raincoat, and with Lassie by his side, he left the library.

Evan remained standing until the door settled closed. Then he went back to the atlas and found a map of Great Britain and located Rosslyn about seven miles south of Edinburgh. "I'm not waiting around here another day," he said aloud and planted his finger on the map. "Before dawn tomorrow, I'm leaving for Rosslyn Castle!"

He began making notes of the lacework of roads northward but stopped to measure the distance between Lyme Regis and Edinburgh. *Over five hundred miles!*

Noticing the straight railway lines, he sighed. *If only I had the money to take a train.*

He sat forward, put his fingers to his chin, and stared at the floor. That's when he noticed his fine boots.

CHAPTER 14

November 29, 1914

Lyme Regis

IAN COWAN hurried to the pub through light rain with Lassie at his side. Skirting muddy puddles, he hoped to arrive before the ale delivery, though his progress was slowed by gusts of wind and paroxysms of coughing.

Exhausted and drenched with rain and perspiration, he reached the tavern and called to his bartender, "Logan! Bring me a pint of the ten-year-old brandy and a snifter." In the warmth of the hearth, he pulled off his raincoat and collapsed into a chair.

After the brandy, he felt better apart from a tightness in his chest.

"Logan!" he called again as he reclined in the chair. "Wake me when they come with the ale." Looking down at Lassie curled up by the fire, he smiled and closed his eyes. As he drifted into sleep, his thoughts turned to Evan, *I'm glad I convinced the lad to stay in hospital. He's in no condition to be traveling about . . .*

"They're here, sir."

Ian felt the bartender's hand on his shoulder. He'd slept, though not enough.

Pushing himself out of the chair, he pulled on his raincoat, and stepped to the tavern door. Waiting on the muddy road was a van drawn by two horses with two young men struggling to unload the first cask of ale as wind-blown rain pelted against the side of the van.

"You took your good time, lads." Ian called out as he studied the sky.

"We're in for more dirty weather so we'd best unload quickly." Turning, he called, "Logan! Lend a hand!"

Ian stayed dry, supervising the work from the doorway, but after a few minutes, the sky opened, and frigid rain sheeted down. At that point, he joined in the effort.

When they finally finished, he was spent and chilled to the bone. Paroxysms of coughing returned with a vengeance. Between them, he could scarcely catch his breath.

"Send for Margaret," he managed to gasp. "Have her bring the cups." Struggling to breathe, he waited by the fire.

"What's it this time, Ian?" Margaret asked as she bustled into the tavern. "Have you caught a cold?"

He had no voice to reply.

She quickly listened to his lungs using her wooden tube "You're barely moving air. How long have you been like this?"

"Two days," he managed to gasp.

"Logan!" she shouted. "Bring me a candle and get Ian onto the table."

He soon felt Logan's hands, pulling him up and onto the table near the hearth.

Lying face down, he felt Margaret's hands pulling his shirt off and he realized it was the same table where Margaret had examined Evan.

"Call the hospital!" Margaret shouted. "Have them bring the ambulance about!"

With a surrendering weariness, he watched Margaret arrange cotton balls and a row of glass cups on the table. He watched her douse the cotton balls with alcohol and ignite them with the candle. He watched as the bright flames banked and felt the warmth of the cups on his back.

He began to feel a little better.

Beyond the edge of the table, he saw Lassie sitting up, watching. "Goodbye, girl," he whispered.

He let his eyes close as a calm oblivion settled over his mind. Though he still couldn't catch his breath, he no longer cared.

CHAPTER 15

November 29, 1914
Boulogne-Sur-Mer, France

GERTRUDE BELL moved through the gathering dusk after another long day of work. Once in her room, she took off her coat, shoes, and hat, and fell back onto the bed. Though completely spent, her mind raced with thoughts of Richard, still at his posting in Addis Ababa. Though they hadn't seen each other in several years, their correspondence had grown increasingly intimate, even though he was still married. But Gertrude took some solace in the fact that it was not she, but the war that had separated Richard and his wife—he was in Ethiopia, and she was serving as a nurse in France.

Another letter from Richard had arrived that morning, which she had read and reread throughout the day. She pulled it from her bodice and thrilled at the last lines:

So many memories, my dear queen, of you and your splendid love and your courage and the wonderful letters you have written me, from your heart to mine . . .

The missive included the news that Richard would be leaving Ethiopia in the first days of February to return to England before his next deployment. He would be spending several days in London and urged Gertrude to be with him there.

Holding the letter against her beating heart, she was determined to do just that, and wondered how she might arrange the tryst. The solution appeared in a flash of clarity; in a letter from her father, she'd learned that

Lord Robert of the London Red Cross had bitterly complained of disarray in his office.

I'll offer to set things right in London just as I did here!

Moreover, David Hogarth had written her to express his concern about the mapping of Arabia at MO4 once Lawrence left for Cairo.

And I'll volunteer my services to Whitehall. Not even Lawrence knows the terrain and tribes of Arabia as I do!

She went to her writing table, determined to provide her father and Hogarth with ample and very legitimate reasons for her to leave France and serve the war effort in London beginning early in February, which would nicely coincide with Richard's plans. Indeed, her first letter would be to Richard. Uncapping her fountain pen, she began to write:

Dearest Richard,

I give this year of mine to you and all the years that shall come after it. Will you take it, this meager gift—the year and me and all my thoughts and love? You fill my cup, this shallow cup that has grown so deep to hold your love and mine.

Dearest, when you tell me you love me and want me still, my heart sings—and then weeps for longing to be with you. I have filled all the hollow places of the world with my desire for you; it floods out, without measure to creep up the high mountains where you are. And when you walk in your garden, I think it touches your feet. Take my love as your own, hold it and keep it—fold me into your heart.

I know the fates will bring us together in February, and my heart turns from despair to joy at this knowledge. If our time together is but one night or a lifetime, I'm intoxicated by the thought of your loving touch.

Oh, Richard, I live only for you!

Your Gertrude

CHAPTER 16

November 30, 1914
London's East End to Hampstead, Borough of Camden

CHAIM WEIZMANN awoke in his lonely flat on Oswald Road, stretched and looked out the window as the rising sun attempted to shine through the mist hanging over London's East End. Though up early, he wouldn't be going to work at the pilot plant today since the shipment of maize from the United States had yet to arrive. Apparently, the cargo ship had been delayed several days so that it could be included in a large convoy to provide a measure of protection from the German U-boats lurking in the Atlantic.

The main thing is that the maize gets through! Weizmann thought, knowing that all else was in readiness at the distillery to begin acetone production for making munitions-grade cordite. And once the pilot plant was fully operational, Churchill had already charged Weizmann with converting other distilleries from the production of spirits to the production of acetone. Much to the chagrin of distillery owners, the need for munitions in the grim struggle with the Central Powers trumped all. Even spirits.

The dreary morning didn't dim Weizmann's excitement at the certainty that his discovery of acetone synthesis would have a pivotal effect on the war effort, providing his new home country with something of immense and immediate value.

And I must admit, he thought, *it's also given me access and leverage with the British Admiralty and at Whitehall for the sake of Zionism.*

But he also understood that having leverage and knowing how to use it were two different things. And for this, Weizmann needed the advice of his old friend, Asher Ginsberg, one of the original leaders of the Zionist movement. Now that Weizmann was splitting his time between Manchester and London, he was able to see Ginsberg frequently—to seek his counsel and to enjoy a home-cooked meal prepared by Asher's wife, Rivke, at their home in Hampstead.

The increased proximity had also given Weizmann a glimpse of Ginsberg's inner turmoil and his predilection for melancholy—a side of him he'd never seen before. And the situation had grown worse. Having decided to help his old friend, Weizmann considered that he always looked to Ginsberg for support, and now he was in position to support him. This was the reason he'd arranged for Ginsberg to come with him on his next trip home to Manchester. And that day was today.

Checking his timepiece, Weizmann saw that the taxi would soon be at his door. He quickly washed up and got dressed. *I may have time to do some paperwork while I'm in Manchester,* he thought and lifted his brown leather briefcase from his desk. Undoing the clasps, he began arranging stacks of invoices and notes when he noticed the broadsheet he'd been handed at the train station in Paris by the police a few months before—the broadsheet with drawings and descriptions of the four fugitives suspected of being German spies.

Sitting on the edge of his bed, he unfolded the broadsheet and looked again at the drawing of the young man, Evan Sinclair. *He certainly seems out of place here,* he thought as he scanned the text and came to the name of "a known associate," Clive Sinclair. *That must be the boy's father—the professor that Vera and I heard lecture at Oxford a few years ago.* He shook his head as he refolded the broadsheet and placed it in his briefcase. *I should bring this to the attention of people at Whitehall . . .*

Weizmann started as a horn sounded from the street.

He headed out the door carrying his briefcase and an umbrella. Stepping into the taxi, he said, "Glenmore Road, number 12, please."

"Is tha' Haverstock Hill in Hampstead, sir?"

"It is."

The cabbie whistled. "Over ten miles 'guv—that'll cost you."

"Not a problem. And there will be an added fare since we'll be stopping in Hampstead to pick up a friend of mine before going on to Waterloo Station."

"Wha' time is yr' train, sir?"

"Half ten."

"I'll 'av ya there in time."

The taxi pulled away from the curb and followed the cobblestone road along the Thames.

Weizmann watched warehouses give way to tenements as his thoughts turned to Vera with a sudden frown as he realized that he had forgotten to cable her that he'd be bringing Asher. *Oy gevalt! With everything going on at the pilot plant, I completely forgot. How to make amends? I know—once we reach Manchester I'll stop at a bakery, pick up a nice honey cake and some rugelach. And after dinner, I'll insist on cleaning up and doing the dishes. That should do the trick.*

As houses and telegraph poles ticked by the window, he leaned back in the embrace of the taxi's upholstery as his thoughts turned to Asher Ginsberg—how he had shaped the Zionist movement starting at the end of the nineteenth century when he was in his early twenties. At that time, Ginsberg had just moved from a small Ukrainian village to Odessa, where he had encountered two stark and conflicting realities—a vibrant Jewish enlightenment and a rising tide of virulent antisemitism.

Faced with the specter of deadly czarist pogroms, Ginsberg was drawn to the Zionist promise of safe harbor for Jews in Palestine, and he joined the first and only Zionist organization of the time, Lovers of Zion, enthusiastically embracing the group's goal of finding sanctuary for Russian Jews in Ottoman Palestine. However, when he had traveled to Palestine in 1891, what he observed in some Jewish settlements shocked him to the core: Jews who had lived like slaves beneath the iron fist of czarist Russia suddenly found themselves free, and many of them used their new-found freedom to inflict a ruthless tyranny over the native Arabs of Palestine.

Ginsberg had referred to their behavior, quoting Proverbs: *Eved kee yimloch*—a slave who reigns. He expressed his dismay in the Hebrew essays he wrote, essays with titles such as "This is Not the Way," and "Truth from the Land of Israel." With self-effacing modesty, Ginsberg used the pen name *Achad Ha'am*—"One of the People"—in all his writings. These critiques of Zionism were widely read by Jews throughout the Russian Empire, and Weizmann was one of many young Jews whose ideas about Zionism were shaped by Ginsberg.

In the gently rocking backseat of the taxi, Weizmann let his eyes close as he drifted off to sleep. The next thing he heard was the cabby's voice.

"Wake up, sir. We're in Hampstead."

Looking out the window, Weizmann saw that the driver had pulled to the curb in front of Ginsberg's home.

Shaking his head clear, he said, "Excellent! We'll be picking up my friend here." Stepping out of the taxi, he added, "It shouldn't take more than ten minutes."

Moving beneath the bare branches of one of the many plane trees lining the quiet street, he mounted the steps to the front stoop of the brownstone, lifted the brass door knocker and brought it down twice, hoping that Asher was packed and ready to go.

After a moment the door opened.

"Good morning, Chaim! What a lovely surprise." Rivke gave him a bright smile as she tied the belt of her robe. Even more diminutive than her husband, Rivke was slender, vivacious and wore her graying hair short. Though living in the shadow of Asher, she shone brightly, and on such a dreary day, her warmth was welcome relief.

Weizmann took off his fedora and smiled down at her. "Good morning, Rivke."

"Please come in, Chaim. Warm yourself by the fire and I'll tell Asher you're here."

"Is he ready to go?" he asked as he stepped into the vestibule.

"Go?" Rivke asked. "Go where?"

"Didn't he *tell* you?" he asked in disbelief. "I invited him to come with me to Manchester for a few days." He waved his hand toward the street. "I have a taxi waiting to take us to Waterloo Station."

Rivke's smile faded. "He didn't mention it." She sighed. "But with his melancholy of late, Chaim, he's barely been speaking to me." She paused and set her jaw. "A trip with you will do him good."

"Can he be ready in fifteen minutes?"

"Most definitely!"

"Good. I'll tell the driver." He went back out the front door, wondering, *how could he have forgotten?* After telling the taxi driver they'd need a bit more time, he returned to find Asher waiting at the door.

"Chaim! I'm so sorry. It slipped my mind!" Ginsberg spoke around the cigarette in his mouth, squinting through his oval wire-rim spectacles.

"Are you still planning to come?" Weizmann asked as he studied his old friend. With his high forehead and short graying beard, Ginsberg had always appeared older than his years, which now numbered fifty-eight. He looked older and thinner—the cuffs of his dressing gown were frayed, and it appeared to Weizmann that he hadn't bothered to dress in several days.

"Of course, I'm coming! I've been looking forward to it."

"Good! Go get dressed."

"I'll be ready in five minutes," he said and hurried away.

As he watched him go, Weizmann smiled and shook his head. *It never fails to surprise me that after a lifetime speaking Yiddish, we now speak to each other only in English. But these days it makes sense—Yiddish sounds too much like German.*

With a few minutes to himself, he wandered into the living room where a bright fire burned in the hearth. Pacing along Asher's crowded bookshelves, he saw they included the substantial religious tomes of the Babylonian and Jerusalem Talmud along with a large set of the Zohar.

Strange to think of Asher in his youth—a prodigy and one of the most renowned Talmudic scholars in the Ukraine. He reached out and touched the dark leather spines, recalling his own years studying Talmud. *Though we're both now completely secular, those religious studies forged the bedrock of our moral principles.*

Weizmann thought back to Ginsberg's essays, where he'd emphasized that the solution to the settlement of Ottoman Palestine involved an imperative to create a Jewish consciousness beyond the basic need of sanctuary, an imperative to internalize and live by the core Jewish values of compassion, truth, and justice, especially when it came to dealing with the local Arab population.

Having read and reread the essays, he remembered Asher's exact words—his unrestrained honesty in exposing what he had witnessed among some of the settlers in Palestine: *They treat the Arabs with hostility and cruelty, deprive them of their rights, offend them without cause, and even boast of these deeds.*

Weizmann sighed as he recalled the way Ginsberg expressed his despairing sadness at witnessing this cruelty; *I can't put up with the idea that our brethren are capable of behaving in such a way to another people, and if it is so now, what will be our relation to the other if we shall achieve power in the Land of Israel? And if this be the Messiah: I do not wish to see his coming.*

As Weizmann peered at shelves crowded with books in Hebrew, he was reminded that Ginsberg also believed that the rebirth of the Hebrew language was vital for a successful return to Zion, believing that Hebrew was central to a Jewish national identity—that only Hebrew, as its medium of culture, could unite Palestine's Jewish inhabitants. Drawn as they would be from the four corners of the world, only Hebrew could serve as their common and ancient language, capable of making them feel that a Jewish past was speaking through them and connecting them to their roots as well as their deepest selves in the present.

Remembering Ginsberg's core beliefs, Weizmann sighed and thought, *He's right—Palestine must be more than a haven from antisemitism. The men and women of Palestine speaking Hebrew will become the conduits of Jewish history, Jewish values, and Jewish culture, which was precisely why he referred to his stream of Zionism as Cultural Zionism..*

"Asher's bag is packed, Chaim," Rivke announced from the arched salon doorway. Weizmann turned from the bookshelves. "That's wonderful, Rivke. Thank you."

"Shall I prepare some sandwiches and hard-boiled eggs for your trip?"

"Thank you, but we really should be going."

"*Nu*," she shrugged, "do you at least have time for tea?"

"I'm afraid not, but don't worry, we'll take tea in the train's dining car."

"I'm ready for that dining car!" announced Ginsberg, neatly attired in a black frock coat and holding his valise. "Goodbye, darling," he said and gave Rivke a kiss.

Weizmann gestured toward the door. "After you, my friend. Our taxi awaits us below."

CHAPTER 17

November 30, 1914
By rail from Lyme Regis to Birmingham

TWO HOURS out of Lyme Regis, Evan was thankful he had a compartment to himself. He glanced at his watch and saw that it was just after eight o'clock. *By now, they'll know I'm gone. But at least I left a thank you note.* He looked out the window and sighed. *I just couldn't spend another day staring at the blank slate where my memories used to be. I had to do something about it, and that's what I'm doing—making progress. And who knows? Maybe by meeting my cousin and hearing about my parents, it'll all come back to me.*

As he settled back in his seat, he thought about Ian and how poorly he had looked when they had said goodbye. *I sure hope he's okay,* he thought and chastised himself. *I should have gone to the tavern before I left, but I had to catch the early morning train, and he wouldn't have been there. But first chance I get, I'm going to write him.*

He looked at the train schedule and rechecked his route—the connecting branch lines that would bring him to the mainline station in Birmingham where he would board the train to Edinburgh. Looking out the window, he watched houses and hedgerows passing by, and for the first time since waking up in the tavern, he felt a surge of hope.

He put his feet up on the opposite upholstered bench seat, looked down at his worn brown leather shoes, and thought of the fine boots he had managed to sell to one of the orderlies. He smiled and thought, *But, in addition to these old shoes, he gave me two pounds sterling, a sixpence, and a handful of copper pennies. Even after paying the fare from Lyme Regis to Edinburgh, I have plenty leftover.* With a final glance at his shoes, he shrugged. *And what good were those boots if I couldn't go anywhere?*

Pulling the coiled whip from the knapsack, he held it in his hand—the texture of the leather so very familiar, like it belonged to him. Holding the whip in his hand, he waited, hoping for a clear memory to emerge. When none came, he put it back in the haversack and fished out the oilskin bag with his cousin's letter.

He studied the earl's name and title. James Francis Harry St. Clair-Erskine, 5th Earl of Rosslyn, and sighed. *I sure hope I'm actually related to this guy—even if only a fourth cousin once removed—because that would mean I really am Evan Sinclair, son of Clive Robert Sinclair.* He stared at the names, saying them out loud, but he still felt nothing. He reread the words, "His Lordship is quite certain that he met Evan along with his parents during their visit to Rosslyn Castle some ten years ago." And as the train entered a covered bridge, Evan studied his reflection in the darkened window, wondering if "His Lordship" would even recognize him after ten years.

The train emerged from the covered bridge, and darkness gave way to open fields where cows grazed within hedgerows and walls of gray boulders. And as the train sped forward, his heart swelled with joy—to be out of hospital, out in the world, where he would make new memories—even if he never regained those he had lost. But when the train suddenly slowed and came to a stop, he frowned. "What's this then?" he wondered as he studied a long stretch of green fields sloping up to a forest of autumn trees beneath a cloudy sky. "There's no sign of a station." He released the window's metal pins and pushed it open, feeling cool morning air on his face. Up the track he saw a dozen heavy sheep with matted coats skitter across the rails with a signpost that read: *BATH—2 miles.* "Bath," he whispered. "Why does that place sound familiar?"

He opened the oilskin bag and found the folded slip of paper with the woman's address: *Sharon Anne Meehan, Cloud House, The Avenue, Bath*

2, Somerset, England. Staring hard at the name he sighed and wondered, *Who are you, Sharon?*

❉ ❉ ❉

By rail from London to Manchester

WATERLOO STATION was nearly deserted as Weizmann and Ginsberg boarded the train. With a compartment to themselves, they sat across from each other on worn upholstered bench seats as the train rocked gently on the rails.

Weizmann looked out the window as they passed through open countryside outside London. He turned at the sound of Ginsberg's voice.

"This is like a tonic, Chaim," he said as he struck a match and lit a cigarette. Blowing out the match, he dropped it into the heavy porcelain ashtray that stood on the wooden ledge beneath the window. "I've been so gloomy lately."

"Why, old friend?"

Ginsberg exhaled the smoke with a sigh. "You have to *ask*? You of all people should know."

"Please don't tell me that you're still upset about your daughter's marriage—"

"But she married a non-Jew!"

Weizmann had to tamp down a flash of irritation. "Really, Asher? Mikhail is a wonderful young man, and he willingly converted to Judaism."

"Only *after* the fact, and even then, he was converted by a Reform rabbi!"

"Since when do you care? You haven't seen the inside of a *shul* in years! You want he should have a second conversion with an Orthodox rabbi?"

"No. For me, not even Orthodox conversion would suffice."

"How can you say such a thing? Conversion brings with it complete and legitimate entry into every aspect of Jewish life—"

"But it doesn't change a person's soul!" Ginsberg shouted, exhaling a plume of cigarette smoke. Shaking his head, he took off his glasses and rubbed his eyes. "I know I'm not making sense, Chaim."

"Then why do this to yourself?"

Ginsberg shrugged. "For me intermarriage, even *with* conversion, equals assimilation, and assimilation equals our *extinction* as a people."

Weizmann winced. "That circular logic isn't even logical!"

"Please understand, Chaim. For me, Zionism represents a Jewish nationalism that binds us together as a people despite and because of antisemitism, despite and because of the threat of assimilation, with or without a national homeland. For years I've lectured others about the importance of preserving cultural Judaism, but with my own child, I've failed!"

"Stop with this ridiculous self-flagellation." Weizmann said sharply, unable to contain his ire. "Surely you accept the fact that Jewish law is a vital part of our cultural heritage, and according to Jewish law, you cannot discount the complete legitimacy of conversion. But, putting that aside, if the notion of assimilation in an increasingly enlightened world is a fact—and it *is*—then it's also a blessing—all the more reason to strive for a national Jewish homeland where our physical and cultural survival will be in our own hands—living as Jews, among Jews, in a Jewish state. This is the Zionism we both seek, and your efforts to infuse that state with Jewish cultural values have not been in vain."

"Not so." Ginsberg sighed. "In this, I've also failed."

"What are you talking about?" Weizmann was exasperated with Ginsberg's negative and convoluted thinking. "You've always promoted Jewish values—"

"What about the value of caring for the stranger in our midst?" Ginsberg cut it. "If we are to coexist with the Arabs in Palestine, we must reach out to them in cooperation and friendship."

"But we *have*! You conveyed my letter through your tea envoy to Hussein and Faisal."

"But there's been no response—"

"It's only been a month!" Weizmann shouted and immediately regretted raising his voice. "Asher," he continued quietly as he leaned forward and patted Ginsberg on the knee. "Please forgive me for my belligerent tone. It's just that, as my mentor and my best friend, I care about you, and it hurts me to see how you blame and punish yourself. You know how difficult postal and even courier services are these days, and we're certainly *trying* to contact Hussein and Faisal. Please understand, Asher—I agree with you about coexisting in Palestine with the Arabs. However, with all the obstacles we face to establish a refuge for Jews in Palestine, and with the continuing threat to our very existence in Eastern Europe, it's . . ." Weizmann paused, searching for the right word, "it's *exhausting* . . . to speculate if the Arabs of Palestine will even accept the leadership of Sharif Hussein—or alternatively, if and when they'll develop their own central leadership."

"I'm *also* exhausted." Ginsberg sighed out a plume of tobacco smoke. "Exhausted by my personal disappointments, and by the dangers we face as a people."

"If it's any solace, Asher, I will join you in supporting this Jewish value—to honor and respect the stranger—whether we hear back from Hussein or Faisal. I *swear* to you that at the very next Zionist conference, I'll have the executive committee declare our firm intention to live in harmony with the Arabs of Palestine based on mutual respect and coexistence."

"Thank you, Chaim," Ginsberg said and managed a wan smile. "But when will we even *have* another Zionist Congress? We skipped this year because of the war . . ."

Weizmann nodded. "This is, indeed, a difficult and precarious time, especially living as we do on the edges of these empires. We'll have to wait until the war ends and the great powers sort things out before we'll be able to see the new contours of the world."

"In the meantime, we live in a world where pogroms threaten our physical existence, and assimilation threatens our spiritual existence."

Ginsberg sighed. "Only when we have a homeland of our own will we know who we are."

"And then we won't need pogroms to *remind* us who we are," Weizmann said as he took out his pipe, placed a pinch of tobacco in the bowl, and pressed it down with his thumb. "And we won't have to worry about assimilation where we *forget* who we are."

Ginsburg nodded. "That notion of forgetting who we are—that's the blessing and curse of leaving the *shtetl* and entering an enlightened society where we lose the insularity of separateness." He took a last puff of his cigarette, then tamped it out in the ashtray. "It reminds me of a joke. Stop me if you've already heard it—"

"Not a chance! It will do me good to hear you tell a joke instead of *kvetching*!"

"I heard this joke one Friday evening from a house guest when he and I were desecrating the Sabbath by smoking in the salon while Rivke was lighting the Sabbath candles in the kitchen." Ginsberg leaned forward and seamlessly switched from English to Yiddish. "A young man returns to the shtetl from his secular studies in the big city. He's walking down the street on a Saturday morning with a cigarette in his mouth. A childhood friend comes up to him and says, 'Yankel, aren't you ashamed? A Jew walking down the street and smoking on *Shabbes*?' The young scholar replies, 'Oh, I completely forgot.' 'What? You forgot that it's forbidden to smoke on *Shabbes*?' 'No, I forgot that I was a Jew!'"

Weizmann laughed and glanced out the window as the steam whistle sounded "Birmingham Station," he said as he lit his pipe. "Next stop, Manchester."

The train rocked to a halt and the locomotive wheezed out a cloud of steam, followed by the clatter of opening doors and the footsteps of passengers leaving and boarding the train.

The compartment door opened.

A sturdy young man wearing a leather jacket hesitated at the door. In one hand he held his ticket, in the other a worn haversack.

CHAPTER 18

November 30, 1914
By Rail from Birmingham to Manchester

"SORRY, BUT my ticket says I'm in here," Evan said to the two well-dressed middle-aged gentlemen looking up at him through a haze of tobacco smoke. He nodded toward the space on one of the upholstered bench seats. "May I sit there?"

"Certainly, young man!" The thinner and more diminutive of the two smiled and slid toward the window making room. "We'll be glad for the company."

"Is this the train for Edinburgh?" he asked, placing his haversack at his feet. "It is," said the man opposite Evan, "by way of Manchester, our destination."

Smiling, he extended his hand. "I'm Chaim Weizmann."

"Pleased to meet you sir." Evan shook his hand, noticing that the two men spoke with an accent he couldn't place.

"And I'm Asher Ginsburg," said the man next to him and extended his hand.

"I'm . . . I'm Evan Sinclair," he stammered, "or . . . or so I've been told." *Damn! Why did I say that? Now I get to wait until one of them asks me what I meant by that . . .*

He didn't wait long.

"Whatever do you mean by that—or so you've been told?" the man called Weizmann asked and exhaled sweet-swelling smoke from his pipe as his smile faded.

"All aboard!" The voice of the conductor knifed through the air and the train lurched forward.

"What I meant is that I don't really know who I am."

Weizmann sat forward. "Are you saying you have *amnesia*?"

A nod was all Evan could manage with Weizmann peering at him through the smoke.

"And you're certain your name is Evan Sinclair? You're sure of *that*?"

"I'm not sure of anything!" Evan replied, a bit too sharply, feeling an unsettling suspicion in Weizmann's question and in the way he was looking at him. "I have no memory of anything before a week ago."

"No memory at all?" asked Ginsberg.

"Nothing," Evan said, reassured by what sounded like genuine sympathy in Ginsberg's voice. "All I know is that I came to Lyme Regis in a lifeboat about a week ago. I was in a hospital there until this morning. Everything I know about who I might be was gathered from papers found in this haversack." He reached down and lifted it onto his lap.

"What papers?" Weizmann probed.

His sharp tone made Evan feel uncomfortable. And angry. "Mostly from a single letter," he shot back. "Want to see it?"

"Certainly!" Weizmann's reply came quickly.

Evan undid the straps of his haversack wondering why he had opened himself up to these two strangers. But he was proud of what the letter said about him, and he wanted them to know that they weren't sharing the compartment with some deranged hobo.

"And, if I may inquire, Evan," asked Ginsburg. "Why were you in hospital?"

"Apparently, I was on a ship, sunk by a U-boat in the Channel——"

"A hospital ship?" asked Ginsberg.

"Yes."

"The *Austrium*," Ginsburg took out a cigarette and lit it. "Such a tragedy!"

"Yes, it was." Evan was relieved that at least one of them knew of the sinking.

"So, you do remember the sinking?" Weizmann asked pointedly, his head wreathed in tobacco smoke.

"Actually, no." Evan snapped. "I told you—I don't remember anything before I woke up in Lyme Regis." He didn't bother to mask the angry edge in his voice. "All I know is that I came ashore in a lifeboat three days after the *Austrium* sank, and the fishermen who found me said I was the sole survivor. The five other men in the lifeboat were dead." He drew out the letter and thrust it toward Weizmann. "Here. This was found in my haversack."

"We'll read it together," Ginsburg said as he got up and sat next to Weizmann. Bending forward, they peered through their spectacles and the tobacco smoke, studying the letter.

Evan coughed. "Mind if I open the window?"

"Go right ahead," Ginsberg said without looking up.

Evan slid the window open a few inches and cool air filled the compartment along with the sound of the train clicking over the rails. His ire at Weizmann ebbed away as he savored the wind on his face and watched open fields bordered by hedgerows fly past the window. After a minute one of the men cleared his throat. Evan turned to see Weizmann looking at him.

"This is impressive—" he began.

"So, I've been *told,*" Evan cut in with more than a hint of sarcasm.

"I see that this is addressed to the head of the War Office, Major-General Charles Callwell. I've met him . . ."

"You *know* him?" Evan asked, noticing that Weizmann's suspicious tone was gone.

"I don't actually *know* him," Weizmann shrugged. "I work for the War Office, and he's been at some of our meetings."

Ginsburg looked up from the letter. "According to this, you're a sixteen-year-old British subject. Forgive me, Evan, but you don't sound British."

"That's one of several things that don't make sense. Like the part where it says that I was wounded while with the Flemish resistance. I don't sound *Flemish,* do I?"

"No, you don't," said Weizmann. "And what about being wounded?"

"I have proof of that." Evan opened the top two buttons of his shirt to reveal a purplish wound over his right chest a few inches below the collarbone. "The doctors in Lyme Regis said this looks like a healed bullet wound."

Weizmann and Ginsberg peered at the scar and nodded.

Ginsberg handed the letter back to Evan. "So, you're supposedly a British subject fighting with the Flemish resistance, but you don't sound like a Brit, a Walloon, or a Dutchman. You sound like an American."

"Or I could be Canadian, which ties in with this." He pulled a second sheet of paper from the folder and handed it to Ginsberg. "They also found this poem in my haversack—'In Flanders Fields.'"

Leaning together again, the two men silently read the handwritten poem.

After a minute, Ginsberg looked up. "This is very moving, but what does it have to do with Canada?"

"The poet who wrote it is Canadian." Evan tapped the signature at the bottom of the page. "John McCrae was a surgeon with the Canadian Expeditionary Force who also wrote poetry."

"And since he was a Canadian, they think you might be as well?" asked Weizmann.

"I suppose . . ." Evan shrugged.

"Has this been published?" Ginsberg asked.

"I don't think so since no one in Lyme Regis had seen it in print." Evan sat back and added, "And according to the newspapers, McCrae didn't make it. He was lost at sea."

"That's very sad." Ginsberg drew thoughtfully on his cigarette. "Given the way the war has gone through the fall and winter, a poem *this* inspiring, *this* uplifting . . . must be published! I'm a writer myself and I have a few contacts in the British literary world." He looked at Evan and asked, "Do you want me to see to it that this gets published?"

"Sure! Especially if it helps the war effort."

"I'll make a copy right now." He turned to Weizmann and asked, "Is there enough time before we reach Manchester?"

Weizmann glanced at his timepiece. "We'll be there in ten minutes."

"Plenty of time." Ginsberg moved along the bench seat to the writing shelf beneath the window. He put out his cigarette, uncapped a fountain pen, flipped open a notepad and began writing.

Weizmann leaned toward Evan and whispered, "With Mr. Ginsberg busy with the poem, I want to speak with you—privately." He nodded toward the compartment door.

Evan stood up, worried about what the man had to say. *What the hell is this about?* he thought as Weizmann took a leather briefcase off the luggage rack and turned to Ginsberg.

"Asher, Evan and I are going to step out for a few minutes."

"Fine," Ginsberg said without looking up.

Evan followed Weizmann into the corridor, and once the compartment door was closed behind them, Weizmann fixed Evan with his eyes.

"I want you to know that I believe you are innocent of any wrongdoing."

"*Innocent?*" Evan couldn't believe his ears. "What are you *talking* about?"

"I'll show you," Weizmann whispered. He reached into his briefcase, took out a folded sheet of paper and handed it to Evan. "At the beginning of the war I was passing through the main train station in Paris and the police were circulating this broadsheet—four men suspected of sabotage and espionage for the Germans." Weizmann pointed at one of the men. "As you can see, you're one of them."

Evan looked at the broadsheet in disbelief. "How can this be?" he whispered, his heart racing as he stared in horror at his likeness and the text. His head was spinning, and he was barely able to catch his breath. "This is crazy! They thought I was a *spy?* A *saboteur?*"

"Clearly a misunderstanding, considering your letter of commendation from the BEF surgeon. That changes everything. And I understand how it happened. I witnessed the chaos and panic that gripped Paris in those days—during the Battle of the Marne with the Germans at the city gates.

It was probably just a mistake on the part of the Paris police that you'll be able to clear it up when you regain your memory."

"But I don't know if I'll ever regain my memory." Evan said as the steam whistle shrieked and the train slowed. "What am I going to do?"

"Since I work at Whitehall, perhaps I can help. Where will you be in Edinburgh?"

"No!" Evan shook his head. "Until I regain my memory, I can't trust anyone," he said with mounting dread. "How can I defend myself if I don't even know who I am?" His hands shook as he refolded the broadsheet. "I'm keeping this, okay?"

Weizmann nodded and together they reentered the compartment.

Oblivious to Evan's agitation, Ginsberg handed him the poem. "Here you go. I'll see to it that John McCrae receives the recognition he deserves."

Evan nodded and put the poem and broadsheet in his haversack.

"Please take my business card," Ginsberg said and handed it to him. "Contact me at this address, and once McCrae's poem is published, I'll let you know."

Weizmann also handed Evan his card, and whispered, "Contact me also, Evan. I'll help make this right."

The train pulled into Manchester station. Puffing steam and with the clanking of couplings, it came to a stop. As the two men disembarked, Evan stuffed the business cards into his jacket pocket, having no intention of contacting either of them, wanting only to disappear until he could be sure who he was.

With Weizmann and Ginsberg gone, he had the compartment to himself. He collapsed onto the bench seat, still stunned by what he had seen on the broadsheet. As the engine labored out of the station, he unfolded it and looked at his likeness and the text again. He saw that it listed the names of two known associates: Clive Sinclair and Mervin Smythe. He didn't recognize the second name, though from Harry's letter, he knew that Clive Sinclair was his father. Looking back at his own likeness in disbelief, he fought to control the panic surging through his chest.

Since I'm wanted in France, perhaps I'm also wanted in England. And what if it's true? What if I really was a spy and saboteur? What if everything about the Flemish resistance and the polders was just an elaborate cover story for the hospital staff in France? I simply can't be certain, and until I can, I need to disappear. He considered that Scotland might be the perfect place to do just that—especially at a remote castle in Rosslyn miles away from Edinburgh. As his plans took form, he began to feel a little better.

He folded up the broadsheet and fished the two business cards out of his pocket.

Looking at Ginsberg's, he was surprised to see the neat calligraphy stating that the deferential and diminutive elderly man was no less than the "Executive Director of the English-Asiatic Tea Company." Looking at Weizmann's card, he was impressed to see that he was "Professor and Chair, Department of Biochemistry, University of Manchester."

Two impressive gentlemen, but despite what Weizmann said, he can't really help me—no one can. Until my memory returns, I'll lie low at Rosslyn Castle. Weizmann and Ginsberg don't know where I'm going, so I have nothing to fear from them revealing my whereabouts to the authorities. The only one who knows about my cousin Harry and Rosslyn Castle is Ian, and he promised not to tell anyone, and I know he'll keep that promise.

He glanced at his watch. It was three o'clock, which meant it would be dark when they reached Edinburgh. Since he couldn't very well appear at the castle in the middle of the night, he'd find a park in Edinburgh where he could sleep before going to the castle in the morning.

As he returned the broadsheet to his haversack, he realized that he was humming to himself, though he had no idea what the tune was. *Whatever it is, I remember humming or whistling it on my long walks in Lyme Regis.*

The compartment door opened, and the conductor announced, "Tickets, please."

"Pardon me," Evan said as he presented his ticket, "but do you recognize this tune?"

He whistled a few passages as the conductor punched his ticket.

"Of course. That's a well-known Irish tune—'Brian Boru's March,'" he said and left the compartment.

Evan jumped up and leaned into the corridor. "Who is Brian Boru?"

"Not *is*, my young friend, *was*! Brian Boru was a high king of old Ireland." With that he stepped into the next compartment. "Tickets, please."

Evan smiled and sat back down. *So that's the melody that goes with the words of the song in my haversack! Which can only mean that it's my haversack. Which means that I'm Evan Sinclair!*

He put his feet up, looked out the window and hummed "Brian Boru's March" as the train sped toward Edinburgh. For the moment, he put the broadsheet out of his mind.

CHAPTER 19

December 1, 1914
Roslin in Midlothian, Scotland

"THIS IS Roslin's main street," the cab driver announced as she pulled to the curb. "Like most, I imagine you'll be wanting to see Rosslyn Chapel. It's about a hundred yards down that lane."

"What about the Rosslyn Castle?" asked Evan from the back seat. "Do you know where that might be?"

"Sorry." She shrugged. "Never been there. Still waiting for an invite."

He had spent the night on an uncomfortable park bench in Edinburgh, worried about being identified from the broadsheet. Though he hadn't slept much, he felt no fatigue, and with no memory of ever having ridden in an automobile, his mind was bursting with questions. "I say ma'am," he began. "In the taxi queue this morning, it seemed that all the drivers were women. Why is that?"

"My dear boy," she said quietly, her smile fading, "we drive because our husbands are gone—in France fighting against the Huns. Someone's got to pay the rent and put food on the table."

"Of course—I'm sorry," he replied, and as he reached for the door handle, a vague memory arose in his mind. "I've seen this automobile before," he murmured.

"I shouldn't wonder! You've probably seen hundreds of them. The Tin Lizzie is the most popular car in America!"

"Tin Lizzie?" asked Evan.

"This beautiful Ford Model T." She beamed and stroked the steering wheel.

"This came from *America*?"

"No, sir—we make them here now. My hubby purchased this beauty at the Ford factory in Manchester a few months before the damn war began."

Evan searched his mind for a clear memory that might connect with the automobile, but to no avail. "Thanks for the ride, ma'am." He leaned forward and paid the fare.

Stepping out, he pushed the door closed.

"Have a good day, laddie!" The driver called out, and with a quick wave, she pulled away from the curb.

Evan glanced at his watch. *Half eight.* Looking about, he saw small single-story shops lining the street—most still shuttered, the sun peeking over thatched roofs.

Before anything else, I've got to record the partial memory of that automobile—that Model T. He crouched down, took his notebook from his haversack, and made the entry.

Straightening up, he drew a deep breath, tasting the cool morning air along with the unmistakable aroma of freshly baked bread. Suddenly hungry, he shouldered his haversack and followed his nose to the opposite side of the street. The sign above an open storefront read *Roslin Bakery*.

Coming to the castle unannounced, I don't want to be empty handed when I show up. He opened the bakery door, and a tinkling bell broke the fragrant silence.

A middle-aged woman wearing a white apron stepped forward and rested her flour-covered hands on the counter. "How may I help you, my boy?"

"What are those, ma'am?" Evan pointed at a bin next to the counter.

"My Bath buns with currants! Fresh baked this very morning."

"Why are they called Bath buns?"

"That's where the recipe hails from."

And that's where the woman, Sharon Meehan, hails from, he thought and said, "I'll take a dozen."

"Fresh churned butter would go nicely with them," the woman said as she placed the buns in a bag. "Care for some?"

"Yes, please. How much would that be altogether?"

"A tanner," she replied and wrapped a cube of butter in white paper.

"A *tanner*? How much is that?"

"Sixpence." She smiled. "You're an American, aren't you?"

"Is it that obvious?" he asked and placed the coins on the counter.

"Charmingly so." She tossed the money into the till. "We do love you Yanks, but we'd love you more if you'd lend us a hand against the Huns." She handed him the bag. "There you are my boy. Where are you bound today?"

"Just seeing some sights."

The woman's smile faded. "An odd time to be sightseeing . . . what with the war."

Feeling uncomfortable, he said, "I was wounded in Flanders—discharged from the hospital yesterday."

"You *volunteered*, did you?" The woman sounded surprised.

"Yes."

"There's some extra buns for you, then!" She put them in the bag. "I wish there were more Yanks like you!"

Hoping to change the subject, he pointed up at the bakery sign above the counter. "Why the different spellings of Roslin?"

"You're not the first to ask, nor the last. The name of the town is spelled like it is on our sign. On the other hand, the chapel is spelled R-O-S-S-L-Y-N, and the same holds true for Rosslyn Castle. As to the title of the Sinclairs of Rosslyn, it goes either way—but no one much cares about them nowadays, not with the scoundrel who occupies the castle, despoiling the noble peerage, however you spell it."

Shocked to hear his cousin called a scoundrel, he stammered, "Now . . . now that you mention the castle, ma'am, how might I get there?"

"I'll show you." She dusted powder off her hands, stepped out the door, and pointed. "Take that lane between the hedgerows for a hundred yards and you'll see Rosslyn Chapel. Before you reach it, there's a small track on your right that runs downhill. Follow that for a few minutes as it passes between two cemeteries. The castle is two hundred yards further on, across a stone bridge." After wishing him well, she returned to the shop.

Before setting out, Evan knelt on the wooden walkway, took a couple of buns out of the bag, and put the bag in his knapsack. He finished off a bun as he walked down the road, wondering why the woman had referred to his cousin as a scoundrel. By the time he saw the spires of Rosslyn Chapel, the second bun was also gone.

The narrow track leading downhill was crowded on either side with evergreen holly growing among ancient oak trees. Glad for the warmth of his leather jacket, he moved quickly through the cool shadows and soon came within sight of a narrow stone bridge spanning a deep chasm. At the far end of the bridge, a ruined gatehouse stood as a mute sentinel. A looming gray wall of the castle beyond the remains of the gatehouse was equally bleak, dotted with caper brush and dry weeds.

This place looks deserted, he thought with mounting concern as he crossed the stone bridge. On either side of the bridge were bare branches of maple trees with a few remaining golden leaves. Stopping to look down into the darkness between the branches, he could see the trees' trunks rooted in the earth of the shadowed glen far below.

Once across the bridge, he paused at the gatehouse—the gaunt scaffolding of weathered stones rising to a height of about thirty feet. On his left was the desolate castle beyond an unkempt hedgerow and a ruined keep. On his right was a partially intact curtain wall and a garden overgrown with weeds. With rising alarm, he couldn't help but wonder, *Was the letter Ian received just a flimflam concocted by a scoundrel pretending to be my cousin?*

He moved along the tangled garden path, warily studying the dark castle. He came to a richly carved doorway. On the arched lintel above were the initials SWS and the year 1622. Iron studs lined the thick-grained door with a brass lion's head door knocker at eye level.

Well, I've come this far. He reached out, lifted the knocker and brought it down twice. The sound echoed in the silence behind the door.

CHAPTER 20

December 1, 1914
War Office at Whitehall, London

TOWARD THE end of a long day working alone on the map of Mesopotamia, Clive had had enough. Without Lawrence, who was now away making arrangements to leave for Cairo, the map room was at best a minor distraction from thinking about Evan—at worst, intolerable drudgery.

I've had enough of this bloody keetch! He gripped a stack of notes in his fist, wishing that he was also going to Cairo. *However,* he quickly reminded himself, *being here gives me the best chance of finding Evan.* He sighed and wondered, *But did he really survive the sinking of the* Austrium?

"Of course, he survived!" he shouted and threw down the notes.

But doubts immediately crept back; *But why no word from him? Was he captured by the Germans?*

He shook the thoughts away. *I need to stop driving myself insane and get back to mapping Mesopotamia!*

He pieced his notes together and forced himself back to the map. An hour passed, the electric lights taking hold as the winter sunlight faded toward evening.

As he was getting ready to leave, a knock sounded at the door. "Come!" he shouted, expecting it to be a boy scout with a message. But looking up, he saw Hedley.

"Colonel Hedley, sir!" he saluted, anxious about why he was there.

Instead of returning Clive's salute, Hedley smiled and came toward him, holding out a sheet of paper. "A letter from Lyme Regis, Captain!"

Lyme Regis? Clive thought as he took the letter and began to read, his eyes widening with disbelief. "He's alive!" he shouted as words jumped off the page—*near drowning, amnesia, healed from his wounds, seeking any information to confirm the identity.* But the words soon blurred, and he had to shut his eyes against the tears.

He felt Hedley's hand on his shoulder and heard his voice speaking. "The letter arrived along with this."

Clive opened his eyes and, and wiping them dry, he saw that Hedley was holding out a small square of paper. A photograph of Evan—smiling and comfortable in what appeared to be a hospital bed.

"Yes, Sinclair! Your boy is alive—alive and well!"

For a few moments, Clive couldn't speak. When he found his voice, he straightened up and said, "Thank you, sir. Request permission to travel to Lyme Regis."

"Granted!" Hedley laughed and patted him on the shoulder. "Your train leaves Waterloo Station tomorrow morning at 0600 hours." He handed Clive an envelope. "Rail passes and branch line connections, Captain. Go get your boy!"

❖ ❖ ❖

Back in his tent, Clive quickly packed a bag, his heart bursting with gratitude, his mind racing. *I'll leave here at 0500 hours with plenty of time to hire a taxi for Waterloo Station.*

Too excited to sleep, he sat to write a letter to Mervin Sykes in Oxford. He'd last seen his old friend about two months before, soon after arriving back in England, and at a time when he had no idea where Evan had gone after leaving home. Now that Hedley had given him the final piece of the puzzle, he wanted to share the news with Mervin, who was something of a brother to Clive, and something of an uncle to Evan.

The words flowed easily into a cursive portrait of Evan arriving by steamer in Nice, arrested upon reaching Paris, escaping from the Paris police, somehow joining the Flemish resistance, wounded in the flooding of the polders, recovering at a BEF hospital in Boulogne, and crossing the Channel by hospital ship, which had been sunk by a U-boat, with Evan reported lost at sea and presumed dead for an excruciating ten days. Clive finished the portrait with the final and wonderful brushstrokes of Evan's deliverance.

> And today, my dear friend, I'm more relieved than you can imagine to report that I've received word from a hospital in Lyme Regis that Evan is alive! I'll be leaving London on the first train tomorrow morning to finally see him. While it's possible I'll travel with him to Oxford to see you, though next steps will await directives from the hospital medical staff.
>
> With more gratitude, love, and
relief than I can express,
Clive

CHAPTER 21

December 1, 1914
Rosslyn Castle Midlothian, Scotland

EVAN WAITED for a long minute after knocking at the castle door. There was no response. Putting down his valise, he noticed the dead leaves covering the paving stones. He put his ear to the door. No sound came from within the castle. *I'll give it one more try,* he thought, reaching for the door knocker, but at that moment, the door creaked open.

"Good morning . . ." said a slender middle-aged man with a neat mustache, a gray dressing gown over white linen pajamas with a paisley ascot, and a guarded look on his face.

After peering at Evan for a few seconds, his eyes flew open. "My dear cousin, Evan!" he exclaimed. "How very good to see you! Do come in!" He opened the door wide, his eyes sparkling with pleasure.

"You . . . you *know* me?" Evan stammered.

"Of course, I know you, though I must admit, the cable and photograph I received from Ian Cowan did prime my memory. Please come in!"

Though relieved at the confirmation of his identity, Evan hesitated in the doorway, his heart pounding. "It's just that . . . I wasn't certain you'd recognize me—"

"Not recognize you? Even without the photograph, I would have recognized you! Though you *have* grown—a full head taller, I daresay." He stepped out, picked up Evan's valise and extended his right hand. "It's so grand to see you again!"

Evan carefully took his cousin's hand and was startled as he vigorously shook it, then pulled him forward into the shadowed foyer and pushed the door closed. He looked at Evan and his smile faded. "Ian mentioned amnesia. So, tell me, does returning here jog your memory? Do you recall being here with your lovely parents? Do you remember *me*?"

Confused and mildly alarmed, Evan shook his head. "I'm sorry."

"No matter, dear cousin!" Putting a hand on Evan's shoulder, he said, "You've been through a rough patch, and I want you to know you're welcome here for as long as you like—until your memory returns or what have you."

Reassured, Evan replied, "Thank you . . . your . . . your Excellency?" he stammered, then blurted out. "Cousin, what should I call you?"

"Pardon my lack of propriety!" he said and made a little bow. "Call me James Francis Harry St. Clair-Erskine, fifth earl of Rosslyn." He burst out laughing. "Or just call me Harry." He motioned grandly with his hand toward the far end of the hallway. "Please, join me in the dining room for tea. Or would you prefer coffee?"

"Tea would be fine and would go nicely with the fresh-baked buns and butter I just bought in town." He lifted the bag out of his knapsack and handed it to Harry.

"Delightful! The buns will add a nice touch since I haven't much in the way of food about at the moment . . ."

What? Evan felt confused. *Not much in the way of food? He lives in a castle, for God's sake!* He followed Harry down the hall for a few paces, passing framed photographs lining the wall. One caught his eye—someone in a safari hat with a scarf covering his nose and mouth standing by an odd stone structure on a hillside. "Is that you here in this photograph?" he asked.

Harry glanced back at it. "Yes! Searching for treasure outside Nice."

"What's this *here*?" Evan asked as a faint memory hovered at the edge of his mind.

"The remains of a stone pyramid. According to local legend it was built by Knights Templar returning to Europe after the Crusades.

The pyramid was built over a cave—the opening is just here, close to the ground beneath the pyramid." He drew a deep sigh. "A nice little adventure, though it came to naught."

"What do you mean?"

"I was in a bit of pickle at the time." He drew up his shoulders in an embarrassed shrug. "During one of my gambling binges, I lost a small fortune at the roulette tables in Monte Carlo. Retreating to Nice, I was drowning my sorrows at a little bar on the promenade, when I heard a gentleman speaking loudly about knowing the whereabouts of the Templar Treasure, claiming it was buried in the hills above Nice near the village of Falicon.

"Having just lost much of my *own* treasure, I was intrigued and spoke with him for the better part of an hour. Due to the extremity of my economic desperation and an advanced degree of inebriation, I agreed to fund the quest with the little credit I had left. As you might imagine, the expense of such an undertaking is *prodigious*!" He nodded at the photograph. "This was taken just before we rappelled down into the cave beneath the pyramid, expecting to possess the Templar treasure! Sadly, all we found was bat guano, stalactites, and an illegible inscription. We dug about for a month until the money ran out. Then we parted ways with every intention of resuming the quest once I could scrape enough money together."

"Have you?"

"No, but like many gamblers, I considered that the best way to get out of debt was to continue gambling. I moved from the roulette tables of Monte Carlo to the Kelso Racecourse in the Scottish Borders. But sadly, my luck didn't improve." He exhaled a sigh and headed down the hallway as he continued talking.

"Though I had inherited title, properties, estates, coal mines in Dysart, a splendid steam yacht, and assets in excess of fifty thousand pounds, I managed to lose almost everything. I declared bankruptcy about two years ago." He stopped and turned. "Not what you probably expected from your noble cousin, I daresay! However, by selling the family silver, gold, and fine China at a three-day auction in Edinburgh, I managed to retain my coal mines, the family chapel, this delightful castle, and *these* priceless artifacts!" He motioned to his right. "Regalia of Scottish Freemasonry going back centuries!"

Evan saw that framed photographs had given way to box frames displaying richly embroidered vests, bejeweled aprons, and glittering medals. He stopped at the last one, his attention drawn to a scrap of parchment mounted below a frayed vest. Studying the parchment, he could see lines defining an equilateral triangle with an inverted obtuse triangle overlying its base. Looking closer, he saw letters of an alphabet he didn't recognize. *I've seen this before!* he thought, his heart pounding. "What is *this*?" he asked.

"*That*, my dear cousin, is a most ancient and enigmatic relic—passed down in our bloodline for a thousand years!"

"I've seen this before! Could it have been when I was here with my parents?"

"Not possible, Evan. You were here, but *this* wasn't. None of the display cases were here! Up until a few years ago, all the Freemasonry regalia, including the parchment, were locked in a vault. I had the display cases constructed after the bankruptcy, thinking to also sell them at auction." Harry made a guilty shrug. "Thankfully, I came to my senses and kept them."

"That's so strange . . ." Evan rested a finger on the glass over the parchment. "I have the distinct feeling I'd seen this before."

"Perhaps you have! Your father told me he'd been to that very pyramid and made a rubbing of the inscription in the cave—identical to the one on this scroll."

"But why would he mention the inscription, if this parchment wasn't on display?" "Because," Harry pointed back down the hall, "he saw my photograph of the pyramid and told me about the rubbing he'd made there. When I told him that I had the actual scroll with the original inscription, he insisted I show it to him—which I did. We went to the vault, he examined the scroll, and confirmed that the inscription on the scroll was identical to the inscription in the pyramid, based on the rubbing he had made."

"Wow!" Evan exclaimed. "But did he understand what it meant?"

"No. He believed it to be an ancient Hebrew script, and despite numerous attempts, he hadn't been able to find anyone able to decipher it."

"Did he know where the scroll came from? Do you?"

"No one knows for certain. Though St. Clair family traditions tell us that it came from the Holy Land. However, no one knows who brought it here and when."

No one knows. Evan stared at the parchment as the words echoed in his mind—*no one knows.* Somehow, he found that reassuring. *No one knows—not just me! Everyone has a point where knowledge ends, and no memory exists.* He startled when Harry patted him on the shoulder.

"Come along, cousin! You must be famished. I know I am!" He went to the end of the hall, turned right, and disappeared.

Evan lingered over the scroll a moment longer, then followed. But at the end of the hall, he stopped again, spellbound by three ghostly pale stone statues, each four feet high and bathed in the sunlight that glowed through a window. There were two bearded male figures each holding a scroll, one also holding a sword. The other figure held a large key. The third statue was a forlorn-looking young woman, her face upturned, hands clasped at her waist.

Evan flinched when Harry's voice cut through the silence. "In here, Evan!"

Stepping away from the statues, he entered a large dining room where Harry was pouring tea. "Room for milk?" he asked.

"Yes, please." Evan placed his knapsack next to his valise on a rich oriental rug. "Were those statues here when I visited with my parents?"

"Most definitely! They've been here since the seventeenth century!"

"They look like they belong in a church," Evan said.

"So, they were—in Rosslyn Chapel until Oliver Cromwell became lord protector. He didn't much like Catholic iconography. However, our ancestors saved these from Cromwell's minions by hiding them here. They've been here ever since."

"Who are they supposed to be?"

"The Apostle Paul is the one with the sword. Peter's got the key," Harry looked over the table. "Drat! I've forgotten the jam!" He disappeared back into the pantry.

"What about the woman?"

"Mary Magdalene," Harry said as he returned with a jar of jam.

"Who was she?"

"A woman who traveled with Jesus—one of his closest followers. She witnessed his crucifixion and burial, and she was the first to witness his resurrection." Placing the buns on a plate, he inhaled and exclaimed. "Fresh Bath buns with currants—how lovely!"

As Evan sat down, he felt anxious that he had no knowledge of the names and words Harry casually mentioned: Jesus, crucifixion, resurrection, Mary Magdalene, Peter, and Paul. He decided to compile a list and, when the time was right, ask Harry for explanations. He was also puzzled by the complete absence of any kitchen staff or family members. "Sorry for asking, Harry, but in a large castle like this, don't you have any help?"

"Had to let them go. Dreadfully expensive keeping staff about."

"But the letter Ian received was from your personal secretary—"

"That *was* a nice touch, wasn't it?" Harry said. "Actually, I wrote that myself." After a sip of tea, he smiled at Evan. "One must keep up appearances, don't you think?"

Evan appreciated Harry's candor. "Another thing I was wondering—the initials, SWS, and the date, 1622, on the lintel above the door. What's that mean?"

"Sir William Sinclair and the year this east range was restored. William is the most popular given name among the generations of Sinclairs. On the other hand, I believe that I'm the first Harry and you're the first Evan."

"I hope you'll let me know how I might make myself useful."

"Any assistance would be appreciated." Harry prepared a bun with butter and jam and raised his eyebrows. "You're no doubt also wondering why there's no family about."

"The thought did cross my mind . . ."

"By way of an explanation," Harry said as he took a bite and chewed, "I'll invoke the great Jane Austen. In the very first sentence of her masterpiece, *Pride and Prejudice,* she writes, ' . . . a single man in possession of a good fortune, must be in want of a wife.'" He sighed and added, "Conversely, since I'm no longer in possession of a good fortune, my wife left. She's on an extended visit with her parents in London with our two children."

"Will she be back anytime soon?"

"Not bloody likely!" Harry paused to take a bite of the Bath bun. "And speaking of Austen, you've read some of her books, I trust?"

"I wouldn't know." Evan shrugged.

"Of course! How silly of me!" Harry tapped himself on the forehead. "As to your loss of memory, another line of Austen comes to mind, ' . . . but in such cases as these, a good memory is unpardonable!' Therefore, dear cousin, according to Jane Austen, your *lack* of memory is a virtue!"

"A virtue I could do without," said Evan.

"We do have outstanding doctors in Edinburgh. Why not see one about this?"

Evan shook his head. "The doctor I had in Lyme Regis was trained in Edinburgh and was certain that the only treatment for me is 'tincture of time.' Besides, I'm not comfortable being seen . . ." He didn't want to tell Harry about the broadsheet.

"You're not comfortable being *seen*? Whatever do you mean?"

After a moment of uncertainty, Evan plunged forward. "Apparently, I was involved in an incident two months ago in Paris and escaped from the police while being questioned. I've been told that there's a broadsheet with my likeness and name circulating in France. For all I know, I may be wanted here as well."

"With the war raging along the Western Front, I cannot imagine that anyone would be concerned about you." Harry shrugged. "That being said, broadsheets are regularly posted at the constables' station and at the post office. If you like, I'll be happy to pop into Roslin and see if there are any posted there. Eventually, I'll also check in Edinburgh. If I don't see any, that should put your mind at ease, and we'll be able to get you care at the Royal Infirmary—one of the best hospitals in Great Britain."

"I had good care in Lyme Regis, Harry. It didn't help at all."

Harry's smile faded. "I suppose there's another option . . ."

"What other option?"

Harry raised his shoulders. "It's a bit . . . peculiar . . . unusual, perhaps . . ."

"What?"

Harry leaned toward Evan and, with no trace of levity, said in a low voice, "The Gypsies of Rosslyn Glen. Many of the older women have a wisdom—a gift of *knowing* things. Some are adept at potions—concoctions of herbs and plants for healing—"

Hearing the word *healing*, Evan asked, "Would you take me to them?"

"They're not here now. They'll only return in the spring."

"When does spring come here? April? May?"

"We'll know that spring has come when the white blossoms of the wild onion bloom in Rosslyn Glen. That's when the Gypsies will return."

CHAPTER 22

December 1, 1914
Rosslyn Castle Midlothian, Scotland

WITH HARRY gone to Roslin, Evan was alone. Leaning on the balustrade at the top of the scarlet-carpeted staircase, he looked down at the pale statues of Peter, Paul, and Mary Magdalene, feeling a certain kinship with these fugitives of Cromwell. *I'm a bit of a fugitive myself—in hiding here with them,* he thought and felt grateful that Harry had gone to see if there were any broadsheets in Roslin accusing him of treason.

With that, a recurrent and terrifying thought rose in his mind. *But what if I really was a German spy? What if they erased my memory so I wouldn't inform on anyone. What if Ian and Harry are part of this, and German spies, themselves?*

He shook the thoughts away and scolded himself: *That's what you get from reading too many* All Story Magazines . . .

"That's a memory!" he said aloud with a shock of realization. He paused to admire the bright shard of remembrance emerging from the opaque darkness of his mind. He turned on the landing and headed for the bedroom to record it in his journal.

Before Harry had left, he'd given Evan a tour of the castle, asking him to select one of the upper floor bedrooms. Evan had chosen that of Harry's five-year-old son, now living with his estranged wife in London. Evan chose it for the view it offered from the window, and for the lurid poster advertising the moving picture, *Broncho Billy's Last Holdup.*

He entered the recovered memory of the *All Story Magazine* in his journal along with the recognition he had felt on seeing the Falicon pyramid and the inscription on the ancient scrap of parchment. Closing his notebook, he looked up at the larger-than-life image of a masked Broncho Billy, a six-gun in each hand—a poster Harry had admitted to bringing back from a trip to America and pasting to the wall above his son's bed. Smiling, he reread the text; *Now showing at Tally's Electric Theater—a new place of amusement, Los Angeles, California.*

He opened the window and looked out. Beyond an expanse of forest canopy along a winding river, he could see the spires of Rosslyn Chapel, which he had glimpsed from the road in Roslin. He leaned out and breathed in the cool air, as bracing as the view.

He closed the window and went downstairs, his footfalls quiet on the scarlet-carpeted steps. Turning from the three fugitive statues on the lower landing, he entered the library, warm at midday with sunlight streaming through a high window. Shelves crowded with books lined the walls, arranged by author with the name of each on a neat label affixed to the shelves.

With Harry having mentioned Jane Austen, Evan pulled out the first of her books on the shelf—*Sense and Sensibility, Volume I.* Opening it to the title page, he saw that, in place of her name, were the words *By A Lady.*

That's strange, he thought. *Why wouldn't an author have her name listed in her own book? Probably because she was a woman . . .*

He sat down to read, but after a few pages, he decided to look for something else. "Perhaps an *All Story Magazine,*" he said aloud and returned the book to its place.

Scanning down the shelves, he came to a large section of books marked by the nameplate, *Burton, Richard Francis.*

"Wow!" he exclaimed. "Twelve volumes of *The Arabian Nights!*" He removed the first volume and ran his fingers over the shining gold embossed lettering on the rich burgundy cover. Sitting on the divan, he carefully opened the book and touched the smooth marbled endpaper.

He read the title page aloud, "A plain and literal translation of the Arabian nights entertainments, now entitled *The Book of the Thousand*

Nights and a Night with introduction and explanatory notes on the manners and customs of Muslim men by Sir Richard F. Burton."

"Sounds interesting," he said and turned the page. The frontispiece painting took his breath away—a crowded courtyard with strangely dressed men and sparsely dressed beautiful women. He turned to the first tale, "The Story of King Shahryar and His Brother."

He began reading, but long passages of flowery prose soon conspired with the warm room, the comfortable divan, and the lack of sleep in the park to produce a profound and dreamless sleep.

Startled awake by the sound of a key turning in the front door lock, he had no idea how long he had slept.

"Evan! I've got good news for you!" Harry's voice echoed from the foyer.

"What is it?" Evan shouted and ran out of the library, the book in his hand.

"You'll be happy to know that there are no broadsheets with your name or likeness *anywhere* in town!"

"That *is* good news. Thank you!"

"You'll also be happy to know I've got some lunch for us!" Harry held up a bag, then saw the book in Evan's hand. "What do you have *there?*"

"*The Arabian Nights*. I found it more interesting than Jane Austen."

"I'm sure you did—perhaps a bit *too* interesting!" He sighed and extended his hand. "May I?"

Evan handed him the book.

"I would be beside myself if I ever had to explain such an indiscretion to your parents. You see, this book is simply a bit *risqué*. Actually, *far more* than a bit."

Evan was confused since he hadn't sensed anything strange in the few pages he had read before falling asleep. "What does risqué *mean?*" he asked.

"Racy," said Harry.

Evan shrugged.

"What about lewd? Salacious? Smutty? Ribald? Naughty?"

"Naughty! *That* I understand."

"Good!" Harry said and returned the book to its place in the library. "Allow me to recommend the *Adventures of Tom Sawyer*—a good book to start with." He guided Evan to the far side of the hearth. "Here it is—under Mark Twain." He handed the book to Evan.

"Having access to my library while you're on the lam—as you Americans say—affords you the opportunity to read *everything*." He winked at Evan. "Well, *almost* everything. And since you have no memory of having read *anything*, you'll be able to experience all this delightful prose for the first time! If I must say so myself, I do have a *magnificent* library! In addition to all of Mark Twain's books, you'll find all the masterpieces of Charles Dickens, Arthur Conan Doyle, Sir Walter Scott—"

"Harry," Evan cut in, "I need to speak with you about my *parents*."

"Absolutely! Let's talk while I prepare the haggis—a veritable feast!"

Evan followed Harry through the dining room into the galley kitchen, where he persisted. "Please tell me everything you remember about my parents."

"Could you be a bit more specific?" Harry asked as he unwrapped the haggis and put it to warm in the oven.

"What did they look like?"

"They were a handsome couple. Your dad had dark hair, a full beard, nicely trimmed. Your mum, Janet, was a beautiful and gentle creature. I remember that she wore her long blond hair in a bun." Harry paused. "If I'm not mistaken, I had an old Eastman Kodak Brownie at the time." Turning, he looked at Evan, his eyes wide. "I may actually have some *photographs*! Wait here—I'll go see."

Evan's heart pounded with excitement. He took the potatoes out of the shopping bag, washed and began to peel them, careful not to cut himself as his hands shook. He had just put them to boil when he heard Harry shout.

"Found them! But, sadly, only three."

Evan rushed into the dining room, drying his hands on a dishtowel. Barely able to catch his breath, Evan stared at the first photograph.

"That's you with your mum and dad." Harry said and put his hand on his shoulder. "Take your time with these, Evan. Meanwhile, I'll go prepare our luncheon."

To steady himself, Evan sat at the table as he looked at a shorter version of himself standing between his parents at the ruined gatehouse with the castle behind. Minutes passed as he studied his parents' faces, hoping to coax a memory to life. But he felt nothing. *How is it possible I don't remember them?* He looked at a second photograph; two men at the ruined gatehouse. He recognized Harry, and now knew the other man was his father. "Clive Sinclair," he whispered aloud, but no memory surfaced.

With a feeling of growing despair, he sighed and looked at the last photograph, taken at the dining room table where he now sat; his ten-year-old self in front of an opened tome, his finger on a page, his father by his side. Evan stood up, went into the pantry and asked, "Harry, what's this?"

"The daily Latin tutorial with your dad and my rare copy of Dryden's *Aeneid*—still in my library if you'd like to peruse it."

Flipping back through the photographs as he leaned on the kitchen doorway, Evan drew a deep breath, trying to lift away the heavy feeling of sadness weighing on his heart. "I have no memory of them, Harry. How is that *possible?*"

"Don't be discouraged, Evan. Your healing will come in time."

"Perhaps in the spring? When the Gypsies return to the glen?"

"Hopefully, before that." Harry checked the potatoes with a fork. "These will need a few more minutes."

"What about the family pedigree you mentioned?" asked Evan. "May I see it?"

"A capital idea! We'll look at it right after lunch!"

"Why not while we eat?"

"Heavens no!" Harry wrinkled his nose. "It's recorded on large bolts of linen, much of it dusty and frayed—not the kind of garnish you'd want with this fine cuisine—delicious haggis sausages!" He opened the oven and put one on each plate.

"I remember haggis from the hospital," Evan said. "What's actually *in* it?"

"I should consider *not* knowing the contents of haggis a *benefit* of amnesia, Evan! Are you sure you want to know?"

"Yes!"

"It's all things minced sheep—heart, lungs, liver, and what have you cooked up with suet, onions, and oatmeal—and all brought together and boiled in the sheep's stomach. Thankfully, it's heavily seasoned." Harry spooned a few potatoes onto each plate. "The good thing about haggis is that it wastes *nothing* and will never be rationed. But do try not to think about what's in it, and just enjoy its tasty economy."

Hungry as he was, Evan found the nonhospital version of haggis reasonably good.

While he ate, he studied the faces of his parents, with no sense of recognition.

When they were done eating, he asked, "Might we see the family tree now?"

"Certainly!" Harry led the way up the long flight of stairs, and reaching the landing, pointed upwards. "There it is."

Evan looked up at what he had thought were faded tapestries, and watched as Harry used a winch fixed to the wall to lower them down.

"Here we are!" Harry carefully lifted the edge of the nearest linen to eye level and pointed. "Here's your family—right here."

Evan saw that his father's entry included his mother's name and his own, along with dates of birth. Staring at his parents' names, he again searched his mind, but felt an almost tangible obstruction blocking his path. "Where does the family tree begin?"

"A thousand years ago, and not with these," Harry said as he used the winch to raise the sheets back into position. "The first recorded years of the St. Clair bloodline are framed on the hallway wall. Do you want to see them?"

"Yes, please," Evan replied with an odd sense of urgency.

"Come, I'll show you."

Once downstairs, Harry tapped the glass over one of the box frames. "Our pedigree begins with Henri de St. Clair, born in 1065, a soldier of the First Crusade—one of the original Knights Templar."

Again, those words I don't understand; First Crusade, Knights Templar. More to add to my list.

Harry moved his finger down. "Several generations later we have the Knight Templar Jonathan St. Clair, born in 1245, who died at the end of the Crusades. See the date of his death? May 30, 1291— the day Acre fell to the Saracens. What's interesting is that his wife also died that day—Zahirah, a woman with a Saracen name."

"What's a Saracen?"

"A Muslim. The other thing is this; the Templars were a monastic order, sworn to celibacy. But, despite his vows, Jonathan St. Clair married this Muslim woman, and they had a child—William—named for Jonathan's father."

Evan sighed, frustrated at his lack of comprehension. "These words, Harry—Crusade, Holy Land, Knights Templar, Muslims—it's like I don't understand English!"

"In that case, I suggest you direct your reading in keeping with your desire to understand your ancestry. Forget about Mark Twain for now—concentrate on the history of the Crusades to understand your family history."

Evan nodded as he squinted at the Jonathan St. Clair entry. "There's a detail here I don't understand; Jonathan and his wife died on May 18, 1291, and their son, William, was born in March of 1291, making him only two or three months old when they died! And within a year, baby William comes to Scotland." He fixed Harry with his eyes and asked, "With both parents dead, how did he survive, and who brought him to Scotland?"

"No one knows!" Harry whispered. "And those questions are at the heart of the greatest mystery of the St. Clair family! And *you* might have an advantage in solving that mystery since your mind isn't cluttered up with preconceived notions."

Excited by the prospect, Evan nodded. "I'll need some books—"

"You may have noticed, Evan, I *have* some books! In particular, some excellent histories of the Crusades and the Sinclair family."

"What about *The Arabian Nights*?" Evan asked with a sly smile.

Harry shook his head. "We don't want your mind cluttered up with that!"

CHAPTER 23

December 5, 1914
Oxford

AFTER NOT finding Evan in Lyme Regis, Clive made the journey to their Oxford home, hoping to find him there. He fished the house keys out of his pocket, and with shaking hands managed to open the front door. He stepped into the foyer and shouted, "Evan!" He dropped his valise and called out again, "Evan!" His heart was pounding.

"Clive?"

He turned at hearing Mervin's voice and looked up to see him leaning over the balustrade on the upper landing. "Is he *here*? Is Evan *here*?"

"I haven't seen him, though I'm delighted to see you at long last," Mervin said as he descended the stairs. "I received your letter just yesterday, and I'm so relieved that he's alive and in Lyme Regis. But if he's *there*, why are you *here*?"

"Because he isn't there anymore!" Clive snapped. "I got to Lyme Regis from London as quickly as I could, only to find that he'd left the day before. And if he's not *here*, I don't know *where* he is."

"But surely he'll come here—this is home!"

Clive's shoulders slumped. "He doesn't know where home is, Mervin—he has amnesia!"

"If that's so, why was he discharged from hospital?"

"He wasn't. The attending consultant told me that Evan had become frustrated and slipped away. No one knows where he's gone!" He reached into his shirt pocket. "The hospital had this photograph taken of him as they were trying to establish his identity." He handed it to Mervin. "That was taken a week ago."

"He certainly *looks* well! The last time I saw him, he was a boy—now he's a handsome young man!" Mervin shook his head and handed the photograph back to Clive. "And no one knows where he's gone?"

"No one." Clive exhaled a deep sigh, fatigued from the travel and the crushing disappointment of not finding him—not in Lyme Regis and not at the house. "Do you have any coffee?"

"Come. I made a pot this morning." Mervin led the way to the kitchen. "Do you want anything to eat?"

"No. Just coffee," Clive collapsed into a chair, took off his cap and placed it on the table.

"Here you are, old chum." Mervin put a cup down "I must say, you do look dashing in your officer's uniform. Did you bring any civilian clothing?"

"Not really, but I still have an entire steamer trunk from Utah I have yet to open."

"Did Evan say anything to the nurses, the doctors, or to any of the other patients?"

"No. They investigated. But there was one thing of interest. When Evan washed ashore, he was wearing a pair of expensive Italian boots, and the evening before he left, he sold them to one of the orderlies. I spoke to the man myself. Evan didn't tell the orderly why he needed the money or that he was planning to leave. But at least we know he's got some money—more than two pounds sterling."

"When did you leave Lyme Regis?" Mervin asked.

"Two days ago."

"It took you two days to get here?"

"I stopped in Bath for a day."

"Why?"

"In piecing together information from the effects they found in Evan's haversack, there was a bit of paper with the home address of a VAD nurse."

"A *what* nurse?" Mervin asked.

"VAD—Voluntary Aid Detachment—civilians providing nursing care for military personnel. It appears this young woman, Sharon Meehan, may have been romantically involved with Evan at the BEF hospital in Boulogne. She apparently gave him her home address in Bath before he left the hospital. The hospital had noted the address in his file as part of the description of the contents of the haversack found with him. Since Bath is only about sixty miles from Lyme Regis, it seemed logical that, with Evan having no memory of his own home, he might have gone there." Clive heaved a deep sigh and took another sip of coffee. "The young woman is still in France, but her parents were at the house and very gracious. They showed me a recent letter where she mentioned Evan—*a handsome young American*—as she described him. But after a full four days since leaving Lyme Regis, he hadn't yet made an appearance there." Clive took another sip of coffee, and added, "On the off-chance he does, I left my contact information."

"What are the chances of the amnesia going away?"

"The consultant told me that there's no way of knowing. He believes it was caused by a combination of head trauma, near drowning, and something called shellshock."

"What's that?"

"Apparently, it's a psychological response commonly seen in soldiers serving along the Western Front, and one of its expressions can be amnesia."

"Is there a cure?"

"Time." Clive said and finished his coffee. "But how much time? No one knows." He looked at Mervin and managed a wan smile as he loosened his necktie. "But at least he's alive—and in England."

"And with a chance he'll regain his memory."

"Yes, Mervin, and when he does, he'll remember Oxford and Marston Street and he'll come home." Clive put his hand on Mervin's shoulder. "Which is why I'm so glad *you're* here. Because when Evan comes home, you'll be here to greet him!"

He felt Mervin cringe beneath his hand. "What's wrong?" he asked.

"Unfortunately, I'm leaving here in a week. I was meaning to tell you. I've been offered a tenured position at Boston University in their archeology department." Mervin shrugged and added, "As you know, what with the war, my classes in Teutonic archeology are about as popular as cholera. All grant funds here have disappeared, but Boston is more promising." He looked up at Clive. "I'm sorry, Old Chum."

Clive patted him on the shoulder. "Completely understandable. I'll leave a note for Evan on the front stoop with my contact information at Whitehall. I'll also leave word with the neighbors." Clive sighed and fixed Mervin with his eyes. "So now I'm also losing my best friend . . ."

"I'll be your best friend no matter where I am, Clive. And, who knows? Perhaps you'll join me in Boston someday."

"Perhaps . . . after the fighting ends, and after Evan comes home." He drew a disconsolate breath. "This war has aged us, Mervin—not only has it robbed us of our youth, it's also robbed us of our young. I just hope I get him back."

CHAPTER 24

December 8, 1914
London

CLIVE REMAINED at the Oxford house for several days, mostly in the hope that Evan might appear, but barring that, to make sure that the neighbors knew how to contact him should he return. Clive also wanted to spend time with Mervin before he left for Boston, not knowing when they might see each other again. But in order to see Lawrence before he left for Cairo, Clive took an early morning train to London, and by eight o'clock he was making his way among the canvas barracks crowding the parade ground outside Whitehall. The first snow had fallen during the night, and only his own solitary footsteps disturbed the silence and the clean blanket of white snow. His thoughts centered on Evan—praying he might find his way home.

Reaching the barracks, he wondered if Lawrence had finished packing. He hadn't.

Despite the cold morning, the door stood open, and Clive could see him from behind—barefoot in khaki shorts and a shapeless gray undershirt. A steamer trunk sat on his bunk, the mattress sagging beneath its weight.

Clive put down his valise and leaned on the doorpost, silently watching Ned pack. In contrast to his frequently disheveled appearance, his packing was unrelentingly neat—like his mapmaking—with unyielding attention to detail and precision in every perfectly folded article of clothing and in the placement of every book and folio. Watching him, Clive felt sad.

Perhaps it was a similarity in the hair color—rebellious brown edged blond by the sun—like Evan's. Finally, he stepped forward. "Just a few hours now, Ned."

Lawrence turned and his eyes opened wide. "Welcome back! What news of Evan? Did you find him in Lyme Regis?"

"No. By the time I arrived he was gone." Clive took off his cap, tossed it on the empty bunk across from Lawrence and sat. He proceeded to tell him all that had transpired in Lyme Regis, Bath, and Oxford, concluding with, "At least I know he's alive and somewhere in England. I only hope the police will solve the missing person case and find him—or that his memory will return, and he'll find *me*."

"I know how hard this is. Not hearing from my brothers is driving me mad!" Lawrence went back to packing. "If there's any news, please cable me in Cairo."

"I will."

Watching him pack, Clive considered that Lawrence was a living anachronism—comfortably at home in the past but not merely a spectator in the present. Clive had long admired his encyclopedic knowledge of medieval Middle East history and knew that he was determined to seize this moment and somehow bend it to his will.

He cleared his throat and asked, "What are you up to, Ned?"

"Whatever do you mean?"

"Just that; what are you up to?"

"Obviously, I'm *packing.*"

"No, I mean, what are you up to? With you there's always a larger plan. For starters, why are you so keen on going to Cairo?"

"*Am* I?" Lawrence grinned as he placed a shirt in the trunk. "It's just that I simply *must* get out of London; the weather is *ghastly,* the city is *swarming* with Belgian refugees, and there's been no decent theater for *months.*" Turning, he took down the last of his books from a makeshift shelf next to his bunk. "In short, I *seriously* disapprove of London, but London seems curiously unmoved." His smile faded and he tossed the books on the bed next to the trunk. "Damn it all, Clive, I should already *be* in Cairo!"

"It's just another desk job—"

"But it's closer to the real action!" Lawrence cut in, his eyes shining. "The clash of civilizations in Arabia! I've been dreaming of this all my life. *That's* what I'm up to! Do you recall what you told me the first time we met in France back in '08? That I was a *dangerous man*? Do you remember?"

"Of course, I do." Clive smiled at the memory. After you told me how you spent summers walking and biking about Great Britain and France—studying, drawing, and photographing Crusader castles, making rubbings of knights' tombs, and doing the same in the Holy Land—I told you that while most people *study* history, you *dream* history, and you dream of things past and what might be in the future, and not at night, but wide awake during the day. *That's* what makes you dangerous!"

Lawrence took a folded piece of paper from among the pages of one of the books and handed it to Clive. "After that conversation six years ago, I wrote this."

Clive read the words aloud; "*Those who dream by night in the dusty recesses of their minds wake in the day to find that all was vanity; but the dreamers of the day are dangerous men, for they may act their dream with open eyes, and make it possible.*"

Clive felt a shiver up his back as he handed the paper back to Lawrence. "What dream would you make possible?"

"To help the Arabs win their freedom from the Turks—from *all* colonial domination."

Clive looked sideways at Lawrence. "You're serious?"

"Yes, and I want to help England atone for its colonial excesses—"

"Would that be with English assistance?"

"Ironic, but yes."

"Then you *are* a dreamer, Ned. England has no intention of ending its colonial enterprises. We glory in being the largest and most powerful empire on earth!"

"Not anymore. England has been like a glutton at a buffet gorging herself. I believe we've had quite *enough* of that fare."

"Do you suggest Britain *abandon* her colonies? Are you *that* seditious?" Clive nearly shouted at Lawrence, surprised at the degree of his irritation.

"If it's seditious to believe that England is capable of learning from history, then, yes, I'm guilty as charged! After all the bloodletting of recent years—Khartoum, the Boxers, the Boer War—I believe that most Englishmen have had quite *enough* of empire!"

"My dear Ned, while I share some of your exhaustion with the enterprise, you must agree that empire is a vital part of who we *are*." Clive interlaced the fingers of his hands. "The colonies are entwined with the very *fabric* of Great Britain."

"Like a malignant cancer!" Lawrence shot back. "I submit we must cut away this cancer before it kills us, and before it kills more of our colonials. I know it won't be easy. But if England is to survive, it's a surgery that *must* be performed."

Lawrence raised his upturned hands toward Clive it what seemed a distinct gesture of supplication as he continued speaking.

"How many more riots, massacres and dead English boys will it require before we learn that for every foreign leader who appeases our imperial designs, there are millions of their subjects who will have none of it! And the more we try to impose our traditions, the worse it gets. It's happening throughout Asia and Africa—a growing hatred of 'foreign devils.' Why should we be surprised? Why should they want to be like us? In the end, they'll fight to preserve their own traditions."

"Come now, Ned! You exaggerate the actions of a few troublemakers. Many colonials are profoundly grateful for our efforts and look upon the Union Jack with love."

"Really? I believe they look upon the Union Jack as a *butcher's apron*—"

"Ned!" Clive cut him off. "Promise me you'll never repeat that hyperbole to anyone! Instead of going to Cairo, you'll end up in the brig and charged with treason."

"I'll try to tone it down. But driving you to distraction has given me quite an appetite." Lawrence began getting dressed as he continued talking. "Let's celebrate my transfer to Cairo over breakfast. I'm looking forward to a nice bowl of porridge."

With Lawrence wearing a clean shirt, jacket, and trousers, they walked across the snow-covered parade grounds to the officer's mess.

Not wanting to part ways on an acerbic note, Clive offered an olive branch, "In many respects, I agree with you, Ned. We British can be insufferably arrogant—as I've heard it said, 'the English are a race of self-made men and have thereby relieved the Almighty of a dreadful responsibility.'"

"A simple thank you from God would be nice," Lawrence said as they reached the officer's mess. "Porridge for you as well?"

"No thanks. I'm dying for coffee." Clive put his cap down on an empty table. "See you back here."

By the time Lawrence brought his bowl to the table, Clive was half-finished with his coffee. "When do you leave?" he asked.

Lawrence glanced at his wristwatch. "Thirty minutes." He took a spoonful of the farina, looked across the table at Clive and sighed. "I'm sure we'll see each other soon enough in Cairo."

Clive shook his head. "Not with Evan still missing."

"Will you be staying in MO-4?"

"Heavens no! Without you there, it's intolerable."

"But Gertrude might be coming aboard. Hedley finally relented to our pressure. She'll soon be coming for an interview."

"It's about bloody time!" Clive exclaimed. "Her knowledge of Arabia is vast, and I'll be delighted to hand her the reins. She'll certainly be able to correct our work and fill in the blanks." Clive shrugged his shoulders, "But I'm done with it, and I'm sure Hedley will find some other sphere where I can help."

"And once Evan surfaces, perhaps then you'll come to Cairo."

"That's my fondest hope."

"After all," said Lawrence, "*that's* where the real war will be—"

"Really, Ned? Everyone at Whitehall sees the war as a purely European affair. While you and I have a fond connection with the Middle East, everyone here calls that front a sideshow. For God's sake—consider the horror of the killing fields of Europe!"

"Sadly, plenty of killing, but not the real show in my opinion, just Kaiser Bill seeking leverage." Lawrence leaned forward. "Listen well, most excellent Theophilus, and I will declare to you in order the things that I have seen and heard."

"Now you're quoting the Book of Acts? Are you about to witness to me about Jesus?"

"No, I want to witness to you about Kaiser Bill. When you and I were together in Carchemish, do you remember Consul Rössler, the head of the German diplomatic mission with the German archeology team?"

"I do."

"After you left for America, the Germans got into a big dust-up with their Kurdish laborers—almost open combat. But I was able to make peace, which saved lives on both sides. Rössler came over to express his gratitude with a bottle of an excellent single malt Glen Scotia—far better than the stuff I was using to preserve those giant desert spiders I collected for my youngest brother. Anyhow, I opened the bottle, hoping the good whiskey would loosen his tongue. And it did." Lawrence paused to take another spoonful of farina.

"The drunker he got, the more he talked—and mostly about Kaiser Bill. Rössler had been with him during the visit to Jerusalem before the turn of the century, when Wilhelm rode into the walled city wearing white robes and mounted on a white steed—styling himself as king of Jerusalem!"

Clive grimaced. "And to think he had a large section of the Old City wall torn down so photographers could record his entrance. Such an arrogant show-off!"

"I wish he could be so easily dismissed as that, Clive. What I learned from Rössler was quite shocking. We've known that Kaiser Bill is after the rich oilfields of Arabia and Mesopotamia as well as control of the Persian

Gulf and the Suez Canal, but there's much more. Rössler spoke of the kaiser's secret wishes for a vast new Holy Roman Empire well beyond that . . ." Lawrence stopped speaking and fell uncharacteristically silent, his eyes fixed on Clive.

"West Asia and North Africa?"

"Bigger . . ."

"World domination?"

Lawrence nodded.

"That's insane. The kaiser is more practical than *that*."

"Is he? According to Rössler, the kaiser is advised by a lunatic named Guido von List who promotes something called Armanism—Aryan superiority with pseudoscientific theories of racial purity and a dash of mysticism. List is stoking the kaiser's grandiose imperial designs. He established an organization in Austria and Germany called, *Ordo Novi Templi*—Order of the New Templars, dedicated to reclaiming Aryan racial purity and world domination. The kaiser is an active patron."

"*World domination*? Do you hear how that sounds? It's *insane!*"

"Perhaps, but before Rössler passed out from the whiskey, he told me that the kaiser is looking to reclaim property of the Holy Roman Empire; the scepter, crown, and orb—the imperial regalia of the Hapsburgs—symbols of power and national pride. And while he's looting the Hofmuseum in Vienna, he also looks to take possession of the Spear of Destiny."

"Well, that changes *everything!*" Clive said in a voice dripping with sarcasm. "After all, the Spear brings its owner the power to conquer the world!" He rolled his eyes and sighed. "Really, Ned! Do you actually believe this silliness makes the kaiser any more dangerous than he already is?"

"There's more, old chap. While you were in Lyme Regis, I had a visit from our mentor, David Hogarth, who told me that the kaiser has sent List to Jerusalem. And you'll never guess who's with him—our favorite treasure hunter, Montagu Walker!"

"Again? The last time he tried digging on the Temple Mount it was a complete failure. Please don't tell me he's trying again."

"Not yet, but Hogarth's contacts report a good deal of surveying in the Kidron Valley—especially just southeast of the walled city."

"Would that be near those second century funerary monuments?"

"Precisely! In particular they've seen activity around the Tomb of Zachariah. Hogarth also reports surveyors at the Great Pyramid in Giza." Lawrence fixed Clive with a knowing gaze. "It's also happening at a third site—outside Falicon in the South of France—at that little truncated pyramid we visited together."

Clive began to feel uneasy. "What does it all mean?"

"Hogarth thinks it has something to do with *ley lines*—invisible energy pathways throughout the world connecting ancient monuments in some grand geometrical pattern."

"Ancient monuments, such as pyramids?" asked Clive.

"Yes. The surveyors in Jerusalem, Giza, and Falicon seem to be mapping ley lines."

Could it be? Clive felt a cold dread tighten around his chest. "Mad and improbable as it seems, Kaiser Bill may be on to something!" He leaned forward and asked, "Do you recall the rubbing I made of the inscription in the cave beneath the pyramid?"

"I do," said Lawrence.

"Do you think that has anything to do with this?"

"It just might."

CHAPTER 25

December 15, 1914
Mediterranean Sea Off the Egyptian coast

FIVE DAYS out of Marseille, Lawrence stood at the weathered gunwale and watched Egypt emerge from the low horizon beneath a gray sky. Gripping the railing, he leaned forward and watched the bow wake foam along the rusting hull.

"I hope you're not contemplating jumping."

Lawrence recognized the speaker before he turned. Lieutenant Colonel Stewart Newcombe, twenty years his senior, stood by his side, attired in khaki drill.

"No, but if you're going to push me, Stewart, please wait till we're closer to Alexandria."

"Not to worry, Ned. You're far too valuable an asset!" Newcombe patted Lawrence on the shoulder. "By the way, I meant to thank you for remembering me in your survey of Southern Palestine. How did you phrase it? . . . *for showing us the way wherein we were to walk and the work that we must do.*"

"It's the least we could do, Stewart. After all, you and Kitchener began it all, and after K went back to Cairo, you stayed on and worked on it alone. To be sure, you would have finished the survey had the Turks not suspected you of spying."

"You can hardly blame them—between K and I as two high ranking British officers, the stench of military espionage was overpowering. We needed to quickly allay Ottoman fears and hope they'd join us if war began, or at least stay neutral. Which is where you and Woolley came into the picture—two unblemished archaeologists fresh from Carchemish."

"And, conveniently, with no connection to the military!" added Lawrence.

"Indeed, and you lads did a wonderful job—hitting the ground running and finishing the thing in five months. I especially appreciated the way you combined all the crucial military intelligence about wells, springs, and topography with detailed allusions to archaeology, native Arab culture, geology, and natural science." Newcombe smiled. "And a wonderful touch, if not a somewhat tedious one, was the way you finished the survey with an analysis of pottery shards and inscriptions in Nabatean and Aramaic."

"It wasn't all tedious, Stewart. Didn't you appreciate the passages describing the exodus of the Hebrews through Kadesh Barnea led by Moses?"

"And lucky for you Moses is venerated by Turkish Muslims!"

"But in the end, Stewart, we merely finished what you began. When we arrived in Beer Sheba last January, you had everything working to perfection—good relations with local Arabs who were ready to act as guides and helpers, support of local Ottoman officials, and well-organized supply caravans from El Arish and Gaza. In short, you were the skillful and prime begetter of the whole operation!"

Newcombe shrugged. "Thanks, Ned, but what I also appreciated about the two of you was your work ethic—"

"That was *your* work ethic, Stewart. In Carchemish Woolley and I tended to lie about a good deal, reading, drinking, and playing chess. But when we saw how you attacked each day—off at dawn with guides and instruments, returning to camp at dusk and then working till midnight to arrange, evaluate, and record—that's what we emulated, and were able to finish the job that you began."

"Thanks, but you went far beyond what I would have been able to accomplish."

"If the truth be told, though, Kitchener had hoped our little deception would have kept the Turks neutral for the duration of the war. No one could have predicted that Kaiser Bill would *shove* them into the war—"

"Kaiser Bill shoved the Turks into the war?" Newcombe cut in. "Whatever do you mean? The Turkish Navy did that on their own."

"You really don't know?" Lawrence asked in disbelief.

"Of course, I know—Turkish battleships fired on Russian positions along the shore of the Black Sea."

"But you know those weren't really *Turkish* battleships, don't you?"

"What are you talking about? Of course they were Turkish."

Shocked that someone with Newcombe's intelligence background didn't know the truth, Lawrence silently reasoned, *no doubt he just relied on newspaper accounts.* "Actually, Stewart, it was like this—while the two battle cruisers *did* have Turkish registry, they were both commanded by German officers with a fair number of German crew—still training the Turks on operational issues."

"How is that possible?"

"Those two battleships, the *Goeben* and the *Breslau*, were the ones Kaiser Bill gave Turkey to replace the two ships England had built for the Turks but didn't deliver in retaliation for the Turks signing a treaty with Germany just before the war."

Newcombe appeared thunderstruck. "You're saying that after three months, these two battle cruisers were still commanded and partially crewed by *Germans*?"

"Precisely! German officers and German sailors were still training and instructing the Turkish crews on the ships' maintenance and care." Lawrence shrugged. "Actually, I'm surprised Kaiser Bill didn't do it sooner, considering his short temper. And, who knows? If he hadn't pulled that stunt, the Turks might still be neutral."

"But here we are now—with a Middle East Front of the Great War." Newcombe turned and nodded toward shore. "Have you been to Egypt before?"

"Two years ago. I took a break from Carchemish to work with Flinders Petrie at the Kafr Ammar excavation."

"Where is that exactly?"

"Forty miles south of Cairo."

"Did you manage to spend any time in Cairo?"

"Whenever I could!"

"What impressed you?"

"Where to begin?" Lawrence shrugged as he ran his hand over the railing, sending flakes of white paint flying aft in the wind. "The Great Pyramids, wide boulevards, the riverfront promenade along the Nile—all amazing! The *suk* of Cairo's Old City was particularly fascinating—a jangling place with incessant bells and bustle. But what I loved most were the mysterious silences of the Old City's labyrinthine alleyways and tiny shops, deserted old palaces, and mosques tucked into back streets." He breathed out a sigh. "A deeply exotic and unknowable place!"

"I'm looking forward to seeing Cairo through your eyes, Ned, as well as working with you."

"Are you quite sure? I have a reputation of horrifying my superiors."

"Because of your charming youthful irreverence?"

"Actually, the adjectives I recall were *insubordinate, intolerable* and *infuriating*."

Newcombe exhaled a short laugh. "In military intelligence, we don't give a damn about arcane notions of rigid discipline. We prefer the suppleness and exuberance of youth!"

"As in Whittier's *Barefoot Boy*?" Lawrence asked.

"Exactly!" He reached out and mussed up Lawrence's already tousled hair. "Blessings on thee, little man!"

"Which can only mean that you were once a barefoot boy!"

"Still am! I daresay my own primitive ways of living might be a bit below yours!"

"Which means I must lower my standards even further!"

"Yes." Newcombe raised his arms and shouted into the wind.

"Together we'll infuriate every stuffy bureaucrat in Cairo!"

"Sounds lovely, Stewart, but won't you just become another dead serious soldier of the empire once you're ensconced as head of the Arab Bureau?"

"Absolutely not. This is who I *am*—who *we* are! Besides, it's the best way to connect with the mischievous spirit of the Levant—the Arabs, Bedouin, and even the intellectuals and revolutionaries of Amman and Damascus. Who cares what official sensibilities we offend? In this war, we need the Arabs on our side!"

"I couldn't agree more, Stewart. Moreover, I'm certain that our fortunes in Europe will turn on victory here. Which is why we're also seeking to forge an alliance with another disaffected and highly motivated population that groans beneath the Ottoman yoke."

"Which one? There are so many fitting that description."

"I was referring to the Jewish Zionists."

"An interesting notion, but to forge any alliance you need to deal with recognized leadership. That's what British Egypt feels they now have with the Arabs—specifically, with Hussein, the sharif of Mecca. As I'm sure you know, McMahon and Kitchener have been trying to convince him to lead an Arab rebellion against the Ottomans. But as for the Jewish Zionists, who's their leader?"

"Chaim Weizmann—a gentleman I heard about during my stint in London," Lawrence replied. "He's been an active proponent of the Zionist movement for years and garnered considerable influence at Whitehall based on his work as a chemist. He's developed a method to produce the cordite we need for munitions production—an invaluable contribution to say the least."

"Is he British?"

"He is now—chairs the department of organic chemistry in Manchester, though originally, he's from somewhere in the Russian Empire."

"As a Zionist, I suppose he's hoping for British support for the Jews' national aspirations in the Holy Land." Newcombe frowned. "That's likely to produce friction with Arab nationalists, don't you think? After all, they're both interested in the same property!"

Lawrence nodded. "There may be overlapping territorial expectations, but these points of contention might be reconciled through direct negotiations." He gave Newcome a sly smile. "Perhaps under our auspices."

"Of course, and I know just the chap to bring the two sides together . . ." Newcombe fixed his eyes on Lawrence.

"Me?"

"Who else? When the time comes, we'll need your youthful exuberance to convince these Semitic cousins to share the Holy Land once the Turks are vanquished."

"And if we play our cards right, Stewart, we'll then have two additional allies on the Middle East Front against the Turks."

"Excellent!" Newcombe exclaimed and put an arm around Ned's shoulders. "The more I see the world through your eyes, the better it looks!"

As Lawrence watched Alexandria emerge from the mist along the shore, he felt an enthusiastic validation in Newcombe's embrace.

CHAPTER 26

December 24, 1914
German Army Headquarters Hotel de Ville
Charleville-Mézières, Occupied France

KAISER WILHELM nodded with satisfaction as he surveyed the ballroom, filled to capacity with German officers. Resplendent in one of his dress uniforms, a blue tunic edged with gold bullion floral brocade, his withered left hand rested on the hilt of his jewel-encrusted golden sword in its white scabbard. The kaiserin stood by his side, elegant in a gown of soft flowing crepe with velvet trim and ropes of pearls.

The royal couple paused at the top of the red-carpeted staircase as the officers below stood at attention and saluted. A herald at the bottom of the steps brought his staff down twice and bellowed, "Kaiser Wilhelm II, German emperor, king of Prussia, Holy Roman emperor and king of Jerusalem!"

Thunderous applause erupted and the kaiser bowed in acknowledgment, then raised his wife's hand as the herald shouted, "Kaiserin Augusta Victoria, German empress, queen of Prussia!"

Applause and cheering continued as the royal couple descended the staircase and strode to their places at the head table. When the applause subsided, Wilhelm raised his glass in a toast. "Down with all enemies of Germany. Amen."

The kaiserin raised her glass and joined the officers in shouting, "Amen! Amen!"

The toast was followed by a boisterous rendition of *Deutschland Über*

[157]

Alles with the royal couple joining in lustily, as waiters fanned out among the tables serving a red lentil soup.

The kaiser and kaiserin were, of course, the first ones served. Wilhelm was half-finished with his soup when an aid handed him an envelope.

"An urgent cable, Your Excellency."

He opened the envelope and read.

Holiday greetings to Your Excellency from the Augusta Victoria Hospice in your future capital. I would bring your royal attention to a delicate situation I face in Jerusalem. As you know, I've made considerable progress in accessing the Temple Mount through a secret entrance, but, alas, the doorway remains sealed. I am certain that the individuals who possess the knowledge to unlock this portal are sheltering in the American Colony, and I seek your advice as to how vigorously I may act in order to enter the colony and acquire these important assets.

Your loyal servant, Guido von List

Excusing himself, Wilhelm left the table and made his way to the hotel's telegraph room where he wrote out a short reply.

Holiday greetings to you, faithful servant. While I fervently hope that you secure all the information we require, it is imperative not to offend American sensibilities lest this cause the United States to enter the war on the side of our enemies. I suggest you consult Djemal Pasha, the Turkish governor of Greater Syria about this matter. In this capacity, he oversees all military and civilian affairs and often comes to Jerusalem. You must rely on his judgment in finding a diplomatic manner to enter the American Colony and acquire the assets you seek.

With gratitude for your service
—KW

When Wilhelm returned to the ballroom, the main course was being served. As he sat next to his wife, he nodded at her plate and asked, "What do we have here, my dear?"

"Bavarian goulash. Not bad, under the circumstances," she said and took a sip of champagne.

❂ ❂ ❂

Ploegsteert Wood—Occupied Belgium

ON CHRISTMAS Eve, the guns fell silent. Fritz Wunderlich, a nineteen-year-old conscript in Germany's Royal Saxon Army, looked up at the dark sky from within the muddy trench as snowflakes drifted down, falling lightly on his face.

Wunderlich had seen a good deal of action during the Battle of the Frontiers, but over the past month his trench within the Ypres Salient of the Western Front had been relatively quiet.

Kaiser Wilhelm and the kaiserin had generously sent lanterns and small fir trees as Christmas gifts, though Wunderlich would have preferred sausage and chocolate.

As he had seen others do, he lit the lantern's candle, crept up the ladder and, keeping his head low, placed the lantern and fir tree on the lip of the trench. Once back down the ladder, he looked up at the small light and thought about his favorite Christmas carol, "Stille Nacht." His mother had always told him that he could be a great German lyric tenor, and standing in the frozen mud of the trench, he began to sing, though very softly.

Stille Nacht, heilige Nacht, Alles schläft; einsam wacht . . .

As Wunderlich sang, the other men joined in—hands on shoulders, swaying as they sang. He sang louder, his voice rising in the night sky beneath the falling snow.

They finished the first verse, but before beginning the next,

Wunderlich paused, raising an index finger to his lips for silence. From the British trenches fifty yards away, he could hear singing.

Silent night, holy night, All is calm all is bright...

He led the men in the original German version, joining the British soldiers. As they sang, he crept up the ladder to the lip of the trench, keeping his head low. There he led the caroling of the soldiers on both sides as he watched light snow dust the frozen mud of No-Man's-Land strewn with corpses, and shell craters filled with rainwater.

Together with the British, they sang a dozen carols, finishing with "Adeste Fideles" in Latin, though many of the English soldiers only knew it as "O Come, All Ye Faithful."

Once the caroling ended, the cold night air rang with shouted greetings from the opposing trenches—Happy Christmas! *Fröhliche Weihnachten!*

"We are Saxons!" A German soldier shouted in heavily accented English. "You are Anglo-Saxons! What is there for us to fight about?"

From the English trench someone shouted, "Kaiser Bill and King George are bloody first cousins for Christ's sake—grandsons of Queen Victoria! Why are we fighting at *all*?"

A German soldier shouted, "You no shoot, we no shoot!"

After that, both sides fell silent, waiting for something to happen, something impossible, something miraculous.

Standing on the ladder near the lip of the trench, Wunderlich saw that the snow had stopped falling. The sky had cleared and a bright quarter moon had risen. He finished climbing up the ladder, ignoring shouted warnings from his comrades. Standing on the highest rung, he slowly raised his arms.

From the British trenches he could hear the metallic clicking of their rifles. But he didn't stop.

Wunderlich took a step, then another. Slowly he moved toward the English trenches, arms high, his hands open. He began singing the third verse, which was his favorite.

"*Stille Nacht, heilige Nacht, Gottes Sohn, o wie lacht*

Lieb' aus deinem göttlichen Mund..."

Passing the bodies of dead German and English soldiers, indistinguishable in the mud, he moved toward the British trenches. Midway across, he stopped singing and shouted, "They told us we would be home by Christmas!"

An English soldier appeared out of his trench, arms raised. "They told us the same bloody thing!"

Others came, and within minutes a few dozen young men stood in the middle of No-Man's-Land—shaking hands in the moonlight, sharing flasks of whiskey and schnapps, trading cigarettes and chocolate, and proudly showing off photographs of family or girlfriends.

A British soldier said, "We should gather back here tomorrow morning—spend Christmas Day together—play some football and have a Christmas feast!"

"Yes!" Wunderlich agreed. "But the first thing is to honor our dead brothers—yours and ours—give them a proper burial."

"Certainly. That's the right thing to do," the British soldiers. "That way we'll also have a proper pitch for our match."

"Wunderschön! And after der Fußball, we'll have a Christmas feast!"

"We'll see you mates tomorrow," the soldier replied.

After shaking hands, the soldiers separated and returned to their trenches for the night.

"This might be a good Christmas after all," Wunderlich whispered as he climbed down the ladder, and very quietly, began singing again...

❋ ❋ ❋

German Army Headquarters Hotel de Ville Charleville-Mézières, Occupied France

GENERAL ERICH von Falkenhayn, chief of the General Staff had observed Kaiser Wilhelm fuming all morning. Now, as the kaiser stared at the cable in his hand, he was furious.

"What the hell is this about? Fraternizing with the enemy? Disobeying orders?"

"I'm certain things will return to normal after Christmas, Your Excellency."

"This is a lack of discipline in the extreme!" the kaiser continued to rant. "It can't be tolerated—not for a second!"

"What would you propose, Your Majesty?"

"In the face of this treasonous behavior? Only the most severe punishment will do! These cowards will face court-martial! The hangman's noose! The firing squad! This disgusting behavior must stop!"

"How would you recommend we do that, sire?"

The kaiser paused in thought, then blurted out, "Snipers!"

Taken aback, Falkenhayn asked, "Snipers, sire?"

"Yes! Have snipers positioned behind our trenches with orders to shoot any soldier—British or German—who ventures into No-Man's-Land and engages in this seditious behavior!"

"Very well, Your Excellency. I'll convey your directive to the company commandeers. I quite agree with you—such a thing should never happen in wartime!"

Once the kaiser had stormed out of the telegraph room, the operator looked up at Falkenhayn, his pencil poised over a pad of paper. "I am ready to record your message, General."

Falkenhayn smiled beneath his elegant mustache. "There will be no message, Private. This is Christmas Day! Let the poor conscripts have a break from killing and dying. They'll get back to it soon enough."

"But . . . but," the private stuttered, "what about the kaiser?"

"I'll make sure that he doesn't get any further reports about this." He patted the telegraph operator on the shoulder. "Don't worry about the kaiser, my boy. His attention span is as short as his temper. He'll soon forget all about this."

CHAPTER 27

January 7, 1915
Rosslyn Castle Midlothian, Scotland

DESPITE THE foul weather, Harry had insisted on going out for a midday constitutional.

Though Evan was alone in the castle, he was content to stay indoors and use the time to solve the St. Clair family mystery. For the past month, he had actually enjoyed inclement winter weather since on halcyon days he felt conflicted—partly yearning to be outdoors, and partly wanting to remain in the library. But on blustery days like this, there was no conflict.

But apart from the weather, another reason he preferred to remain indoors was because of the anxiety he still felt about being a wanted man. Despite Harry's reassurance that there were no broadsheets in Roslin accusing him of treason, he had no way to exonerate himself. With no memory, he couldn't be certain that he really wasn't a traitor.

Standing in the comfortable warmth and silence of the library, he watched the rain sheeting against the windows, hoping that Harry had managed to find shelter.

To provide the information Evan needed, Harry had furnished him with histories of the Crusades and of the St. Clair bloodline from his extensive library. He'd also included Sir Walter Scott's *Ivanhoe*. Though a historical novel and chivalric romance, Harry thought *Ivanhoe* would give Evan a perspective of some of the Crusade's historical figures and an entertaining respite from the tedium of research.

As Evan sat to review his notes, he remembered how, on his first day at the castle, he had felt compelled to learn all he could about the St. Clair family from the moment he had seen the family tree. And this feeling had only increased when presented with the family mystery in the form of the unanswered questions: how had the infant William St. Clair survived after both his parents were slain during the fall of Acre, and who had brought him from the Holy Land to Rosslyn Castle?

Evan was determined to answer these questions.

But as he studied the crowded pages of his notes, his mind was gripped by the vacant emptiness of his amnesia, and his heart ached with a hollow and profound sadness—a rising dread that, without any memory of who he was, he didn't really exist at all.

He closed his eyes and reminded himself that, if he could just illuminate the darkness surrounding his family history, he might feel less alone, and with this the hope he might yet uncover the knowledge that he was Evan Sinclair and part of this family.

Opening his eyes, he was able to smile as he considered the irony; unable to unlock the mystery of his own identity, he was intent on solving the mystery of his ancestry. He shook his head and thought, *How crazy is that? Here I am with amnesia, trying to recall some forgotten family history when I can't even remember my own. But I am making progress!*

He looked down at the notes in his hand, heartened that in five weeks he had succeeded in clarifying a number of facts—and all cross-referenced from a variety of primary and secondary sources. He was confident that he'd soon be ready to present Harry with a compelling narrative. With a renewed sense of purpose, he sat forward to review and edit his notes. After an hour, he was just finishing when he heard the front door open and the sound of Harry's voice calling out to him.

"Evan?"

"In here!" he yelled back.

"You hungry? I've picked up some lamb chops and vegetables for dinner."

"I can't think about food right now. Please come to the library!"

He heard Harry's footsteps down the hall and the sound of packages being deposited on the dining room table. Once in the library, Harry took off his wet jacket and hung it to dry near the hearth. "You were wise to stay home. The weather is absolutely *beastly*—"

Unable to contain himself, Evan cut him off. "Wait till you hear what I've found!"

"Sorry. I simply *must* have some hot tea!"

"Tea can wait." Evan dragged Harry to the divan. "Please! Have a seat by the fire. Give me twenty minutes, then we'll both have tea."

"Alright . . ." Harry sighed as he sat down.

"Okay," Evan began, his notes in his hands. "The questions are: how did our two-month-old ancestor William St. Clair survive after his parents died, and who brought him from the Holy Land to Rosslyn? Let's begin with what we know—his parents, Jonathan St. Clair and the Saracen woman, Zahirah, both died the day Acre fell to the Saracens—May 19, 1291. And what do we know about them? While we know nothing about Zahirah, we know a good deal about Jonathan, and, for that matter, Jonathan's father, William de St. Clair, Scottish nobleman, commander during the Scottish-Norwegian War, and later, the Scottish ambassador to France, which is why he moved the family to Paris in 1260.

"At that time, Jonathan is sixteen years old, and Paris is buzzing with all sorts of thrilling notions about the Crusades and the Holy Land. Jonathan apparently becomes hooked. The Knights Templar are recruiting, and he volunteers . . ." As Evan spoke the words, he had another moment of recognition—a vague memory from his own past. "He volunteers . . ." he repeated, then fell silent.

"What's wrong, Evan? Why did you stop?"

"Another memory . . ." he murmured.

"Yes, and I know which one! Sixteen-year-old Jonathan Sinclair volunteers for the Crusades just as *you* volunteered at that age and ended up with the Flemish resistance!"

He looked at Harry and smiled. "Thanks. I didn't see that. I'm glad you did." He looked back to his notes. "So . . . Jonathan St. Clair makes his way to the Holy Land and is sent to the Templar outpost of Safed in the Galilee. We know this because in 1266 the Mamluk sultan Baybars overwhelms the Safed garrison, and every Templar is put to the sword, with the sole exception of . . . Jonathan St. Clair."

"You actually found Jonathan's name in a primary source?"

"Yes!" Evan exclaimed, barely able to contain his delight. "His name is referenced in Templar manuscripts recovered from Acre and in a Mamluk soldier's diary."

"My word—that is amazing! But how did he survive?"

"Local Jews are forced to bury the dead Templars, and they discover that Jonathan is wounded but still alive. Since Sultan Baybars wants there to be a survivor—to tell the Templars in Acre what befell the Safed garrison, he allows the Jews to nurse Jonathan back to health and to take him with them to Acre.

"The next we know of Jonathan is twenty years later—one year before the fall of Acre. In 1290 the Templars send Jonathan on a reconnaissance mission to evaluate Mamluk preparations for the impending attack on Acre. On this mission in Mamluk territory, it would appear that he met Zahirah, since she would have become pregnant in June of 1290 for baby William to be born in March of '91."

"Any idea how they died?" asked Harry.

"Not exactly, nor any record how baby William escapes, though the histories do paint a very chaotic picture of the fall of Acre to the Mamluks; there's a mad scramble for boats leaving the quay, there are boats too close to shore bombarded with clay jars of burning naphtha, there are boats that sink when already full and swamped with desperate people trying to escape . . ."

Evan fell silent for a moment, then continued in a low voice, "I've imagined this so many times—sometimes I see Jonathan and Zahirah leaving their boat at the quay to keep the Mamluks at bay—to let the boat with their infant son escape. Could that have been how they died, and how baby William St. Clair lived?"

Harry shook his head. "There's nothing in the genealogy about that."

"But we *do* know that whoever is carrying baby William, *does* manage to get away, and is able to reach one of the Templar galleys anchored in Acre's outer harbor."

"True, but we still don't know who that is."

"Granted, but it's safe to *assume* that it was someone Jonathan knew he could trust to bring baby William back *here* to Rosslyn. And there's also this—you told me that the scrap of parchment framed in the hallway with the ancient Hebrew lettering came to Scotland with one of our forebears from the Crusades. So, whoever brought baby William here *also* brought that piece of parchment!"

"How do you know that?" Harry asked. "How do you know it wasn't some other St. Clair who fought in an earlier Crusade? Indeed, Henri de St. Clair was a knight of the First Crusade and one of the original Knights Templar. Perhaps *he* brought it here."

Evan smiled. "Have you forgotten the pyramid outside Falicon?"

After a second, Harry gasped out, "You're right! The pyramid outside Falicon was built by Knights Templar after the fall of Acre—"

"And the inscription is in the cave below the pyramid." Evan cut in. "The rubbing my father made matched the parchment! You both saw that inscription and the parchment."

Harry's eyes grew large. "Right-o! Whoever brought baby William from Acre must have sailed to the South of France and must have been among those who constructed the pyramid and helped carve the inscription from the parchment into the wall of the cave beneath the pyramid. They must have then sailed to Scotland, bringing baby William and the parchment here."

"Exactly!" Evan exclaimed. "Jonathan St. Clair entrusted his son *and* the parchment to someone who was able to escape Acre, someone he could trust to bring his son and the parchment here to Rosslyn Castle."

"That had to be a very *special* someone." Harry sighed. "But who?"

"Again, it had to be someone that Jonathan knew well and trusted, but also someone known and trusted enough by the St. Clairs here at Rosslyn so they would accept baby William as the rightful heir."

"Let me try to recall which St. Clair was at Rosslyn around that time—1292 or so," Harry said and crushed his eyes closed. "Of course," he opened his eyes. "Jonathan's father—William de St. Clair, Baron of Rosslyn."

"Exactly," said Evan. "William de St. Clair was living here along with his youngest son, Henry. After all, it was Henry and his wife, Alicia who adopted baby William and raised him as their own. It's right there in your genealogy—baby William is listed as Jonathan's son *and* as Henry's son!"

"Amazing!" Harry exclaimed "And what became of baby William?"

"That's a great story in itself," Evan said and consulted his notes. "Baby William became known as Sir William 'the Crusader' Sinclair, Lord of Rosslyn. He married a woman named Isabel and they had three sons and a daughter."

"Why was he called *the Crusader*?" Harry asked. "The Crusades were over."

"That's what I wondered, and the answer is this: he left Scotland on a Crusade—"

"*Which* Crusade?" Harry cut in.

"It's like this, William the Crusader was a friend of Robert the Bruce, who died in 1329. And after Bruce's death, William was one of the knights chosen to accompany Sir James Douglas to the Holy Land to honor Bruce's dying wish, that his heart be buried in *Jerusalem*." Evan took a breath. "*That* was his Crusade, Harry—to bring the heart of the Bruce to the Holy Land! But sadly, the Scottish knights never made it. As they were passing through Spain, they joined forces with the Castilian army besieging the frontier castle of Teba. Outnumbered and separated from the main Christian army, they were overwhelmed and wiped out."

"How heartbreaking!" Harry sighed. "William 'the Crusader' St. Clair came so close to returning to his birthplace—to coming full circle." He fixed Evan with his eyes. "But you still haven't told me *who* brought William as a wee bairn ta' Alba!"

"I have my suspicions, but let me put it *this* way," Evan said with a sly smile. "Do you have any histories that include the early life of William Wallace?"

"William Wallace . . ." Harry repeated, his eyes wide in a dawning realization. "As a matter of fact, I do."

CHAPTER 28

January 13, 1915
British Intelligence Offices, Cairo

LAWRENCE AWOKE as a smoky Cairo dawn filled his hotel room with muted light. As was his habit, he had slept in his clothes on the hardwood floor next to the bed. He slipped on a pair of scuffed shoes, brushed his teeth, splashed water on his face, and left his room.

Having arrived in Egypt three weeks earlier, Lawrence occupied a luxurious room at the palatial Grand Continental Hotel. It was almost more than he could bear. Though he couldn't deny the convenience of the hotel's proximity to the British Intelligence offices at the adjacent Savoy Hotel on the east bank of the Nile, he detested the lavish appointments—especially the bed—it offended his ascetic sensibilities.

Lawrence was one of thousands of British and territorial troops held back in Egypt to counter the anticipated Turkish assault on the Suez Canal. To accommodate them, the British had taken over most of the city's finer hotels to provide office space and lodging for officers. Foremost of these hotels were the Grand Continental and the Savoy.

Lieutenant Colonel Stewart Newcombe, who had arrived in Cairo with Lawrence, had set up the military intelligence unit in a three-room suite of the Savoy. Lawrence eschewed the lift and took the stairs, two at a time. He found Newcombe at his desk.

"Good morning, Stewart," he said and plopped onto an upholstered settee. "I'm ready to continue our practice of the black arts—intelligence and counterespionage."

Newcombe looked up. "Good to see you're sort of in uniform, Ned, though you forgot your Sam Browne belt."

"Shall I have my batman fetch it?"

Newcombe smiled. "I'm also pleased you haven't lost your gift of irritating our superiors. One paid me a visit last evening—grumbling about the disappearance of a large sectioned map of the Ottoman Empire from the senior officer's mess. It somehow ended up plastered onto an entire wall in the mapping room."

"It looks better there." Lawrence pouted. "Am I to be court-martialed?"

"No, but you won't be working in the mapping room for the foreseeable future."

"As punishment?" Lawrence asked, genuinely surprised.

"Hardly. What I have in mind for you is far more interesting than collating maps—"

"What?"

"Our patrols in the Western Sinai picked up some Syrian refugees trying to reach our lines—Arab urban liberals infused with European ideas of nationalism and self-determination. One of them was a physician who recently escaped from a Turkish prison in Damascus. They finished debriefing the good doctor yesterday." Newcombe lifted a sheet of paper off his desk and handed it to Lawrence. "He speaks of having met with Prince Faisal about an Arab revolt . . ."

"Faisal—as in the son of Hussein, the sharif of Mecca?"

"The same." Newcombe stood up and stepped out from behind his desk. "It appears that Faisal was sent by his father to sound out the secret societies in Damascus about the Hashemites leading a revolt against the Ottomans."

Lawrence stood and read the document, and once finished, handed it back to Newcombe. "Though he's Hussein's third son, I believe that Faisal is the best-suited to lead the revolt. He's the leader I've been hoping for."

Newcombe sat on the edge of his desk and nodded. "And there's this—Kitchener finally cabled Hussein with a clear promise of support."

"So, the revolt might begin soon?" Lawrence asked and began to pace.

"Yes, and with the guarantee of British gold and British guns."

"Good," said Lawrence, pacing faster. "With the Bedouin on our side, we'll be advantaged throughout the Levant. I'm convinced that our fortunes in Europe will turn on what we accomplish on this front of the Great War, and the Bedouin are the key! They hate the Turks far more than Kitchener realizes. Gertrude recently wrote me that she's met many of the sheikhs and knows which are most likely to join the revolt."

"Miss Bell is, indeed, a vital asset," said Newcombe. "Is she still stuck at the Red Cross in France doing secretarial work?"

"Yes, but not for long. Clive Sinclair and I hounded the MO-4 chief, Hedley, for months to bring her aboard. It appears he's finally relented. She's to have an interview at Whitehall in a month."

"A *month?*" Newcombe winced. "Such a colossal waste of time. We need her *now*—at Whitehall or here." He fixed Lawrence with his eyes. "But in the meantime, we have *you*."

"What do you have in mind for me?" Lawrence stopped pacing, his heart pounding in anticipation.

"Nothing less than a meeting with Faisal—and the sooner the better."

Lawrence rubbed his hands together. "I'm very much looking forward to that."

Newcombe frowned. "But that might be a problem."

"What do you mean?"

"He's disappeared." Newcombe whispered.

"Isn't he in Mecca?"

"Not for months. We have no idea where he is and, apparently, neither do the Ottomans. They're actively hunting for him . . ."

Lawrence flashed a mischievous grin. "I'll have better luck."

"Really? You have information the Turks lack?"

"I do. Faisal is a Bedouin and no doubt being sheltered by other Bedouin loyal to the sharif. While doing the desert survey, I spent a fair amount of time living among tribes of the Arabah and Eastern Sinai. I'm certain they'll trust me enough to lead me to Faisal."

Newcombe sat back in his chair. "Good. You'll be pleased to know that I've consigned you a Triumph motorcycle for your use in the endeavor—"

"Are you daft? I'll be delighted to tool about Cairo on the motorbike, but it won't last a mile in desert sand. To cross the Sinai, all I require is a camel."

"And you shall have one. I was just joking about the motorbike, though perhaps we'll get you one when you return." Newcombe paused and added, "You should know that our forays into the Sinai have been limited to no more than thirty miles. We're asking you to go very far beyond that. As the Mesopotamian crow flies, it's over a hundred and fifty miles from Suez to Akaba."

Lawrence stepped to a window and looked out over the Nile and the hard-stone crowns of the Giza pyramids on the far bank, his heart beating wildly.

"And you'll be going alone."

He turned to Newcombe, grinning. "I wouldn't have it any other way!"

CHAPTER 29

January 18, 1915
Sinai Desert

FOUR DAYS out of Cairo, Lawrence left the Pilgrim Road at Wadi Taba to steer clear of the Ottoman garrison at Aqaba. The waning crescent moon faded as the sky brightened toward dawn, the jagged coastal mountains like ruined castles.

Before setting off across the desert, he had purchased Bedouin clothing in a Cairo *souk*—a loose-fitting white cotton *kandura* and a red *keffiyeh* for protection from the unforgiving sun—but above all, to blend in.

Having ridden all the previous day and much of the night, he was exhausted, and the skin of his hands and forearms had turned crimson. He had finished the last of his water hours before. Though his throat burned with thirst, he knew he'd find sweet water in the springs along the Red Sea. And there, he also hoped to find Faisal.

He guided his camel into a bone-dry wadi, covered by a pavement of parched earth and loose stone. His face creased into a smile at seeing evidence of hidden subterranean water channels in an acacia tree and a melon field just off the path. *How lovely! I shall breakfast on something other than boiled camel meat and dates!*

Dismounting, he let his camel forage among the green leaves while he cracked open a few ripe melons to slake his thirst and cool his chapped lips. As he ate, he reflected on the quest that had brought him across the Sinai.

He knew that Faisal was in hiding from Ottoman agents and could only hope to find shelter among Bedouin loyal to the Hashemites. He also knew that he would only find Faisal with the help of these Bedouin—his old friends of the Tarabin tribe who had grown to trust him from the years he'd lived among them during the desert survey. And he knew that the most likely place to meet the Tarabin would be along the shore of the Red Sea south of Taba.

Remounting, he lifted his camel to a steady trot, and soon reached the point where Wadi Taba met the coast road bordering the Red Sea. He continued south as the sun rose over the granite mountains, and after a few miles he reached the wash where Wadi Marukh met the sea.

That's when he saw them—two riders trotting on thoroughbred camels. Both were young, one dressed in a rich Cashmere robe with a heavily embroidered headcloth, the other in white cotton with a red *keffiyeh* like his own. He raised his hand in greeting.

They came to a halt and the one in the Cashmere robe asked, "Your presence is from Syria?"

"Nay—I am four days out of Cairo from the Haj Road," he replied in traditional Bedouin Arabic, which was far more familiar to him than the colloquial Egyptian Arabic he struggled with in Cairo.

The Arab smiled. "You are also four months late for the Haj."

"I seek my friend among the Tarabin."

"We are of the Tarabin. Who do you seek?"

"One called Mirzuk el Tikheimi."

The two exchanged glances, then one said, "He is our cousin."

"I have important business to discuss with him. Will you bring me to him?"

"No, but we will inform him that you wish an audience. What are you called?"

"El-Orenz." He replied with the Arabic form of his name. "Tell him el-Orenz would speak with him."

"I swear that I will." The Arab bowed, and in a fluid motion, brought his hand to his lips, then his head, then his heart, then back to his lips.

"Shall I await him here?"

"No. He will meet you at the place where Wadi Muhas meets the sea, about forty furlongs hence." He waved his hand to the south, then bowed his head and said, "May Allah richly requite the Arabs."

"And may Allah bless you," Lawrence called back.

With that, they reined their camels about and moved swiftly away.

Lawrence urged his camel after them, but they were soon out of sight with only a faint cloud of dust marking their progress. Then that too disappeared.

His spirits soared as he anticipated seeing Mirzuk. He had been a lad of nineteen when he helped with the desert survey, and Lawrence was certain he'd know Faisal's whereabouts.

By the time Lawrence reached the designated intersection of the wadi with the coast road, the morning was well on and warm, though there was a cooling breeze off the water. He dismounted and watched the camel forage among shrubs near the shore while he waited for Mirzuk to appear.

He didn't wait long.

Moving swiftly toward him on a magnificent camel came a lean, good-looking young man with sharp features and long braided hair that issued from beneath a white *keffiyeh*. Beneath his striped robe he wore two crossed bandolier bullet belts.

"Ya Orenz!" he flashed a bright smile as he slid off his camel. "Ya Habibi!" Rushing forward, Mirzuk wrapped Lawrence in his arms. "I am so pleased to see you again, my friend. Do you require more of my assistance with mapping?"

"I require your assistance, ya Mirzuk, but not for mapping."

"Anything you wish, Orenz. For you, I will do anything!"

"I come in search of Prince Faisal ibn Hussein."

Mirzuk's face lost all expression. "No one knows where he is," he muttered. "I am sorry, but with this I cannot help you."

Lawrence reached up, rubbed the young man's shoulder, and smiled. "I know you too well, Mirzuk, and I know when you're lying. You know where he is."

Mirzuk stared at the ground and said nothing.

"Tell me, my friend, have I not always been honest with you?"

Mirzuk nodded silently.

"Then listen well. I am working now with British Intelligence in Cairo. It is known to us that Hussein the sharif of Mecca has acquired the support of the British government for a revolt of the Arabs against the Turks. He has designated Prince Faisal to lead the uprising. It is imperative that I meet with the prince so that the British can understand how best to support him—with weapons and with gold. That is why I must speak with him. Will you help me?"

A silence stretched between them as Mirzuk studied the ground. Finally, he looked up. "I will be honest with you, ya Orenz, I jealously guard the prince since the Turks seek to destroy him. They have put a price on his head, and there are many who would betray him. However, with the trust and love I have for you, I will bring you to him. But, only with strict conditions."

"I will do whatever you say."

"Good." Mirzuk reached into his saddlebag and pulled out a black cloth. "You must switch your red *keffiyeh* for this."

"A black *keffiyeh*?" asked Lawrence.

"A black hood—for the prince's protection, and your own."

Nodding his assent, Lawrence removed his red-checkered *keffiyeh* and stuffed it into his saddlebag.

"This will also be kind to your eyes," Mirzuk said as he slipped the hood over Lawrence's head and tied it about his neck. "Protecting you from the sun's glare,"

"Thank you," Lawrence replied and groped blindly for the pommel of his saddle on his kneeling camel. Once he found it, he mounted "Perhaps I'll use this hood always since camels require so little guidance and usually go where they will!"

He heard Mirzuk laugh. "Nonetheless, I will guide your camel today."

No more words passed between them as Lawrence felt the sway and pacing of his camel along the coast road. From within the hood, he could see nothing, but he knew they were continuing south since he could hear the breathing of the Red Sea along the shore to his left. After a long while the sound of waves faded away, and as more time passed, he heard the splash of water and understood they were fording a stream. Then the pacing of the camel slowed, and he heard the bleating of sheep and muted greetings to Mirzuk.

Certain they had reached their destination, Lawrence's excitement grew. After a minute, they came to a halt, and he heard Mirzuk's voice close by "I'll help you down, ya Orenz."

Lawrence felt his camel kneel and strong hands guiding him off the mount to the ground. With the hood still in place, he was led forward, and after another minute he heard the voice of someone he didn't recognize.

"I am told that you would speak with me."

The hood was removed and squinting into the half-light, Lawrence found himself standing in a large tent lit by torches. Before him stood a striking figure of a man—tall and pillarlike, slender in a long robe of white silk with a brown headcloth bound with a brilliant scarlet and gold cord. His eyelids were drooped, and his black beard and pallid face were like a mask against the still watchfulness of his body. His hands were crossed and rested on the hilt of a golden dagger tucked into his sash.

With a pounding heart, Lawrence recalled words of the American author Mark Twain; *The two most important days in your life are the day you are born and the day you find out why.* He bowed his head. "Thank you, O prince. It is an honor to speak with you."

Faisal stepped back and gestured for Lawrence to sit with him.

He saw that the tent held many silent figures surrounding and studying him. He waited for Faisal to sit before taking his place on the carpet.

Faisal seemed to stare at his own hands, twisting slowly about his dagger. At last he spoke. "I am told you have traveled here from Cairo. How did you find the journey?"

"Long and hot, Your Lordship." Lawrence replied. "But I am pleased to be back in the desert and honored to be granted an audience."

"How do you like our place here?" Faisal asked.

"Blinded by the hood, O Prince. I know not what place this is."

"That is well." Faisal gestured with his hand. "How do you like our tent?"

"Well," Lawrence replied, "But I fear it is far from Damascus."

With a short laugh Faisal asked, "You have business in Damascus, ya Orenz?"

"Yes, Your Lordship. I should very much like to ride into Damascus by your side with a thousand Bedouin warriors."

Faisal laughed again and was joined by those around him in the tent. "Praise be to God," he said. "There are Turks nearer to us than Damascus."

"I know, sire." Lawrence drew a deep breath and added, "I come as an Englishman with my government's firm offer of British gold, British guns, and British support for your revolt against the Turks."

Faisal smiled and winked. "We are now of necessity tied to the British, grateful for their help, and expectant of our future profit. But we are not British subjects and never will be. We do not wish to trade one colonial master for another."

"As you know, O Prince, there are thousands of Englishmen now in France, yet the French don't suspect we will stay there."

"You compare France to the Holy Land of the Hejaz?"

"Of course not, Your Lordship, but allow me to assure you—Great Britain accepts the Damascus Protocol, and the principle of Arab hegemony in Arab lands including the Hejaz after the defeat of the Turks."

Faisal seemed to muse a little, then said, "I am not a Hejazi by upbringing, and yet, by God, I am jealous of it. And though I know the British do not want it, yet what can I say when the British took the Sudan, also not wanting it? The British seem to hunger for desolate lands, to build them up; and so, perhaps one day Arabia will also seem to them precious." He paused and added, "Your good and my good, perhaps they are different, and either forced good or forced evil will make a people cry out in pain. Does the ore admire the flame which transforms it?"

Lawrence nodded before replying. "By God, O Prince, I will do everything in my power to see to it that the British will honor their promise to you of freedom."

"That is well, for what we want is a government that speaks our language and will let us live in peace." He shrugged and added, "Also, we hate the Turks."

CHAPTER 30

January 26, 1915
Crossing the Sinai to Suez

AFTER A week in Faisal's encampment, Lawrence was looking forward to leaving. Though he had been graced with daily and extended meetings with Faisal, and was in all ways very well-treated, he had been completely confined to his tent and had no idea of his whereabouts. And though he completely understood the rationale, he found his extended isolation intolerable.

In all his years of living and working in the Levant, Lawrence had only known unbridled freedom. Likewise, he had dealt easily with the Turkish bureaucracy both at Carchemish and during the desert survey. As he packed up his haversack, he shook his head. *While I totally comprehend how this isolation underscores the mortal danger I would face as an enemy of the Ottoman Empire, and while I completely agree with Faisal's necessity to keep his family's and his own whereabouts unknown, I've had enough of this quarantine and I'm quite ready to leave. But I do hope to say goodbye to Faisal...*

As if on cue, he heard Faisal's voice at the tent door. "May I come in, ya Orenz?"

"Certainly, Your Lordship," Lawrence replied and turned his back to the door to avoid even the appearance of sneaking a look at the encampment.

"I wanted to wish you well on your journey, and to show you something." He held out a sheet of paper. "Please read this."

Turning, Lawrence saw it was a handwritten letter. He read it aloud.

*"To His Excellency Sharif Hussein ibn Ali,
with respect and salutations,*

I, Chaim Weizmann, greet you in peace on behalf of the World Zionist Organization.

In the hope that the Axis Powers will be defeated in the current war and the Ottoman Empire undone, I write to you in recognition that an independent Arab state may be created in West Asia. Insofar as Your Excellency is Islam's greatest prince and guardian of the Holy Places, and believing you and your son, Faisal, will be leading a rebellion of the Arabs against the Turks, I wish to offer, on behalf of the World Zionist Organization, any assistance you may require to achieve success.

In offering our support, I am mindful of the racial kinship and ancient bonds existing between the Arabs and the Jewish people. In this spirit, I offer to meet with you, or your son, at any time and place of your choosing to discuss our common cause and our mutual aspirations—for Your Lordship, an independent Arab state—for us, an independent Jewish homeland.

Desirous to create a good understanding between us, I look forward to hearing from Your Eminence.

*With all respect and admiration,
Professor Chaim Weizmann
General Zionist Council."*

Finished reading, Lawrence looked up.

"Do you know this Weizmann?" Faisal asked.

"I have never met him, sire, though I have heard that he has some influence at the War Office in London because he is a chemist who has contributed his discoveries to British munitions production. I also know that he is active in the Zionist movement." He handed the letter back to Faisal and asked, "Are you interested in my opinion about his proposition, O Prince?"

"From our conversations over the past week, I already know your opinion, ya Orenz. You believe, as I do, that the Arabs should make common cause with other peoples who have also suffered for centuries under the Ottoman yoke. Is this not true?"

"Even so, Your Lordship."

"This is also the opinion of my royal father. He believes that the Jews are our cousins as sons of Abraham, and as such we are the two main branches of the Semitic family. He also believes that the Arabs and the Jews would be advantaged to cooperate in our efforts toward self-determination. If, in the aftermath of the current war, the Ottoman Empire is defeated and dismantled, he believes there will be ample room for an independent Arab state and an independent Jewish state in what is now Greater Syria. When I read this letter with my father, he was fully supportive of a meeting between myself and Professor Weizmann to discuss future areas of collaboration and cooperation."

Faisal smiled and handed an envelope to Lawrence. "I have therefore composed a letter to Weizmann in response to his proposition. I have not sealed the envelope so that you may read it. You will see that I have suggested we meet in Aden on May 5, and that I would hope that you, ya Orenz, will facilitate his transportation and that you would also attend this meeting." Faisal canted his head. "Would that be agreeable to you?"

"With all my heart, yes!"

* * *

Lawrence left the encampment as he had entered—with a black hood over his head and accompanied by Mirzuk. When the hood came off after a few hours, Lawrence saw they were in the Sinai Desert, moving northwest.

Mirzuk led the way through the arid wastes and dry wadis. Nearing midday, he reined his camel about where a wadi ended in a rubble of boulders at the foot of a low rise. "Ya Orenz! This is as far as I am able to go with you."

"*Mashkur kathir, ya Mirzuk!*" Lawrence said and they shook hands. "I am grateful to you for guiding me to Prince Faisal."

"I am pleased that the prince loves you as I do. If God wills it, we will meet again. Come, my friend." Mirzuk nodded toward the ridge above them. "From the ridge I will show you the way you should go."

Lawrence urged his camel over the boulders and up the hill. On reaching the summit, he was alarmed to see the northern horizon completely obscured by a low gray cloud. "A sandstorm?" he asked, his voice edged with concern.

"Something worse! It's the Turks. They apparently left Gaza and are already moving along the Pilgrim Road toward the Canal. If you wish to warn the English in Cairo before they attack, you must make haste!"

"When do you believe they will reach the Canal?"

"Five days."

"How many are there to raise a cloud like that?"

"More than ten thousand mounted troops—perhaps fifteen thousand."

"How long would it take you to reach the Canal from here?"

"Me?" Mirzuk shrugged. "Three days—perhaps less."

Lawrence smiled. "I will make the journey in two days."

Mirzuk laughed. "I believe you will, ya Orenz!" He raised his arm and pointed. "For now, you must stay to the south along this ridge. Only when you are beyond the Turkish column may you turn north and take the Pilgrim Road." Mirzuk bowed. "I bid you farewell and success, ya Orenz!" Then he turned and guided his camel back into the wadi.

Lawrence rode along the hillcrest, finding the terrain good for quick pacing. After an hour, a wind lifted away the dust to reveal the Ottoman convoy—stretching along the Pilgrim Road from east to west as far as he could see.

If I am able to see them so clearly, they might see me, he thought and decided to guide his camel further south, though this brought him into the arduous Sinai scarp with its wild and broken terrain.

Lawrence cursed under his breath as the camel plunged and strained upon loose stones and undulating dunes. The saddle creaked and his body ached beneath the merciless sun, now at its zenith. On steep ascents, he dismounted and coaxed the camel along, laboring uphill, sweating, and trembling with fatigue. Finally, he reached the high cliffs at a safe distance from the Turks.

With his field glasses he was able to identify details of the convoy—motorized units, infantry, mounted cavalry, artillery, and pontoons—streaming westward for the assault on the Canal. Fatigue forgotten, a singular imperative energized body and mind, *I must reach Cairo and inform the War Office well in advance of the Turks reaching Suez.*

Toward evening, Lawrence saw that the Turkish convoy had reached the fortress of *Nekhel*, and was apparently stopping there for the night. *That is well,* he thought and began traveling to the northwest. After several hours, and with the setting of the sun, he was able to reach the Pilgrim Road well beyond Nekhel.

Pausing beneath scarlet banners of clouds, Lawrence listened to the perfect stillness of the desert. Recent rains had brought up a thin growth of grass creating the appearance of a green mist. With a light tapping of his crop on the camel's flank and the exhortation of "hut, hut, hut," he soon had her at a brisk trot, heading west—toward Suez, toward Cairo. Before him, the road was illuminated by the scarlet sunset and a bright quarter moon.

As he rode, his thoughts turned to Faisal, certain he was the ideal leader for the coming revolt. He was also certain that Newcombe would be able to help obtain the rifles and gold Faisal would need to arm and pay his Bedouin fighters.

Lawrence was also gratified that Faisal was completely receptive to the idea of obtaining the support of Jewish Zionists for the Arab Rebellion with the understanding of allowing the Zionists to realize their dream of an independent homeland following the defeat of the Ottoman Empire. He had raised this possibility in a brief letter he had written to Weizmann before leaving Faisal's encampment. Having placed Faisal's letter to Weizmann along with his own note in a single envelope, he looked forward to reaching Cairo and sending both letters to Weizmann in England by diplomatic pouch. He especially looked forward to meeting with Faisal and Weizmann in Aden.

Once the moon set and darkness descended, he drew rein and bivouacked by an acacia, tying the camel's reins around the tree's trunk as an old Arabic expression rose in his mind—*trust in Allah but tie up your camel!*

He spread his blanket on the sand and decided that, when he was back at the Grand Hotel, he would sleep in the bed rather than on the floor. He was also looking forward to a breakfast of cream of wheat, rather than green dates and camel sinew.

Sleep came quickly, but he awoke to the sound of chattering laughter, which he recognized as the sound made by hyenas.

Known to feed on dead camels that fell by the wayside during the Hajj, hungry hyenas were also known to attack solitary travelers. Fortunately, the sound was coming from far away.

But not for long.

As the sky lightened toward dawn, the laughter grew louder and his camel became restless, straining at her tether. He sprang to his feet and tried to calm her, but in the half-light, he saw a dozen striped hyenas, skittering about in the sand—a hundred yards away and drawing nearer. His camel lurched in terror, bleating, and grinding her teeth.

Trying to control her while drawing his pistol, he saw them circling closer—not twenty feet away. He turned round and round, waiting for a clear shot.

A young hyena charged forward. He fired and missed. He fired again. The animal buckled and rolled to a stop at his feet.

A large female slouched forward, snarling. He aimed and fired. She yelped and limped off into the desert. The others scattered.

Lawrence knew they'd return. He quickly repacked the camel and rode away.

It wasn't until well after dawn when he felt safe enough to stop at a patch of thorn bush in the mouth of a wadi that led to the Mitla Pass. There he gave the camel pasture while he breakfasted on his usual fare. Crouching as he ate, he considered the Mitla Pass—a twenty-mile defile of sand dunes— and beyond the pass, his goal, the port of Shatt on the banks of the Suez.

Back in the saddle, he entered Mitla as the morning sun revealed limestone strata along the southern cliffs, shining crystalline like snow. Though anxious to reach Cairo, he relished these final hours in the desert, the sea breeze cool upon his face as the camel trotted swiftly forward, gliding up each wind-sheltered leeward dune and switch-backing down the other, the fine sand spray cascading like delicate lace.

By midday he was well past Mitla, the camel pacing swiftly along a flat plain where the ground air grew hot. Dust devils sprang up—some hundreds of feet tall and moving over the desolation like unsettled Jehovahs.

Reaching the trench lines of Shatt, he passed the sentry post and was shocked to find it empty. *What the hell is going on here?* He entered the outpost without challenge.

Cautiously, he slackened the pace. Treading slowly forward into a section of offices and living quarters, all seemed abandoned. The silence was complete, apart from the sibilant hissing of sea breeze through opened windows. *Where is everyone?*

Passing blocks of silent barracks, he was startled by the sudden sound of loud tapping from somewhere close by. He rounded a building and found the source—loosened wainscoting moving in the sea wind.

Looking through a window, he saw that it was an office. Entering, he found a telephone and, lifting the earpiece off the stand, he was pleasantly surprised that it appeared to be working. *Thank God,* he thought and, using the directory by the telephone, he rang up the number listed for the Inland Water Transport.

"How may I be of service?" asked the British subaltern.

"Second Lieutenant Lawrence calling from Shatt. I need to come across the Canal."

"So very sorry, sir, but that's not our business."

"Not your *business*?" he asked, his voice rising. "Could you at least connect me with the War Office in Cairo? I just arrived back from the desert with urgent military intelligence—"

"Sorry, sir, but this exchange is not for Canal crossings."

"So, how do I get across the bloody Canal?" he shouted.

"The Embarkation Office manages transit across the Canal after its own methods." The man sniffed and rang off.

Furious, Lawrence connected to the Embarkation Office. The phone was quickly answered. "Halo?"

"Good afternoon, I'm Lieutenant Lawrence of British Intelligence in Cairo. I've just returned from the Sinai, and I'm marooned in Shatt. I have critical information for our Cairo office, and I must get across the Canal with all dispatch. I've just spoken to an incompetent jobsworth at Inland Water Transport who was completely useless. Can *you* help me?"

"It's no bloody good talkin' to them fookin' water boogers, sir!" came the reply in a thick Scottish brogue. "They've got nothin' better to do than fret about who gets to dip in their sacred canal. I'll personally ready your launch and be at Shatt in a few hours."

"Wonderful! And as a reward, I'll give you my camel—a stalwart beast."

"Thank you, sir."

"While I have you on the line, might you tell me why Shatt is abandoned?"

"Pulled out yesterday, sir—rumors the Turks are gettin' near the Canal Zone."

"Those aren't rumors, my good man. That's precisely why I must reach Cairo with dispatch!"

There was a pause on the line. Then the response. "I'll be there in twenty minutes."

❖ ❖ ❖

Once across the Canal, Lawrence headed straight to the railway station at Ismailia. While he waited to board the late-evening train to Cairo, a mixed body of determined British military police came round the train, scrutinizing passes.

Oh, Lord, he thought, glancing down at his dusty Bedouin robe. *In these rags and without papers, how the bloody hell do I navigate this bureaucratic gauntlet?*

Pushing forward, he boarded the train before the inspectors got to him on the platform. He found an empty seat, sat down, and looked up. "Damn!" he whispered as he saw a perspiring officer in khaki drill board the car.

"Be ready to show your pass!" the officer called out and began moving down the aisle, checking papers.

I've got no bloody pass, but I know that all Allied troops in uniform may travel without a pass. I also know that this dolt doesn't know all the allies, much less their uniforms. My Lord—this is the second bloody jobsworth today! I'll just tell him that my robes and red keffiyeh are the uniform of a native Bedouin army allied with the British . . .

The officer approached Lawrence and asked in halting Arabic to see his papers.

"Staff of the sharif of Mecca," Lawrence replied crisply in perfect English.

Astonished, the officer begged his pardon. "And your *uniform*, sir?"

Raising his shoulders, he replied, "This *is* the staff uniform of the sharif of Mecca."

He gave Lawrence a look of disbelief. "But . . . what army would that be, sir?"

Lawrence parried with, "Meccan."

"Not familiar with the uniform . . ."

Then Lawrence delivered the home thrust. "My good man, would you recognize the uniform of a Montenegrin dragoon?"

The officer shrugged. "Very well, sir. Good night and have a pleasant trip."

With the bench seat to himself, Lawrence stretched out and, after the long ride and little rest, he fell into dreamless sleep.

❀ ❀ ❀

From the Cairo railway station, Lawrence went straight to see Newcombe at the War Office. His sandaled feet slip-slapped along the Savoy corridors in the quiet of early morning. Reaching the office, he opened the door and was relieved to see Newcombe already at his desk.

Newcombe didn't look up more than a glance as he worked. "*Lais el'an. Ana mashgul,*" he muttered, brushing off someone he thought was an Arab by saying he was busy.

Lawrence loudly cleared his throat.

Newcombe looked up and his jaw dropped. "Ned?"

"Back from the Sinai, sir." Lawrence saluted smartly.

Newcombe jumped up, rushed round the desk, and caught Lawrence up in his arms. "How very good to see you, my dear boy! I was so worried."

"I have much to tell you."

"But you're covered with dust! Wouldn't you like a nice bath and some less publicly exciting clothing?"

"I do need a bath, Stewart, and I very much want to change out of these robes that are sticking to my saddle sores in filthiness. But right now, there are two things I must do." He extended the envelope. "First, these letters from Faisal—I need sealing-wax and the very next diplomatic pouch to England."

"Done." Newcombe said and took the letter. Squinting at the addressee, he asked, "Are you serious? Professor Chaim Weizmann c/o The Russian Tea King, Wissotzky Tea Company, London?"

"It appears that there is some enigmatic jest between the correspondents."

"What else do you have?"

"I must unburden myself to you with vital news."

"Yes?"

"The Turks will likely attack the Canal in two or three days!"

CHAPTER 31

February 2, 1915
German Army Headquarters Hotel de Ville
Charleville-Mézières, Occupied France

"AN URGENT cable from Palestine, Your Excellency," the courier announced and entered the palatial suite that had been converted to the kaiser's war room.

Turning from a large map festooned with small flags and wooden blocks that occupied the center of the suite, the kaiser rolled his eyes as he took the envelope. *Please, not another tiresome appeal from that fool, List.* He tore it open and was immediately relieved to see that the cable was from Friedrich Kress von Kressenstein, his military liaison with the Turkish Army. Quickly perusing the cable, he exclaimed to his chief of staff, "Excellent news, General Falkenhayn—the Turks are within a few kilometers of the Suez Canal and will likely attack before dawn tomorrow."

"Has their presence not been detected by the British?" asked Falkenhayn.

"Apparently not—they've generally been moving at night and seemed to have avoided discovery. See for yourself." The kaiser handed him the cable.

Falkenhayn nodded as he read. "Interesting." He smiled beneath his mustache. "Ottoman scouts actually observed British officers playing football—seems they're completely unaware." He handed the dispatch back to the kaiser. "Promising news, sire. If we're able to establish a secure beachhead on the western shore using the pontoons von Kressenstein fashioned, we'll likely take the Canal."

"And that, my dear General, will be a deathblow to the Entente!"

"Indeed, so, sire. At the very least, an extended battle in the Canal Zone will be to our advantage. The British will divert resources from the Western Front and dramatically improve our fortunes here."

"Quite so, General, quite so. I should imagine that by this time tomorrow, we will have the first reports from Suez, and we will learn of our smashing success!" But even as he spoke these words, he saw a hesitant shadow of doubt cross Falkenhayn's face. "You harbor some reservations, General?"

"Certainly not, Your Excellency—certainly not. Between the element of surprise and General Kressenstein's leadership of the campaign, we will certainly prevail."

"But more than that, we also have Oppenheim's gambit."

"Oppenheim's gambit, sire?"

Seeing the General's look of confusion, Wilhelm patted him on the shoulder. "The fact that you haven't heard of this covert operation attests to our capacity to keep it secret. But now that we are on the cusp of its success, all will know its value to our purpose."

"What value, sire?"

"A most significant one," The kaiser said and began to stride along the length of the map. "Max von Oppenheim left his legal career and position with the Oppenheim banking dynasty to pursue a life of delicate diplomatic missions and covert operations in the Levant. Though a half-Jew, I must admit that, over the last twenty years, he has proven a faithful servant of our person and of the Fatherland. He is apparently fluent in several Arabic dialects and frequently poses as an archaeologist. In this guise, he has made many contributions to the discovery and securing of antiquities for German museums. Most notably, while charting the course for the Berlin to Baghdad railway, he discovered the site of Tell Halaf in northern Syria." The kaiser took a long wooden pole from its place by the huge floor map and placed its black rubber tip on the map. "That would be here, near the Ottoman border."

Resting the pointer on his shoulder, he continued to pace. "Excited by the discovery of a site rich in antiquities, Oppenheim cabled me with the news, and requested my permission to begin excavations, which I granted straight away.

"However, within a few months and with the nasty business in Sarajevo, we all witnessed the rising tensions in Europe. It was then I cabled Oppenheim and summoned him to meet with me in Berlin, and it was then we developed a secret plan to weaponize Islam against our enemies."

"How so, Your Highness?"

Wilhelm waved the pointer over the map. "Throughout the Levant there are millions of Muslims living in colonies and protectorates controlled by France and Great Britain. Here in Morocco and Tunisia," he exclaimed and slapped the pointer down twice along the North African coast. "Here in Egypt, Aden, Kuwait, Oman, and India," he shouted and slapped down the pointer again and again. "Given these large populations of Muslims, I convinced Oppenheim that Islam could be our most lethal secret weapon!"

"Islam, a secret weapon, Your Majesty? I don't understand."

"Elementary, my dear General. With a well-orchestrated propaganda campaign, I knew that we might stir up mass Muslim uprisings against our enemies. Indeed, soon after Turkey entered the war, I convinced the Ottoman Sultan to further this mission by declaring a 'holy war'—calling on all Muslims to rise in arms against the French and British infidels."

Wilhelm turned to Falkenhayn and smiled. "Oppenheim assures me that this strategy has been very effective. And just for good measure, I also had him spread the fiction that I secretly converted to Islam and made pilgrimage to Mecca—Hajji Wilhelm they call me!" The kaiser guffawed and slapped Falkenhayn on the back. "Can you believe that—Hajji Wilhelm?"

CHAPTER 32

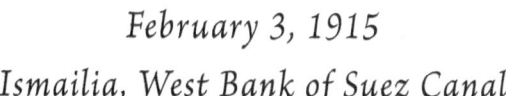

February 3, 1915
Ismailia, West Bank of Suez Canal

L AWRENCE AND Stuart Newcombe lay in the sand at the edge of the shallow trench they had dug, each scanning the Canal with their binoculars. They were flanked by a bristling array of defenders: closest to them on the left were four platoons of New Zealand infantry, and on their right flank was a brigade consisting of Gurkha Rifles and Queen Victoria's Own Rajput Light Infantry. Behind them on a bluff was a battery of British artillery with four mountain guns and two Maxim machine guns.

"I don't see anything yet," Newcombe whispered. "But we know they're out there, and we know they'll be coming for us soon."

"Indeed," Lawrence replied as he lowered his binoculars and rolled onto his side to face Newcombe. "I still can't believe how quickly they made the Sinai crossing with a force of that size."

"True, thank heaven you made it across in time to bring word so we could get our aircraft up and locate the main force."

Lawrence smiled. "And I'm impressed you were able to push through the usually constipated bureaucratic loitering and put ample defenders in place. Lacking the element of surprise and with our defensive line in place, we should be able to send them back across the Sinai in short order."

"I wouldn't get too confident, Ned. You may be ignoring another important element . . ."

"You mean the call to holy war?"

"Exactly," Newcombe replied and gestured to the troops around them. "It's no accident that our main forward defenses don't include our considerable Egyptian or Indian Muslim troops. But even in the rear and flanking positions they could do considerable damage if they were to mutiny."

Lawrence shrugged his shoulders. "Kaiser Bill certainly put plenty of effort and resources into spreading the word about the call to jihad. Interesting how they framed the call to only include the French and British as infidels—as if the Germans aren't. And I don't think anyone bought the rubbish that Wilhelm had secretly converted to Islam."

"Nonetheless, it was an innovative maneuver." After a short pause, Newcombe asked, "Do you think it will work?"

Lawrence could hear the apprehension in his voice. He actually felt some anxiety himself and repeated Newcombe's question. "Do I believe our Muslim colonial troops will rise up in a holy war against us? I honestly don't know, Stuart. I met Max von Oppenheim when Wooley and I were digging alongside the Germans in Carchemish. We considered him an intelligent and decent chap, and I'm sure he can be very convincing." Lawrence sighed as he scanned the Canal. "We can only hope that their propaganda ploy will come to naught—"

Their conversation was cut short by the sudden glare of British searchlights illuminating the Canal followed by the pounding of artillery and the clatter of Maxim machine guns.

Looking up from their defensive position above the Canal, Lawrence saw Turkish soldiers on the far bank scurrying for cover as machine-gunners cut swathes through those at the water's edge. But all the while teams of engineers were quickly assembling the pontoon bridges, and Turkish troops, seeming to ignore the fusillade, were already beginning to hurry across to the western shore. For a moment his breath caught as he saw three pontoons and their crews reach the west bank with a few hundred Turkish troops immediately establishing a beachhead.

Peering through his binoculars into the shadows across the Canal and beyond the searchlights, Lawrence was horrified to see more troops massed and ready to charge forward.

Damn if they're not making a decent show of it, Lawrence thought with mounting anxiety as more Turkish infantry crossed the Canal.

With the help of spotters, the artillery began to find its mark, and the pontoons were splintered in short order. Turkish soldiers were thrown into the Canal or plunged in as the water roiled with the shelling. All the while Maxim machine-gun fire raked the Turkish troops now stranded on the western bank of the Canal.

Cries of the wounded and dying filled the air when not drowned out by the roar of artillery and the sharp clatter of machine-gun and small arms fire. With the pontoons destroyed, shelling was redirected to the farther shore, and the Turkish troops there, illuminated by searchlights, were now panicking and in full retreat, clearly abandoning any attempt to cross. Lawrence watched them scatter into the desert, seeking shelter away from the Canal.

He felt Newcombe's hand on his shoulder.

"I'm going to see how our defensive line is faring along the ridge," he shouted.

Lawrence could barely hear him over the thunder of the artillery. He looked down at the Turkish beachhead below the ridge and saw British infantry advancing on the relatively small Turkish force—no more than two companies. Some were surrendering, but most appeared either wounded or killed with scores of bodies floating in the Canal. As the big guns fell silent, cries of the wounded Turks rose in the predawn air.

On the far side of the Canal, the confused retreat left dead and wounded everywhere—exposed by the cold eyes of the sweeping searchlights.

He blew out a sigh as he looked down at the devastated Turkish force, impressed by their bravery and saddened by the slaughter. But at the same time relieved that they had utterly failed.

He turned to see Newcombe slide into their trench. "What news?" Lawrence asked.

"The same as here." Newcombe nodded down at the Canal below them. "The Turks are routed. Our radio boys have picked up chatter about

Djemal Pasha trying to direct an orderly retreat to Beersheba."

"Will there be any pursuit?"

"Probably not. We've taken very few casualties, and from what I hear, our good General John Maxwell will probably let them bog off across the Sinai."

"That's well," said Lawrence, then asked, "And any word about a mutiny of Muslim troops?"

"Not a one. Companies of Jodhpur and Kashmiri Muslim Lancers fought valiantly. Indeed, they had to be restrained from pursuing the Turks into the desert. So much for the kaiser's hope of weaponizing Islam for his own benefit."

Lawrence looked down at the carnage along the Canal and shook his head. "At least for this round."

CHAPTER 33

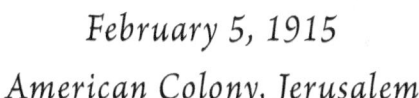

February 5, 1915
American Colony, Jerusalem

ANNA SPAFFORD was reading in her bedroom in the early afternoon following a long morning in the Colony's soup kitchen when a knock sounded at the door, quickly followed by a voice she knew as that of her daughter, Bertha.

"Mother, are you awake?"

"I am, darling. Come in."

Bertha stepped in, still wearing her apron. "I just had to tell you, Mother," she whispered breathlessly and pushed the door closed. "Frank just returned from meeting with the Spanish Consul Ballobar—"

"Wonderful! Has he agreed to represent American citizens since the Turks closed our consulate?"

"He has, Mother. But while Frank was there, Ballobar was given news about a huge Ottoman attack on the Suez Canal. Apparently, the British, Egyptian, and colonial forces were waiting for them, and the Turks didn't stand a chance. According to the dispatch there are many hundreds of Turkish dead and wounded."

"Oh my lord!" Anna sighed and shook her head. "It's likely many of them will be sent to us for treatment. I only hope that our little hospital won't be overwhelmed."

"There's also this." Bertha took a postcard from her apron pocket and handed it to her mother. "Frank received a hundred of these at the Colony store from his German supplier this morning—even before he heard about the attack on the Canal."

Anna squinted at the postcard in disbelief and her heart began to pound. She saw a crowded photomontage showing the Canal beneath a fluttering Turkish flag with floral German script next to the flag proclaiming, *Der kampf um den Suezkanal.* On the right side of the postcard was an oval bust of Enver Pasha in military dress regalia wearing a neat fez. Along the bottom of the postcard was a long segment of the Canal's eastern shore filled with mounted Turkish and Bedouin troops as far as the eye could see, with infantry filling a long trench line next to the water and a single cannon in the foreground. She couldn't help but laugh. "Bertha," she whispered, "these postcards were probably printed a month ago. This is just good, old-fashioned propaganda."

"Are you certain? It looks so convincing . . ."

"Look here." Anna pointed at the bust of Enver Pasha. "Enver is in Istanbul and could not have been involved in the campaign at all since it's Djemal Pasha who commands the Middle East Front. Enver Pasha is simply better known to the Germans since he was a military attaché in Berlin for many years. That's why they stuck him in there. Trust me, my dear, it's rubbish." Anna stood up. "Come, Bertha. We have work to do."

"We do? But we've been working all day."

"As Isaiah tells us, 'You who call on the Lord, give yourselves no rest.'"

"But, what remains to be done, Mother?"

"We need to begin planning for more bed space and how to increase the nursing staff to care for the Turkish wounded. I should imagine they'll begin arriving from the Sinai by way of Gaza in droves within a week." With her hand on the door latch, Anna paused and added, "We'll also need to prepare for wounded Turkish pride."

"What's your meaning, Mother?"

"This resounding defeat at the Canal will be a significant blow to the Turkish military, and specifically a blow to the prestige of Djemal Pasha. They might look for scapegoats to blame—such as members of the American Colony. Though Djemal has always treated us with respect and affection, he's known to have mood swings, and given this defeat, he may well be angry, and more likely to invade the Colony."

"Why would he do that, Mother?"

"Djemal has come under pressure from a certain disagreeable Austrian by the name of Guido von List, who seeks to seize two of the fugitives hiding in the catacombs beneath the Colony—Gunter and Rahman. Djemal, in anger, might yield to List, invade the Colony, and seize them. We cannot allow that to happen . . ."

"How can we stop them?"

"We can't. We can only make certain that, when the breach occurs, the fugitives will no longer be here—that they'll be hidden elsewhere."

CHAPTER 34

February 14, 1915
London's East End

CHAIM WEIZMANN stared at the cable in his hand. **PLEASE COME QUICKLY, ASHER.** "What the hell is that supposed to mean?" he wondered aloud as his heart pounded, anxious that either Asher Ginsberg or his wife, Rivke, had sustained a medical emergency.

He had just signed for the cable and, looking up, saw that the telegram messenger was still by the curb in his automobile.

"Please, my good man!" he shouted and crossed the walkway. "Could you give me a lift to Hampstead?"

The young man frowned. "The General Post Office wouldn't approve, sir, but . . ."

Weizmann heard in his hesitation an opportunity to reach the Ginsberg home quickly. "I'd be happy to compensate you—how much would it cost?"

The young man scratched the stubble on his cheek. "That's at least ten miles, guv' . . . a shilling and six I should think."

"Done. Just give me a minute to close up and we'll be off."

Weizmann grabbed his coat and secured the lock on the distillery door. Once in the automobile, he sat next to the messenger in the small two-seat Ford, and announced, "Glenmore Road, number 12 in Hampstead."

"I know th' place, guv'. He pulled slowly away from the curb.

"Do hurry, please."

"What's th' rush, if I may ask?"

"I'm afraid an old friend of mine is ill."

"I'll do my best t' get ya there double quick."

"Thanks very much." He settled back in the cushioned seat, hoping to avoid any further conversation with the driver as his thoughts turned to Asher and his wife, *God, I hope they're alright* . . .

Weizmann closed his eyes as he considered that, up until receipt of the cable, he had really been having a very good day. For one thing, he was gratified that pilot-plant production of acetone was going well. Between homegrown wheat and regular imports of maize from the United States, there was adequate starch for the fermentation process.

Finally, acetone production was rising to meet the needs for the cordite required for British munitions.

Most importantly, First Lord of the Admiralty Winston Churchill wanted the program expanded and had given his blessings to the conversion of other distilleries throughout Great Britain for acetone production. Churchill had also charged Weizmann with the training of personnel for the other distilleries.

And that instruction is to begin tomorrow, Weizmann thought with satisfaction. *I so look forward to training the young chemists who will go on to expand the program throughout England. However,* he thought and shook his head. *What happens tomorrow might well be affected by whatever is going on with Asher and Rivke.*

He pulled the cable from his pocket and reread the terse message, **PLEASE COME QUICKLY, ASHER.**

Perhaps it's not a medical emergency at all, maybe something else—perhaps a pogrom in Russia, or something about the Ottoman attack on Suez . . .

Weizmann looked out the window with no idea why Asher had summoned him. "Is it much further?" he asked.

"Not at all—we'll be there in a few minutes."

When the driver turned onto a street Weizmann recognized, Ginsberg's house soon came into view. "That brownstone on the left," he said pointing.

Once the taxi slowed to a stop, he asked, "How much do I owe you?"

"As I said, guv', a shilling and six, and I do hope your pal is alright." The messenger paused, then added, "If you like, I'll wait here for a minute . . . so's you can see if I can be of any help."

"That's very kind of you, thanks." Weizmann paid the fare. "If there's no problem, I'll wave to you from the front door." He stepped out of the auto, ran across the street, and took the brick steps two at a time to the front door. He knocked quickly and was relieved when Rivke opened the door after a few seconds.

"We're glad you're here, Chaim—"

"Is something wrong?" he asked anxiously. "Is everything alright?"

"Everything's fine," she said, closing the door. "A letter came for you—delivered by courier to Asher's office and brought here by his secretary."

"Good morning, Chaim!" Ginsberg called out from an overstuffed brown leather chair in the library, waving the letter over his head, his feet up on a matching ottoman.

Weizmann sighed and shook his head. "I'll be right back." He stepped out the front door and waved to the messenger, who waved back and pulled away from the curb.

Returning to the flat, Weizmann collapsed into the armchair next to Ginsberg. "You summoned me all the way from East London for a *letter*, Asher? I was worried sick—I thought it was an emergency! All this for a *letter?*"

"A letter you might want to see immediately. A letter closed with sealing-wax." Ginsberg handed it to him.

Weizmann whispered, "Could it be?" His hand shook as he broke the seal, opened the envelope, and unfolded the letter. "Yes! At long last—a reply to the letter I sent to Sharif Hussein and his son, Faisal over two months ago."

He began to read aloud.

"29 Rabi al-Awal, 1333 AH Mecca
My dear Professor Weizmann,

I write to you in my own name and in the name of my royal father, Hussein bin Ali, the Sharif and Emir of Mecca and Keeper of the Holy Places. I am in possession of the letter you sent to us in Mecca late last year which arrived by courier and which we read with great interest. My royal father wanted me to commend you for the discreet manner whereby you conveyed the missive since such caution is vital in these dangerous times. I also wish to express my gratitude to His Excellency, the tea king of Russia, for facilitating our correspondence."

"Did he really write that?" asked Ginsberg.

Weizmann held up the paper for Ginsberg to see. "Just as he did on the envelope." He shook his head and returned to the letter.

"I share with my royal father the belief that Arabs are not jealous of Zionist Jews, since our two branches of the Semitic family understand one another and understand that we will both be advantaged to cooperate toward the realization of our mutual aspirations for self-determination.

"Insofar as I share your belief that the Central Powers will be defeated in the current war, I also share your hope that the Ottoman Empire will be dismantled, and in the areas of Greater Syria and Arabia there will be ample room for an independent Arab state and an independent Jewish state. As you, I am also mindful of the racial kinship and ancient bonds existing between the Arabs and the Jewish people. In this spirit, my royal father has charged me to contact you about meeting at a time and place that will ensure our mutual safety and secrecy.

"Since your letter two months ago there have been two momentous events: the official entry of the Ottoman Empire into the war effort on the side of Germany, and the proclamation of holy war by the Sultan-Caliph from Constantinople. These events in no way detract from the importance of our collaboration; indeed, they strengthen it. The time is at hand for

us to communicate about an agreement of cooperation between us so that we may realize our individual and shared dreams of national liberation and independence. It is in this spirit that I suggest that we meet to discuss areas of mutual assistance toward future coexistence.

"*Also, since your letter, I was sent by my royal father to Jeddah, where I prepared the Bedouin troops of the Hejaz and of the Sinai for battle.*

However, insofar as I am now being hunted by the Ottomans, I am now elsewhere and in hiding until the revolt begins. An envoy from the British Empire, one Captain T. E. Lawrence, is with me for a short time and, upon leaving, will convey this letter to a point where it may be safely brought by courier to you in England. I would add that Captain Lawrence is very sympathetic to our cause.

"*I believe it is safest for us to meet at the Port of Aden within the British Protectorate. There is a coffee shop next to the Francis of Assisi Church in the Tahiri section of the city. Let us meet there at noon on May 5. Captain Lawrence has assured me that he is willing and able to help arrange your transport to Aden and if you like, to accompany you. In that regard, he will contact you soon.*

"*With hope for friendship and cooperation toward the realization of our shared and sacred goal of national independence, and with blessings of the One God,*

Emir Faisal ibn Hussein"

Once Weizmann finished reading, he could barely catch his breath. He refolded the letter and as he was replacing it in the envelope, he stopped. "There's another slip of paper here." Taking it out, he glanced at it and smiled. "It's a brief note from Captain Lawrence to let me know that he will arrange my passage to Aden and will accompany me on the journey. He's also provided his address in Cairo. I shall write him forthwith!"

He pushed up from the armchair and turned to Ginsberg. "Over the years we've argued about reconciling our need for a national homeland with the need to respect the rights of the people of Palestine, but after all the squabbles, the one thing we've agreed on is the need for a bridge of communication between us—Jews and Arabs." He held up the envelope in his hand. "I believe Faisal is that bridge!"

"True, Chaim, but bridge or no, it doesn't change how I feel about your use of British munitions production to curry favor with Whitehall—"

"Stop with the lecturing, Asher!" Weizmann said, laughing. Then, pointing to the envelope, he asked, "But how should I address you since you're apparently the 'tea king of Russia?'"

"No need to make a fuss—it's only an honorary title. On the other hand, it's a clever device and not completely inappropriate since the courier was my tea envoy to the Middle East."

Weizmann laughed. "At some point we should inform Hussein and Faisal that your employer, Kalman Zev Wissotzky, was the true Russian tea king. You were merely a member of his entourage—a gentleman-in-waiting, perhaps."

"I beg to differ, Chaim. As director of the London office of Wissotzky Tea, it was I who stood first in the line of succession to Wissotzky's throne, and with his death, I had no choice but to accept the crown." Ginsberg stood up, looked at Weizmann over his spectacles and placed a hand on his shoulder. "Do you at least forgive me for summoning you all the way from East London?"

"I do. It was well worth the trip." Weizmann breathed out a sigh. "To think I'll be sitting down with Faisal in a couple of months—speaking with him about Arab-Jewish cooperation in Palestine! It's like a dream. And all this is *your* doing. If you hadn't nagged me this wouldn't have happened."

"So, I have your permission to continue to nag you about my misgivings regarding your moral quandary about munitions production?"

"Yes, Asher. You've earned the right to nag me, and I reserve the right to ignore you."

CHAPTER 35

February 15, 1915
Whitehall, London

GERTRUDE BELL looked up at the soaring columns of the War Office Building. *Certainly, a far cry from my dreary office in France!* She gripped the handle of her suitcase, lifted her long skirt, and carefully mounted the marble steps, slick beneath a dusting of snow.

Glad to be back in England, she harbored no regrets at leaving the Russell sisters and several new volunteers to manage the Red Cross office in France. Satisfied that she'd created a first-class catalog system to monitor the dead and wounded, now it was up to them to maintain it.

Certain that her firsthand knowledge of Arabia would benefit the Geographical Intelligence Division of the War Office, she'd written Colonel Hedley, the MO-4 director, and after almost three months he had finally responded with an offer to interview her for possible employment. *It's about bloody time!* she thought with umbrage and pushed open the heavy doors of Whitehall.

Finding herself in the marble foyer of a grand atrium with pillared alcoves, soldiers were everywhere, their boots tapping on the smooth stone floor. They all seemed intent on being somewhere else and double quick about it. She stood for a moment, watching them in their starched khakis, mustaches waxed to a point, faces immobile.

She considered her own uniform—a feathered hat, fur boa, white skirt, and a string of pearls highlighting a dark crepe de Chine shirt.

"I say, mum, may I help you?"

The voice sounded close at hand, but looking about, there was no one in sight. Then she looked down.

A young scout stood in front of her looking up. "May I help you, mum?"

"Why yes, my dear boy," she replied, quickly regaining her composure. "I should like to check my bag."

"Certainly, mum." The boy took her suitcase and disappeared into the crowd, returning after a minute with a numbered brass tag. "Here you are, mum. Might I help you with anything else?"

"Yes. I'm to meet with Colonel Hedley in MO-4. Could you direct me to his office?"

"I'll take you there myself, mum." He turned and pelted into an alcove that housed an iron staircase.

"Wait a moment, young gentleman!" she called out. The boy stopped and turned.

"Can't we take these stairs?" She motioned a gloved hand toward the grand marble staircase in the main hall.

"Sorry, mum. Those aren't for us."

"Who are they for?"

"Generals and members of Parliament, mum. This way if you please." He turned and labored up the steel steps.

How perfectly idiotic, Gertrude thought with a final glance at the elegant and empty central staircase. Turning, she followed the scout into the stairwell. As she watched him climbing the steps, her heart clenched—a little boy in oversized khaki shorts, his chubby legs so short, he required two paces to mount each rise. *Oh, for a child of my own,* she thought. *Perhaps when Richard gets his divorce.* She mounted the steps to an arcade that opened into an expansive landing crowded with soldiers and bordered by a stone balustrade.

The boy stopped in front of an oversized oak door with neatly stenciled words—*Geographical Division.* He pushed at the heavy door and it creaked open. "Colonel Hedley's office is just through here, mum."

The air was filled with the clatter of typewriters and tobacco smoke. The boy stood aside to let her pass.

Gertrude bent down. "You've been very kind, and I thank you."

"I'm just doing my job, is all."

"And, indeed, you do a very *good* job."

The boy grew serious and fixed her with his brown eyes. "We must all do our part, mum." He made a little bow and disappeared, lost among the soldiers filling the arcade.

Gertrude made her way through the gray haze of cigarette smoke filling the outer office where soldiers and civilian women worked at their desks. Reaching a door with Hedley's name stenciled on the opaque glass upper panel, she raised her hand to knock.

"Sorry," a soldier said sharply. "The colonel is quite busy. Might I be of service?"

Turning her head, she took in the young sergeant in a cold glance. "Thank you, no. I have an appointment with the colonel."

"Let me just check his schedule, Miss . . ."

"Bell. Gertrude Bell." Her tone barely hid a mounting irritation—a sensitivity to condescension heightened by years of dealing with men who presumed that their sex imbued them with superiority or even competence. Far from growing used to it, each perceived slight stung like salt on an open wound.

The soldier scanned a ledger. "Ah, yes! Here we are. I'll announce you." He tapped a knuckle on the glass panel of Hedley's door.

"Come!" a deep voice called from within.

The sergeant opened the door just wide enough to admit his head. "A Miss Gertrude Bell to see you, sir."

"Yes, yes, Sergeant. Do show her in."

Head held high, she lifted her skirt slightly, brushed past the sergeant and approached the desk. "How good to meet you, Colonel Hedley." She extended her hand.

"It is, indeed, an honor to meet *you*, Miss Bell."

Hedley pushed back his heavy chair, stood up, and they shook hands, a little awkwardly, over his desk.

"Please," he pointed to a chair. "A spot of tea perhaps?"

"That would be lovely." Gertrude sat in an upholstered chair facing the desk.

"Sergeant, we'll take tea now."

"Yes, sir. Of course." The door settled closed.

"As I'm sure you might imagine, Miss Bell, your reputation precedes you."

"Thank you, Colonel. I'll take that as a compliment."

"So intended, Miss Bell. So intended." Hedley sat back down behind his desk. "The recently foiled Turkish attack on the Suez Canal created quite a stir around here, quite a stir, indeed. Whitehall is finally paying attention to us."

"Only *now*?"

"Sadly, yes. Up until the attack on the Canal, our work here was regarded with skepticism, even a certain amusement, I daresay. But the possibility of the Canal falling to the Turks dramatically raised our profile."

Gertrude sensed Hedley's smug satisfaction at finally being relevant after apparently cooling his heels for months.

"Your expertise in Arabia will be put to good use here, Miss Bell. Of that, you may be certain. And with war on this front, we're hoping our maps will be up to par."

"I'm anxious to be of help, Colonel. As I wrote you from France, my expertise in Arabia will serve the Empire well."

"We enthusiastically concur." Hedley flipped through a desk calendar. "When might you be able to begin?"

"I should like some time to visit family in Yorkshire and to find a nice flat here in London. I'll also need to visit the London office of the British Red Cross London office since, as I wrote you, I'll also be volunteering there to set up systems for recording the wounded, missing, and dead—just as I did in France."

"Indeed, very important work, Miss Bell. Shall we say a week from today, then?"

"That would be perfect, Colonel." She was relieved at having a full week to accomplish what was, indeed, a full schedule, and she felt less guilty about her plans to spend a good measure of that time with Richard. She struggled to retain her composure as her body tingled with anticipation of a union planned for that very afternoon. After years of chaste correspondence, Richard had arranged for their lodging at a small hotel, and with that thought, her heart began to race.

The sergeant appeared at the door with a tray and Hedley waved him forward. "One lump or two, Miss Bell?"

"Two, thank you."

"Your trip across the Channel was tolerable, I trust?"

"Pleasant enough, Colonel. At a moment's notice I was able to find room on a troop ship." She smiled, adding, "The ship's cat and I were the only two not in uniform. Thank you, Sergeant," she murmured, accepting a cup and stirring as she settled back in her chair.

"Will there be anything else, Colonel?"

With satisfaction she detected barely concealed resentment in the sergeant's voice.

"No, that will be all," Hedley said with a curt dismissal.

As the office door clicked closed, Hedley looked at Gertrude over his teacup. "I read your book, The Desert and . . ." His voice trailed off, as he struggled to recall the title.

"And the Sown," Gertrude offered.

"Ah, yes. *The Desert and the Sown.* Quite good—brilliant, really. One of the best Eastern travel books I've read."

"Thank you, Colonel," she said pleasantly, though she hated hearing her book referred to as an Eastern travel book.

"Never actually been to those regions myself. I recall you were quite taken with Damascus. Capital of the desert, you called it."

"I did, didn't I? I suppose I took a measure of poetic license with that description."

"How so?"

"Damascus isn't actually in the desert, Colonel. To be sure, the desert comes almost to its gates and the breath of it blows in with every wind and with every caravan. But it's the *contrast* that makes Damascus a truly luxurious oasis, bounded on three sides by mountains, filled with orchards and running streams." She sighed. "I yearn to return someday. Soon, I hope."

"That will, of course, depend on the course of this war."

"Indeed, and I believe the course of the war will be determined in Arabia."

"Really?" Hedley raised his heavy eyebrows. "Notwithstanding the business with the Canal, I fear the Middle East Front is still considered something of a sideshow."

"I think not, Colonel. I believe the Germans will go to great lengths to maintain Ottoman hegemony, and with it their own dominance throughout the Levant."

"What do you make of Kitchener's notion of hitching our wagon to an Arab uprising against the Turks? Some contend that the Arab's nature renders it a vain hope."

"Would the source of this opinion be Mark Sykes, sir?"

"Indeed, so, Miss Bell. He's written extensively of their nature, noting they are eloquent and cunning, but at the same time diseased and insolent. What chance of a successful rebellion with the likes of these?"

Sykes! She silently screamed his name. *Another arrogant man with an oversized self-image to hide his undersized intellect.* She smiled and said, "I wouldn't put much stock in his caricature of Arabs, Colonel. Mark has a fertile imagination but lacks the knowledge and discipline of a scholar. To put it plainly, Sykes doesn't know the Arabs as I do."

"Alright, then, what do *you* make of them?"

What do I make of them? Gertrude resented the breathtaking generalization of the question. She sipped her tea and considered the years of traveling and living among the Arabs. *What do I make of them?* Any answer would be imprecise, but she had to provide some counterweight to Sykes's simplistic and grotesque misrepresentation.

"The Arab is practical, though his utility is not ours. His actions are guided by traditions of conduct that go back to the beginnings of civilization, at times unmodified by the passage of time. These things apart, I can assure you that human nature does not undergo a complete change east of Suez. The friendship, hospitality, and honesty I have known among the Arabs equals or surpasses that which I've experienced among Europeans."

"What about their treatment of women, Miss Bell? Doesn't that concern you?"

"I'm not sure what you mean, Colonel. But before we focus on the treatment of women in Muslim societies, we might acknowledge our own patriarchal shortcomings—"

"Our own shortcomings?" Hedley cut in. "What could you possibly mean?"

Gertrude paused before answering as she recalled the painful memories of her time at Oxford University where she was among a few women begrudgingly allowed to attend. She recalled how she was obliged to sit with her back to the lecturer, constrained to remain silent in class discussions—not allowed to speak with professors or male classmates. And even though she graduated with highest honors, she wasn't awarded an academic degree because these were given only to men.

But she didn't wish to share these memories with Hedley, fearing it might antagonize him and jeopardize her opportunity to work at MO-4.

With a sigh, she pushed away the buried rage. "It's just that I'm not sure what you mean about the Arab's treatment of women," she said pleasantly. "I will tell you that, as an English woman, I was proud to represent the British Empire everywhere I went in Arabia—from camel-hair tents of desert sheikhs to the medieval ramparts of Ibn Rashid in Hayil and the royal courts of Ibn Saud in Riyadh. And I'll never forget how Ibn Saud complimented me and the British Empire after we spent some hours together. He said, and I quote, 'If the Britons' women are so strong and energetic, imagine the power of their men!'"

"Well played, Miss Bell, well played. Hedley exclaimed, laughing. "So, you feel comfortable with the notion of supporting and financing their revolt against the Turks?"

"With all my heart, Colonel."

"Even becoming involved with conflict in Mesopotamia?"

"Absolutely."

"As regarding that, Miss Bell, I have my doubts. Mind you, I'm quite keen about protecting the Canal, but I believe we have it wrong in Mesopotamia. I believe it's bloody folly for our boys to become further entangled in Basra and Baghdad—bloody dangerous if you ask me."

"The environs of Baghdad and the port of Basra are of *vital* importance, Colonel," she replied, "with grain supplies to feed an army, and oil to fuel a navy."

She sat up straight in her chair, satisfied at parrying Hedley's assertion with facts of her own. "One might argue that the only way we can win the war in Europe is by doing all we can to deny Mesopotamia and its resources to Germany. Simply put, sir, if *we* don't control Arabia and Mesopotamia, the Germans will, and they'll win the war."

Hedley frowned. "I do find myself agreeing with you, Miss Bell, certainly on the basis of military strategy—"

Oh, for heaven's sake! she thought and asked, "What other basis is there?"

"Just this—our presence in India and Egypt already gives the British Empire the largest Muslim empire in the world—*tens of millions* of them. If we become entangled with administering Mesopotamia, we'll have millions more. What will happen if these millions of Muslims decide to follow their holy leader, the sultan of Turkey, against us?"

"A fair question, Colonel. My answer is this: ten days ago, Muslim soldiers in Egypt, fighting under the Union Jack, fought bravely against the Turks at the Canal without paying any attention to the sultan's call for holy war. None. The Arabs will ally with us because we have committed to giving them what the Turks have denied them for five hundred years. We'll give them their freedom!"

"An admirable notion, Miss Bell," Hedley said and drew an impatient breath. "But if we win this bloody war with the Arab's help, would you suggest we simply give them home rule? Self-governance to people who have never known it?"

"As an experienced soldier of the Empire, Colonel, you know this calling far better than I. We have rich experience in overseeing new nations in fairness and benevolence. We would clearly have to help the Arabs develop their own leadership and institutions of self-governance. I'm sure we'll have great success in dealing with the independent Arab countries that will emerge from the rubble of the Ottoman Empire."

"But that's exactly the *problem*, Miss Bell," Hedley exclaimed. "Arabia and Mesopotamia aren't *countries*! You've described this aptly in your writings. How did you put it—*unwieldy collections of tribes and families*? With this sort of hodgepodge, how can you propose to create Arab states in Arabia and Mesopotamia? Who would decide where to place the borders? I should think that if you attempt to foist a national identity on a bunch of feuding tribes, the thing will just fall to pieces."

"That's where I come in, sir."

"*You*, Miss Bell?" Hedley's heavy eyebrows arched in surprise.

"Myself, and others with extensive knowledge of the Arabs. Those of us who know their traditions, languages, and customs will be able to work with tribal leaders and city dwellers to decide where to form national boundaries. We'll also be positioned to help them build the democratic institutions of a civil society with hospitals, schools, and good jobs. In this manner, we'll help them move toward self-governance and prosperity."

"I certainly hope your optimism is well-placed, Miss Bell." Hedley stood up and straightened his uniform. "But now, let's deal with the mundane practicality of winning this bloody war. Let me show you to the map room."

"Excellent." Gertrude stood up. "I assume you already have extensive maps of Arabia along with Basra, Mosul, and Baghdad . . ."

"We do, but they're probably not up to date. You see, Lawrence did much of the work based on his recollections from a few years ago."

"And, from what I hear, Colonel, he's now in Cairo."

"Correct, and the officer in the map room now, has even less current information. On the other hand, *you* have a wealth of recent experience in these regions."

"Quite so. I was there less than a year ago, and I should be delighted to work with your current staff to update the maps and fill in any gaps."

"I'm counting on that, Miss Bell." Hedley held the door open for Gertrude. "When will you be leaving for Yorkshire?"

"Early this afternoon, Colonel. That way I'll be with my family before dark," Gertrude lied, blushing as she thought about meeting Richard that afternoon.

At a door marked *Middle East Cartography*, Hedley stopped, turned the knob and opened the door into a large room with a polished wooden floor. Sunlight filtered through beige curtains that covered a large bay window at the far end of the room, the light falling over a huge table where an officer stood, his back to the door, bending over a map.

Hedley cleared his throat, and the man turned. Gertrude's breath caught.

"Miss Bell, allow me to introduce your partner here, Captain Clive Sinclair."

"*Captain* Sinclair?" Delighted to see Clive, Gertrude stepped quickly forward. "The uniform suits you well, professor!" She effused as they shook hands.

"Please, Gertrude, none of this *professor* business. Captain will do nicely."

"I see no introductions are required." Hedley chuckled. "I'll let you two catch up." He went to the door and paused before leaving. "Miss Bell," he said with a little bow. "Welcome aboard. I look forward to seeing you when you return from Yorkshire."

When the door closed, Clive turned to her. "Yorkshire?"

"Yes. I haven't seen my mum or dad in months. I arranged to spend some time with them before I start here in earnest."

"Soon, I hope."

"A week from today." She didn't volunteer any information about her plans to see Richard. "Before I go, however, I'd love to see what you and our dear boy, Lawrence, have accomplished with the maps—"

"*Dear boy?*" Clive laughed. "When we were at Carchemish, you generally found him infuriating. I distinctly remember you calling him *that little imp!*"

"He sometimes *was!*" she replied, laughing. "Though it did make me sad to hurt his feelings—the way his ears and face would turn red, and he'd retreat in silence!" Beaming, she looked over the map table and said with genuine enthusiasm, "I can't begin to tell you how happy I am to be here!"

"I hear you did a smashing job with the Red Cross in France."

"Thank you, Clive, I did." She paused and fixed him with her eyes. "You received my letter about Evan?"

"The letter with no news of him? Yes."

"I'm so sorry, Clive. I wish—"

"That was two months ago, Gerty, and much has changed! Let me catch you up about where things stand now!"

Gertrude was heartened to hear all that Clive had discovered about Evan since he had left home in Utah. He finished the recitation with the disturbing fact of Evan's unknown whereabouts. Her heart was heavy as she saw Clive's eyes glisten with tears. She wanted so much to comfort him.

"But he's alive, and in England, Clive. I'm sure you'll find him, or he'll find *you.*"

"That's my hope, Gerty. In the meantime, your work here will be vital! No European has your knowledge of the current state of the tribes and terrain of Arabia." He raised his shoulders. "Truth be told, my contribution to the mapping has been minimal, and the main reason I'm here is that Whitehall offers the best resources to find Evan."

"And God willing, you will."

"But I'll be leaving MO-4 soon—"

"Why?" Gertrude asked, dismayed by what she was hearing. "I was so hoping we could work together."

"That would be lovely, but with you here, I literally have nothing to contribute."

"But it's *imperative* you stay. Don't you understand?"

He looked surprised. "No, I don't."

"As a woman, I have no official capacity. I'm only able to be here as an assistant to a man."

"Are you joking?"

"I'm afraid not."

"I honestly don't know how you put up with this garbage, Gerty!"

She nodded and for a long minute said nothing. She appreciated Clive's succinct choice of words—*this garbage*. Her thoughts strayed back to the unpleasant years auditioning for a husband as a debutante; the coming-out parties she endured for three difficult years starting at twenty—the marriage market that felt more like a meat market—standing in line with other debutantes to be inspected by potential suitors for appearance, manners, bearing, and to be judged as too headstrong or too opinionated or too smart, or not sufficiently pretty. Her heart ached when she recalled the hurt she had felt at failing the process. Because three seasons was all the time allotted for a young lady to find a husband. And she'd run out of time.

Clive broke the uncomfortable silence. "They'll easily find some other man to replace me here, and besides, Hedley has already promised to help me find another job. And . . . speaking of changing jobs, I had a wonderful dinner last evening with our dear friend, Richard. He just finished his job in Addis Ababa, and he's back in London for his next deployment. I told him I might be seeing you today, and he sends his warmest regards."

"How delightful," she exclaimed, and her heart began pounding. She struggled to maintain her composure and asked, "Is he here with his wife, Lillian? She's such a dear."

"Sadly, no. She's working as a nurse in France and couldn't get away, so it was just the two of us. I took him for a lovely dinner at Simpson's, which also included a game of chess." Clive smiled. "He let me win, which I suspect was because I paid for dinner!"

"Do you know how much longer he'll be in London?" She asked, trying to sound natural though her face felt hot, and she feared she might be blushing. "I do hope to see him—perhaps we can all go out together!" She glanced at her timepiece. "But look at the time." It was almost noon, and she'd arranged to meet Richard at one o'clock. Looking over the map table, she shook her head. "I was so hoping to look over your maps, but I must catch the train for Yorkshire."

"Not a problem, Gerty. We'll go over them when you get back. Do give your folks my very best wishes, won't you?"

※ ※ ※

As Gertrude made her way down the iron steps, her heart pounded with shame. Lying to Hedley had been easy, but lying to Clive was another matter; they knew each other all too well. She felt ridiculous and humiliated at her attempt to provide a pretext with such an obvious lie.

She retrieved her suitcase from the cloakroom, pushed open the heavy doors and left the War Office building. Feeling the frigid outside air, she shuddered as she made her way down the snow-covered steps.

Entering a waiting taxi, she instructed the driver to take her to the Monte Carlo Hotel in Leicester Square. As the taxi moved away from Whitehall, the burning cold in her cheeks dissipated and was replaced with a burning ardor—spreading out from the very quick of her—knowing she would soon be in Richard's arms.

CHAPTER 36

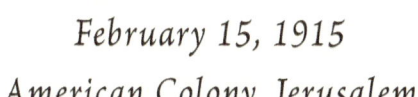

February 15, 1915
American Colony, Jerusalem

"GUNTER! GUNTER!" Anna Spafford shouted and pounded on the door with her fists. "There are two Turkish soldiers at the gate!"

The door jerked open, and Gunter gasped, "They know we're here?"

"Yes! They're asking to speak with you and David Nathanson. And they told me to give you this." She held out a notebook. "It looks like Hebrew. Do you know what this is?" She could see his hands shake as he turned the pages.

"It's the handwriting of my wife, Rachel—her Hebrew lessons. Did they say anything else?" he asked, still staring at the notebook.

"Yes." Anna struggled to catch her breath. "They wanted me to tell you . . . that they were the ones . . . who helped David survive his torture . . . at the hands of Guido von List . . . who got the whole family away from him . . . so you could bring them here."

"Have you told David they're here?"

"Not yet. He's helping in the kitchen."

"These soldiers—did you tell them we're in hiding here?"

"Of course not! But they seem to be certain that you're here and they won't leave without speaking with you."

"How did they *find* us?"

"They saw the car you drove the night you brought the Nathansons here. With so few cars in Jerusalem, they said it wasn't hard to trace." Anna steadied herself, trying to think of a way out. "Listen, Gunter! There's a

[221]

warren of hidden caves beneath the compound. While the soldiers wait, I'll take all of you to the caves. My children will bring your things—"

"Not yet, Anna." Gunter cut in. "David and Sarah may actually know these two soldiers. They can help us decide what to do."

"Good. You wait here, and I'll bring them."

Anna quickly went to the kitchen and fetched the Nathansons. She explained the situation to them on the way back to the commons room where Gunter waited.

Sarah spoke first. "If they're really the Turkish soldiers who helped us, we're happy to speak with them."

"But, how do you know these are the same ones?" asked Gunter.

"We'd have to see them," said David.

Gunter turned to Anna, "Is there a way David and Sarah might get a look at them without being seen?"

"Yes. There's a balcony with a good view of the gate." She turned to David and Sarah. "I'll take you there once I fetch a pair of opera glasses from my room." Turning back to Gunter, she added, "Wait here until we know it's safe."

As Anna led Sarah and David through the compound's labyrinthine limestone passages, she felt a small measure of hope, though she feared the worst.

❖ ❖ ❖

With anxious anticipation, David watched Anna slowly open the green double door shutters onto a second-floor balcony overlooking the front gateway of the compound.

Stepping back, she handed him a pair of mother-of-pearl inlaid opera glasses. "Have a look, David. See if those Turks are really the ones who helped you."

He raised the glasses to his eyes. "With their backs turned and wearing those black checkered *keffiyehs*, I can't see their faces . . . wait . . . they're turning . . . okay! The one on the left is definitely Mustafa, and the other is Yusuf. Where can we meet with them?"

"Wait here. I'll bring them to you."

After a few minutes, Anna entered the room followed by the two Turkish soldiers.

David rushed toward them and, without speaking, embraced each in turn. Fighting back tears, he raised his shoulders. "What can I say? We owe you our lives!"

"Yes," Sarah said, beaming at them. "We're so very grateful to you for helping us get away, and for everything you did for David. We can't thank you enough."

Mustafa made a little bow. "We're pleased to see you're safe and well. We were very worried we'd never see you again. Now we're just *worried* . . ."

"About what?" asked David.

"Rumors," said Yusuf. "That's why we're here. At Augusta Victoria, it's whispered that Mrs. Spafford is hiding fugitives here, and Guido von List is trying to convince the Turkish commandant to send in troops to search the compound."

"But we're an *American* institution! Anna exclaimed. "Any intrusion would be a violation of American neutrality."

"The commandant is aware of that. Especially since it's also the sultan's policy that nothing be done to provoke the United States to enter the war on the side of the Entente."

David made an audible sigh of relief. "So, there are no plans to search the compound—"

"No *current* plans," Mustafa cut in. "But Djemal Pasha will soon be coming to Jerusalem to set up headquarters at Augusta Victoria."

"Will that make things worse?" asked Sarah.

"If anything, it might be better," said Anna. "Over the years, we've had an excellent relationship with Djemal on the occasions he's visited Jerusalem. He's even gone out of his way to play with my grandson, Horatio."

David saw that the two Turkish soldiers appeared dumbstruck. "Djemal al-Saffah has played with your grandson?" Mustafa asked.

"Yes," said Anna. "What does that mean—Djemal *al-Saffah*?"

"Djemal the *butcher*." Yusuf replied. "That's how he's known among the Arabs since he's killed thousands of those he has suspected of treason against the Empire."

"How horrible!" Anna said, a hand over her heart. "I've heard such rumors, but he's always treated us kindly, and Horatio adores him." She frowned and shook her head. "And he's always appreciated and supported our work here. I just can't believe he'd allow List to raid the Colony."

Mustafa shrugged. "List can be very persuasive . . ."

"Which is why you're here," said David. "To warn us."

"Yes. Since the Turkish defeat at the Canal, Djemal is said to be dispirited and angry. In situations like this, he's known to behave erratically. He's already ordered the evacuation of all Arabs and Jews from Palestine's coastal towns and villages, and it's said that he plans to put Jerusalem under martial law. There's no telling what else he might do."

"In that case," said David, "we should prepare for the worst."

"That would be prudent," said Yusuf. "As a precaution, you should have most of your things packed and ready to go."

"Where would we go?" asked Anna.

"I've asked Gunter that very question," said David. "He has a number of ideas—"

"I'll fetch him," said Anna. Turning to the Turks, she added, "Gunter also wants to thank you for bringing the notebook with his wife's writing."

"Good, but please hurry. We must return to Augusta Victoria before anyone realizes we're not there."

❀ ❀ ❀

Alone in the commons area, Gunter paced nervously, waiting to hear if David and Sarah had been able to identify the Turks at the gate. Hearing footsteps, he turned. "Anna! Thank God! I've been so worried."

"No need to worry, Gunter. They're indeed the young men who assisted David and Sarah before you picked them up in West Jerusalem—"

"Good. But why are they here *now*?"

"They came to warn us. They believe that List might instigate a search. David told us that you had some ideas about finding safe sanctuary elsewhere. Please come, they're waiting to hear from you."

"Certainly, especially since these are the soldiers who studied Hebrew with my Rachel." He held up the notebook. "I really want to meet them. Please, Anna, lead the way."

Gunter followed her through corridors he'd never seen before to a limestone cavern where the Nathansons and the Turkish soldiers were gathered. Once Anna introduced the soldiers to Gunter, Yusuf stepped forward.

"Shalom, Gunter," he said in Hebrew with a nod at the notebook in his hand. "Mustafa and I wanted to bring that to you—from the lessons we had with your wife, Rachel. She was a wonderful and kind teacher, and we're very sorry for your loss."

"Thank you," said Gunter. "She was very impressed by the two of you—how hard you worked and how quickly you learned. I'm sure she would want you to continue your studies, so keep this as you go forward—and to remember her."

"We will." Mustafa and Yusuf nodded their thanks.

Switching to English, Gunter included Anna in the conversation. "I understand that the time has come to discuss another place of sanctuary. From my experience, *Ain Jiddy* is the best option—an oasis by the Dead Sea and home to the Rashida Bedouin. Over the years, Rahman, Fatima, and I have stayed with them during our digs near Qumran."

"I've never heard of the Rashida Bedouin or Ain Jiddy," said Sarah.

"That's what makes it ideal—few people know of it. Ain Jiddy is an island of green in an ocean of sand. Though it's only thirty miles from Jerusalem, it's a place apart—isolated and remote with poor, unpaved roads."

"How would we get there?" asked David.

"Camels," said Gunter.

"We can help with that," said Mustafa. "After the failed attack on the Suez Canal, many transport camels were brought back to Jerusalem. They're being kept in Barracks Square—not far from here. How many would you need?"

Gunter thought for a moment. "Six and a few more for baggage. Let's say ten."

"Tomorrow we'll begin bringing them, a few at a time, so as not to draw attention."

"Excellent!" said Anna. "We'll have a separate paddock for them in our stables." Turning to Gunter, she asked, "Is Tirzah old enough to have her own camel?"

"Most definitely," said Gunter.

"Excuse me," Mustafa said to Gunter. "Your daughter, Tirzah, does she by any chance have a beautiful singing voice?"

"She does. Why do you ask?"

"A few months ago, rumors began circulating at Augusta Victoria about a mysterious young girl at the American Colony Sunday gathering. It was said that she had an exquisite voice, but she'd never been seen there before, nor since."

"But how could they know that at Augusta Victoria?" asked Anna.

"You have a spy here, Mrs. Spafford," whispered Mustafa. "How many of the colony members know about the fugitives?"

"None outside of the immediate family."

"List must have learned of Tirzah from a spy in your midst. Perhaps that added fuel to his suspicion about the Colony."

Gunter nodded. "The spy must have been in contact with Montagu Walker—"

"You needn't worry about Walker anymore," said Mustafa.

"Why?"

"Walker is dead, and at the hands of List."

Gunter nodded silently, groping to understand, his mind racing. *If*

List could kill Walker, he'll truly stop at nothing—

Anna's voice cut into his thoughts. "My dears, we mustn't keep our Turkish friends away from Augusta Victoria any longer. Come! I'll guide you back to the front gate."

Gunter stepped forward. "Thank you for your kind words about Rachel, and for all you've done for us. You've put yourselves at great risk, and we're all in your debt."

"We're grateful and honored for the opportunity to help you," said Yusuf.

"And we'll find a way to warn you as soon as we hear anything of List planning to enter the Colony," said Mustafa. "We promise you that."

CHAPTER 37

February 20, 1915
Rosslyn Castle Midlothian, Scotland

WITH HARRY gone, Evan was alone in the castle. Though heavy rain had fallen through the night and well into morning, Harry had left for Edinburgh on a vague errand; *to speak with my solicitor*, was all the explanation he offered.

As Evan usually did when blustery weather buffeted Rosslyn Castle, he spent the morning sitting on a divan in the library. There, warmed by a bright fire that burned in the hearth, he studied the histories of the Crusades, the Sinclairs, and for the past few weeks, all available accounts of William Wallace.

Toward noon he was finished. Using his notes, he sat for another hour and wrote out a summary, weaving all the histories into a tapestry he believed would demonstrate the centrality of William Wallace in the Sinclair family mystery.

Researching the life of Wallace had proved challenging; almost everything about him derived from a wandering minstrel called Blind Harry who had collected songs, poems, rumors and embellished recollections into book form sometime around 1480, more than 150 years after Wallace's death. The original title of Blind Harry's book, *Actes and Deidis of the Illustre and Vallyeant Campioun Schir William Wallace*, was later and mercifully shortened to *The Wallace*. And for hundreds of years *The Wallace* was second only to the Bible as Scotland's most popular book.

Evan found it mostly unintelligible, even when presented in modern

English. Beyond that, it lacked factual detail and demonstrably included events that never happened. Notwithstanding, he had managed to piece together details of Wallace's life by supplementing *The Wallace* with English and French histories and documents.

And now he was done.

He put down his pencil, leaned back and listened to the voiceless wailing of the wind, rain pelting the windowpanes and thunder rolling over Rosslyn Glen. Looking out the window as lightning flashed within black clouds, he hoped Harry had found shelter and would soon return.

"And while I wait, I'll review my summary." Sitting forward, he read aloud. "THE CENTRAL QUESTION: could it have been William Wallace who brought two-month-old William St. Clair from Acre to Rosslyn Castle?

"FACTS ABOUT Wallace: Born 1272 in Ellerslie, a village sixty miles west of Roslin. The second son of a minor lord, Sir Malcolm Wallace, sixteen-year-old Wallace sent to study for priesthood in Scotland in 1288, then at a scriptorium in La Rochelle, France.

"FACT: La Rochelle was a seaport on the French Atlantic coast serving English and Scottish Knights Templar at the beginning of the overland route to the Mediterranean seaport of Collioure, and from there they sailed to the Holy Land.

SUPPOSITION: Since La Rochelle was full of knights bound for the Holy Land to defend Acre, Wallace would have felt the tug to join them—"

The words struck home: *the tug to join them—that memory again*! It had first surfaced when he had told Harry how Jonathan St. Clair had been drawn to join the Crusades as a teenager in Paris. "The same tug I felt to join the Great War for Civilization," he said aloud, and continued to read.

"Leaving La Rochelle with a group of knights sometime in 1289, he made the overland crossing to the Mediterranean seaport of Collioure and sailed for the Holy Land.

"FACT: Wallace was known to have loved the idea of the Holy Land and always carried a copy of the Psalms in his pocket.

"UNCERTAINTY: What did Wallace do in the Holy Land? Arriving with the Knights Templar, he probably received military training, and may have been involved in combat. Indeed, Wallace showed military expertise during the Wars of Scottish Independence.

"UNCERTAINTY: Upon arrival in Acre, Wallace might have met the Knight Templar Jonathan St. Clair since he was garrisoned there. The two of them would have been likely to connect with each other as fellow Scots. Also, since St. Clair was from Rosslyn, he might have known of Wallace's father, Sir Malcolm Wallace, who hailed from Ellerslie, only sixty miles away. Given all this, St. Clair would have seen Wallace as someone he could later trust with the parchment, with instructions about building the pyramid, and most importantly, someone he could trust with protecting his infant son and bringing him to Rosslyn Castle.

"FACT: Wallace's presence in the port city of Dundee in December 1291 is documented by an English account when he is charged with killing the son of an English constable, perhaps in revenge for his father's murder at the hands of an English knight a few months before. According to the English warrant, Wallace escaped Dundee, was declared an outlaw, and was last seen in Dunipace before disappearing from history until 1297—at the beginning of the Wars of Scottish Independence.

"UNCERTAINTY: Wallace's presence in the port city of Dundee in December of 1291 might suggest that he had recently returned from the Holy Land by ship. But would it have been possible for Wallace to leave Acre with baby William when the city fell on May 18, 1291, to disembark at the port of Nice, help other knights construct the pyramid outside Falicon, and then sail to Dundee, arriving there in late December? Using nautical maps for a galley traveling at an average speed of five knots, the sailing time from Acre on the Mediterranean coast of Palestine to the port of Nice—a distance of 1,859 nautical miles would take about sixteen days . . ."

Looking up, Evan realized that the rain had stopped, and sunlight was streaming in through the window.

He also realized that he was hungry.

He took his notes and went to the kitchen where he fried up some eggs with onions and mushrooms. He sat at the dining room table, eating while he finished reviewing his summary. As he was washing up, Harry called from the front door.

"Evan, I'm happy to report that the weather has cleared. It's a beautiful afternoon."

"And I have good news for *you*," Evan said as Harry appeared in the doorway. "I believe I've solved it!"

Harry's eyes widened. "You have?"

Evan nodded. "I'm dying to show you, but I'm also dying to go outside. Could we review my summary while we go for a walk?"

"I was hoping we might, but you'll need your rubber wellies. The roads are a mess."

"Why do you call them *wellies*?"

"In honor of the Duke of Wellington—he came up with the idea."

Once Evan pulled on his wellies, he grabbed a jacket, folded his notes and put them in his pocket. Following Harry down the hall, he asked, "How was your meeting with your solicitor in Edinburgh?"

"Fine," Harry said as they stepped into the sunlight. "I also went to the conscription center." He sat in the sun on the low wall bordering the bridge over Rosslyn Glen.

"The conscription center?" Evan asked, confused.

"I've re-enlisted for active service."

"Re-enlisted?" The news struck Evan like a blow to the chest. *What will that mean for me?* He drew a deep breath and stuttered, "But . . . but, aren't you . . . too old?"

"*Heavens* no! They're conscripting men up to forty, and I'm a lad of thirty-six." Harry patted the stones beside him. "Have a seat. Before we go for a walk, there's something I need to tell you." Once Evan was seated, Harry continued, "I had actually tried to renew my commission right after the war began, but the induction officer who interviewed me believed that my sketchy gambling history wasn't consistent with the behavior of a respectable British officer."

"What changed?" asked Evan.

"What changed?" Harry's perpetual smile faded. "The decimation of the officer corps on the Western Front. That's what changed. Now they're happy to have me."

"So . . . you'll be *leaving*?" Evan asked, alarmed at the thought.

"Yes. Tomorrow morning for orientation at Gailes Camp in the dreary moorlands north of Troon. And *you* shall be master of Rosslyn Castle!"

Evan felt bereft, panic rising in his chest, "Will you be coming back?"

"No. The camp is miles away and I'll only be there for a few weeks—training with Royal Scots Fusiliers before they ship me off to France to assume my command."

Trying to control his voice, Evan paused before he spoke. "I'm proud of you for serving, Harry, I am. But I'm *really* going to miss you." He fixed Harry with his eyes. "You're the only person I know."

Harry placed his hand on Evan's shoulder. "I thought about that in the taxi all the way from Edinburgh. But don't forget, *spring* is almost here!"

"You mean the business about the Gypsies?"

"Yes, and I must explain how you'll find the woman who might help you. But first, tell me about your solution to our family mystery."

Evan pulled the folded pages from his jacket pocket and handed them to Harry. "That's my summary. After you read it, we'll talk."

Harry read the first lines aloud, "The central question: could it have been William Wallace who brought two-month-old William St. Clair from Acre to Rosslyn Castle?" He looked at Evan and smiled. "Intriguing!"

"Read the rest to yourself, and when you're done, I want to hear what you think."

Sitting with Evan on the low wall of the stone bridge, Harry read silently.

Evan raised his face to the sun and closed his eyes. *I'm sick about him leaving. I'm afraid to be alone here and afraid for him—that he might get badly hurt or killed. But I do understand the tug he must have felt to volunteer. I must have felt it myself.*

With his hands on the warming stones, he took a deep breath of the cool air welling up from the glen below. After the long cold nights of winter with overcast days and frigid rain, the sun felt wonderful, and he was happy that spring was at hand. *When the Gypsies return to the glen, I'll meet that woman who might be able to help me come out of the night that covers me . . .*

There it was again. Familiar words that rose in his mind, words remembered from a poem he once knew, words he now recited silently: *Out of the night that covers me, black as the pit from pole to pole.* Another bit of memory to record. He took his journal from his back pocket and was writing the words down when Harry tapped his arm.

"Finished already?" Evan asked.

"Yes, and I'm thrilled by what you've done! But allow me to offer a brief critique." Harry pointed. "The narrative drags here with your calculation of nautical miles and estimated travel times. The calculations are marvelous, but you should include them as a separate addendum. The same holds true when you go into Wallace's possible routes from Dundee to Dunipace and then to Rosslyn. Interesting, but . . ."

"Boring?" Evan asked.

"Yes. That should go to an addendum as well. But your overarching *analysis* is gripping. I especially like this bit." Harry read aloud.

"Whoever brought baby William to Rosslyn Castle also brought the parchment, and that person also helped build the pyramid near Falicon since the inscription within the cave beneath the pyramid matches that on the parchment. But what is the evidence that this person was William Wallace?

"We know that baby William is listed in the genealogy as the son of Jonathan and as the adopted son of Henry, Jonathan's younger brother. From this we know that Henry trusted the person who brought baby William to Rosslyn enough to list the information he provided about Jonathan and Zahirah in the genealogy. Henry also trusted him enough to adopt baby William as his own son, making him heir to the St. Clair family fortune.

"There's also the connection between William Wallace and the St. Clairs that continued for subsequent years; the father of Jonathan and Henry, William de St. Clair served as a commander under Wallace at the Battle of Stirling Bridge in 1297. And Henry fought alongside Wallace at the Battle of Roslin in 1303, and after Wallace was executed in 1305, the St. Clairs remained true to the struggle for Scottish independence; Henry joined Robert the Bruce to defeat the English at the Battle of Loudon Hill in 1307 and at the epic battle of Bannockburn in 1314. Finally, we know that it was the grown-up baby William—William 'the Crusader' St. Clair of Rosslyn, who, after the death of Bruce in 1329, was one of the knights who died at Teba in Spain, trying to bring Bruce's heart to the Holy Land for burial.

"While all these facts point to William Wallace as the person who brought William 'the Crusader' St. Clair back to Rosslyn as an infant, a central question remains: how does a nineteen-year-old William Wallace take care of a two-month-old baby?"

"Stop here, Harry," Evan cut in. "You should know that question is still a big stumbling block for me."

Harry smiled and handed the pages back to Evan. "I may be able to help with that."

"You *can*? How?"

"Let's go down to the glen, and I'll tell you what you need to know."

They stepped from the stone bridge, carefully descended the steep slope into Rosslyn Glenn, and began walking a shaded path beneath the twisting branches of ancient yew trees. As the minutes crawled by, Evan found Harry's silence maddening. "When are you going to tell me?"

Harry paused in a patch of warm sunlight. "I will soon, but first, I have another important fact about Wallace to share with you—a persistent rumor about his secret cave somewhere here in Rosslyn Glen—a cave where Wallace took refuge during the Scottish Wars of Independence. It's supposedly on a steep cliff face on the far bank of the North Fork of the Esk, well-hidden and high above the river. Though I've never been able to find it, the Gypsies *swear* by it."

Harry placed his hand on Evan's shoulder, his eyes sparkling with pleasure. "And then there's the stumbling block which I'll remove when we speak of the Gypsies. But allow me to show you where you'll find their encampment."

Harry continued speaking as he led the way through the glen in alternating sunlight and shadow. "They'll be camped in a clearing beyond a loop of the river, which you cross here at the rope bridge. You won't be able to miss them—not with the caravans, the cooking fires, and the smell of their sheep and goats."

As they crossed, the rope bridge swayed back and forth with each of their steps. "As for Madame Shelta, she'll no doubt remember you, since you spent a good deal of time playing with the Gypsy children when you were here with your dear parents. And the best time to find her is when the clan gathers toward evening in their encampment. That will be over there, in the clearing beyond those trees."

"That's another reason I wish you weren't leaving, Harry. I'd want you to be with me when I meet Madame Shelta."

"Trust me, Evan, you wouldn't want me around when you meet Madame Shelta. I burned my bridges with her a long time ago."

"How?"

Harry shrugged and seemed embarrassed. "I hate to admit it, but I used to beg her to use her clairvoyant gifts to advise me on the horses at Kelso. Worse yet, I offered her considerable amounts of money. But she always refused. These were her exact words," he straightened up and spoke with a strange accent. "What you ask of me is sacrilege, Harry! If my gifts were to be so misused, Madame Shelta would be unworthy of having them!"

Evan laughed, then asked, "*Shelta*—what kind of a name is that?"

"An Irish Gypsy name, meaning *a voice that moves*. But the strange thing is that the clan doesn't consider themselves Irish, nor Scottish for that matter. Indeed, these Gypsies call themselves Pharaoh's People or Egyptians."

"Are they really from Egypt?" asked Evan with mounting confusion.

"So, they say—Egypt or Palestine. To be sure, many have skills known to be well developed in the Levant—silversmiths, tinkers, tin workers, and horse groomers. Shelta herself is adept at fortune telling and is very knowledgeable in the medicinal use of plants and herbs. What's also true is that as long as the Sinclairs have been here, we've had a close connection with these Gypsies. Over the centuries we've welcomed them to camp in the glen—giving them freedom to forage, hunt, and fish."

"Is that unusual?"

"Decidedly. City dwellers and landed gentry throughout Europe have regarded Gypsies with suspicion and hatred, considering them shiftless vagabonds and thieves, but not so with the Sinclairs. We've had a special bond with them for centuries."

"Why is that?"

Harry smiled. "The answer to *that* question involves that vital bit of evidence I promised you. So, listen well! These Egyptians had been the craftsmen, the nannies, the healers, the servants, and the mercenary men-at-arms of the Scottish Knights Templar in the Holy Land. When Acre fell to the Saracens, the loyalty and love between them was such that they would not be separated. Many surviving knights and their families brought the Egyptians with them out of the Holy Land, settling with them in Scotland.

Evan drew a deep breath and exhaled it with a sigh. It felt as if a veil was lifting with each word that Harry spoke. "I'm beginning to understand . . ."

"Of course, you are! These are the fruits of your research, Evan. You established that Wallace was from Ellerslie, a few days' walk from here. So, he would not only have known where to bring baby William, he would also have been able to guide the Egyptians who were in that boat that left the quay in Acre—to guide them here to Rosslyn. Wallace would also have told the St. Clairs of Rosslyn of the service these Egyptians rendered to Jonathan St. Clair and to the other Knights Templar during their long years together in the Holy Land. Because of *that,* they would have been welcomed here, as they are to this day."

"Why aren't they here now?"

"Our beastly winter weather! The Egyptians were a desert people and would have found the dark time of year in Scotland intolerable. So they migrate to southern climes in the winter and return to Rosslyn Glen in the spring."

Evan felt a sudden rush of exhilaration. "That explains it! Nineteen-year-old William Wallace *couldn't* have taken care of baby William, but there must have been an *Egyptian* wet nurse with them. *That's* how he survived!"

"Exactly," Harry whispered as he stood in the clearing with a broad smile. "You solved it, Evan. You solved it. And when spring comes to the glen, I trust you'll find Shelta, and with her help, you'll recover your memory, reclaim your past, and fully face your future with all the power and knowledge of who you are—a St. Clair! By bloodline and in your own right!"

CHAPTER 38

February 21, 1915
British Intelligence Offices, Cairo

LAWRENCE HADN'T slept well. Still dressed in his rumpled fatigues, he got up from his hotel room floor, put on his shoes, and splashed water on his face. Looking more disheveled than usual, he left the Grand Continental Hotel and headed to the Savoy.

As he walked, he took deep breaths of the still-fresh morning air, pleased by the interlude of blue sky before the bustle of human activity stirred up the dust of centuries, turning Cairo's skies a gray brown. The clear air, however, was small comfort to Lawrence given the plans afoot for British and French battleships to bombard Turkish installations followed by an assault on Gallipoli. He feared a disastrous failure.

Once in Newcombe's office, Lawrence collapsed onto the upholstered Victorian settee. "I'm sick about Gallipoli, Stewart. It's absolutely the wrong thing to do."

Behind his desk, Newcombe sat back and drew a deep breath. "I agree with you, Ned, but it's simply not our business. We have our hands full with Egypt, Arabia, and Greater Syria—not to mention Mesopotamia. Beyond the topographic maps of Gallipoli we supplied to Camp Mena, all else is quite simply beyond our charge."

"However, it will profoundly *affect* us."

"True, but you know as well as I that the War Office at White Hall is planning all aspects of the offensive."

"Damn it all, Stewart!" Lawrence sprang to his feet and pointed at the wall map behind Newcombe. "We *should* strike at Turkey, only *not* at Gallipoli, rather at *Alexandretta*!"

"Alexandretta?" Newcombe swiveled in his chair and looked up at the map. "Why would *that* be preferable to Gallipoli?"

"A *host* of reasons. Its capture would cut the Ottoman Empire in two—severing Constantinople from Syria, Palestine, and Egypt. Plus, Alexandretta is the bloody center of their railway network. Also, and this is key, it has a large Christian Arab population who would willingly join the fight for their freedom from Turkey. And more local Arab troops mean fewer British troops; and fewer British troops means fewer British dead!"

Newcombe turned back to Lawrence and shrugged his shoulders. "Have you appealed to Whitehall?"

"Of course. I wrote to Kitchener, asking him to speak with Churchill, but nothing appears to have come of it."

"What about asking Hogarth?"

"Does he have access to Churchill?"

"He does *now*. He was just promoted to lieutenant commander in the Royal Naval Volunteer Reserve. He's now based at Whitehall."

"Then I shall write to him!" He jumped off the settee. "May I borrow paper?"

Once in a small side office, Lawrence wrote:

Dear Professor Hogarth,

The Mediterranean Expeditionary Force that's been training at Camp Mena outside Cairo will soon be off to Gallipoli, and I'm sick about it! I fear the MEF will be beastly ill prepared. Newcombe and I have taken pity and sent them maps, but I fear it won't end well. As I've told anyone who will listen, the best place to attack Turkey would be at Alexandretta. It's the hub of the Baghdad Railway line, its port is the natural outlet for the northern reaches of Syria and Mesopotamia, and it's the only place from which a fleet might operate against us in Egypt and the Canal. It's therefore crucial we take Alexandretta and its harbor.

I've written K of K about this matter with all rational arguments, asking him to convey this singular message to Churchill: To defeat the Ottoman Empire, Alexandretta must be the point of attack, not Gallipoli! However, Winston seems hell-bent on this wrong-headed approach. It appears he's deferring to our French allies, apparently afraid of hurting their feelings, since the French insist that Greater Syria is their show, their "sphere of influence," perhaps based on romantic notions of their thirteenth-century Crusader legacy in the region.

I'm hoping you might intercede—perhaps lubricate a shift in his opinion with the promise of oil! Though I personally consider oil detestable stuff, tell Winston that it would be simple to tap into the oil reserves of Alexandretta since it's already been advised on by engineers, though the Turks have refused to grant drilling concessions. Also, let Winston know that it's a splendid natural naval base. If Churchill settles on a thing, he gets it, and I can only hope that, with your gentle nudging, he'll change his mind.

I'm certain we could occupy Alexandretta with only ten thousand men, since there would be more than forty thousand local Arab troops who would be happy to fight on their own land, for their own homes, and for their own freedom. In that way, a victory at Alexandretta would hand over much of Syria to the native Arab population—a thing that ties in nicely with a general Arab rebellion, though I do realize it will enrage the French.

I believe the logic is overwhelming. A successful attack at Alexandretta will cut the Ottoman Empire in two, severing communication between Turkey and her southern reaches: Syria, Palestine, Arabia, and Mesopotamia. It would also compel the Turks to immediately dispatch reinforcements from Gallipoli to Alexandretta, where they'll fritter themselves away against the

Arabs and not against us. And THAT would be the moment for the Dardanelles naval assault.

In your conversations with Winston, please try and push it through because I think it's our only chance. I hope my letter is clear, but I dashed this off in such a sweat, I had no time to think!

With Salaams,
TEL

Finished writing, Lawrence returned to Newcombe's office. "Already done?" he asked as Lawrence strode in.

Lawrence nodded as he folded the pages and put them on Newcombe's desk. "Please make sure this goes out in the very next diplomatic pouch." He sighed as he sat back on the settee. "The other reason I'm out of sorts, Stewart, is that I haven't heard from Weizmann about meeting with Faisal."

"Weizmann?" Newcombe repeated the name. "That Jewish chemist with connections at Whitehall?"

"Yes. Faisal was very receptive to our offer of British support and to the notion of receiving support from the Zionists. You remember—we sent out the letter from Faisal along with my note to Weizmann right after I got back from Sinai." Lawrence blew out a discouraged breath. "I would have hoped to have heard from him by now . . ."

"Come now, Ned—that was just three weeks ago. Even letters sent by courier must contend with U-boats and travel restrictions."

"I know, but there are arrangements to be made for Weizmann's meeting with Faisal in Aden . . ."

"When's that supposed to happen?"

"May 5."

"My word, Ned—you've got plenty of time. I'm sure you'll hear from him soon."

CHAPTER 39

February 21, 1915
Whitehall, London

After two quick knocks on the mapping room door, Clive heard the voice of one of the scouts.

"Captain Sinclair, Colonel Hedley wishes to see you in his office."

"Thank you," Clive called back. He grabbed his cap and headed for the door, his heart pounding in anticipation of what he might hear from Hedley. *Perhaps news of Evan.*

Pushing open the door of MO-4, he went straight to Hedley's office and tapped on the upper section of frosted glass. "Captain Sinclair to see you, sir."

"Come in!" Hedley's voice boomed out.

Clive opened the door to find the colonel sitting behind his desk, beaming. "Is this about my son, Colonel?" Clive asked with an upwelling of hope.

"I'm afraid not, Sinclair—it's about your transfer—it just came through." Hedley gestured toward one of the upholstered chairs in front of the desk. "Have a seat." Leaning back, he tented his fingers together. "Actually, what you have is an *interview* about your new assignment."

"An interview, sir?" *What the hell? A transfer doesn't require an interview . . .*

"Yes—tomorrow morning at 0900 hours."

Confused, Clive asked, "And where is this interview to take place, sir?"

"I'm not at liberty to tell you."

"Is it here at Whitehall?" he asked with growing exasperation.

"Yes, but I can't tell you where."

"And you can't tell me where because . . . ?"

"Because I don't know where the interview will be held."

Taken aback, Clive asked, "Do you know what my new assignment is, sir?"

"I do, but I can't tell you." Hedley sat forward. "Damn it all, Sinclair, with everything you've been through, I'm finding this very difficult, quite bizarre really . . ."

"I appreciate your candor, sir, but I'd very much like to know what the job is!"

"And I want to tell you because I want you to get the bloody job. I know how much you want to remain here at Whitehall—it's the ideal place for you to contribute to the war effort and to search for your son."

"Correct, sir. So please tell me what the job is." Clive couldn't hide his frustration. After a moment's hesitation, Hedley sat forward and whispered, "The Foreign Section of the Secret Service Bureau."

"The Secret Service Bureau, sir? I've never heard of it."

"Almost no one has," Hedley held an index finger in front of his mouth. "It's all very hush-hush—exceedingly classified. The government denies that the Bureau even exists. It began about six years ago—an initiative of the Admiralty and the War Office to keep an eye on German aspirations to challenge us on the seas—"

Clive frowned. "Let me make certain I heard you correctly, sir—I'm to interview at an unknown location for an unknown job at an agency that doesn't officially exist . . ."

"That's the size of it. But I *can* tell you that the Bureau is known by two other names—MI-1 or C's organization."

"'*C's organization*'? Who's C?"

"C is the last initial of the director, Major Mansfield George Smith-Cumming—affectionately known as C."

"So," Clive said slowly, "C will be my new boss."

"Yes, but *only* if you get through the interview with him tomorrow."

"Why would that be a problem, sir?"

When Hedley didn't respond, Clive asked, "Is there anything you might tell me that might be helpful?"

"There is, Clive. I really should tell you something about him—no secrets, mind you, just information." Hedley stood up and began to pace. "C served as captain in the Royal Navy, saw action in Egypt and against the pirates of Malay. But he had a bit of a problem—severe seasickness—an unfortunate malady for a sea captain. He was ultimately deemed unfit for service."

"So, he was reassigned to the secret bureau?" Clive asked.

"Yes, and apparently, he's done a smashing job. However, there are a few things you should know about him for your interview tomorrow. For starters, he uses a gold monocle, and though it looks rather amusing, he hates when people stare at it."

"Duly noted, sir. I won't stare."

"Also, he had a serious road accident in France about a year ago— terrible, really— his son was killed and both of C's legs were broken, one so badly it had to be amputated below the knee. He was fitted with a wooden leg and gets about with a cane."

"So, I shouldn't stare at his leg."

"Yes, but that's not it." Hedley stopped pacing. "C has a novel way of interviewing prospective agents. First off, during the interview, he'll be sitting opposite you, and there will be no mention that the conversation is about a job in the Secret Service Bureau."

"Right. Since it doesn't officially exist."

"Correct. C will go on and on with a bunch of bureaucratic mumbo-jumbo for about ten minutes, when suddenly, in midsentence and without warning, he'll violently stab himself in his wooden leg with a penknife."

"What?" Clive asked, barely able to stifle a laugh. "Why would he *do* that?"

"That's the test, Clive! C calls it the *flinch test*. He'll be watching your reaction. If you flinch, the interview is over. You'll be asked to leave, and you won't get the job, because C believes that flinchers aren't secret agent material."

"And if I don't flinch?" Clive asked, unable to believe what he was hearing.

"If you keep your composure, he'll reveal to you the true nature of the interview as well as the existence of the agency. In a word, you get the job."

"Thanks for telling me, sir." Clive raised his shoulders. "I would have flinched."

"Who *wouldn't*? It's a completely natural response. C apparently finds it so amusing he's taken to doing it during regular staff meetings."

Clive smiled. "Is there anything else I should know?"

"I suppose—that cane I mentioned?"

"The one he uses to walk, sir?"

"Yes. He's got a very sharp sword inside the cane, so if he draws it, I should get away double quick."

"Will do, sir!"

"Just make sure you're there at 0900 hours."

"W*here*, sir?"

"At the Secret Service Bureau at Whitehall."

"Is there a room number?"

"I believe that's—"

"A secret, sir?" asked Clive.

"Yes, but I shouldn't worry about that—he'll find *you*."

CHAPTER 40

February 28, 1915
American Colony, Jerusalem

ANNA SPAFFORD awoke to frantic knocking on her bedroom door. She groped for the box of matches on the table by her bed, lit the candle in her lantern holder and checked the time. It wasn't yet six o'clock. The knocking came again, insistent.

"Who is it?" she called out and rolled out of bed.

"Lewis Larson, Mrs. Spafford. I'm sorry to disturb you, but it's an emergency!"

Lewis had come to the Colony more than twenty years before as a young boy with his family from Sweden. Now the Colony's photographer, Anna knew him to be a steady and meticulous young man, not one given to anxious outbursts.

She pulled on her robe and opened the door. In the candlelight, she saw that he was wearing a knapsack over his jacket. "What's going on, Lewis?"

"I was photographing in *Wadi al-Qilt* yesterday, when I heard a strange sound—like the rumble of ocean waves. I thought there might be a flash flood through the wadi, but there hadn't been any rain. Then I noticed that the sound was coming from above. I looked up and saw swarms of locust! A few fell to the ground dead." He held out his hand. "Look."

Anna raised the lantern to examine the three large grasshoppers in his hand and asked, "Where were you exactly?"

"At *Ayn Fara*, the upper spring in *Wadi al-Qilt*. There were so many—in thick clouds that covered the sky and blocked out the sun. I took some photographs and after an hour, they moved off to the southwest. I knew I had to get word to you about this, so I packed up my things and made my way out of the wadi. When the sun set, I was able to keep walking since the moon was almost full, and I came straight here."

"You did well, Lewis. Come. Let's get you some breakfast." She took her lantern and led the way down the hallway. "As soon as it's light, we'll spread word in Jerusalem about this locust visitation."

"Has this ever happened before?"

"About every ten years, but rarely bad enough to call them a plague. The last locust plague was about fifty years ago—before I arrived in Jerusalem. I heard it was terrible—vineyards and orchards were stripped bare, and all the melons, grain, and vegetables were consumed. Even the date palms weren't spared."

Reaching the kitchen, Anna put down the lantern. "If you saw a locust cloud that darkened the sky for an hour, this one will be bad." She lit the stove and continued speaking. "If you saw them in *Wadi al-Qilt*, they could be here within the next few days, so we'll need to work quickly. With first light, you'll inform the Spanish Consul Ballobar so he'll be able to get word to all the other consular authorities in Jerusalem. We'll send others to spread the word among the merchants and farmers in and around Jerusalem. I'll send a note by courier to Djemal Pasha and schedule to meet with him later today."

"What can the farmers do, Mrs. Spafford?" Lewis asked as he collapsed into a chair in the kitchen. Anna could see he was exhausted.

"They must harvest what they can and protect whatever they can't harvest. Smoke fires around their fields will keep the locusts at bay. Djemal will use the army to help farmers and to alert merchants. I'll also let him know that we'll need help with the soup kitchen—the poor of Jerusalem are already starving; this will just make matters worse."

"But, surely, Mrs. Spafford, the locusts will eat and move on."

"No, Lewis. This is only the beginning. After the adult locusts feed, each of the females will lay about a hundred eggs, and when they hatch, there will be *millions* of larvae crawling over the ground and eating as they become adults. I've heard that this becomes literally a tide of larvae, and they'll consume everything in their path—all remaining plants as well as any animal or person unable to escape them."

"How long will this go on?"

"For months. Our only hope is to work together—to save and protect food stores and crops, and to find and destroy the locust eggs before they hatch. This will require the participation of all people of Jerusalem—Turks, Christians, Arabs, Jews, Armenians—everyone. This is the war that matters now. We can't stop the plague from happening—we can only hope to shorten it."

Setting eggs to boil, Anna patted Lewis on the back. "You've done well in giving us early warning, my boy, so after you bring word to the Spanish consul, come back here and get some sleep.

"How can I sleep at a time like this?"

Anna smiled. "Don't worry. If you can't sleep, I'll find more for you to do."

CHAPTER 41

February 28, 1915
Camp Mena, Outskirts of Cairo

LIEUTENANT COLONEL Richard Doughty-Wylie looked at the Great Pyramid looming over the tent city of Camp Mena and thought, *Such a lovely plan. Pity it won't work.*

Throughout the morning the commander of the Australian Imperial Force, Field Marshal William Birdwood, had provided details of the naval bombardment of Gallipoli that had been going on for a week with long-range British and French naval guns shelling fortified Turkish positions. The Entente battleships would soon sail from the Aegean, through the Dardanelles, and into the Sea of Marmara. Assuming all went smoothly, the ships would approach Constantinople at the mouth of the Bosporus, and the big guns would be leveled on the Ottoman capital. At this point it was expected that the Turks would capitulate and sue for peace.

But Richard didn't believe these optimistic expectations. Not for a second. From his years of service as British vice-consul in Turkey, he knew the Turks to be judicious and careful in military matters, and he feared that the Dardanelles would be heavily mined. *The naval assault will stall,* he thought with a heavy sigh. *The narrow straits of the Dardanelles will be our own dreadful version of Scylla and Charybdis.*

He also feared that the British contingency plan, with ground troops in a full amphibious landing at Gallipoli, would be a disastrous failure... *a bloodbath, God help us!*

But that wasn't the only troubling issue on Richard's mind as he stood outside the mess tent. He turned his eyes from the Great Pyramid to look down at the neat tent rows of Camp Mena. Then he looked down at Gertrude Bell's unopened letter in his hand—newly arrived with the morning mail call. Since the rendezvous with Gertrude in London had not gone well, he was in no hurry to read her letter.

Heading toward his tent, he descended a low hill dotted with scrub brush, nodding and smiling at the high-spirited greetings from Australian troops—one of them playing with their platoon mascot, a baby kangaroo. Calls of "*You right, sir?*" "*G'day, mate,*" and "*How's it going, sir?*" filled the morning air. Morale was high, the atmosphere in camp almost festive.

Pushing through the flaps of his tent, Richard tossed Gertrude's letter onto his bunk, loosened his tie, and sat down. He looked at the envelope and sighed.

After years of passion-filled correspondence, his expectations for the meeting were high, and he now understood that no simple reality could possibly measure up. Indeed, after three days and nights, there had been no consummation—Gertrude had been unable or unwilling to give herself to him.

He sighed as he reflected on his high expectations. He had selected the Hotel Monte Carlo based on its elegance and close, but not-too-close, proximity to Whitehall. On the day she arrived, he had risen early, bathed, dressed, breakfasted, and whiled away the hours trying, without much success, to read a book he'd brought along: *Geographic Features of the Gallipoli Peninsula*. Given his imminent deployment, it seemed a good choice.

On hearing an automobile pull to the curb, he had looked out the window to see Gertrude alight from a taxi. Pacing back and forth in the foyer of his room, he had waited—to kiss her at the door, draw her forward, close the door after hanging the *Do Not Disturb* sign on the knob, and take her in his arms.

Now, as he sat alone on his bunk in Egypt, he shook his head. *I should have left the hotel without seeing her.*

He tore open the envelope and read.

My Dearest Richard,

I've had time to reflect on our meeting, and I wish to bring some clarity to what, at the time, was inexplicable. When you greeted me at the door of our hotel room, I was enraptured, more certain than ever that you were everything I wanted in a man—intelligent and understanding, gentle and caring, protective and strong. I took refuge in your arms, and as we embraced my smoldering dreams burst into flame. With your lips against mine, I nestled against your muscular body.

You told me that I was life itself, a fire that burned with passion.

You told me that you needed me, that you hungered for me, and I listened in ecstasy. More than anything, I wanted to give myself to you, and I willingly began to yield.

But then, as I later told you, a force even stronger than the desire burning inside me, rose up and held me back. In a panic, I recoiled. But again my yearning for you overwhelmed me and we embraced again and kissed, again and again. But once more the force rose up and held me back.

I want to explain it to you, my darling—the fear, the terror of it.

Every time it surged up, I wanted you to brush it aside. It was only a ghost, the shadow of a ghost. I wanted you to exorcise it, but I couldn't tell you then, because I wasn't certain. Only now can I see clearly. Only now do I know that you and only you can free me from it—drive it from me.

Now listen, my love—I won't write to you like this again. If you want me, you must obtain a divorce and marry me. If you want me for a lifetime, you will have me. It's that or nothing. If you only desire me for an hour, it cannot be. We know that now.

I would have you, before all the world, claim me and hold me forever and ever. Furtiveness I hate! In the end I should go under and hate myself and die. I can't live without you. But not the other way. Not to deceive and lie and cheat, and at the last be found out. If it's honor you think of, this is honor, and the other dishonor. If it's faithfulness you think of, this is faithfulness. And I beg you, keep faith with love.

And oh, for the greatest gift to you—a greater gift even than love—the divine pledge of fulfillment, a child created in rapture—the handing on of life in fire, to be cherished and worshipped and lived for!

Please don't miss the fire that burns in this letter—a clear flame, a bright flame fed by my life. Oh, my dear, it might be ecstasy.

There is an eternal secret between you and me. No one has known, no one will ever know, the woman who loves you. Mind and body, a different creature from she who walks the common earth before the eyes of men—newborn and new fashioned out of our joined love. Only you know her and have seen her. You gave her life, but I made her, bone by bone. I ask you now to be without fear and to scorn convention with me, ignore the stigma of divorce. Marry me and be with me. It's that or nothing. I can't live without you. I would that you love me without fear.

And, my dearest love, you will.
Gerty

Richard put the letter down, lay back and closed his eyes.

Life in the desert was simple and he was glad to be away from Gertrude's complexity. After years of an increasingly intimate correspondence, and after their unconsummated meeting, he was exhausted and at his wits' end. His wife had warned him she would kill herself if he left her, and Gertrude had warned him she would kill herself if he didn't leave his wife.

Resting on his bunk, he considered the narrow straits he was navigating, and the Dardanelles and Straits of Messina again came to mind—the latter with the lurking terrors of Scylla and Charybdis. Shaking the image away, he sat up. *What a perfectly appalling metaphor!*

He checked his wristwatch and saw that it was almost eleven o'clock.

Time to review contingency plans for the ground assault with a company of the Australian Light Horse.

Pushing up from his bunk, another unbidden thought rose in his mind.

A consummation devoutly to be wished . . .

What the hell is that supposed to mean? he thought as he hurried out of the tent to meet with the Australian Light Horse officers.

But in his heart of hearts, he knew exactly what it meant.

CHAPTER 42

February 28, 1915
Jerusalem

THOUGH ALMOST a month had passed since the failed attack on the Suez Canal, Djemal Pasha was still seething, his anger even now white-hot. Newly arrived in Jerusalem from Gaza, he flung his suitcase onto the bed in his suite at the Augusta Victoria Hospice and pummeled the valise with his riding crop. "Idiots!" he shouted, "What a humiliating catastrophe!"

Still wearing his gray uniform, he slumped on the edge of the bed, twisted the riding crop in his hands and stared at his black woolen fez that had fallen to the floor. *All the months of careful preparation, all the meticulous plans to cross the Sinai undetected, the careful construction of pontoons to cross the Canal, fifteen thousand troops poised to attack from the east, with thousands of Muslims within the British ranks ready to heed the call to holy war and attack from the rear . . .*

He couldn't stop reviewing the events in his mind; the soaring optimism during the months of painstaking planning, the precise coordination of engineers tapping wells for the oncoming troops, building rainwater reservoirs, laying in depots of ammunition, using teams of oxen to haul heavy artillery and pontoon bridges, twelve thousand camels ferrying supplies; a perfectly coordinated 120-mile crossing of the Sinai.

And in the end, a colossal failure!

His fury erupted again, and he sprang to his feet, shouting and striking the suitcase with the riding crop again and again, thrashing it with every few words.

"I *spoke* to the troops every *night* about the victory in store. What a *glorious* victory it would be, nothing less than the complete *liberation* of Islam from British *imperialism!*" The riding crop snapped with the last blow. Exhausted, he flung away the fragments, collapsed onto the bed, and buried his face in his hands.

Somehow, they knew we were there. But how could they have known?

He turned onto his back and stared at the ceiling. In his mind's eye he again saw the engineers assembling the pontoon bridges at the water's edge, infantry massed behind ready to charge across. Then the sudden glare of British searchlights, and the roar of pounding artillery.

He closed his eyes, but the images remained; pontoon bridges splintered, soldiers who had crossed over now cut off, the thunder of exploding British shells, thousands on the eastern bank seeking cover, scores of dead, cries of the wounded, and finally the confused retreat.

With a bitter laugh, he sat up, rubbed his eyes, and remembered the rosy predictions of widespread Muslim support for the sultan's call to jihad. But that, and all the pamphlets and radio broadcasts had yielded no deserters. Worse yet, most of the Turkish Army's Arab units fled as soon as the shooting began, and their Bedouin guides vanished into the desert.

So much for the pan-Islamic jihad against the imperial infidels!

But, beneath his anger about the Canal debacle was Djemal's unspoken rage at the kaiser for having tricked them into the war—how Wilhelm had directed the German officers of the two battle cruisers flying Turkish flags to attack Russian Black Sea ports ending Ottoman neutrality. He shook his head. *But what's the use thinking about that? Even though the reason for going to war was a shameless hoax, now we're in it!*

With a sigh, he stood, picked his fez off the floor, and put it on his head. He straightened his uniform and began to unpack.

It vexed him that he was obliged to obey Kressenstein and remain in Jerusalem and closer to the Southern Front rather than return to Damascus. *But I suppose it makes sense, and he did sweeten the proposition by giving me his Mercedes staff car.*

As Djemal finished unpacking, he began to feel better. He considered that the Canal disaster was not without some positive results; by calling off the engagement when he did, he kept the Fourth Army intact to fight another day. And the threat of another Suez attack forced the British to keep more troops in Egypt, making fewer available for Gallipoli.

A knock on the door interrupted his thoughts and, to his consternation, the door opened without his sanction. An old man with a bushy beard and a formless cap over wild hair leaned into the room, eyes invisible behind sunlight reflecting off round spectacles.

"Is this a bad time?" he asked in German-accented English.

"Who are you, sir, that you dare invade my private quarters?"

"My apologies, Excellency." The man stepped into the room and bowed. "I'm Guido von List. The kaiser told me to expect you, and bid you welcome."

Reassured but wary, Djemal replied, "Thank you, Herr List. General Kressenstein has spoken to me of your valuable role, and I would hear further details. Let's have lunch together and talk."

"Excellent!" said List as he lingered in the doorway, craning his scrawny neck and looking about the residence.

"If you don't mind, Herr List, I need to get settled."

"Of course, General. Shall we meet in the dining room at about noon?"

"That would be fine."

List left and drew the door closed.

Djemal frowned. *Given the apparent connection of this irritating old fool with the kaiser, how do I assert my authority?*

❖ ❖ ❖

Guido von List stood outside the dining room waiting for Djemal Pasha and checked his timepiece. *How ironic! The Übermensch waits upon the Untermensch!*

Looking up, he saw him approaching, short in stature with a striking black beard and upturned mustache. List shook his head. *With the braided epaulets on his shoulders and the sword at his side, he could pass for a short tenor in a bad opera.*

"Your Excellency, I'm so glad you are able to join me." List bowed. "I'm certain you'll find the cuisine here outstanding. And if you don't mind a Russian dish, I recommend the Beef Stroganoff!"

The men shared a laugh as List led the way through the main dining area filled with tables and a smattering of diners. "This section serves the general public—the *sans-culottes*," he remarked in a barely concealed stage whisper. Grasping the ornate balustrade of the staircase, he mounted the steps. "Private dining rooms on the mezzanine are reserved for royalty and members of state—with commanding views of Jerusalem."

"Thank you, Herr List. It's very gracious of you to welcome me to the hospice. General von Kressenstein has spoken highly of the Augusta Victoria, as he has of you, and I'm anxious to hear of your efforts."

"Your Excellency, it's an honor to serve the Fatherland and to support our common goals in alliance with the Ottoman Empire."

On the landing, a waiter in formal attire and a red fez bowed. "Your dining room is ready, Herr List." He led the way to a door along the landing, opening it with a flourish. "Please make yourselves comfortable and peruse the menu. I shall return—"

"No, my good man," List cut him off, "I'll order *now*. We'll share a half liter of the Radeberger Pilsner, and we'll each have the Beef Stroganoff."

"Very well, Herr List."

Enjoying Djemal's vexed expression at his having arrogated ordering lunch, List smiled. "After you, Your Excellency." He watched Djemal walk stiffly to an expansive window, which occupied the entire west-facing wall of the private dining room, where he stood, looking out over the Kidron Valley and the walled city.

"Magnificent!" Djemal exclaimed. "I've never seen Jerusalem from such a height. The Mosque of Omar within the Sacred Precinct is quite impressive. And those buildings to the north . . . is that the American

Colony compound?"

"It is, sire, and I indeed wish to speak with you about the Colony." List waved a hand toward the table. "Please, Your Excellency, let's get down to business."

Once they were seated, he fixed Djemal with his eyes. "General, allow me to be blunt. Kaiser Wilhelm is very concerned about a fifth column that infects your empire in Syria and Palestine. Subversives poison the attitude of an otherwise compliant populace against us. This situation will create very serious difficulties for us during the current war." As List spoke, he raised his voice. "It is imperative that this infestation be *eradicated!*" He smacked the table with his hand, rattling the flatware.

Djemal shot up to his feet, but before he could respond, the dining room door opened, and the waiter entered with a tray.

"Your Radeberger Pilsner, my masters." He began to pour.

"Herr List," Djemal whispered through clenched teeth, "I don't require suggestions from you or anyone else as to how to maintain order in my domains—"

"*Suggestions*, my dear General?" List cut him off, raising his hand to suspend further conversation until the waiter left the room. Once he was gone, List continued, "These are not suggestions. These are *directives* that come straight from Kaiser Wilhelm himself. It is vital that you maintain order."

"Maintain order?" Djemal snarled. "I am known to the Arabs as 'the Butcher'! I don't require a lecture from you about how to handle traitors. I've virtually eliminated all Arab nationalists, bringing them by trainloads to Damascus for public hangings!"

List raised his hands in mock surrender and did his best to smile. *Now that I've put the apeling in his place, it's time for flattery.* "My apologies, Your Excellency! The kaiser is, overall, pleased with your efforts, which is the reason he wonders why you haven't gone further—to *other* subversive elements. But now, if it pleases Your Excellency, let us drink a toast." He stood up and raised his glass.

Still standing, Djemal snatched his glass off the table.

"To the good health of the kaiser and his royal consort, the German empress, queen of Prussia, and namesake of this wonderful edifice, the Kaiserin Augusta Victoria." List drank down the glass in a few swallows, watching Djemal take a sip.

Wiping beer from his mustache, List added, "Lest you take offense, Excellency, please be reassured—the kaiser is *very* pleased by much of what you have accomplished here. He, of course, extends his condolences on your recent defeat at the Suez Canal and is certain that, with the help of General Kressenstein, your fortunes will improve. However, as I already mentioned, the kaiser remains concerned about *other* elements—"

"*What* other elements?" Djemal cut in as he sat down.

To his satisfaction, List noted a petulance in Djemal's tone. He paused to pour himself another glass of beer. "More for you?" he asked.

Djemal shook his head.

List repeated Djemal's question, "What other elements?" He looked at him through his spectacles and made a little shrug. "The Armenians. The kaiser believes you should begin with them. Make an example of them for the others—the Jews, Assyrians, and Kurds. Start with the Armenians—they humiliated your troops in Val and did so to help the Russians, which has impeded us on the Eastern Front. The kaiser insists they pay for this treason. He believes that the misdeeds of Armenians *anywhere* is the responsibility of Armenians *everywhere*—especially in Palestine, where they will likely rise against us at the first opportunity. Therefore, the kaiser wants you to start with them."

"You should know, sir, that I've already communicated my plans for the Armenians to the kaiser. I will now put them into action."

"When?"

"This very afternoon. Armenian men are already doing forced labor, and I will now have them removed from their homes and moved into work camps. We will then evict the women, children, and old ones from the Armenian Quarter—moving them to camps close to the Turkish border where we can keep an eye on them."

"Excellent!" List exclaimed. "The kaiser will be pleased by your decisive action." He took a sip of beer and nodded toward the American Colony compound. "As for the Americans, Your Excellency, we have pressing business."

"Pressing business with a few American Christians? I should think our armed struggle with the Triple Entente would be pressing enough—"

"Don't make light of our concerns, Excellency. We believe the Americans harbor fugitives we must acquire and interrogate."

"Herr List," Djemal replied. "You're obviously unaware that the kaiser and I have communicated specifically about the Colony. Neither of us wishes to create a diplomatic incident that would bring America into the war against us."

"Certainly not. There's no question about that."

Djemal appeared to study the glass in his hand before he spoke. "I may have a way to enter the Colony without ruffling American feathers. As we speak, we are moving many of our wounded from Gaza to Jerusalem for hospital care—many to the American Colony. It would be entirely appropriate for me to conduct a full inspection of the Colony before our soldiers are admitted to determine the condition of their hospital."

I'm impressed by the apeling's initiative! List thought and exclaimed, "Wonderful, Your Excellency!" When might you conduct such an inspection?"

"Tomorrow. Would that be soon enough?"

"Indeed!"

"However," Djemal continued, "to avoid offending American sensibilities, I will communicate in writing with the Colony's founder, Mrs. Anna Spafford, beforehand—"

"Quite out of the question!" List cut in. "If she is forewarned, our rats will escape." He took a sip of beer and watched Djemal stroke his beard as he seemed to be formulating a reply.

Leaning forward, Djemal said, "An unannounced and sudden intrusion into the Colony is precisely the type of incident the kaiser wishes to avoid. However, there is a way to do this without allowing your rats to escape. I'll pen a personal note to Mrs. Spafford, explaining the need to conduct an inspection, and send it by courier early tomorrow morning. I'll indicate that her consent to inspect the Colony should be immediately conveyed to the courier. Even if she is harboring fugitives, I'm certain she'll agree, believing that she'll have time to warn them and facilitate their escape before I arrive. However," Djemal leaned further forward. "We'll already *be there*—having arrived with three platoons *before* the courier's arrival. We'll take up positions out of sight, surrounding the Colony while she's reading my friendly note. Once the courier steps away, we'll wait a few minutes, then appear with a few soldiers at the Colony gates to conduct our inspection in a very respectful, though thorough manner. In the meantime, all other soldiers will maintain a perimeter. If there are fugitives that attempt to escape, they'll be easily apprehended—either by us within the Colony or by the large force surrounding it." Djemal took a swallow of beer and asked, "Would that be acceptable, Herr List?"

"It would, Your Excellency!" List exclaimed and thought, *What a clever apeling—able to solve complex problems. He must have Aryan blood . . .*

The door opened, and the waiter pushed a serving cart forward. "Lunch is served, my masters." He set the plates before them and withdrew.

"Gutten Appetit!" said List and stabbed a chunk of beef with his fork. But before bringing it to his mouth, there was a tap at the door. "What is it now?" he shouted.

The door opened and a Turkish soldier announced, "I have an urgent communiqué for His Excellency, Djemal Pasha."

List watched as Djemal took the sealed envelope, opened it and, after glancing at it, tucked the communiqué into a pocket of his uniform.

"Have my staff come to my office in thirty minutes," Djemal said to the soldier.

"Something important?" asked List, the chunk of beef and a large noodle suspended on the fork inches from his mouth.

"Quite! There have been locust sightings east of here. We'll need to mobilize to fight yet another enemy."

Concerned that the raid on the American Colony might be delayed, List snapped. "That's all well, Your Excellency, but I insist we move forward with the Colony inspection as planned. Are we in agreement?" he asked and stuffed the forkful into his mouth.

"Absolutely. As I plan our defense against the locusts, I will also put our plans for the Armenians into action, and early tomorrow morning we'll descend upon the Colony."

"Good! I look forward to informing the kaiser of all your efforts to exterminate all the insects infesting Jerusalem!"

※ ※ ※

Once back in his office, Djemal's hands shook with rage as he took the note from Anna Spafford from his pocket. *Given the manner List sticks his nose into my affairs, I should be thankful he didn't demand to see this. As the kaiser's personal representative in Jerusalem, he clearly fancies himself my master. At the same time, he pretends to be subservient.* He sighed and shook his head. *I have no patience for this eggshell dance—it makes matters more difficult than they already are!*

He reread the note from Anna Spafford alerting him to a locust sighting in Wadi al-Qilt, and reporting steps she had already taken—warning foreign consular authorities and contacting merchants and farmers about protecting goods, crops, and grain stores.

There's no time to waste. He shouted to his secretary, "Come here please. I have an urgent dispatch to send by courier."

Once the secretary was ready, and with a courier standing by, Djemal dictated a note to Anna. He thanked her for reporting the locust sighting and for her initial efforts and told her he was mobilizing the army along similar lines. He also indicated that they would soon meet to coordinate further measures. As the courier departed, he thought, *Of course, I'll wait until tomorrow morning to inform her about inspecting the Colony—*

"Will there be anything else, Your Excellency?" the secretary asked.

Djemal thought for a moment, then smiled to himself. *What a sublime idea! I shall contact the Jewish agricultural expert in Atlit, Aaron Aaronsohn, about dealing with the locust plague. And by involving a Jew, I'll infuriate List!* Turning to his secretary, he said, "Yes. I want you to send an urgent cable."

He proceeded to dictate a communiqué to Aaronsohn, informing him of the looming locust plague and inviting him to Jerusalem with an offer to serve the Ottoman Empire as scientific consultant for management of the plague.

As he finished dictating the cable, his senior staff arrived at his office. Rising to begin the meeting, he smiled inwardly. *Two can engage in this eggshell dance!*

CHAPTER 43

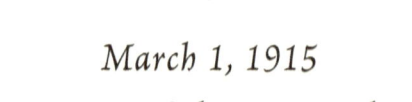

March 1, 1915
American Colony, Jerusalem

IN NORMAL times, visitors didn't come to the gate in the middle of the night. But these weren't normal times.

Anna Spafford startled at the knocking on her bedroom door but was reassured upon hearing the voice of the Colony member on guard duty.

"Mrs. Spafford?"

Anxious about the impending locust threat, she was already awake and dressed.

Opening the door, she asked, "Have the locusts arrived?"

"No. But there's someone at the gate who insists on speaking with you."

"Who is it?"

"I don't know, but he sounds like an American. I told him you were asleep, but he said it was urgent. What shall I tell him?"

"Nothing. Go back to your rounds. I'll go to the gate myself."

I'm certain it's one of the Turkish soldiers who attended that American high school in Constantinople—they all come out speaking like Americans, Anna thought as she put on a coat and hurried out of her room.

At the gate, she looked through wrought iron bars into the shadows of the fan palms beneath cypress and olive trees. She couldn't see anyone. "Who's there?" she whispered.

"Mrs. Spafford?"

Certain it was one of the Turkish soldiers, she whispered, "Mustafa? Yusuf?"

"Mustafa."

"What is it?"

"Guido von List and Djemal Pasha are coming to search the Colony later this morning. The fugitives must leave quickly and leave no trace they were ever here."

"But he sent me a note yesterday about the locust sightings, and he didn't mention a word about a visit. Does he know you're here?"

"It was Djemal who sent me."

"How much time do we have?"

"Two hours, and you should know that, a few minutes before his arrival, a courier will come with a letter from Djemal requesting your permission to inspect the Colony. Your guests should leave now." And with a quick movement of shadow in the darkness, he was gone.

Anna went straightaway to the hidden apartments, and went from door to door, knocking. "Wake up! Quickly my dears! Quickly!"

They emerged from their rooms in dressing gowns and were all soon gathered in the commons area.

"Is it locusts?" Gunter asked.

"No. Not yet. It was Mustafa with a warning. Djemal Pasha and Guido von List will be here in two hours to search the Colony. So, my dears, the time has come for you to leave." Anna paused, fighting back tears. "We'll help move out the beds and other furnishings. Anything you leave behind will go into the furnace, since they mustn't find any trace that you were *ever* here. Bertha will bring you the Bedouin clothing we bought for your journey and Frederick and my son Jacob will bring the camels to the rear of the compound. Please hurry!"

In less than an hour, they were ready. By the cold light of a full moon hanging low in the southwestern sky, they mounted their camels, and after a brief but tearful farewell, the little caravan moved out from beneath the twisting branches of olive trees and down the road toward Jericho and the Dead Sea.

Saddened, but with a hopeful heart, Anna watched them go.

Jerusalem to Qumran

FATIMA, HOLDING baby Mahmoud in her arms, nestled comfortably in the camel's upholstered saddle. She, like Sarah, was dressed as a Bedouin woman in a long black *thobe,* richly embroidered on the chest and the arms. Her hair was covered by a black *usaba,* wrapped around her head and tied at the back.

They headed east, toward the descent into the Rift Valley and their ultimate destination—*Ain Jiddy* on the shores of the Dead Sea.

Fatima felt comforted by the gentle motion of the camel's gait and was pleased that Mahmoud didn't stir as the hours passed. In the pale moonlight, all she could see of their caravan was the hindquarters of Tirzah's camel, but overhead the sky was alive with stars. As dawn approached and the stars faded, she could make out the two camels at the forefront carrying Rahman and Gunter.

The sun rose as they reached the northern tip of the Dead Sea. Fatima smiled at the sight of smooth blue water stretching to the haze below the mountains of Moab. They followed the barren shoreline to the south and came upon a copse of date palms that stood like silent sentinels above a shaded understory of green shrubs. From prior trips, Fatima knew that the oasis was fed by a spring of cool water.

Rahman reined his camel about and announced. "We'll water the camels and rest here before we continue to Ain Jiddy."

In the unhurried silence, Fatima heard the murmur of flowing water from within the oasis, pleased that it appeared deserted. Her camel kneeled for her to dismount.

Tirzah approached. "May I help you with Mahmoud?"

"Certainly, my child." She eased Mahmoud into Tirzah's outstretched arms. "May I carry him until you're ready to nurse?" Tirzah asked as she swayed back and forth with the child in her arms.

"Of course, my dear. As I've told you, I look upon you as my own daughter and Mahmoud's big sister." Fatima dismounted and called to Sarah, who held Isser in her arms, "Come, Sarah! I'll show you a place where we may comfortably nurse our little ones." She followed a path between palm trees and a clutch of green jujube and acacia shrubs to flat limestone boulders beside a little stream. Together they sat to nurse their babies.

Fatima sighed. "Though I'm very grateful to Anna Spafford for the months of protection, I'm so relieved to be out in the open air."

"I agree," said Sarah. "And I'm also relieved with the comfort of our journey. The movement of the camel was like the rocking of a cradle. Isser slept like a baby."

"He *is* a baby!" said Tirzah and sat on the flat rock next to Fatima.

The women laughed and Sarah asked, "How much further to Ain Jiddy?"

"Seven hours with a steady pace."

"What's it like there?"

"Quite lovely! This time of year, Ain Jiddy is green with sweet water. There are even waterfalls and pools for bathing."

"And the Bedouin?"

"The Rashida are gracious hosts and well-known to us. Over the years, we've stayed with them many times . . ." Hearing approaching footsteps, Fatima fell silent and half-turned, startled briefly to see two robed Bedouin men she quickly recognized as Rahman and David.

"I see you found the best place to nurse," said Rahman and handed Fatima a waterskin. "Have you finished?"

"On this side, yes," she replied. "What about you, Sarah?"

"Me, too." Sarah passed Isser to David, who put the baby over his left shoulder. "Has he already burped?" David asked.

"Not yet, darling, but since he takes after you, I'm sure he will!"

Rahman smiled as he placed his son over his shoulder. "I will also bring out the best in Mahmoud."

Fatima raised the waterskin to her lips and froze. Someone was moving behind an acacia shrub, not fifteen feet away.

"Quiet!" she whispered.

"What is it?" asked Rahman.

"There!" She pointed, her hand shaking. Springing to her feet, she called out, "You there—show yourself!"

Hesitating, a woman dressed in rags, stepped forward, holding a baby in her arms, her eyes wide with terror. "You . . . you are Bedouin?" she asked in accented Arabic.

"*Ta'aban!*" Fatima shot back as she approached the woman. "*Wa inti?*"

"Armenian."

"What are you doing here? Where are your people?"

"They're gone. I . . . I have no people anymore. Just my baby girl . . ."

"What happened?" Fatima asked, her voice softening.

"My husband was taken to a labor camp yesterday. Now, I . . . I don't know where he is. At the same hour, I was put out of our home in the Armenian Quarter with my baby and three-year-old . . . my son, Krikor. The Turkish guards told us we were to walk to Damascus." The woman began to cry.

Fatima didn't see the woman's son and she swept through the foliage with her eyes as she approached the woman. "I don't see you son—where is he?"

"Dead."

Stunned, Fatima placed her hand on the woman's shoulder. "How?"

"The guards gave us nothing to eat, not even water to drink. We walked and walked . . . all afternoon. It was hard . . . so hard to keep up. I was carrying my baby. Krikor was walking as fast as he could, but he couldn't keep up. The guards said they were of the Special Organization, with orders to kill anyone who delayed the march. I tried to make Krikor walk faster, but he couldn't. I tried to carry him with my other arm, but I . . . I couldn't. We walked the best we could, but it wasn't fast enough. The guards cursed me. We tried harder. We passed Jericho and went into the desert. Krikor said his feet hurt and he wanted to rest. He sat down on the road. A guard beat him. Krikor fell back. He hit his head on a rock and cried. There was blood on his head. Then . . . they left us there."

The woman hunched her shoulders, tears streaming down her cheeks. "I tried to stop the bleeding from his head. When night came he fell asleep. With my body, I kept Krikor and the baby warm. I also fell asleep. In the morning he didn't wake up. He felt cold. I tried to wake him up . . . but I couldn't." Her shoulders shook, then raising her face, she whispered, "I didn't know what to do. I saw the palm trees. I came here for water . . ." The woman heaved a deep sigh. "My Krikor is dead, and I have no people."

Fatima put her arm around the woman's shoulders and led her back to where the others stood by the flat boulders near the stream. "What is your name?" she asked her.

"Arsine . . . Arsine Sarkisian."

"*We* are your people now." She hugged the woman close. "We are also fleeing from the Turks. I lied to you when I told you that we are Bedouin. None of us are—this is just the best disguise we could use to travel to a place where we will find refuge among *real* Bedouin. And there, you also will be welcome! My name is Fatima. This is my husband, Rahman, and our baby, Mahmoud." After introducing Arsine to everyone else, she stated, "We are all one family, and now that includes you." She gave Arsine a final hug and said, "Take us to where your Krikor lies, so we might give him a fitting burial."

Arsine led them into the desert, where her son lay on his side, as if asleep. The sun was well up. Overhead, a buzzard floated on the wind. Fatima took Arsine's baby in her arms so she might carry the body of her son back to the oasis. And there, by the flat boulders and next to the little stream, they laid him to rest.

CHAPTER 44

March 1, 1915
American Colony, Jerusalem

WITH THE fugitives gone, Anna found herself looking forward to the Colony's inspection by Djemal. While waiting, she sat in the parlor with her daughter, Bertha, and son-in-law, Frederick. She poured herself a cup of coffee and took a deep breath. "I imagine the letter from our friend, Djemal, will arrive any minute now."

"How can you call him 'our friend' mother?" Bertha asked and buttered a piece of toast. "I've heard that Djemal Pasha is a thoroughly wicked person!"

"He's always been polite and kind when visiting with us, my dear. And your little Horatio has been quite fond of him!" Anna took a sip and raised her shoulders. "I'm not sure how much stock one can put in rumors—"

"Sadly, mother," Frederick cut in, "I have it on good authority that the rumors are true. Not only has he executed scores of Arab nationalists, just yesterday he sent hundreds of Armenian men to a forced-labor camp and evicted their families from the Armenian Quarter. It's quite scandalous."

"How terrible!" Bertha exclaimed. "Where are the families to go?"

"It's said they're being resettled north of Aleppo."

"That's positively *beastly*." Bertha said and snapped off a bite of toast. "How can you be so naive, mother?"

Anna put down her cup with a force that rattled the saucer. Bertha and Frederick froze.

"I have no illusions about Djemal Pasha," Anna said quietly, her voice edged with steel. "He is a determined politician and a brutal dictator—otherwise he wouldn't be one of the three Young Turks ruling the Ottoman Empire. However, he's consistently supported our relief work, starting when we first met four years ago. At the time, Turkey was at war with Greece, Italy, and Russia, and his aide-de-camp, claiming to be acting at Djemal's behest, accused us of caring for Turkey's enemies and threatened to deport us!"

"What did you do?" Bertha asked.

"I told the aide-de-camp that the American Colony doesn't take sides—we serve *humanity* and always will." Anna shrugged. "I had no idea what Djemal might do, since I had also heard rumors—that he had a dual personality and a penchant for cruelty—capable of lunching with a man one day and lynching him the next. So, when Djemal appeared here four days later, I feared for my life. And since your little Horatio was with me, I feared for us both.

"Nonetheless, I invited Djemal in, and we sat at this very table—sharing tea and gingerbread cookies. Horatio couldn't stop staring at Djemal and asked him if could touch his beard. I was aghast, but Djemal said yes and took him in his arms. Before I knew it, Horatio was sitting on Djemal's lap and running his little hands through his beard. Horatio also noticed a medal on Djemal's chest and squealed, 'Pretty star,' as he pulled at it.

"As you might imagine, I was petrified—watching Horatio with this man who I had heard was a monster. But words of the Prophet Isaiah rose in my mind . . . *and a little child shall lead them.* I began to feel better, especially when Djemal told me how he missed his own children and his wife, who were still in Turkey. When I asked him about his reputation for cruelty, he admitted that, though he was conflicted about the use of extreme measures, he was ultimately compelled to confront resistance to the Ottoman Empire with brute force since the Central Committee, the German advisors, and the other Pashas expected that of him.

"Djemal didn't bring up the threats made to me by his aide-de-camp, and neither did I.

"At the end of our tea, he politely said goodbye and left, promising to visit again. Afterward I saw that he had pinned his medal to Horatio's shirt. And that aide-de-camp? I later learned that Djemal had him demoted and sent to a remote outpost in the Sinai!"

Anna fixed Bertha and Frederick with her eyes. "So, my dears, please understand why I regard Djemal as a friend. Indeed, the truth about anyone can be complicated. After all, it was Djemal who sent Mustafa to warn us about the inspection today, allowing our fugitives ample time to escape. Living in this lion's den of the Ottoman Empire, do remember— the lion is sometimes a lamb."

Bertha reached out and touched Anna's hand. "I'm sorry, Mother," she whispered. "I didn't realize—" She fell silent as a Colony guard entered the parlor.

"Mrs. Spafford—a courier at the gate with an urgent message."

"I'll be right there," said Anna, and once the guard left, she whispered, "This must be the courier with a letter requesting my permission to inspect the Colony. Mustafa said it would arrive just before the inspection."

At the gate, Anna saw a thin Turk in a red vest with broad white pantaloons. "I'm Mrs. Spafford," she announced.

The Turk bowed. "I am honored to convey this letter from my master, General Djemal Pasha, to your hand, Mrs. Spafford. He requires an immediate response, so I will wait here."

Anna opened the envelope and read the formal request to conduct an inspection in advance of transferring Turkish wounded to the Colony hospital. *He's smart to avoid any appearance of anti-American action,* Anna thought as she finished reading.

Looking up, she smiled, "Please inform the general that we'll be delighted to have him grace us with his presence!"

"The general will be pleased to hear that, Mrs. Spafford. I will tell him forthwith." With a short bow, the Turk ran off in the direction of the walled city.

"Your Excellency, Djemal Pasha!" Anna smiled and curtsied as she welcomed him at the Colony gate. "How delightful to see you again!"

Djemal bowed. "And I am so very pleased to see you again, Mrs. Spafford."

He was accompanied by a small entourage of armed soldiers and an elderly man with a large scraggly beard.

Anna gestured with her hand. "I'm certain you remember my daughter, Bertha, and her husband, Frederick."

"I do." Djemal made a bow and seemed to search the parlor with his eyes. "And Mr. Horatio? I trust that he has grown considerably?"

"He has, indeed, Your Excellency. Might you have time to see him today?"

"He probably wouldn't even remember me . . ."

"But he does, Your Excellency! He treasures the star you gave him and speaks of you quite often!"

"In that case, we'll find the time!" But, as a cloud slides in front of the sun, Djemal's smile vanished. "But first, official business. We must conduct a full inspection of the compound, then speak of your hospital's readiness to look after our wounded."

"And then some time for Horatio?" Anna asked playfully.

Djemal leaned forward and the cloud lifted. "That's the part of this visit I'm looking forward to!" Almost as an afterthought, he waved a hand toward the old man with the wild beard. "This is Guido von List, the kaiser's personal envoy to Jerusalem."

Anna's blood froze. *This is the monster who directed David's torture!* She forced a smile. "Delighted, Herr List."

"The pleasure is mine, Frau Spafford," he said and kissed her hand. She cringed as she felt his lips on her skin.

List straightened up, still holding her hand. "If I'm not mistaken, I am now in the presence of a strong woman of proud Norwegian stock. Would you mind telling me your maiden name, my dear?"

"Larsen-Øglende, Herr List. You're indeed perceptive—I was born in

Norway and immigrated to America as a child."

"I knew it!" he laughed and released her hand. "How I delight in meeting other Herrenvolk, especially in these dark lands!"

Anna nodded agreeably, though inwardly she felt ashamed and sickened at having to maintain appearances.

Turning to Bertha, List bowed, "And I'm charmed to meet this beautiful Nordic maiden, Bertha, is it?"

"Yes, sir."

After planting a lingering kiss on her hand, List smiled at Frederick. "And I am also happy to meet you, my young friend . . ."

"Frederick Vester, sir." He made a little bow and extended his hand.

"Vester?" List repeated. "Another proud member of the Herrenrasse?"

"If by that, you imply that I am German, sir, you would be correct."

"How delightful!" List squealed as he shook Frederick's hand. "I have been in this horrid country for months, surrounded by Untermenschen. But now I finally feel at home in the charming company of fellow Aryans of purest stock!"

Anna was horrified. *I've heard these disgusting notions of racial superiority before, but never so brazenly.* She saw that Djemal was also irritated as he stepped forward.

"It's time we began our inspection, Herr List."

Frederick bowed his head to Djemal. "I'd be honored to show you the compound, sire."

Djemal nodded. "Thank you, Frederick. Please, lead the way."

Anna watched them leave, and breathed a sigh of relief, knowing that they would find nothing. But she suddenly felt an intense desire to wash her hands, especially the one List had kissed.

❃ ❃ ❃

The inspection lasted almost two hours, concluding with an extended conversation about the number of hospital beds to be allotted for the

Turkish military, and the Colony's need for governmental support of the soup kitchen.

There had also been time for eight-year-old Horatio to become reacquainted with Djemal Pasha. Horatio had insisted on taking him to the Colony stables to show him his pony, and how well he could ride. List had gone along.

When the visit was over, Anna stood with the others, waving goodbye as Djemal and List departed in a sleek black automobile.

Once the car disappeared down Nablus Road, Anna turned to her extended family and exhaled the word, "Finally!" Shaking her head, she said to Frederick, "Before we begin preparing today's soup kitchen, you *must* tell us about their tour of the compound."

"There's not much to tell," Frederick replied. "I showed them everything—including the area where our guests had been quartered. We spent a fair amount of time there since Djemal felt it would be well suited for hospital isolation rooms. All the while List took notes. They stopped at every door, explored every closet, and poked their noses into every cupboard. In the end Djemal seemed happy to be done with it, though List appeared agitated."

Anna sighed. "I believe we know why . . ."

"Grandmother," Horatio cut in. "I should tell you about *my* tour with Djemal and Mr. List."

Anna crouched down and smiled. "Djemal told me that you were the one person he really wanted to see today, and I told him that, even though you were very young then, you haven't forgotten the time you sat on his lap."

"I remember that quite well—especially touching his beard—though I didn't ask to touch it today. But I did tell him that I still have the beautiful silver star he gave me, and I offered to show it to him. So, the first place we visited was my secret treehouse, where I keep the star in my treasure box. He seemed quite pleased to see that I've kept it safe."

"Did you show him anything else?"

"Oh, yes! Mr. List asked to see my hiding places around the compound, so I showed them my little cave in the outer wall by the kitchen, and the secret cemetery in the garden where I bury dead baby birds. But the *most* fun was the stables. I showed them my pony and how well I ride. Mr. List also picked out a horse to ride, and I must say, he's quite a good horseman!" Horatio frowned. "But there *was* something strange . . ."

"What was that dear?" asked Anna, suddenly fearful.

"While Mr. List was riding about, Djemal was in the stables looking at the horse droppings. It was very odd—"

"Oh my God!" said Frederick. "Djemal saw the camel droppings!"

"And no *camels*!" Anna said, her heart pounding.

"What does that mean?" asked Horatio.

"The droppings of camels and horses are quite distinct, Horatio," Anna said quietly, trying to control her own fear and not frighten her grandson. "Camel droppings are small and dry—it's how they conserve water." She raised her shoulders. "I believe that's what Djemal was curious about." She smiled and tickled his tummy. "Did he say anything about that to Mr. List?"

"No. He didn't say anything."

Not wanting Horatio to hear anything further about List, Anna kissed Horatio on the nose. "There are some delicious cookies for you in the kitchen, my boy. Go have some!" When he was gone, Anna straightened up. "I don't believe Djemal told List anything about camels, and I don't believe he will."

"How can you be sure, Mother?" Bertha asked, her voice rising with fear.

"Because it's clear to me that Djemal despises List just as we do—with his arrogance and all that bragging about the Master Race, the *Herrenrasse*. I'm also certain Djemal doesn't want List to make our lives difficult, especially when he depends on us to tend to his wounded and feed the poor." Anna sighed and shook her head. "And wouldn't it be just too bizarre for our fate to turn on camel droppings?"

CHAPTER 45

March 1, 1915
American Colony to Augusta Victoria

DJEMAL LOOKED out the window of his black Mercedes staff car as they passed Damascus Gate. He was making a concerted effort not to listen as List prattled on about his suspicions concerning Anna Spafford. Finally, he'd had enough.

"Really, Herr List!" Djemal said sharply. "We inspected every inch of the Colony compound with no shred of evidence your fugitives were ever there."

"I'm a clairvoyant, sir, and I know that Spafford woman is hiding something. I feel it in my very bones!"

Djemal could barely suppress a smile at List's ravings. *I could tell him about the camel droppings and what they mean—that the fugitives he so desperately seeks are already miles away—most likely on their way into the Judean Desert by way of the Dead Sea. But why should I? Why would I punish Anna for harboring them? She's a brave and admirable woman. Besides, with the coming locust plague and our wounded to be cared for in the Colony, I depend on her more than ever! Why would I tell List anything? To further the kaiser's insane designs? To help that madman rule as king of Jerusalem? Never!*

"Please," Djemal said loudly, interrupting List's ranting. "I must request quiet to review these reports of locust sightings." He tapped the folder on his lap.

"Of course, sire." List exhaled in petulant frustration and fell silent.

Allah be praised! I never thought he'd shut up.

Djemal reviewed the reports he had already studied the night before—

locust sightings from Es-Salt and throughout the Jordan Valley. Thanks to Anna's forewarning, he had already sent soldiers to instruct farmers around Jerusalem to gather and protect what crops they could harvest, and to assist in setting smoke fires around their fields to ward off the locusts.

There's undoubtedly much more to be done and I'm certain Aaronsohn will advise us well. As an agricultural scientist, he'll know exactly what else we must do. Djemal smiled to himself in anticipation of seeing the expression on List's face upon introducing him to the Jewish expert hired to direct all efforts against the locust plague.

Reaching the hospice, a Turkish soldier ran to meet the automobile as Djemal and List stepped out.

"Herr List!" The soldier handed him a cable. "This just arrived from Berlin."

As List opened the envelope, he called to Djemal, "Your Excellency, don't you wish to hear what the kaiser has to say?"

Djemal waited in mounting irritation while List slowly unfolded the buff-colored paper.

"The kaiser extends his congratulations for your punitive measures against the treasonous Armenians and encourages you to continue!"

"Thank you." Djemal turned away, hoping to avoid any further conversation. He strode into the huge atrium of the hostel, with List running to keep up.

"Your Excellency," the old man gasped, out of breath from the effort. "Shall we meet for supper?"

Before Djemal could reply, his secretary came running toward him, waving an envelope. "From Haifa, Your Excellency!"

Opening it, Djemal saw to his satisfaction that the cable was from Aaronsohn. He planned to arrive that very evening at five o'clock. Looking up at List, Djemal smiled. "I'm afraid I won't be available for dinner, Herr List. I'll be meeting and taking dinner with the agronomist, Aaron Aaronsohn, who will lead our fight against the locusts—"

"Aaronsohn?" List cut in. "A Jew?"

"Yes, very Jewish," Djemal replied, amused by the way List's widely opened eyes were magnified by his thick glasses, giving him the appearance of a monstrous insect. "Why don't you drop by my office after dinner and have a glass of sherry with us?"

"I think not," List snapped. "Good day, sir."

A fine eggshell dance, this . . . Djemal thought as he headed to his office. Pausing at the secretary's desk, he said, "I'll be having a dinner meeting with Aaron Aaronsohn at five o'clock. Please have the kitchen send up supper." He took a step and stopped. "Have them prepare a goodly amount. I'm told that Mr. Aaronsohn is a man of large appetites."

❊ ❊ ❊

American Colony

THE AFTERNOON sun blazed in a clear blue sky over the courtyard of the Colony as distribution of soup and bread ended, though the crowd lingered, enjoying full bellies and the warm weather. As Anna and Bertha gathered the pots and ladles, the courtyard suddenly darkened. Above them, a strange dark cloud obscured the sunlight.

"They're here," Anna whispered, her heart racing as she studied the darkening sky.

All looked up as a sound emerged, at first barely audible, but rising—like distant thunder. Then the cloud descended, and the thunder grew louder and louder. The courtyard erupted in cries of terror as the darkness expanded with a roaring shower of black pellets falling like hail in a storm.

Anna knew it wasn't hail, but a deluge of locusts and their droppings, covering the paving stones, balconies, and roofs of the Colony.

"Everyone inside!" Anna shouted as she and Bertha bolted for shelter within the walls of the main building.

"Mother!" Bertha shouted. "Have you ever seen anything like this?"

Anna shook her head as she looked out at the dark tempest.

"How long will it last?"

"Not long," Anna shouted back. "There's little for them to eat here."

"And then it will be over?"

"No! This is only the beginning."

Anna watched the horde rise, moving westward—toward the open fields of West Jerusalem, the orchards of Jerusalem's foothills, and the farmlands of the coastal plain.

Words of the Prophet Joel rose in her mind—*A day of cloud and thick darkness—a blackness spreading over the mountains* . . .

"Now as then—these wretched little animals!" she said aloud, though no one could hear her.

CHAPTER 46

March 4, 1915
Jerusalem to Jaffa

AFTER WORKING closely with Djemal Pasha for three days, Aaron Aaronsohn was anxious to get back to his experimental agricultural fields and his home in Atlit. Guiding his 1912 Mercedes Landaulet down the Pilgrim Road from Jerusalem to the coastal plain, he was saddened to see the locust-devastated orange, lemon, and olive groves. As he had anticipated, the trees had been stripped bare, their pitiful skeletal branches stretched toward heaven in desolate supplication.

Driving down the steep defile just beyond West Jerusalem, he passed the carriage road leading to the village of Ain Karim, and after another hundred yards, he pulled off the road in the valley between the small Jewish farmstead of Motsa and the Arab village of Qalunya.

Taking his field glasses from their leather case, he leaned on the hood of the automobile and scanned the rolling hills across the valley, bordered on the western heights by the Arab villages of Nebi Samwil, Kustul and Suba. Everywhere, he saw barren devastation left in the wake of the ravenous adult locusts.

But what do we have here? He adjusted the binoculars' focusing wheel to view a cluster of workers with shovels and canisters. *Excellent! Those folks are clearly extracting locust egg cylinders for destruction by burning. That's encouraging—good coordination between the military and local residents in getting rid of those damned eggs.*

He got back in his automobile and resumed driving, following the road west through the undulating Judean hills. *I'm heartened that Djemal took my advice to fight against the plague as vigorously as he would fight a war, since that's exactly what this is.*

Aaronsohn was gratified as he considered that Djemal had issued a mandate for all male residents of Palestine between the ages of sixteen to sixty years to gather at least eleven pounds of locust eggs per week, with extra stipends to those who gathered more and fines for those who gathered less. *It is well that he took these steps quickly since we cannot afford half measures. We must do everything to stem the tide of this war since this is just the beginning, and not even the end of the beginning!*

While working with Djemal in Jerusalem, Aaronsohn had seen shocking reports coming from Transjordan, where the plague had begun a week before. Despite their eradication efforts, hosts of crawling and hopping larvae had already hatched, and the black swarms were now expanding—one measured a mile wide and seven miles long—so vast that nothing could escape its ravenous destruction. Orchards, fields and vineyards were stripped bare as the larval flow consumed everything in its path including goats, sheep, and horses that weren't able to get away. There were even reports of small children and the lame enveloped by the voracious larvae.

As Aaronsohn guided his Mercedes carefully forward, he frowned. *While Djemal himself is very supportive, the responses from local bureaucrats and military officers range from helpful, to indifferent, to defiant. Nonetheless, it's my mission to enlist everyone in the effort. The survival of the people of Palestine hangs in the balance.*

Beyond the town of Abu Gosh, the road descended through the Jerusalem foothills and soon reached the caravansary at Bab el-Wad, marking the gateway to the Maritime Plain of Sharon. As he continued driving, the air became hazy with smoke, and Aaronsohn smiled.

Excellent! They've heeded my advice about protecting their crops with smoke fires.

With visibility poor, he slowed down as he passed fields of sugar beets, melons, and grain, as well as orange, lemon, and olive orchards—all viewed with difficulty through the thick smoke, and from what he was able to see, the fields and orchards had been spared.

Reaching the town of Ramle, he decided to get away from the smoke and took a road leading to Jaffa on the Mediterranean coast. There the heavy sea breezes kept flying adult locusts at bay and no smoke fires were required.

And sure enough, as he approached Jaffa, the air cleared. Aaronsohn cranked down the side window, taking deep breaths of fresh ocean air as he searched for the area's only petrol station. *I'll get the Mercedes serviced, then spend the night with friends in Tel Aviv before taking the coast road home to Atlit tomorrow.*

As he passed orange groves with rich foliage, he saw that they were untouched with oranges still to be harvested.

Beyond the groves, he reached a filling station on the western outskirts of Jaffa. Leaving the automobile to be serviced, he entered a small café attached to the station. He ordered Turkish coffee and a thick slice of *halva*. While waiting for the coffee, he took the plate of halva to an outdoor table shaded by a spreading pine tree. Taking a handkerchief from his jacket pocket, he brushed away pine needles from the table and chair before sitting down. The shade was welcome relief, and he breathed out a sigh. He restrained himself from tasting the halva since he wanted to enjoy it with his coffee.

While he waited, he thought back to the last full day he had spent with Djemal. They had left Jerusalem and gone together to the Jordan Valley to speak to government administrators in Jericho about recommendations for locust eradication. Aaronsohn had to laugh when he recalled how Djemal had introduced him to everyone as his "Locust Czar." *I can't wait to add that to my résumé!*

While in Jericho, Aaronsohn had taken every opportunity to obtain soil samples, and he was encouraged by what he had found; samples from Jericho and wide swaths of the Jordan Valley showed levels of salt and alkali such that any locust eggs deposited there would not hatch. *That's good news!* he thought. *Between the salty soil of the Jordan Valley, and the* ocean winds along the coast, we might have enough citrus, vegetables, and dates to avoid mass starvation. We can only hope . . .

But as he thought about Jericho, he recalled something he had seen that made his heart clench—a group of about a hundred people walking through the desert outside the city. With his field glasses he was able to see that they were mostly old people and women with children, including babies on their mother's backs. Many carried bundles and suitcases, and there were a few mounted Turkish soldiers scattered among them.

When he had asked Djemal who these people were, he received no immediate response. But after several minutes, Djemal leaned over and whispered, "They're Armenians being relocated to Aleppo. Though I find this appalling, I'm under pressure from Talaat and Enver Pasha in Constantinople to execute this program."

"But, Your Excellency," Aaronsohn had countered, "There can be no rationale for such inhumane treatment."

To which Djemal had replied, "The rationale, my dear Aaronsohn, lies not in the directive from Constantinople, but rather in the relentless and insane ravings of Kaiser Wilhelm in Berlin. He insists that Armenians living along the Eastern Front near Russia are guilty of treason, and if Armenians anywhere are so accused, Armenians everywhere are also guilty of treason, and they must, like locusts, be eradicated. Again, I find this notion detestable. Indeed, I once had many friends and advisers among the Armenians. But there is nothing I can do to stop this."

Aaronsohn's coffee arrived, and he thanked the proprietor.

Before tasting the coffee and halva, he drew a deep breath. *It's all well for Djemal to say that he feels terrible about the Armenians, but by allowing this outrage, he is complicit and just as guilty as anyone else! And if Armenians are being exterminated today, tomorrow it could be Jews.* He shook his head and thought, *But enough of these thoughts!*

He took a bite of the halva followed by a sip of coffee. The combination of the two—the sweet and the bitter—was delicious. *And what an apt metaphor,* he thought and considered the complexity of life in Ottoman

Palestine. And as he continued to enjoy the coffee and halva, his thoughts turned to the challenges and opportunities at hand.

I suppose I'm thankful that Djemal possesses some admirable qualities, but the central Ottoman government and their German masters pose a clear danger to all ethnic minorities in Greater Syria. There's no escaping the conclusion that I must work in any way possible to break their hold here. And the only way to do that is by helping the British, and I'm now in position to do just that!

With equal measures of exhilaration and dread, Aaronsohn considered how his position as so-called Locust Czar required him to travel the length and breadth of Palestine to assess local conditions and resources. He resolved that he would use this access to document the size and location of Ottoman army camps, troop numbers, supply depots, and gasoline storage facilities—all vital information for the large-scale campaign against the desert locust invasion, and equally, a trove of information that would benefit British fortunes when it came time to attack along the Southern Front of the war.

But the question is—how to contact the British?

He finished the halva, took a final swallow of coffee, and it came to him. *There are evacuation ships leaving Haifa once a week, some bound for Egypt. We could easily place a messenger on board. But, who might we start with? Why not my brother Alex? After his stint living in the US, he speaks perfect English, and can pass for an American. He could convey bits of information straightaway to British military intelligence in Cairo!*

With a spring in his step, Aaronsohn pushed back from the table, paid his bill, and went to the garage. The servicing of his automobile complete, he settled the charges and left, driving through Jaffa on the Mediterranean shore. Parking on a bluff along the beach, he got out of the car, his spirits high, refreshed by the cool sea breeze on his face. He watched a V-shaped flock of storks float by, their outstretched wings skimming the water.

Despite the locust plague and a world convulsed in war, despite everything, Aaronsohn smiled as he watched the storks heading north on their annual spring migration along the Rift Valley flyway, heedlessly crossing all the arbitrary borders from the southern tip of Africa to Europe.

And what a blessing they're here now, in their tens of thousands, to stop and feast on the adult and larval locusts—consuming them by the millions! It's no wonder the Arabs call the stork, Abu Sa'ad—father of good luck!

Aaronsohn wasn't a religious man, but he knew his psalms, and a fragment of verse came to mind as he watched the storks disappear up the coast.

I lift up my eyes from where my salvation comes.

CHAPTER 47

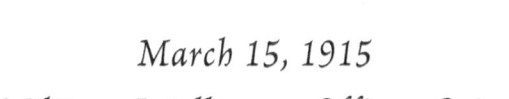

March 15, 1915
Military Intelligence Offices, Cairo

LAWRENCE STOPPED by the mailroom and found a letter in his box. With no censor's stamp he knew it had come by courier, and a glance at the return address made him smile—*Professor Chaim Weizmann, c/o The Tea King of Russia, Wissotzky Tea Company, London*

Sitting on a bench outside the mailroom, he began to read.

18 February 1915 London

My Dear Captain Lawrence,

Thanks so very much for conveying the letter from Prince Faisal to me along with your contact information and your offer to assist me with transportation and, indeed, to accompany me on the journey to Aden.

As an ardent Zionist who seeks coexistence and cooperation with my Arab cousins in Palestine, I am relieved beyond words that Prince Faisal is willing to have this discussion, and equally delighted that you, as a British officer, will facilitate and participate in this vital conversation.

I hope to hear your suggestions as to how I might travel from Great Britain to meet with you in Egypt and travel together to Aden. I'm certain you're well-aware of the details Prince Faisal mentioned in his letter—meeting on 5 May at noon in the Port City of Aden at a coffee shop next to the Church of St. Francis of Assisi.

I look forward to this meeting with Prince Faisal, which I hope will prove historic in reconciling a return of the Jewish People to Zion to live in peace with their Arab cousins.

With affection and all respect,
Chaim

Lawrence smiled as he tucked Weizmann's letter back into its envelope, then ran up the stairs to the Intelligence Office. He approached Newcombe's desk, but before he could tell him of Weizmann's letter, Newcombe pushed a thick brown envelope forward.

"This just arrived in the diplomatic pouch from Whitehall..."

In a glance, Lawrence saw it was from Hogarth. Knowing it was about Gallipoli, he took the envelope and went straightaway to the map room, where he began reading.

War Office

Whitehall & Horse Guards Avenue Westminster, London

4 March 1915

Dear Ned,

I'm writing with a heavy heart since your insights about the Dardanelles campaign have fallen on deaf ears. I've just spoken with Kitchener regarding Alexandretta. He has long favored the idea and shares our frustration that his appeals to Churchill have been ignored.

K provided me with a draft of a letter he sent to Churchill, which I'm including herewith. You won't find any solace in it since the die has been cast—the Entente fleet will soon attempt to traverse the Dardanelles to reach Constantinople.

Lawrence sighed as he turned the page from Hogarth's personal stationary to K's letter to Churchill.

The Rt. Hon. Winston Churchill, MP Admiralty, SW

My dear Churchill,

As we consider options regarding an attack on Turkey designed to neutralize her threat and allow resources to be directed against Germany on the Western Front, I wish to alert you to the ideas of a young 2nd lieutenant at our Cairo bureau, one Thomas Edward Lawrence.

A brilliant Oxford scholar, Lawrence is a most daring and original thinker, and has put forth a well-reasoned plan for seizing Alexandretta with Commonwealth and Arab forces, thus drawing the bulk of Turkish forces away from the Gallipoli Peninsula. This gambit would open the Dardanelles to a combined naval invasion of English and French battleships sailing from the Aegean into the Sea of Marmara with the ultimate goal of bombarding Constantinople into submission.

However, with the current undivided concentration of Turkish forces guarding Gallipoli and the Dardanelles, I shudder to think of a naval or land invasion without the strategic and diversionary attack at Alexandretta as suggested by young Lawrence.

In addition to these considerations, an attack on Alexandretta would yield a host of other advantages; it is a wonderful natural harbor with rich oil reserves along the shore, and most importantly, the participation of local Arab forces in the attack at Alexandretta would diminish the need for British troops, with far fewer casualties among our boys.

I look forward to speaking with you about this promising idea.

Yours sincerely,
K

Lawrence turned the page, where Hogarth's letter continued.

Sadly, K's letter was dismissed out of hand. Churchill remains insistent on the original plan with a naval assault on Constantinople by way of the Dardanelles.

You should know that much of Churchill's churlish resistance to K stems from a long history of bad blood between them. They first clashed before the turn of the century in the Sudan when K was a commanding general and Churchill an outspoken second lieutenant with a megaphone as a war correspondent for the Morning Post.

K was credited with winning the Battle of Omdurman in 1898 and securing control of the Sudan. However, Churchill contributed a few unflattering articles to the Post about K, and that was the start of an animosity that spilled over to the Second Boer War. There K was chief of staff and Churchill, having parlayed a heroic escape from a Boer POW camp into a seat in Parliament, was a war correspondent for the Post. The enmity continues, and we find our war cabinet in dysfunction as K still regards Churchill as an arrogant upstart. and Churchill despises K.

All this is by way acknowledging that, despite the gravity of the current military situation, it's clear that Churchill may have allowed his personal feelings to influence his view on Alexandretta.

What's more, it appears that our French allies have Churchill's ear, and as you know, the French view a British or Arab presence in Syria as anathema. They therefore oppose Alexandretta as the point of attack.

Lastly, Churchill is an ambitious politician and enamored with the notion of a grand naval assault on Constantinople to rival Nelson's attack on the Danish-Norwegian Fleet at the Battle of Copenhagen a hundred years ago. He's convinced that this will quickly win the war, and he'll achieve his ardent ambition of becoming supreme warlord and eventually PM.

Which all leads to the present catch with Churchill having convinced the cabinet to adopt the French plan. I believe they should have been more cautious, especially given France's unhappy history in naval affairs.

So, the attack at Gallipoli is going forward. We can only pray it will be successful, and not too many of our brave boys will be sacrificed for the glory of politicians. One would have hoped that our army of young lions would not be led by asses. But apparently, it is.

Yours ever, my dear friend and colleague,
D. G. Hogarth

Lawrence stared at the letter and his heart sank.

He took a sheet of paper and sat to write, but with nothing further to propose about Gallipoli, he decided to write to Professor Weizmann. *That's at least an arena where I may yet make a difference. Plus, going to Aden will get me the hell out of Cairo.*

He dipped the nib of his pen into the inkwell and began.

Military Intelligence Offices

Cairo 15 March 1915

My Dear Professor Weizmann,

Thank you for your letter, which I received today. I am indeed looking forward to facilitating your journey to Aden and traveling with you for your meeting with Prince Faisal.

As to the logistics of sailing from England to Alexandria, the voyage takes about fourteen days, and I would suggest any Prince Line vessel departing Manchester or London on or about April 13. That should bring you to Alexandria on or about April 27, with ample time for us to reach Aden on the appointed day. I suggest that we meet in Alexandria at the main entrance of the Greco-Roman

Museum a few blocks from the harbor at 5 p.m. on either April 27 or 28 (since there's no telling exactly when either of us might arrive).

I'll secure lodging in Alexandria, and we'll set out by rail the following day for Cairo, thence by a hired cab to Port Said. From there, I'll book passage on a steamer to the Port of Aden.

As Prince Faisal expressed to me, he looks forward to meeting you at noon on May 5 at a small coffee shop next to the Francis of Assisi Church, which is a short walk from the landing on Esplanade Road.

If you must contact me, please cable the War Office at the Savoy Hotel in Cairo.

Looking forward to bringing representatives of the Jewish people and their Arab cousins together for the sake of peace,

With fond regards,
Thomas Edward Lawrence,
2nd Lieutenant

Lawrence sealed the envelope, planning to send it off immediately by diplomatic pouch. As he retraced his steps to Stewart's office, he thought, *I'm certain Stewart will be as pleased as I am about this meeting, but also as sad as I am about the news regarding Gallipoli.*

"God help us!" he whispered and entered Newcombe's office.

CHAPTER 48

March 31, 1915
War Room at the Palast Kurhaus at Bad Kreuznach

KAISER WILHELM, wearing a field-gray uniform festooned with medals, was in poor spirits. Having lost the "race to the sea," the Western Front had ground down to a bloody stalemate. However, having commandeered a palatial hotel in the resort town of Bad Kreuznach, he had some solace as he worked with his chief of staff in a luxury suite converted to a war room. As they reviewed which divisions to redeploy to the Eastern Front, a knock sounded at the door.

Wilhelm shouted, "Come!"

"A cable for His Excellency, the kaiser," the messenger announced.

Having contacted his wife the day before about the many hotel spa amenities, Wilhelm hoped the cable was from her. Before opening it, he turned to Falkenhayn.

"General, please draft a memorandum summarizing the troops we've designated for redeployment and return when it's done."

"Yes, Your Excellency." Falkenhayn bowed and left the room.

Once he had gone, Wilhelm opened the envelope and cursed under his breath. "Damn! It's from that idiot von List!" He rolled his eyes as he scanned past toadying salutations and fawning opening lines to the main point of the message.

... YOUR HIGHNESS, NOTWITHSTANDING THE UNPRODUCTIVE INSPECTION OF THE AMERICAN COLONY I CONDUCTED WITH

DJEMAL PASHA LAST MONTH, I REMAIN CONVINCED THAT THE
AMERICANS ARE HIDING SOMETHING! AS A CLAIRVOYANT,
I'M ABLE TO DIVINE THE PSYCHIC RESIDUE PEOPLE LEAVE
BEHIND, AND I'M CERTAIN THAT THE FUGITIVES HAD BEEN
AT THE COLONY AND WERE APPARENTLY FOREWARNED AND
LEFT. I'M CERTAIN THAT ANNA SPAFFORD, THE WOMAN WHO
LEADS THE COLONY, KNOWS WHERE THEY ARE HIDING.

 I THEREFORE REQUEST YOUR PERMISSION TO RAID THE
COLONY, SEIZE MRS. SPAFFORD AND HER FAMILY, AND BRING
THEM TO AUGUSTA VICTORIA FOR INTERROGATION. THIS IS
THE ONLY WAY TO FLUSH OUT THE FUGITIVES ABLE TO ACCESS
THE HIDDEN PORTAL INTO THE TEMPLE MOUNT. BEYOND THAT,
I ALSO WISH TO BEGIN CLEANSING THE HOLY LAND OF THE
JEWS AS IS ALREADY BEING DONE WITH THE ARMENIANS . . .

Wilhelm had read enough. "That insolent son of a bitch!" he fumed as he sat at a writing table to make an immediate response.

Herr List, my dear and valued counselor!

I just received your cable, and I have taken it upon myself to respond immediately, writing from my war room in the Palast Kurhaus at Bad Kreuznach in the Rhineland—the most luxurious accommodations I've yet known during this bitter conflict.

 As to your request to detain the Spaffords for questioning, my answer is an emphatic NO! Under no circumstances should you pursue any such action against the American Colony.

 While I appreciate your intuition, let me be clear—I absolutely forbid any such intrusion! As I've already told you, such an action might alter the current neutrality of the United States and MUST be avoided. The US, with its almost unlimited resources, must remain on the sidelines. The longer they remain neutral, the better our fortunes for winning the war.

When we have victory in our grasp, or if the Americans ally with the Entente, you will have my full blessing to do with the American Colony as you will. But not before!

As to your second request regarding the Jews of the Holy Land, the same applies. This is not the time to deal with them. As we know from our friend, Henry Ford, Jews in the United States grip the levers of power with influence on the press and government far beyond their numbers. The Jews, trade unionists, and Bolsheviks would like nothing more than to push the US into the war against us. Therefore, this is not the time. But be assured, the time will come!

We are indeed of one mind when it comes to Untermenchen. The Jew, like the Armenian, is a parasite, sucking out the marrow of the host countries where they reside. With your able prompting, the Turks are already in the process of eliminating the Armenians, and once we finish this war, we will disinfect Germany and Palestine of Jews. We will not rest until they have been exterminated from our sacred soil. Personally, I believe the best thing would be gas! But this is not yet the time.

Stay strong and true to our ultimate purpose,
W

❖ ❖ ❖

Falkenhayn finished his summary of troop relocations and, leaving his suite, walked down a mirrored hallway, thinking, *this place is large enough to billet the whole Fifth Army.*

Reaching the war room, he opened the door and saw the kaiser studying the large map of Europe. He cleared his throat. "Beg pardon, Your Excellency. I've finished the memorandum. Would you like to review it?"

"Yes. Place it on that writing table, and while I study it, bring this message to the telegraph office for immediate transmission to Herr Guido von List at the Augusta Victoria Hospice in Jerusalem."

"Yes, Your Majesty." Taking the folded page from the kaiser, he left, and as he made his way toward the telegraph office, he wondered aloud, "An important cable to the deranged Nordic warrior and magician?" He exhaled loudly "Why does the kaiser waste his time on that madman?" Looking down the long hallway, he saw it was deserted. Pausing beneath an electric light, he unfolded the page and scanned the kaiser's message to List, shaking his head as he read. "Thank God the kaiser forbids him from taking American hostages."

Reading further, he came to words that brought him up short. "What's this? Disinfect Germany of its Jews?" He refolded the page and continued down the hall, his heart pounding.

Hundreds of thousands of German Jews volunteered to serve the Fatherland at the start of the war, and tens of thousands have served honorably on the front lines with many wounded and killed. And this is how the kaiser rewards them?

"Disinfect Germany of its Jews? What the hell is that about?" he muttered under his breath.

CHAPTER 49

May 3, 1915
Rosslyn

EVAN HADN'T heard from Harry in over a month, and he was beginning to worry. His last real letter had been from a training camp in western Scotland, followed by a few short and heavily censored notes. When the rain stopped and the sky cleared in the late afternoon, Evan decided to walk into town to check for mail.

Once out the door, he saw steam rising from the garden beneath the warm sunshine. He crossed the stone bridge into the cool air of the shaded path that wound up to the main road. Reaching the post office, he unlocked the box.

"Thank God!" he exclaimed, relieved to find a letter from Harry. He opened it and began to read.

15 April 1915

My Dear Cousin Evan,

I've settled in nicely with my battalion in a place I shall not disclose lest I incur the censor's wrath. I trust all goes well with you at Rosslyn, and I'm happy to leave the family estate in your care.

I must tell you that, on my way to deploy, I stopped at the London home of my in-laws, and my appearance was met with a prodigal's welcome. My wife and her parents were delighted that I was finally "doing my part!" I was also thrilled to see my six-year-

old son, James (whose bedroom you occupy), and my beautiful three-year-old daughter, Mary. Since all appears forgiven, my dear wife, Vera, and I have reconciled and we plan to return to Rosslyn with the children after all this is over . . . that is, if I survive.

Whatever the future holds, it was good to see adoration, rather than contempt in Vera's eyes. Perhaps it was the uniform—and that of a major, no less!

I must confess that I never told you why I visited with my solicitor when I went to Edinburgh to re-enlist. I did so for the purpose of amending the deed of Rosslyn Castle. This is my way of informing you that you are now listed thereon, my dear cousin. So, even if you have no memory, you will always have a home. Though I fervently pray you shall have both.

Do write soon and often.

Your no longer distant cousin,
Harry

He tucked the letter into a pocket, happy to hear the good news from Harry, and excited to be listed on the castle deed.

Seeing that the butcher shop across the street was still open, he picked up some haggis and headed back to the castle. *My castle! At least in part.*

With the sun now low in the western sky, he reached the stone bridge, and paused to admire the lush green grass covering the steep slope down into the glen.

He froze. *Could it be?* He looked closer and saw hundreds of small white flowers scattered among the leaves, glowing in the early evening sunlight. His heart pounded as Harry's words sprang to mind. *You'll know that spring has come when the white blossoms of the wild onion bloom in the glen. That's when the Gypsies will return . . .*

Checking the time, he saw that it was just after seven o'clock. He sprinted across the bridge and let himself into the castle, his mind racing. *Two hours until sunset—I'll have to hurry if I'm to find Madame Shelta . . ."*

Putting the haggis in the icebox, he took the electric torch and a jacket. Heading out the door, he felt anxious about meeting Madame Shelta, but recalled Harry's words: *What have you got to lose? You've already lost your marbles. Perhaps she'll help you find them.*

He locked the door and stepped out to see ruddy evening sunlight shining on the upper red bricks of the curtain wall. He hurried through the garden, trotted across the arched bridge, and picked his way down the steep hill of grass and wild onion flowers into the shadowed glen. Racing along the path to the river, he crossed the swaying rope bridge. Once on flat ground, he broke into a run, but slowed his pace upon hearing the almost human sound of goats bleating nearby. Stepping past a hedgerow, he froze.

The Gypsies had indeed returned to Rosslyn Glen. The grassy clearing was dotted with the cooking fires of a dozen caravans and tents with families of several generations around each.

He approached the nearest one and asked, "I'm looking for Madame Shelta. Can you help me?"

A half dozen men and women by the fire looked at him, seemed to hesitate and said nothing. Some older children warily approached.

"Evan!" A voice sounded from behind.

He turned and saw an older woman striding toward him. She wore a homespun heavily embroidered dress, and her long black braids were streaked with gray.

"Come," she said and walked past him. He didn't need to ask who she was.

Following her along a path of crushed stones through a field of tall grass, they reached a clearing beneath a lone oak tree.

There, she stopped and turned. After holding his gaze for a long moment, she smiled, "You've grown, English boy, but I easily recognize you. Do you recognize me?"

"I don't."

"That's unusual," she said, "Most people remember me."

"I'm sorry—I don't remember . . ."

"Don't be sorry, English boy." She looked into his eyes. "I am Madame Shelta. You came from the castle?"

"Yes. Harry told me to speak with you."

She said nothing, just stared into his eyes.

He found it curious that her steady gaze didn't make him feel uncomfortable.

"I believe it's not just *me* you don't remember, English boy. You don't remember *anything*."

"I don't even know who I am."

"I wonder why that is." And after a long silence, she whispered, "To forget the pain, you forgot *everything*."

"*What* pain?" he asked.

"You see? It worked." She extended her hands toward him, palms upward—the burnished bracelets on her wrists clicking softly in the silent evening. "Give me your hands, English boy."

"Why do you call me 'English boy'?" he asked as she took his hands in her own.

She didn't reply as she studied his palms. Beyond the roughness and strength of her hands, he felt a comforting warmth, spreading up his arms, easing the heaviness around his heart. He breathed out a sigh and asked again, "Why do you call me that?"

She looked up, a deep sadness in her eyes. "That's what I called you during the summer you turned eleven."

"Can you help me remember?"

"Even if it means also remembering the pain?"

"Yes."

"Why?"

"So I can be myself, be who I was."

"Who you *were*? You must find out who you *are*. That lies in the present."

"But the past will give me moorings. Now I have none."

"Yes. But for you the unremembered past is like an anchor, keeping you in a place filled with pain. Your mind holds this closed, so you won't remember, so you won't feel the pain. And that's a bad thing because I see that your heart wants to live in the present." She drew a deep sigh. "That is why I will help you."

"Thank you," he whispered, his vision blurring.

She released his hands, and pulling a brightly colored handkerchief from the folds of her dress, she handed it to Evan.

He dried his eyes.

"Follow me." She turned toward the encampment. "I'll make you a cup of tea."

He put the handkerchief in his pocket and followed.

They came to a solitary tent at the edge of the clearing with a few cushioned chairs around a fire that burned beneath a black pot. She nodded at one of the chairs.

"Sit while I make your tea." She disappeared into the tent.

He sat down and extended his hands toward the fire. The sun had nearly set, and the air had cooled.

After a minute, she emerged holding a basket. Kneeling by the fire, she placed the basket beside her on the ground. Opening a clay jar, she shook some of the contents into the pot. "This is dried Valerian root." She did the same with another jar. "Rhodiola flowers." Taking some dried stalks from the basket, she crushed them into the pot. "Stinging nettle."

Brushing off her hands, she sat next to him. "The tea will make the remembering easier. While it steeps, we have time to talk. I know you have many questions. You may ask me now."

"Harry told me that your name, Shelta, is old Gaelic and means 'a voice that moves.' He also told me that you're not really Scottish Gypsies—but call yourselves Egyptians. Are you Scottish or Egyptian?"

"Both." She stirred the fire beneath the pot. "Six hundred years ago my ancestors came here from Egypt, actually *Little Egypt*, which is now called Palestine. My real name is Zahirah, but when I was younger, I found that my fortune telling business improved when I used the name, Shelta.

I also liked the sound of it. But within the tribe I'm known as Zahirah. You should call me that."

Zahirah, he repeated to himself, *the name of my ancestral mother—the Saracen wife of Jonathan St. Clair.* His vision blurred with tears as he watched her stir the pot. *Now it all makes sense—I know whom she was named for, and I know who the "Egyptians" were.* He dried his eyes and asked, "Do the Scots know that your tribe is from Little Egypt?"

"Most neither know nor care." She peered into the pot. "Whether they call us Bohemians, Tartars, Heathens, or Romani—to them we are all 'Gypsies.' Some find us useful as tinkers, odd-jobbers, horse groomers, soothsayers, and magicians. At best, they look upon us with curiosity and regard as quaint. At worst, they hate us and regard us as spies, kidnappers, and thieves. But *your* people, the St. Clairs of Rosslyn, *they* knew better, which is why they have welcomed us here for hundreds of years."

He met her gaze and said, "I know why the St. Clairs welcomed you here."

"You *do?*"

Despite the disbelief in her voice, he plunged forward. "They welcomed you here because, after the Crusades, they *brought* you here."

"Who told you this?"

"No one."

"Then how could you know? *You*, who don't even know who you are."

"That may be, but I know who *you* are. I pieced it together from Harry's books about the Crusades and the St. Clairs." He left off speaking, not sure if he was violating something to be held in confidence.

After a few seconds, she said, "Tell me what you know."

"I know that during the years the Knights Templar fought the Wars of the Cross in the Holy Land, they required support from the native people—metalworkers, silversmiths, horse groomers, domestic workers, and those with knowledge of herbal elixirs and potions—healers. I know that over the years, many of these people became like family to the knights, and when the Mamluks drove them from the Holy Land, some Templars took these people with them. This is what occurred with my ancestors when Acre fell to the Mamluks. Jonathan St. Clair gathered his family in a boat, and his family included these trusted and beloved Egyptians. But I also know that Jonathan left the boat—leaving his wife and son—to do battle with the Mamluks so the boat might move far enough away from the quay and not be burned by naphtha—"

"Yes," Zahirah cut in and took up the story. "And I know that Jonathan's wife, Zahirah, my namesake, did not remain in that boat." "She left her infant son with a wet nurse and went to fight at her husband's side on the quay." She breathed a sigh and whispered, "Jonathan and Zahirah died there together." She dabbed her eyes with her sleeve. "That story has traveled through our blood over the centuries—how they sacrificed themselves so that their child, William, might live—that *we* might live."

She looked at him, smiling through her tears. "Out of the darkness of your forgotten past, Evan Sinclair, you have managed to raise up a chalice brimming with the memory of that moment—the unbroken bond between the Egyptians and the St. Clairs of Rosslyn. And that moment belongs to both of us—you and I—we are the children of their sacrifice. And because of that, I look upon you as my own child. I always have."

Evan's throat was too tight to speak. He could only nod.

Zahirah wiped her eyes and sniffed at the rising steam. "Your tea is ready." She filled an earthenware cup and held it out. "Here you are, English boy—the first step to remembering." Then she hesitated. "You're certain this is what you want?"

"Yes," he said and took the cup. "How much should I drink?"

"All of it."

He drank the tea down, the slightly bitter taste, feeling the warmth of it. Putting down the cup, he wiped his mouth with the handkerchief and handed it back to her.

"No. You will need it, because the place of remembering is also a place of weeping."

"What place?"

"The cave of William Wallace."

Evan's heart began to pound. "How may I find it?"

"You can't. Someone must guide you—one of my granddaughters."

❊ ❊ ❊

In the gathering dusk, Zahirah's ten-year-old granddaughter led Evan away from the clearing, and onto a heavy-wooded bluff above the Esk River. The sun had set, and scarlet ribbons of clouds streaked the evening sky.

"This is as far as I can take you," the girl said and tightened the bright red sash of her black robe. "The opening to the cave is there." She pointed across the river.

"Where? I cannot see it."

"Those rocks among the leaves—that's the opening." Evan took a step forward and the girl shouted.

"Wait!" She handed him a small paper packet. "First, you must eat this."

"What?"

"Mushrooms that grandmother selected and dried over many days. You must eat all of them."

"When?"

"Now." She waited, watching as he shook the mushrooms into the palm of his hand. In the half-light they looked like any other mushrooms he'd ever seen, only smaller. He brought his hand to his mouth, chewed, and swallowed. They tasted like mushrooms and earth.

"Now, drink." She handed him a water skin.

He drank deeply and handed it back.

"Now go. It will soon be dark."

He looked toward the cave, half-hidden in the heavy foliage on the far bank beyond the narrow river where a swift current flowed. He turned to thank the girl, but she was gone. Turning back, he plunged forward and skidded down the muddy slope toward the river.

CHAPTER 50

May 3, 1915
Rosslyn Glen

HO'S THERE?" Evan called out.

"Who do ye think? Isna this ma cave?"

A giant of a man loomed in the darkness, seeming to reflect bright moonlight. Only there was no moon. Memories began to stir in Evan's mind. "This is *your* cave?"

"Aye."

"Which means . . . you're . . . Sir William Wallace."

"Ye would serve me better to leave off with 'sir.' I ne'er sought nor wanted title."

"But you can't *be* here." The curtain began to lift.

"And why the nae?"

"You're six hundred years dead."

"Oh, tha'." Wallace shook his head. "I ne'er died."

"But you did! King Edward had you killed—most brutally."

"It takes more than tha to kill a man."

"What are you saying?"

"When a man ken he fights for freedom, tha man ne'er dies. So, when they offered clemency if I would but swear fealty to Edward, I refused. I ne're recanted. I stayed true ta' th' end."

"But in the end, you *died*."

"Nae, laddie. I go on. Whe' er' men and women demand their freedom, I'm there."

"What men and women? I'm the only one here—alone in this dark cave."

"Wha' dark cave?"

"What—" Evan left off speaking as he saw light rising, rising without pressure, illuminating a man with a full beard and strong arms, long brown hair cinched up in highlander fashion, the bright pommel of a claymore girded on his back.

"But I'm alone here."

"Are ye? I'm wi' ye now, laddie. Dunna you see tha'? Just as I wa' there when ye sailed from the New World to join th' fight. Just as I wa' there in the polders when ye fought with yer sling against th' German gun."

Evan closed his eyes as memories washed over him. He remembered the machine-gun raking the wood, the sluice gate, the bright water flooding the polders.

"I wa' there when ye were wounded by the canal. And I wa' there when ye were tossed by th' storm in th' wee boat. I saw how ye fought to save each one of them, and how ye could nae do it."

Evan's tears flowed as the horror of the lifeboat buffeted him, a raging storm driving him to his knees. He remembered now how they had taken turns baling, until one-by-one they grew too tired and too weak, and the sea water washed into the lifeboat, until he was alone—trying to bale and keep their heads out of the water. He remembered how each boy struggled to breathe, the sea filling their mouths, gasping their love to a wife they would never see again, to a mother, a father, a child. The weight of the sea-driven deaths washed over him. He pitched forward.

"Ye ken now, laddie, dunna ya?"

He felt Wallace's hand lightly on his head, heard him whisper. "I wa' with ye then, an' I'm with ye now."

Evan wept, his whole body shaking.

Minutes or hours passed. When the tide of weeping ebbed, he heard Wallace sigh, the sound filling the cave.

"I'm glad that's o'er. And I'm glad it happened here."

Evan sat up and wiped his eyes with Zahirah's handkerchief. "What do you mean—here?"

Wallace nodded toward the cave entry, and Evan knew he meant the castle.

"When first I came here, I wa' about yer age. It wa' here I brought the wee bairn, young William St. Clair back from th' Holy Land."

Evan listened, seeing Wallace smile at the memory.

"So many years past. Young William ha' been entrusted ta' my care by his father, Jonathan—my mentor and master, as fine a knight as ere broke bread." He fixed his eyes on Evan. "I see him in ye now, laddie. Yer of his blood. I also knew th' bairn's mother— Zahirah, so full of grace and strength. As our boat left th' landing wi' Acre in flames, I saw them on the landing, through th' smoke an' the mist on the water. I saw their sacrifice wi' my own eyes. They fought tha' *ye* might live, tha' *we* might live. Remember tha'! Wi' everything else, laddie, remember tha'!"

A breeze stirred in the cave and with it the sound of pipes, soft at first, but like a wind, rising. Evan knew the tune well—the bagpipes skirling, keeping time through the centuries, rising in the bright air—"Brian Boru's March."

Wallace placed a hand on his shoulder. "Ye'll go on from here," he whispered.

"Where? Where do I go from here?"

Wallace smiled. "When I wa a young man, I floated about wi' no particular direction—like a feather on the breath o' God. But tha' was gude and fair at tha' time. I'd the chance ta' move in any direction I chose. An' when th' time came for me to choose, I wa' free to do so wi' no cauld nor care, an' I chose Jerusalem! But na' a place o' this world—o' stone an' dust an' bad smells. I chose th' *Upper* Jerusalem. A place where I cud become ma' best self. An' in the end, ma' path led me here, where ma' journey began. But all tha' is history. It's yer turn now. Ye must choose yer path—"

"But how?"

"Dinna fash on it, laddie. When the time comes, ye'll be free to choose. And tha will be easier now."

"Why?"

"Because now ye ken who ye are."

CHAPTER 51

May 4, 1915
Criterion Restaurant Piccadilly Circus, London

GERTRUDE WAS distraught. Even though the Turkish attack on the Canal had failed, the war was not going well for the Entente. British troops slated for transfer to the Western Front had been retained in the Middle East Theater, and the situation in Europe had become a terrible stalemate with mounting casualties.

Defense of the Canal had also diverted Allied attention from the Dardanelles, and over the past month, the naval campaign had proved disastrous. The Allied armada of cruisers, destroyers, minesweepers, and submarines had sustained significant losses from mines and Turkish artillery, and had failed to enter the Sea of Marmara, requiring an amphibious landing at Gallipoli. And that had now begun.

She was also distraught about Richard. She hadn't heard from him since he left Egypt for Gallipoli—his last letter so blackened by the censor's ink it was barely legible. Frantic with worry, she was thankful for a busy work schedule that filled her days; between the MO-4 mapping room and the London Red Cross, she was fully occupied. But she dreaded unattended time outside work—the empty minutes and hours when all she could do was fret about the war and about Richard.

The evening's dinner party was one such gap in her schedule, though one she couldn't avoid since it was hosted by the director of the London Red Cross, Lord Robert Cecil. He insisted she attend.

Attired in a purple chiffon evening gown, Gertrude took her place at the table set for twelve and tried to smile.

Lord Cecil stood and tapped a spoon against a glass of cut crystal for quiet. "It's so very good to see you in this delightful setting, especially at this momentous occasion! As you're all aware, Great Britain's brave boys along with those of Ireland, New Zealand, and Australia, are mounting an unprecedented amphibious landing at Gallipoli. While we await news of their progress in knocking Johnny Turk out of the fight, let us stand and raise a glass and a prayer to those risking their lives in this Great War for Civilization." Lifting his glass, and intoned, "Our Father in Heaven, strengthen the hands of those who defend our blessed land, impart them with salvation, deliver them from evil, and may their heads be crowned with glory on earth as in heaven. And let us say—amen!"

"A beautiful and touching tribute and prayer, Lord Cecil," Gertrude said after adding a silent prayer for Richard and placing her glass down. As she took her seat, she saw Godfrey Whitecastle, the elderly telegraph operator from the Red Cross, enter the private dining room. He sat next to Gertrude. She turned to him and said, "Good evening, Mr. Whitecastle. I'm so glad you could join us."

"Thank you, Miss Bell. With all the dispatches coming in from Gallipoli, I found it quite difficult to leave my station."

Having overheard Whitecastle, Lord Cecil asked, "What's the news, Godfrey?"

Gertrude gripped her napkin, wanting to know but dreading what she might hear.

"I perused a rather lengthy dispatch just before coming, Lord Cecil, and based on firsthand accounts, it's not going well, though conditions vary between the different landing sites—"

"How many landing sites are there?" asked Gertrude.

"Five." Godfrey paused to take a drink of water. "The different beaches are designated by the letters *V* through *Z*. The Aussies and New Zealanders came ashore at Z Beach and, by last accounts, were holding their own, though taking fire from the Turks with moderate casualties.

However, the situation at V Beach has been ghastly!"

"How so?" asked Gertrude, gripping her napkin tighter.

"The first problem was the landing. Having lost the element of surprise when the SS *River Clyde*, carrying about a thousand troops, ran aground too far from shore. Precious lives were lost trying to position pontoons to get men ashore, while others scrambled into rowboats."

"Were these British troops?" Lord Cecil asked.

"Actually, Irishmen of the Royal Dublin and Royal Munster Fusiliers. Though they were commanded by two British officers—Captain Garth Walford and Lieutenant Colonel Richard Doughty-Wylie."

"What?" Gertrude heard herself cut in, her heart pounding in her ears. Unable to speak, she heard Godfrey's voice give way to that of Lord Cecil, but it was difficult to hear what they were saying. Their voices sounded distant, echoing as in a dream or a nightmare. Redoubling her efforts to hear them, she found that they were gossiping about Richard's family.

She heard Lord Cecil ask, ". . . where did that hyphenated name 'Doughty-Wylie' come from anyhow?"

Whitecastle replied, "He added his wife's surname when they married—"

"For heaven's sake, Godfrey!" she cut in, nearly shouting, "What happened after they came ashore?"

Godfrey cleared his throat and continued. "As the fusiliers struggled to reach the shore, the Turks raked them with machine-gun fire from their positions above the beach. As one might imagine, casualties were quite heavy—of the thousand men in the landing party, only three hundred managed to make it ashore . . ." Godfrey cleared his throat and glanced around the table. "Perhaps I've said enough—"

"No, *do* go on. *Please*," Gertrude pleaded. Barely able to breathe, she dreaded what she was hearing, but was compelled to hear more.

"I shouldn't want to upset anyone, sir." Godfrey shrugged apologetically.

"No, Godfrey. I *want* you to continue," said Lord Cecil. "Everyone here is committed to the war effort and dedicated to supporting our brave boys. We should know what they're enduring."

"Very well, sir," Godfrey said and plunged ahead. "The last dispatch I saw was from a war correspondent who interviewed survivors of the V beach landing. They noted something peculiar; one of the officers, Doughty-Wylie, carried no weapon and seemed oddly calm during the battle, almost oblivious to the Turkish guns. Nonetheless, he and Walford led the fusiliers forward and captured the village of Sedd el Bahr and the old castle above it—a remarkable feat under the circumstances. Sadly, neither of them survived." Godfrey took a deep breath and added, "But they've both already been recommended for the Victoria Cross . . ."

Gertrude pushed back from the table, knocking over her chair as she ran from the room. She didn't know where she was going—only somewhere she'd be able to weep for Richard.

CHAPTER 52

May 4, 1915
Ain Jiddy

IN THE heat and stillness of early afternoon, Gunter, Rahman, and David harvested the early figs in the wadi above a haphazard dam of boulders. In defiance of the desert, the Rashida Bedouin had planted fig trees where silt and soil had collected, washed down over decades from rare downpours and saturating gully runs.

During their time with the Bedouin, the fugitives pitched in; Fatima, Sarah, and Tirzah helped with cooking, tending the sheep and goats, mending clothing and the goat-hair tents, and helping to care for the children. Gunter, Rahman, and David tended the vineyards, tilled the soil, and, as they did now, helped with harvesting.

Wearing an ankle-length *thawb* of homespun sheep's wool, Gunter cut the figs away with his penknife, leaving a short stem attached to delay spoilage. He carefully placed each fig in a bag strapped to his shoulder. Pausing, he sampled one. "These are *so* good! How fortunate the locust didn't touch them. It's as if they never reached Ain Jiddy!"

"They did, but they didn't stay long," Rahman said as he worked. "According to the sheikh, migrating storks feasted on them."

"What about the eggs?" asked David.

"They never hatched because of the salty soil here. Between the storks and the soil, no ravenous locust and no hungry larva survived."

"I'm delighted the figs survived." David said. "They're delicious."

Gunter looked up and saw David sitting in the shade of one of the trees, eating a handful of figs, apparently having decided to take a break.

"It is with me as Micah prophesied," David announced, "*Each man shall sit beneath his fig tree, and no one shall terrify him!*"

Laughing, he threw a fig at David, which hit him on the head then fell onto his lap.

"Thanks," David said and ate the fig.

As Gunter returned to gathering, he heard Rahman shout, "What's that?"

"Where?" Gunter asked, looking up.

"There!" Rahman pointed toward the northern shore of the Dead Sea.

Gunter saw a flag of dust moving along the dirt track bordering the water. "Is that an automobile?"

"I don't know. It's too far away," said Rahman, his voice edged with fear.

"I've got just the thing," David exclaimed and scrambled up the embankment, "Anna's opera glasses!" After training the glasses on the cloud of dust, he shouted, "It's a Turkish military truck!"

Gunter turned and pelted down the wadi with Rahman and David close behind. "Turkish soldiers!" Gunter shouted as he entered the Bedouin encampment. When the sheikh emerged from one of the tents, Gunter pointed. "Turkish soldiers are coming!"

While the Turks generally left the Bedouin alone, there would be dire consequences for harboring fugitives. Gunter knew the Bedouin had a cave they used to shelter from thieves, and he was sure that's where they could hide.

Knowing Tirzah was tending the goats and sheep, Gunter ran to a fenced-off pen of spiny thorn-brush and found her feeding the animals with barley husks.

"Tirzah! Turkish soldiers! We need to hide in the cave I showed you."

"The big one the Rashida use?"

"Yes. Let's go!"

Rounding the tent with Tirzah, Gunter saw David still standing and looking through the opera glasses.

"David!" he shouted. "Let's get to the cave!"

David lifted his free hand and said, "Wait."

"What do you mean, wait?" Gunter yelled, but seeing that David was smiling, he asked, "What do you see?"

"Mustafa and Yusuf!"

"You're sure?"

"One hundred percent."

"But why are they coming *here*?"

"I don't know, though they did promise to warn us if they heard anything . . ."

"Alright then," Gunter breathed a sigh of relief as he stood next to David. "We'll see what this is about."

By the time the truck pulled to a stop in front of the main tent, the whole settlement was waiting. Except for the Armenian woman.

Seeing that she was missing, Gunter whispered to Rahman, "I don't see Arsine."

"Poor thing! She's frightened of the Turks. I'll ask Fatima to find her."

Mustafa and Yusuf were quickly out of the truck and warmly greeted by David and Sarah, who guided them to meet the sheikh, loudly praising the two young men for the kindness and protection they had provided.

Gunter saw the sheikh touch a hand to his forehead, chest, and lips as he bowed his head to them. "I thank you for your beneficence and your bravery. I will explain this to my people." After he had done so, the sheikh gestured toward the main tent. "Please, come inside, that you may rest and drink coffee with us!"

"Soon, ya Sheikh!" Mustafa replied with a respectful bow. "We must first speak with the fugitives about the state of their affairs in Jerusalem."

"Of course. While you converse, we will begin our preparations for coffee."

Gunter joined David with Mustafa and Yusuf a few paces from the main tent. David was the first to speak. "Does List plan to raid the Colony?"

"Not yet," Mustafa replied. "But we're concerned about this." He opened a folded newspaper. "The New York Times from two weeks ago." He handed it to David. "We saw this in the Augusta Victoria library earlier today."

"I don't read English well enough," David said and handed the newspaper to Gunter. "You read it."

"Right here," Yusuf pointed. "A warning from the German government right below an advertisement for the *Lusitania*."

Gunter read out loud. "From the Imperial German Embassy in Washington DC. Travelers intending to embark on the Atlantic voyage are warned that a state of war exists between Germany and Great Britain. The war zone includes the waters adjacent to the British Isles, and in accordance with formal notice given by the Imperial German Government, vessels flying the flag of Great Britain or any of her allies, are liable to destruction in those waters. Travelers sailing in the war zone on ships of Great Britain or her allies do so at their own risk."

Looking up, Gunter saw that Sarah and Tirzah had drawn near to listen.

"The risk is real," said Mustafa. "German U-boats have been sinking British vessels since the end of last year—even hospital ships. And they've recently increased the submarine campaign. That's why they're warning civilian travelers."

"But nothing has happened yet," said Sarah.

"Not yet. The *Lusitania* left New York four days ago, on May 1, with over a hundred Americans on board. She'll enter the war zone in a few days, and if a German U-boat sinks her and Americans drown, American neutrality might end. We thought you should know."

"You're right," said Gunter. "The minute List sees an opportunity he'll enter the American Colony and take Anna and her family for interrogation—"

"But they don't know anything!" Sarah cut in. "David was questioned as an *archeologist* about the portal. Anna doesn't know anything about that!"

"Sarah," said David. "They only questioned me to find Gunter and Rahman."

"Why?" Sarah asked.

"Because," Gunter replied, "List believes we have knowledge of certain secrets of the Temple Mount, and he'll stop at nothing to obtain that information." He handed the newspaper back to Yusuf. "Are you returning to Jerusalem now?"

"Yes."

"I'll go with you," said Gunter.

"What?" Tirzah asked, nearly shouting. "You *can't*!"

"I must, darling—"

"Why *you* Aba?" she cried. "You can't leave me!"

Gunter took Tirzah in his arms. He felt her shoulders shaking as she wept.

Rahman raised his shoulders. "Tirzah asks a good question. Why you?"

"Isn't it obvious? I *must* be the one to confront List! I speak his language, and I'm every bit as much an *Übermensch* as he is!" Gunter said in a voice dripping with sarcasm. "And once he has me, he'll leave Anna and her family alone. Besides, I'll be able to reason with him, and when the time is right, I'll give him what he wants." He fixed Rahman with his eyes. "I'll give him what he *deserves*!" He gestured toward the main tent. "Go ahead and join the sheikh for coffee."

Turning to Tirzah, Gunter put his arm around her shoulders and hugged her. "Come, my darling, Let's speak together in a quiet place. Come." Together, they walked away from the encampment and out into the desert. Coming to a stop, they stood without speaking—looking up at the sky bannered with russet clouds as the sun set over the high cliffs of Ain Jiddy, the air warm and fragrant. Turning from the cliffs, Gunter saw that the sky was perfectly reflected on the smooth water of the Dead Sea—as if they were hovering between two skies.

Tirzah was first to speak. "I understand that you must go, Aba. After all, I'm not a child anymore, I'm fourteen."

He looked at how the twilight shone on her olive skin, so much of her mother in her green eyes and delicate features, her golden-brown hair gathered in a single braid. His heart swelled with gratitude. "My darling," he said. "Fatima tells me that, in addition to cracking barley, sewing, cooking, tending the goats, and helping with Isser and Mahmoud, you've also been learning Arabic."

"Yes. While you're off doing your Bedouin-man things, I've been busy with my Bedouin-lady activities. But to make things more interesting, Fatima has been teaching me Arabic, and I've been teaching English and Hebrew to the Bedouin women."

"Your mother would have been very proud of you!"

"My mother *is* very proud of me!"

Gunter wasn't sure he had heard her correctly. "What do you mean by that?"

"Arabic isn't the only thing Fatima has taught me!"

His breath caught. Taking a step back, he looked into the eyes. "What are you saying?"

"I'm saying that Fatima told me more about the Temple Mount secrets." Looking at him calmly, she whispered, "I'm saying that I know more about your hidden fellowship of Temple Mount Guardians, and more about the connection between the earthly and Upper Jerusalem, than you told me, Aba. Do you remember when you quoted *Hamlet* to me; *'There are more things between heaven and earth than are dreamed of in your philosophy?'* You were right, because there were things you didn't tell me. But Fatima did."

"What didn't I tell you?"

"Something that I needed to hear. Something I needed to know. That Ima is in that place between the worlds," she said with a sad smile. "And when the time comes for me to enter that blessed place, I know I'll see her, and I won't have to miss her anymore!"

❊ ❊ ❊

Returning to Jerusalem, Gunter sat on the truck's front bench seat between Mustafa and Yusuf, watching the headlamps carve a tunnel of light through the empty darkness of the desert.

Parts of his conversation with Tirzah returned to him as the truck rattled forward and the minutes crawled by. He was glad that Fatima had expanded the description of the hidden Temple Mount chamber to include the heartening and miraculous presence of all Guardians, from the present and distant past. Including Rachel.

"Where in Jerusalem do you want to go?" Mustafa asked Gunter, shouting over the noisy clatter of the truck.

"The American Colony." Gunter shouted back.

"Do you plan to meet with List soon?" asked Yusuf.

"Only when I must. First, let's see what happens with the *Lusitania*."

Having changed into his usual khaki shirt and shorts, Gunter reached into his shirt pocket, took a folded piece of paper, and handed it to Yusuf. "Hold onto this, please—it's the name of the husband of the Armenian woman."

"Fatima told us why she was so frightened of us," Yusuf said and put the paper in his pocket. "Completely understandable given what happened to her young son, and with her husband sent to a forced-labor camp."

"Do you know the one?" Gunter asked.

"We do. It's west of Jerusalem, near an-Nabi Samwil."

"Can you get him out?"

"I'm pretty sure we can. We'll use the ruse of bringing him to Augusta Victoria for interrogation. Instead, we'll bring him to Ain Jiddy—"

"Couldn't all that driving around get you in trouble?"

"No. Djemal is *expecting* us to drive around—to bring the villagers petrol and equipment to deal with the locust larvae. That's how we got away today, and that's how we'll get away tomorrow."

"Thanks!" Gunter patted Yusuf on the knee. "With all that poor woman has been through, having her husband back would be a blessing."

"We'll do our best. Mustafa and I much prefer helping people than killing them, though every army strikes a balance I suppose . . ."

"That depends on what army you're talking about." Gunter sat back, silently considering that the two Turks might someday make good recruits as Guardians of the Temple Mount.

CHAPTER 53

May 5, 1915

By Steamer to the British Protectorate of Aden

FAISAL AND his bodyguard, Mirzuk, were the only passengers on a tramp steamer staffed by captain and crew of the sea-faring Bedouin, the Bani Zaranik, providing passage to Faisal because of their love for him along with ten thousand gold sovereigns in compensation.

Leaning on the stern gunwale, Faisal felt the thrumming of the ship's pounding cylinders beneath his hands as he looked back at the widening wake. With the sound of the wind in the aerials loud in his ears, he shouted to Mirzuk. "If you don't know where you are *going*, you must look to where you have *come from*!"

"I cannot hear you, my prince!" Mirzuk shouted back.

With his brown camel-hair robe whipped by the wind, Faisal held his *keffiyeh* in place with one hand and led the way down a curving flight of descending mahogany steps. Once in his cabin, which was actually the captain's stateroom afforded to Faisal for his comfort, he was glad to be out of the wind. "Now that we are able to hear each other, Mirzuk, let us converse." Faisal settled into an upholstered chair and motioned Mirzuk to sit.

"What occurred to me while I was admiring the ship's wake was the imperative of knowing where we come from in order to penetrate the unknowable mystery of where our journey leads." On seeing the lost expression on Mirzuk's face, Faisal added, "As it is said, *el-harakah baraka*—movement is itself a blessing."

"Now I see your meaning, sire—to accomplish anything, we must act. And to act, we must know who we are and where we come from. And that much is clear, sire—as Arabs and as Bedouin, we most decidedly know who we are."

"Well said Mirzuk! This knowledge indeed gives us the strength we will require in the coming days. For more than four hundred years we have strained beneath the Ottoman yoke. However, now that we are poised to rise against them, I am troubled about a lack of Arab unity."

"But, sire, are not all Arabs united in our struggle for freedom?"

"Sadly, no. Some oppose us, and others, like a beaten dog that cowers from his master, are full of fear. We must, therefore, do all we can to unite and gather all possible allies before the revolt begins. Because, when we rise, we must have early success. This is essential, since early success will show our timid brethren who hesitate that we might succeed and triumph. In this manner, our numbers will grow. That is the very reason we have journeyed here."

"That is well, O Prince."

Faisal looked out a porthole and heaved a sigh. After six days, he was anxious to disembark. Despite the comfort of his quarters, he hadn't slept well, thinking about his imminent discussions with Weizmann. To his relief, he could now see the brown coastline of Aden beyond the azure waters of the Red Sea. He checked his timepiece. "I see that we are nearing the port, and it is not yet ten o'clock. This pleases me since we will have ample time to register at our hotel and regain our land legs before we meet with Weizmann and el-Orenz."

"El-Orenz!" Mirzuk exclaimed. "It will do my heart good to see him again!"

Faisal nodded his agreement. "I am hoping he will make fast our connection with the British, and I am gratified that he has facilitated our meeting with Weizmann."

"But what do you really hope to gain from Weizmann, my master?"

"Two things. I believe he will strengthen our position with the British and ally us with the Jews of Western Europe and America." As Faisal spoke, he noticed that Mirzuk was frowning. "But I see that you are displeased, Mirzuk. Tell me why."

"Regarding the British, my prince, is it possible we will only be trading one imperial master for another?"

Faisal knew that many Arabs believed this to be true, and he chose his words carefully. "I have no illusions about the imperial nature of the British and all the great powers. One has only to see how they scrambled for colonies in Africa at the end of the last century, and how they now scramble for influence in the Middle East. However, it is clear to me that neither the Ottomans nor the Germans will ever give us freedom. And while it is true that the British and the French are just as imperialistic, they are currently inclined to be generous with us given their need for our support. This is why my royal father and I are willing to ally with them—but only with the British, since no one trusts the French."

"May Allah utterly reject them." Mirzuk nodded in agreement.

"When el-Orenz visited with me in Nuweiba, he assured me that we now have binding promises in writing from Kitchener and McMahon in British Egypt."

Mirzuk raised his shoulders. "Granted, my prince, but what of the Zionists? It is said that they want all of Palestine—*both* sides of the Jordan River."

"There are indeed such voices among the Jews," Faisal conceded. "But the majority of Zionists, like Weizmann, are committed to developing Palestine without encroaching on the property or the rights of Arabs."

"These are elevated and commendable sentiments, sire, but I worry that the current needs of the British and the Zionists are such that they will say anything to gain our support."

"I appreciate that you are judicious and careful, ya Mirzuk."

"Sire, do you truly believe Weizmann is someone we can trust?"

"I do, and for three reasons: First, both our movements might be strengthened if we support each other in our struggle for recognition by the imperial powers. In this manner we will be better able to counter the pressures arrayed against us. Second, like us, the Jews are from here—*their* Holy Land is not far removed from *ours*. Third, and this is the most important, we and the Jews have a shared inheritance as sons of Abraham, and is it not said, *it-dam ma beysir mai?* Or as the English say, 'blood is thicker than water.' With the Jews we have a family bond—Abraham is their patriarch as well as ours. We are therefore brothers, and it is therefore not only to our *advantage* to welcome them back to their Holy Land, it is our *duty* to do so."

A defiant expression on Mirzuk's face belied his reply. "May Allah bless you for your munificence, sire . . . but . . ."

"But, what?" Faisal prodded.

"What if our Zionist brothers decide to curry favor with the British and turn their backs on us? What then?"

"I do not believe this will happen. If we are generous and become their allies in reclaiming the homeland they lost, the Jews will realize that the future of a Jewish Palestine is linked in close sympathy with us—we who are their brothers and neighbors. They will understand that our acceptance and support will be key in developing and sustaining their homeland. Why would they jeopardize their very existence by denying that bond?"

The steamer pulled into port and the sailors made fast the lines. Faisal disembarked, pausing briefly to shake hands with the ship's captain. Stepping off the wooden pier, he put his hand on Mirzuk's shoulder and said, "We will continue our discussion when time allows. For the present, let us go to our hotel and then get a decent cup of coffee at the restaurant by the church where we'll be meeting Lawrence and Weizmann."

❊ ❊ ❊

The HMY *Osborne* conveying Lawrence and Weizmann the length of the Red Sea was a decommissioned forty-foot paddle steamer that had known better days. As a Royal Navy yacht, the *Osborne* had been favored by Queen Victoria's eldest son, Prince Albert Edward, logging thousands of miles between the Isle of Wight and the British Raj. But after forty years of hard service leaving her with weak rigging, leaking seams, cracked paint, and rotten canvas, she was deemed unseaworthy and decommissioned. Scheduled to be scrapped, she was smuggled out of the Tilbury dock by enterprising German sailors, patched up and taken to Egypt where she enjoyed a few years of service to the Imperial German diplomatic corps on the Nile. However, the *Osborne*'s decrepitude worsened, and she was finally declared unsafe and condemned to be broken-up. But as before, she was spared; Greek sailors bought her for afloat salvage, and, after minor repairs, she was put back into service as an affordable hire.

"I'm so very sorry, Professor Weizmann!" Lawrence apologized as they sat together on a dilapidated cherry wood bench. His rumpled mismatched uniform nicely matched the boat's decor. "The Greek skipper impressed me with the *Osborne*'s pedigree and assured me that, up until three years ago, she was hosting diplomatic parties for the German Embassy in Cairo."

Weizmann, wearing a soiled white shirt and dungarees, laughed. "I find it hard to believe that this steamer could accumulate so many layers of filth in just three years."

"I know." Lawrence sighed. "Grimy sleeping and dining quarters, inedible food, and the head so revolting! I'm sorry, but it was impossible to secure any other vessel—"

"Ned, please!" Weizmann cut in. "My only concern was whether this thing would be able to get us here, and though much-neglected, she has proved sufficiently seaworthy. Now that we are here, I am well pleased. Besides, I've had worse accommodations—"

"You have?" Lawrence asked hopefully.

"Actually . . . no!" Weizmann smiled. "This is absolutely the worst, but we've made it here, and that's all that matters."

"I'll make it up to you, Chaim. Once we make port, we'll check into the swanky Crescent Hotel, and you'll be able to take a proper bath and feel restored."

"I'll settle for feeling clean," said Weizmann. "But will there be time? We're to meet Faisal at noon—"

"Not a problem. Everything in the Port of Aden is within a short walking distance." Lawrence paused and considered the historic significance of the moment at hand. *In a few hours, Weizmann and Faisal will meet as putative leaders of the Jews and Arabs to speak about their national movements, and how they might cooperate with each other. In the sweep of history, this moment is epic.* It took his breath away. After a deep sigh, he asked, "Do you feel ready to present the Zionist program to Faisal?"

"Speaking with people about Zionism is what I do, Ned. It's like breathing. Are you worried how he'll receive it?"

"I am," Lawrence conceded. "Faisal has pinned his fortunes on the rising tide of Arab nationalism, and he can't appear to be the lackey of any imperial power—"

"Such as Great Britain?" Weizmann cut in. "After all, you're here as a representative of the British Empire, the preeminent colonial power in the world."

"True—but Great Britain has promised freedom and independence for the Arabs."

"Be that as it may," Weizmann raised his shoulders. "I'm here as a representative of the Zionist movement, which supports a Jewish homeland in a post-Ottoman Palestine. If Faisal chooses to work with us, would that make him a lackey of world Judaism?"

"I think not," Lawrence replied. "Because you and Faisal represent two dispossessed peoples. And if we are able, at this and in future meetings, to project a clear and positive vision of how you would coexist and share the land, you might be able to convince the British and French to support the idea—that is, of course, if the Entente wins the war and dislodges the Ottomans."

Weizmann nodded. "I believe I can project that vision, Ned." He pushed up from the bench and stood facing Lawrence. "But since you know Faisal, I want your opinion on what I'm planning to say to him. You play the part of Faisal."

"What is this . . . a *rehearsal?*" asked Lawrence.

"Yes."

"Do I have any lines?"

"No. You just listen." Weizmann cleared his throat and bowed. "Prince Faisal, Your Excellency, in promoting Jewish self-determination, I completely and honestly feel common cause with Arab self-determination. Just as the Arabs have faced cultural repression under the Turks, so too the Jews throughout our diaspora. Jews and Arabs can and should rise as one against the same denial of our vitality and intelligence. My hope is that, if Arabs and Jews support one another in their struggle for nationhood, our combined efforts will greatly increase our chances for success. There is also this—since Your Royal Highness is the only representative Arab leader with influence beyond a local level, you have the pedigree and personal qualities that carry great weight in Arabia and with the British authorities. By creating a commonality of purpose, we will more likely achieve our common goals of self-determination and independence, and in the bargain, we'll create good relations between us for years to come." Weizmann smiled and asked Lawrence, "How was that?"

"Perfect!" Lawrence clapped. "And perfectly timed as we arrive in Aden."

They watched as their ramshackle steamer docked at the dusty port, and the disheveled Greek sailors tied onto the posts.

Lawrence leaned toward Weizmann and whispered, "I pray that you will leave Aden with a firm alliance, and in a much better boat!"

CHAPTER 54

May 5, 1915

Aden

AFTER MORE than two hours, it was over.

Lawrence was exhausted after facilitating the wide-ranging conversation between Faisal and Weizmann in Arabic and French. Reclining in the shadowed comfort of the restaurant at a large round table of hammered copper, he was content to watch these two leaders—one of the Hebrews, the other of the Arabs—sipping coffee and chatting together in French.

At Faisal's invitation, Weizmann had donned a striped *keffiyeh* complementing his three-piece white travel suit.

Lawrence allowed himself to smile as he looked at them, together on a cushioned couch in matching headgear. *I may be witnessing the birth of possibility that these two nations might live peacefully in neighboring portions of the Holy Land.*

There had, indeed, been a measure of progress—should the Entente prevail, they had agreed to present a united front regarding their shared vision of Arab and Jewish self-determination within the Ottoman province of Greater Syria. *But this will be a heavy lift. Even before they encounter any external resistance, they'll need to convince their own people!*

He sipped his coffee and recalled the frustrations Weizmann had expressed during their voyage—the virulent anti-Zionism coming from many Jews throughout Eastern and Western Europe: Orthodox Jews who viewed a nonreligious return to Zion without divine intervention as a profane sacrilege; secular, well-to-do Jews who considered themselves good

Germans or Englishmen of the Enlightenment who feared that Zionism would create the suspicion that Jews weren't fully loyal citizens; and lastly, young revolutionary Jews who were strongly anti-Zionist, believing it counterrevolutionary to harbor a separate allegiance to the Jewish people.

For Faisal, the situation was as bad or worse. While there was growing support for unity and nationalism among the Arab inhabitants of the Ottoman Empire, it remained a minority position. *Would the diverse millions of Ottoman Arabs support Faisal's leadership in revolt against a weakened but still formidable Ottoman Empire? Will a large majority of Cairo intellectuals, shopkeepers of Damascus, and merchants of Baghdad ever swear allegiance to a Bedouin prince?* He took another sip of coffee and sighed. *Even among the Bedouin there is no unity, with endless feuds between many of the tribes. Indeed, Ibn Saud and the Rashidis are outright hostile toward each other and toward the Hashemites. How will they ever unite?*

He leaned forward and took a few pitted olives from a nearby plate. *On the other hand, a struggle for freedom after four hundred years of Ottoman oppression might bring disparate groups together under Hashemite leadership.* He ate an olive and frowned. *But what will come afterward? What of Arab unity once the Turks are vanquished? Will it vanish? Is the idea of Arab nationalism just a midsummer's daydream? Is it all just a dream?*

At that, Lawrence smiled to himself, recalling the passage he had written and shared with Clive Sinclair at Whitehall months before... *Those who dream by night in the dusty recesses of their minds wake up in the day to find it was vanity, but the dreamers of the day are dangerous men, for they may act their dream with open eyes, and make it possible.*

"What the hell!" he shouted. "Let's make it possible!" Seeing shocked expressions from Faisal and Weizmann, Lawrence stood up. "A toast!" He beckoned to a waiter. "A bottle of *Arak,* please, and," he nodded toward Faisal, "a glass of iced tea."

When drinks arrived, Lawrence raised his glass. "*Je vous félicite messieurs,*" he proposed in French, wanting both Faisal and Weizmann to understand without translation. "You have made great progress toward future cooperation between your peoples—two great peoples who have contributed so much to world culture, to literature, science, and medicine. Just like my people—the Irish!" Laughing, he raised his glass high. "May your pockets be heavy, may your heart be light, may the Lord keep you in his hand, though never close his fist too tight!"

After everyone drank, Faisal stood up, raised his glass of tea, and made a little bow to Weizmann. With Lawrence translating, he bestowed a traditional Arabic blessing. "I ask Allah to delight you with three things: extended provisions, gratitude for blessings, and a long life!" He then surprised Lawrence with words of the poet, Rumi, which he whispered to Weizmann. *"Beyond the notions of faith and apostacy, there is a field. I will meet you there."*

Then it was Weizmann's turn. He raised his glass and bowed his head to Faisal. "This is for you, my friend—something I read in the *Times of India* from a young lawyer named Gandhi; 'Friendship that insists upon agreement on all matters is not worth the name. Friendship, to be real, must ever sustain the weight of honest differences, however sharp they be.' Let us drink to our friendship, Prince Faisal!"

After they drank, Weizmann added, "I'm grateful to the prince for sharing with me a vision of cooperation for the national aspirations of our people. But, beyond that, I'm grateful to the prince for inviting us to join him for the return trip on his steamer, rescuing us from the filthy deathtrap of a boat we took to get here!"

After the final toast, Lawrence sat back and smiled as he studied Weizmann and Faisal. He knew this was a good beginning and he hoped this first step would lead to a highway of promise. He prayed that the generosity and camaraderie they had shown would light the way to a bright future.

God willing, we'll succeed. God help us if we fail.

CHAPTER 55

May 7, 1915
Oxford

IN THE bright warmth of a spring afternoon, Evan ran up the steps to the front door of the family home on Marston Road in Oxford and knocked. "Dad! Mervin!" He shouted and knocked again. "I'm home!"

Having taken an early morning train from Edinburgh, he'd arrived by taxi from the railway station hoping to find his father at the house, or at least Mervin.

He knocked again, stronger than before—the sound echoing through the house. He listened for footsteps but heard only the sibilant whisper of a light wind through the branches of the plane trees along the street.

He tried the door, jiggled it hard, but it was locked. *Like amnesia—that feeling of being locked out.*

He glanced at his wristwatch. *Almost four o'clock.* He took off his haversack and sat at the top of the steps, looking up and down the street, wondering which neighbor's door to knock on first.

Looking back at the house, he noticed the planter boxes his mother kept below the sitting room windows, empty now but for the dry husks of dead flowers. He thought of her with a stab of sadness, his newly restored memories of her and of her death, sharp and painful.

He drew a disconsolate breath. *How odd to have wandered about witless for so long, and now to remember everything—everything except for what happened in Wallace's Cave. How strange to have no memory of what restored my memory.*

Before leaving Roslin, Evan had gone back down to the glen and thanked Madame Shelta for all she had done in restoring his memories. He also told her that he was leaving Rosslyn Castle but would return.

Thereafter, he went into town and said goodbye to Mrs. Winthrop at the bakery. Crossing the street to the Royal Mail, he posted some letters he'd written the night before; one to Harry, one to Ian Cowan in Lyme Regis, and one to Sharon Meehan. He also sent one to Mike Cope, just to let his old friend know what he was up to, and why he hadn't traveled with him to Moab and the Arches so many months before. Last, he arranged for the post office to hold his mail until he'd contact them with a forwarding address—once he had one.

Now, as he sat on the steps in front of the Oxford family home, his thoughts turned to Sharon, and he sighed. *No doubt she thought I didn't survive the sinking of the hospital ship. This way she'll know—and she'll know I want to see her again. But the person I really need to see is Dad. I'm certain he didn't stay in Utah—not once he knew I had left to join the Great War.*

"Evan? Is it you?"

He looked up and saw an elderly woman walking two King Charles spaniels. He smiled and stood up. "Mrs. Macready?"

"Yes, Evan. How very good to see you!"

"And good to see you." He gestured toward the house. "Have you seen my father lately?"

"I have, but not recently. He stopped by to say hello just after New Years."

A wave of relief washed over him. "Good! So, he's back in England."

"Most decidedly. The professor has an important job at Whitehall and stays at a flat in London. Mervin Smythe had been living here, but he left several months ago for Boston."

"Would you have my father's address?"

"I'm afraid not. He told me that if I needed to reach him, I could cable him at Whitehall."

"Thanks very much, Mrs. Macready," Evan said and shouldered his haversack. "I look forward to seeing you when I'm back this way."

"Your dad left me a key if you'd like to stay here—"

"No need. I haven't seen my dad in months, so I'm off to Whitehall." Smiling, he waved goodbye and moved down the road.

"Goodbye Evan!" She waved. "I can't get over how you've grown."

Moving in the direction of the train station, he began running.

❀ ❀ ❀

The Secret Service Bureau at Whitehall, London

HAVING WORKED at MI-5 for two months, Clive was just beginning to feel useful.

The Bureau's director, C, with his gold monocle and wild eccentricities, continued to be an endless source of amusement, but there hadn't been much for Clive to do in the way of actual intelligence work related to the Middle East. But that had changed.

Clive got up from his desk and stretched. *Aaron Aaronsohn in Palestine has been a Godsend*, he thought and placed a dossier in the office's iron safe. *Since Djemal appointed him as director of the locust mitigation program, he's been traveling along the Mediterranean coast and throughout the maritime plain, and the amount of intelligence he's provided about Ottoman troop strength and installations has been prodigious!*

He turned off his office light, pulled the door closed, and locked it. With an increased workload, he'd taken to working late and was usually the last one to leave Whitehall. But, far from being annoyed, he was happy to be busy—less time to agonize about Evan.

He passed the MO-4 mapping room and saw the light was on. *That's odd—Gertrude's still here?* He knocked on the door and after a few seconds it opened.

Gertrude smiled. "Good evening, Clive. You're here late."

"I'm *always* here late, Gerty. *You're* the one who usually leaves at midday for your work at the Red Cross. Why are you still here?"

"Hedley's in a sweat about maps of the Tigris around the garrison of Kut."

"Anything going on there?"

"Not yet but our friends in the Raj are worried."

Clive paused and said, "Actually, Gerty, I'm glad you're here. I really didn't have a chance to speak with you during Richard's memorial service."

"It *was* a bit awkward, wasn't it? You were the only one who knew about my feelings for Richard." She sighed. "There I was, offering my condolences to his widow when I'd been telling Richard a few months before to divorce her and marry me!"

Clive nodded. "That qualifies as awkward . . ."

Gertrude fixed him with her eyes. "Knowing how very close you and Richard were, I wanted to talk to you about saying goodbye to him properly—something we might do together."

"What do you have in mind?"

"I'm not sure . . ." She paused and took a deep breath.

Clive could see that she was struggling to maintain her composure.

"As you know, he's buried close to where he was killed . . . at Seddel-Bahr . . ." She bit her lip, her eyes shining with tears.

He pulled a handkerchief from his pocket and handed it to her.

She dried her eyes and looked up at him. "I'd very much want to visit the gravesite with you, Clive—to lay a wreath and to say goodbye."

"I'd be honored to join you, Gerty."

"But, how? When?" she asked as she dried her eyes.

"I've been in touch with Hogarth about transferring to Cairo, that is, once Evan's situation is resolved. He also wants *you* there."

"So, there's a possibility we'll eventually go to Cairo?"

"A possibility—and if that comes to pass, I'll arrange a detour for us to Gallipoli."

"Thank you, Clive!" Gertrude blew her nose and held up the

handkerchief, "May I keep this?"

"At this point, I insist!"

"Well, I've got to get back to my maps of Kut. Good night, Clive."

"G'night Gerty."

He headed toward the steel stairwell wondering how the unsentimental Gertrude Bell he thought he knew could be so vulnerable, so romantic.

As he passed the pristine central marble staircase, he asked himself, *Why shouldn't I take these damned stairs?* With that, he headed down the clean white steps, remembering what a young soldier had told him the first day he had come to Whitehall—*the grand staircase is reserved for field marshals and charwomen.*

Crossing the atrium, Clive was on his way out of the building, when he noticed a broadsheet by the door. FIGHT FOR RIGHT was emblazoned across the top in large black letters. Below that; A Rally at Queen's Hall, 7 May, Eight o'clock in the evening.

Despite his doubts about the jingoistic title of the rally, he knew that an infusion of optimism was desperately needed given the toll the war had taken on the home front with thousands dead and badly wounded, the anguish of loss touching every home. And beyond that, there was mounting anxiety about the very survival of Great Britain.

We need rallies like this, he thought and was about to step out the door when the word *Jerusalem* caught his eye. He turned back and read.

> The poem, "Jerusalem" by William Blake, has been beautifully set to choral music by the renowned composer, Sir Hubert Parry, and will be publicly performed for the first time at this event. It is noteworthy that His Royal Majesty, King George V, upon hearing it for the first time in a private performance, stated that he preferred "Jerusalem" over "God Save the King" as Great Britain's National Anthem.

Clive glanced at his timepiece. *The sun doesn't set for another hour and it's a lovely evening. If I walk quickly, I'll be there on time. Besides, I want to hear what Parry has done with Blake's poem.*

❀ ❀ ❀

Evan looked out the taxi window at the soaring columns of Whitehall, but as the taxi pulled to a stop, he saw that the building looked closed.

"Could you wait here for a few minutes?" he asked the driver. Hurrying up the granite steps he saw a light burning in the vestibule. He tried the door, but it was locked. He rapped on the glass and waited.

After half a minute, a sleepy custodian appeared and pushed the door open, "Sorry, mate, building's closed."

"But surely there's someone here I might speak with."

"You can speak with me, if you'd like, but no one else is 'ere, mate—all gone off to the big rally at Queen's Hall."

"What rally?" Evan asked.

"This one 'ere." He pointed to the broadsheet. "Starts at eight. If ya hurry, ya might make it."

Glancing at the broadsheet, he thought, *With Whitehall staff there, I'll be able to ask about Dad. Perhaps I'll even find him there.*

"Thanks," he said and hurried back to the waiting taxi.

❀ ❀ ❀

The sun was low in the sky as Clive neared Queen's Hall. Slowing his gait, he joined pedestrians, automobiles and horse-drawn cabs streaming toward the crowded square fronting the hall.

Crossing the square, he heard newsboys shouting, "Read all about it! *Lusitania* torpedoed by German Submarine! Get your Daily Mirror here! Only a halfpenny! *Lusitania* sunk without warning! Read all about it!"

He bought a paper and stared at a stock photograph of the great ship escorted by tugs. The sinking had taken place about six hours earlier that day and there were no details about survivors—just the photo and a lurid headline; GIANT CUNARDER CROWDED WITH PASSENGERS CALLOUSLY SUNK WITHOUT WARNING OFF THE IRISH COAST.

What a dreadful tragedy! He sighed as he flipped through the paper, but there were no details. *I'll know more tomorrow from the Daily Telegraph* . . .

He bought a ticket to the rally and made his way into the noisy concert hall. He could hear anxious talk of the *Lusitania* sweeping through the crowd, adding to the already charged atmosphere. He found his seat, but remained standing, facing the crowd entering the hall, searching for familiar faces, and for one face in particular. *Everywhere I go, I'm always watching for him.*

After a few minutes, the lights dimmed, and he sat down.

❊ ❊ ❊

It was just past eight when Evan's taxi pulled into the deserted square in front of Queen's Hall. He paid the fare, jumped out, and ran to the box office, only to find it closed.

He approached the door to the hall. "I don't have a ticket, but as a wounded veteran, might I come in?"

The usher snorted. "I'll wager you're as wounded as I am!"

"That's a bet you'd lose," Evan shot back. He pulled down the collar of his shirt to reveal the scar over his left upper chest. "Do you have one of these?" he asked.

"Sorry, mate," said the usher. "I meant no disrespect. Please, take a program and go right in!"

Evan slipped the program into his jacket pocket, crossed the lobby, and entered the dark and cavernous theater. The concert had already begun, the orchestra accompanying a song he didn't recognize. He stood among a crowd tucked under the balcony. On the raised stage a uniformed soldier stood in the spotlight flanked by six others.

"What song is this?" he asked someone standing nearby.

"'Keep the Home Fires Burning,'" came the whispered reply. The soldier's tenor voice filled the hall.

"Overseas there came a pleading,
Help a nation in distress.
And we gave our glorious laddies—
Honour bade us do no less.

"It's going to be a long evening," Evan muttered as the song continued.

For no gallant Son of Britain
To a foreign yoke shall bend
And no Englishman is silent
To the sacred call of 'Friend.'"

He looked about, perturbed that in the darkness, he couldn't see any uniformed personnel he might ask about his father. But, as applause followed the conclusion of the song, the lights came up and he saw a group of soldiers a few yards away.

He threaded a path toward them as the orchestra broke into a boisterous introduction, and the tenor led the audience in a melody Evan recognized.

"It's a long way to Tipperary,
It's a long way to go.
It's a long way to Tipperary,
To the sweetest girl I know!
Goodbye, Piccadilly,
Farewell, Leicester Square!
It's a long, long way to Tipperary,
But my heart's right there."

He waited until the chorus to ask. "Sorry, but are you from Whitehall?"

The soldiers shook their heads and joined in singing the second verse.

❀ ❀ ❀

Clive's initial cynicism had fallen away, and he enthusiastically joined in the final chorus of "It's a Long Way to Tipperary."

Checking the program, he smiled. *Ah! 'Jerusalem' is the next to be performed, and by no less than three hundred members of the main choirs of London!* Looking up from the program, he watched in amazement as a multitude of male and female singers in formal attire filed into tiered rows, filling the stage. When finally in place, they opened their black folders as a pipe organ sent out a few introductory bars. Then the full force of the huge chorale posed Blake's mysterious rhetorical questions:

> "And did those feet in ancient time, Walk upon Englands mountains green:
> And was the holy Lamb of God,
> On Englands pleasant pastures seen!
> And did the Countenance Divine, Shine forth upon our clouded hills?
> And was Jerusalem builded here, Among those dark Satanic Mills?"

Familiar with the text, Clive was thrilled by Blake's allusion to the apocryphal story of a young Jesus traveling to England with his uncle and tin merchant, Joseph of Arimathea, and living in Glastonbury during the silent years before returning to the Holy Land and starting his ministry in the Galilee.

But compounding and magnifying the text, Clive was transported by the power of the chorale and the way Hubert *Parry had transformed Blake's poetry into a beautiful hymn.*

His eyes filled with tears.

❀ ❀ ❀

Evan had never read Blake's poem and, with the lights down, he wasn't able to read the words in the program but, with the hymn's measured pace, each vivid phrase shone as bright as illuminated text:

"Bring me my Bow of burning gold:
Bring me my Arrows of desire:
Bring me my Spear: O clouds unfold:
Bring me my Chariot of fire!"

The words resonated in his heart—the call to spiritual arms, the longing for a Jerusalem not built with hands, a place not of this world. He wiped the tears from his eyes, and wondered, *Is this my true destination?*

"I will not cease from Mental Fight, Nor shall my Sword sleep in my hand:
Till we have built Jerusalem,
In Englands green & pleasant Land."

❋ ❋ ❋

Clive could scarcely catch his breath as the final chords from the pipe organ rose triumphant with the end of the hymn, so exhilarated by the inspiring perfection of music and text. As he stood and applauded, he smiled through his tears and thought, *Indeed, much more inspiring than "God Save the King!"*

As the chorus filed off the stage, Clive was about to slip out of the theater when the lights came up and several kilt-wearing men took the stage—two with bagpipes and one with a traditional bodhrán Irish drum. The pipers inflated the bags of their highland pipes, moving the reeds on the drones to tune them, and a kilted vocalist took the stage.

What's this then? He checked the program. *A tribute to our brave Irish volunteers—"Brian Boru's March."*

"Wonderful!" he said aloud and considered how central the tune was in his own life—as son and as father. He couldn't wait for it to begin. And he didn't wait long.

The drone of the pipes was followed by a slow and measured skirling of the melody, and after one pass through, the bodhrán added a deep and pulsing urgency. Last, the Irish tenor added his voice, weaving a stirring Gaelic tapestry.

Clive's heart ached on hearing words he had sung to Evan—Gaelic remembered though never understood. He listened to the long-beloved tune and thought of him.

Oh, God! How I wish he could hear this! How I wish he were here!

❂ ❂ ❂

Evan was on his way out of the hall when he heard the pipes. Returning, he stood transfixed—his spirits rising with the tenor's voice, his eyes filled with tears, his heart full to bursting with an ecstatic affirmation of love for his father.

And as the pipes droned and skirled, the love grew, connecting in his blood through the generations of St. Clairs, back to Jonathan St. Clair, back to Jerusalem.

The song ended, but he knew that for him, the song would never end—like the unbroken legacy of his bloodline—a fine thread, abiding and bright.

Wiping tears from his eyes, he left the hall. Stepping out to the street, he saw that night had taken hold of London. Looking up, he smiled at the benign indifference of the night sky, crowded with stars, like the vault of his mind, now crowded with memory.

Looking about for a taxi, he asked himself aloud, "Why do I need a taxi? I don't know where I'm going!" He looked back up at the sky and laughed. "But I know I'll find my way, because I know where I've been, and I know who I am!"

Clive was exhausted from a long day at the Bureau and the emotional storm he had just weathered at Queen's Hall. But as he left, he saw a young man standing alone in the street looking up at the night sky. With a shock of recognition, he called out, "Evan?"

Then he heard the word he had all but despaired of ever hearing again. "Dad?"

CHARACTER LIST

PLEASE NOTE: historical figures are listed in all-capital letters and departures from actual historical detail are noted in italics.

AARONSOHN, AARON (1876–1919)
A Jewish agronomist, botanist, Zionist activist, and spy. Born in Romania, he lived most of his life in Ottoman Palestine. Served as a scientific consultant to DJEMAL PASHA during the crop-destroying locust invasion of 1915 and at the same time collected strategic information about Ottoman troop deployment for British intelligence.

AHMED DJEMAL PASHA (1872–1922)
Ottoman military leader and one of the Three Pashas—the Young Turks who ruled the Empire during WWI. He favored entering the war on the side of the Entente but was overruled by Enver Pasha.

BELL, GERTRUDE (1868–1926)
British archeologist, writer, traveler, and political officer central in shaping British policy in the Middle East during and after WWI.

B'SHARA, FATIMA
Wife of Rahman B'shara.

B'SHARA, MAHMOUD
Infant son of Fatima and Rahman.

B'SHARA, RAHMAN
Arab archeologist at École Biblique, Jerusalem.

MANSFIELD GEORGE "C" SMITH-CUMMING (1859-1923)

British naval officer who suffered from seasickness and was therefore retired as "unfit for service" and appointed as chief of the Secret Service Bureau (MI-5). An unusual person, he typically signed letters with a "C" in green ink. Having lost a lower leg in an automobile accident, he was given to vetting prospective agents by suddenly stabbing himself in his wooden leg to see if they flinched. If they failed this "flinch test," they were deemed unfit for service.

CALLWELL, MAJOR GENERAL CHARLES (1859-1928)

Director of operations and intelligence during World War I at the War Office at Whitehall.

CECIL, LORD ROBERT (1864-1958)

British lawyer, politician and diplomat who served as director of the London Red Cross at the beginning of WWI.

CHURCHILL, WINSTON (1874-1965)

First lord of the admiralty in the Asquith government, tasked with overseeing Britain's naval effort when WWI began.

COPE, MIKEL

Evan Sinclair's high school friend in Cedar City, Utah. (Fictionalized after Mikel Cope, author's high school friend in Oakland, California who worked at the actual Bob Pitney's filling station in the 1960s).

COWAN, IAN

Fictional owner of Pilot Boat Inn in Lyme Regis. Historically, the owner was TOMMY ATKINS. The name "Cowan" pays homage to the subject of the historical LASSIE resuscitation of Able Seaman JOHN COWAN—presumed dead after a German U-Boat attack on New Year's Eve, 1914. Cowan's apparently lifeless body lay on the floor of the Pilot Boat Inn beer cellar before transfer to a Lyme Regis mortuary. There ATKINS saw COWAN stir after his collie, LASSIE, nuzzled and licked his face. (see LASSIE)

DOUGHTY-WYLIE, LIEUTENANT COLONEL RICHARD (1868–1915)

British Army officer and diplomat who died at Gallipoli and was posthumous recipient of Victoria Cross. Had also been awarded the Ottoman Empire's Order of the Medjidie for his humanitarian service to Turkey during the Balkan Wars. Had long term romantic correspondence with GERTRUDE BELL.

FAISAL BIN HUSSEIN BIN ALI AL-HASHEMI (1885–1933)

Third son of HUSSEIN BIN ALI, SHARIF OF MECCA, born in Mecca and educated in Constantinople. Historically, met TE LAWRENCE in Wadi Safra, 1916 and met CHAIM WEIZMANN with LAWRENCE at a British-Arab encampment in the Mountains of Moab overlooking the Dead Sea in June 1918. *(In book, Faisal's meeting with Lawrence was fictionalized to Nuweiba in the Sinai, January 1915, and the meeting with Weizmann and Lawrence was fictionalized to Aden, May 5, 1915)*

FALKENHAYN, GENERAL ERICH VON (1861–1922)

Chief of the German General Staff from September 1914 through August 1916.

GEERAERT, HENDRIK

Leader of a group of Belgian partisans.

GINSBERG, ASHER ZVI HIRSCH (1856–1927)

Better known by his Hebrew penname, Achad Ha'am ("One of the people"). A Talmudic prodigy, Hebrew essayist, and one of the earliest and most prominent Zionists in the Russian Empire. Known as the founder of "cultural" Zionism that stressed the rebirth of the Hebrew language and the centrality of Jewish ethics in settling Palestine with respect for the rights of the indigenous residents of the land.

GINSBERG, RIVKE (1856–1931)

Wife of ASHER GINSBURG.

GUPTA, RISSALDAR PRATAB

Wounded soldier of the Raj who befriends Evan Sinclair at the British Expeditionary Force (BEF) hospital in France.

HEDLEY, COLONEL W. COOTE (1865–1937)
Commander of MO-4, British Intelligence, Geographical Division.

HOWDEN, MAJOR RICHARD
Chief surgeon at BEF Hospital, Boulogne-Sur-Mer, France.

HUSSEIN BIN ALI AL-HASHIMI, SHARIF OF MECCA (1854–1931)
Leader of the Banu Hashim Bedouin tribe and direct descendent of The Prophet. As sharif and emir of Mecca, he declared the Great Arab Revolt against the Ottoman Empire in June 1916. Self-declared king of the Hejaz from 1916 to 1924.

KAISER WILHELM II, GERMAN EMPEROR AND KING OF PRUSSIA (1859–1941)
According to German historian, Thomas Nipperdey, Wilhelm was "superficial, hasty, restless, unable to relax, without any deeper level of seriousness, without any desire for hard work or drive to see things through to the end, without any sense of sobriety, for balance and boundaries, or even for reality and real problems, uncontrollable and scarcely capable of learning from experience, desperate for applause and success . . ." On 9 November 1918, having lost support of the military and with a revolution underway, he abdicated his throne and fled Germany for Holland, where he died in 1941.

KAISERIN AUGUSTA VICTORIA OF SCHLESWIG-HOLSTEIN (1859–1921)
Wife of Kaiser Wilhelm II.

KEMAL, YUSUF AND KADIM, MUSTAFA
Two twenty-year-old Turkish friends, graduates of the American high school of Robert College in Istanbul, the oldest continuously operating American school outside the US. Given their English language skills, the two were drafted into the Turkish Army and assigned for service at Augusta Victoria Hostel in Jerusalem.

KITCHENER, HORATIO HERBERT, 1ST EARL KITCHENER (1850-1916)

A British Army officer and colonial administrator. Kitchener came to prominence for his imperial campaigns, his involvement in the Second Boer War, and his central role in the early part of the First World War.

KRESSENSTEIN, FRIEDRICH KRESS VON (1870-1948)

German general who assisted in the direction of the Ottoman Army during WW I as the main leader for the Ottoman Desert Command Force.

LARSSON, LEWIS (1881-1958)

Emigrated to Jerusalem from Sweden with his family, joining the American Colony in 1896. Soon began studying photography and became head of the Colony's photographic department.

LASSIE

Cross-bred collie of Pilot Boat Inn owner Ian Cowan, fictionalized after the collie who revived presumed dead seaman, JOHN COWAN after sinking of British battleship by U-Boat in the English Channel on New Year's Eve, 1914. (See Ian Cowan)

LAWRENCE, THOMAS EDWARD "LAWRENCE OF ARABIA" (1888-1935)

British archaeologist, scholar, soldier, spy, and writer. Helped lead Arab Revolt with Faisal and brought Faisal together with the Zionist leader, CHAIM WEIZMANN.

LIST, GUIDO VON (1848-1919)

Austrian occultist who expounded a revival of the religion of the ancient German race, and in 1910 suggested the swastika as a symbol for all anti-Semitic organizations. Active in Austria and Germany during the war, he oversaw publication of his books promoting ultranationalism and Germano-Nordic racial supremacy. Died in Berlin on May 17, 1919. *List's life is fictionalized to the extent that there is no record of List traveling to Jerusalem or working with the historical Montagu Parker.*

MADAME SHELTA (ZAHIRAH)

An elderly "wise woman" from among the Gypsies of Rosslyn Glen. The Gypsies were welcome guests of the Sinclairs of Rosslyn for hundreds of years, considering themselves as "Egyptians" having come to Scotland from "Little Egypt" or Palestine in the thirteenth century.

MCCRAE, LIEUTENANT-COLONEL JOHN (1872–1918)

Canadian physician, soldier, and poet who wrote "In Flanders Field" on May 3, 1915, first published in the magazine *Punch*. Poem written in homage to his friend Lt. Alexis Helmer, who was killed during the Second Battle of Ypres in 1915 (*fictionalized in book as First Battle of Ypres in October–November 1914*). McCrae died on January 28, 1918, while commanding No. 3 Canadian General Hospital at Boulogne-sur-Mer of pneumonia and pneumococcal meningitis. (*McCrae's death fictionalized in book to November 19, 1914, after hospital ship torpedoed by U-Boat in English Channel*).

MEEHAN, SHARON

Twenty-year-old Volunteer Aid Detachment (VAD) nurse who befriends Evan Sinclair when hospitalized at BEF hospital in France.

MIRZUK AL-TAKHEIMI

Twenty-three-year-old Bedouin. Once a guide for LAWRENCE and WOOLLEY during their desert survey, now an aide-de-camp for FAISAL.

NATHANSON, DAVID

Jewish archeologist at École Biblique, Jerusalem.

NATHANSON, ISSER

Infant son of Sarah and David.

NATHANSON, SARAH

Wife of David Nathanson.

NEWCOMBE, STEWART FRANCIS (1878-1956)

British army officer who served the Empire in South Africa, Sudan, Egypt, and Arabia. Mapped the Sinai and Negev deserts with TE LAWRENCE and LEONARD WOOLLEY in dual capacities of mapping and espionage of the Ottoman Empire's capabilities in advance of WWI. Organized the Military Intelligence Branch in Cairo, was sent to Gallipoli to command an Australian division of Royal Engineers, followed by action in all theaters of the Great War.

PARRY, SIR CHARLES HUBERT HASTINGS (1848-1918)

English composer who set Blake's poem, "Jerusalem," to music as requested by those involved in organizing the Fight for Right rally in London's Queen's Hall on March 28, 1916, to "brace the spirit of the nation to accept with cheerfulness all the sacrifices necessary." Parry was initially reluctant because of the ultrapatriotism of the organization, but relented, and on March 10, 1916, he handed the manuscript to the British poet laureate, Robert Bridges, with the comment, "Here's a tune for you, old chap. Do what you like with it." *(In book, the Fight for Right rally and first performance of "Jerusalem" was moved to May 7, 1915).* In support of his wife, Lady Maude, a suffragette, Sir Parry passed the copyright for "Jerusalem" to the National Union of Women's Suffrage Societies, hoping it would become known as "the Women Voter's Hymn."

PITNEY, BOB

owner of filling station in Cedar City, Utah. (Fictionalized after BOB PITNEY, owner of filling station in Oakland, California).

RUSSELL, FLORA AND DIANA

Sisters who worked at the Red Cross office in Boulogne-Sur-Mer at the start of the war, tracking the dead and wounded from the Western Front, joined there after a few weeks by their friend, GERTRUDE BELL.

SARKISIAN, ARSINE

Armenian woman taken from her home and forced to walk into the desert with her two young children after her husband was taken to a forced labor camp.

SINCLAIR, CLIVE ROBERT

Professor of Near Eastern languages and Archeology, Balliol College, Oxford. Father of Evan.

SINCLAIR, EVAN WILLIAM
Sixteen-year-old son of Clive Robert Sinclair.

SMYTHE, MERVIN
Colleague of CR Sinclair, Professor of Teutonic Archeology with academic appointments at Universities of Oxford and Stuttgart.

SPAFFORD, ANNA LARSEN ØGLENDE (1842–1923)
Norwegian American woman who, with her husband, HORATIO SPAFFORD, emigrated from Chicago in 1881 with a dozen other Presbyterians. Settling in Jerusalem, they were joined by Swedish Christians and established the American Colony, where they engaged in philanthropic work for the poor of Jerusalem regardless of their religious affiliation and without proselytizing.

SPAFFORD, HORATIO GATES (1828–1888)
Prominent American lawyer and Presbyterian church elder who established the American Colony in Jerusalem with his wife ANNA SPAFFORD. Wrote the hymn "It is Well with My Soul" following the tragic deaths of their three-year-old son from scarlet fever followed by the death of their four daughters by drowning on a transatlantic voyage.

ST. CLAIR-ERSKINE, JAMES FRANCIS HARRY, 5TH EARL OF ROSSLYN (1869–1939)
Bon vivant graduate of Eaton College and Magdalen College, Oxford University followed by seventeen-year stint in military, achieving rank of captain in Fifeshire Light Horse Volunteers. Served as war correspondent for the *Daily Mail* during Boer War, where he was captured twice (recounted in his book, *Twice Captured*), held office of justice of the peace in Fife, was private secretary to the secretary of state of Scotland, gambled and lost much of family fortune at roulette tables of Cannes and Monte Carlo (recounted in his book, *My Gamble With Life*), established and toured with Lord Rosslyn's Theatrical Performances, and served as a major in the King's Royal Rifle Corps on the Western Front between 1915 and 1917.

VESTER, BERTHA SPAFFORD (1879–1968)
Daughter of ANNA and HORATIO SPAFFORD, born in Chicago after family tragedies (see SPAFFORD, HORATIO). Bertha served the American

Colony as educator, nurse, and provider of social services. She assumed primary administrative responsibility for the Colony upon the death of her mother ANNA SPAFFORD in 1923 until her own death in 1968.

VESTER, FREDERICK (1869–1942)

Husband of BERTHA VESTER and manager of the American Colony Store just inside Jaffa Gate—a commercial, charitable, and educational enterprise.

VESTER, HORATIO FREDERICK (1906–1985)

Son of BERTHA SPAFFORD VESTER and FREDERICK VESTER. Was doted on by DJEMAL PASHA when he visited the American Colony during the early years of the war.

WALKER, MONTAGU

Soldier, adventurer, and treasure hunter, Walker barely escaped with his life after excavating the Temple Mount in 1911, returning to Jerusalem under the kaiser's patronage three years later. Walker is the fictionalized version of MONTAGU PARKER, a British aristocrat and soldier who truly did serve in the Boer War, searched for treasure on the Temple Mount in 1911, and escaped Ottoman authorities on the yacht of CLARENCE WILSON. But, unlike this fictional version, the historical Montagu Parker did not return to Palestine but went on to fight in WWI and was decorated with the Croix de Guerre. He inherited the title of 5th Earl of Morley in 1951 with the death of his older brother and died in England on April 28, 1962.

WATSON, CLARENCE

A young aristocrat, Boer War veteran, and yachtsman. Friend of and collaborator with Montagu Walker, they were discovered excavating the Temple Mount for treasure in 1911 and managed to escape the mob and Ottoman authorities, sailing away from Palestine on Watson's yacht. Clarence Watson is a fictionalized version of the historical CLARENCE WILSON (just as Montagu Walker is a fictionalized version of the historical MONTAGU PARKER).

WEIZMANN, BENJI (1907–1980)

The eldest son, of CHAIM and VERA WEIZMANN. Born in Manchester, he settled in Clonlara, Ireland, and became a dairy farmer.

WEIZMANN, CHAIM (1874–1952)

Russian-born biochemist and Zionist leader, who met with FAISAL and TE LAWRENCE to work toward Jewish-Arab cooperation in Palestine. (*However, the actual meeting between Weizmann and Faisal facilitated by LAWRENCE portrayed in the book as taking place on 5 May 1915 in Aden, actually took place in southern Transjordan in June 1918*). Weizmann developed a biochemical fermentation method to produce acetone, central to England's ability to produce munitions during WWI. Weizmann would serve as Israel's first president until his death in 1952.

WEIZMANN, VERA (1881–1966)

Russian-born physician and Zionist activist, married WEIZMANN, CHAIM in 1906 and soon thereafter settled in Manchester, England, where their first son, BENJI was born in 1907. Vera received her English medical license in 1913 and directed a public health clinic for mothers and infants.

WERTHEIMER, GUNTER VON

Archeologist at École Biblique, Jerusalem, of German Lutheran Templer parentage.

WERTHEIMER, RACHEL

Wife of Gunter von Wertheimer, a Yemenite Jewess and linguist.

WERTHEIMER, TIRZAH

Daughter of Rachel and Gunter.

WALLACE, WILLIAM (1272–1305)

Scottish knight who became one of the main leaders of Wars of Scottish Independence, though little is known of him during the first twenty years of his life.

WOOLLEY, LEONARD (1880–1960)

British archaeologist who worked with Lawrence at the excavations in Carchemish, then on the desert survey that yielded their report, *The Wilderness of Zin*—all the while reporting crucial geographic details to British Naval Intelligence.

WUNDERLICH, FRITZ

Nineteen-year-old conscript in Germany's Royal Saxon Army and promising tenor.

ACKNOWLEDGMENTS

I want to offer my profound gratitude to all those who read the manuscript in its various forms and offered their comments and encouragement. Foremost among them are the long-suffering members of my critique group, Critical Mass—Margaret Dumas and Claire Johnson, there from the painful beginnings to the final beta reads. Without their cruel, kind, and relentless attention to detail, this book could not have been written.

I'm also indebted to fellow authors, Annamaria Alfieri, Sylvia Boorstein, Matt Coyle, Andrew Kaplan, Ronit Meroz, Penny Warner, and Kenneth Wishnia for their support and friendly reassurance.

Special thanks are due to my loving wife, Teri, who afforded me the time, space, and therapeutic Yoga exercises to enable me to weave multiple storylines into the book's sweeping tapestry.

I also wish to thank John Koehler of Koehler Books for opening his publishing home to *Crossroads of Empire,* the new baby in a growing family; to Becky Hilliker for cleaning him up; and to Lauren Sheldon for his pretty clothes.

SUGGESTIONS FOR FURTHER READING

Anderson, Scott. *Lawrence in Arabia—War, Deceit, Imperial Folly and the Making of the Modern Middle East.* New York: Doubleday, 2013

Baigent, Michael et al. *Holy Blood, Holy Grail.* New York: Dell Publishing, 1983

Bell, Florence – Editor. *The Letters of Gertrude Bell.* New York: Boni and Liveright, 1927

Florence, Ronald. *Lawrence and Aaronsohn and the Seeds of the Arab-Israeli Conflict.* New York: Viking Penguin, 2007

Friedman, Isaiah. *Germany, Turkey, and Zionism 1897–1918.* Oxford: Oxford University Press, 1977

Fromkin, David. *A Peace to End All Peace—The Fall of the Ottoman Empire and the Creation of the Modern Middle East.* New York: Avon Books, 1989

Gardner, Laurence. *Bloodline of the Holy Grail.* Rockport, MA: Element Books LTD., 1996

Garnett, David - Editor. *The Letters of T. E. Lawrence.* London: Jonathan Cape LTD., 1938

Haythornthwaite, Philip J. *The World War One Source Book.* London: Arms and Armour Press, 1992

Hulsman, John C. *To Begin the World Over Again—Lawrence of Arabia from Damascus to Baghdad.* New York: Palgrave Macmillan, 2009

Lawrence, T. E. *Seven Pillars of Wisdom—A Triumph.* New York: Doubleday & Company, Inc., 1935

Lockman, J.N. *Meinertzhagen's Diary Ruse—False Entries on T. E. Lawrence.* Grand Rapids: Cornerstone Publications, Inc. 1995

Maidment, James—Editor for Hay, Father Richard Augustine. *The Genealogy of the Saint Claires of Rosslyn.* The Grand Lodge of Scotland, 1835

MacDonogh, Giles. *The Last Kaiser: The Life of Wilhelm II*. St. Martin's Press, 2001

Mack, John. *A Prince of our Disorder—The Life of T. E. Lawrence*. Cambridge and London: Harvard University Press, 1976

Mackay, James. *William Wallace—Brave Heart*. Edinburgh and London: Mainstream Publishing, 1995

Manchester, William. *The Last Lion—Winston Spencer Churchill—Visions of Glory*. New York: Dell Publishing, 1983

Mazza, Roberto. *Jerusalem in World War I. The Palestine Diary of a European Diplomat—Conde de Ballobar*. London: I.B. Tauris & Co. Ltd, 2011

Morris, James. *The Hashemite Kings*. New York: Pantheon Books, In., 1959

Sicker, Martin. *Between Hashemites and Zionists—The Struggle for Palestine*. New York: Holmes & Meier, 1989

Spafford-Vester, Bertha. *Our Jerusalem—An American Family in the Holy City*. Jerusalem: Ariel Publishing House, 1950

St. Clair-Erskine, James Francis Harry, 5th Earl of Rosslyn. *Twice Captured: A Record of Adventure During the Boer War*. Edinburgh and London: William Blackwood and Sons, 1900

Van der Kiste, John. *Kaiser Wilhelm II: Germany's Last Emperor*. The History Press. Cheltenhham, UK, 1999

Wallach, Janet. *Desert Queen—The Extraordinary Life of Gertrude Bell*. New York: Anchor Books, 1999

Weizmann, Chaim. *Trial and Error—The Autobiography of Chaim Weizmann*. New York: Harper & Brothers, 1949

Whiting, John D. "Jerusalem's Locust Plague." *The National Geographic Magazine*, Dec. 1915, pp. 511 – 550.

Woolley, C. Leonard and Lawrence, T. E. *The Wilderness of Zin—Archaeological Report*. London: Palestine Exploration Fund by Harrison and Sons, 1915

www.ingramcontent.com/pod-product-compliance
Lightning Source LLC
LaVergne TN
LVHW091702070526
838199LV00050B/2253